PRAETORIAN
RISING

J. McSpadden

First Paperback Edition July 2019

ISBN: 978-0-578-53373-5

Published by J. McSpadden Writes
www.jmcspaddenwrites.com

DEDICATION

I'd like to dedicate this book in two parts. First, to those that helped me get through the self-publishing process reminding me to never give up hope on why I embarked on this adventure.

Bjorn, thank you for listening to me read every version of this book to you on our long road trips, working through story and character development. You are my idea board, my most honest critique, and the man I love most.

Laura, thank you for being my first editor and the one to push me to write when I was at a stationary moment in my life.

Ashley, thank you for always politely killing my darlings while shaping my book to perfection. You kept me laughing through the whole editing process. My forever Editor and self-publishing guru I wouldn't be here without you.

Rebecca, thank you for being my most diligent comma hunter and the last eyes on this story before publishing glory.

Mom and Dad, thank you for supporting me and giving me a lifetime worth of experiences. Every vacation, every get away enabled me those moments to dream every dream.

Second, I dedicate this book to every author who was sent a rejection letter and made to believe their story wasn't good enough to be published. This book, this first published piece, is for you my fellow writers. Don't give up on your dreams, don't let anyone say you can't do it. To be a writer is to write, and to be an author is to find your way to a published platform. Fly your own path to your dreams.

CONTENTS

My heart shall love,
My sword protect,
My courage remain,
My strength withstand,
I serve you Ma'Nada.
With every breath,
I praise the day,
We embrace again as equals,
In the great halls of Cydonia.

CHAPTER ONE
LOST MEMORY

Wind whistled through the dense overgrowth of Dun L'er Forest, a high-pitched whir of warning dogging his every step. The rustling maple and stark pine trees hunched like ghostly sentinels, the foggy fingers of breaking dawn stretching toward him as he ran. They were watching him, the ancient eyes of the forest, their aged and weathered limbs creaking against the pressured air. They would hold his secrets in their entombed silence, but the gods knew what he'd done.

Panic slipped down Vesyon's spine, a rivulet of ice pushing his legs to move ever faster. There was no going back now, the deed was done. He had her. They had escaped.

"We're almost there," he whispered as he readjusted the precious form cradled in his arms. Tucking away the young woman's brilliant tumble of red hair beneath the dense fur of his cloak, he pushed through a bramble bush as he continued south toward Sierra Village. Thankfully, the beasts tracking him had lost his scent miles behind his current location. He no longer heard the crash of paw on his heels. Despite the small reprieve, he kept moving. One could never hide from the High Court for long within the depths of Aspera. The eyes of the crown stretched far and wide.

As he pressed into the barrier lines of Sierra Village, Vesyon was vividly aware of the dangers that came with anyone seeing the young woman tucked into his arms. Thankfully his destination wasn't far—just beyond the forest's edge—but he could never be too careful.

Her breath was warm against the crook of his neck, a slow and steady reminder of the depth of her induced sleep. He was grateful for it, wishing she could remain in a peaceful swirl of dreams instead of waking into the harsh reality of her impending future.

A mysterious and silent creature followed him in quick pursuit, dodging between bush and boulder to keep pace with Vesyon's steady gait through the dense forest terrain. Short tufts of black and brown fur camouflaged the creature's every move, allowing him to accomplish his task of the silent companion with pristine perfection. After so many years together, Vesyon couldn't help but think of his small feline friend, Neeko, as one of his closest confidantes.

Up ahead, past the battered wooden fence skirting Sierra Village, he saw a dulled lamp light flickering wildly in the grey of early morning. The orange glow of electricity was like a beacon perched on top of a well-weathered cabin. He hurried toward the sagging walls and ancient, slatted roof with eager anticipation.

An elderly man with a grizzled grey beard stepped out of a low-slung doorway, intrigue and growing curiosity spilling across his creased face. His milky blue eyes and the weight of age contrasted the sharp edges of Vesyon's youthful appearance.

"It's been a long time, my dear friend," the man, Peter Schroder, remarked with a mischievous grin. "I'm surprised the guards let you sneak by." His anxious gaze swept over the deserted village grounds, his caterpillar brows furrowing into a single line. The cracked skin of Vesyon's lips stretched wide with affection as Peter caressed the dagger hidden in his waistband like a cherished friend. Being the town butcher had its positives for Peter; no one questioned his love of sharp blades.

"Too long," Vesyon replied in earnest agreement, readjusting his hold on the sleeping woman as he ducked through the cabin's doorway.

A flicker of shocked bewilderment crossed Peter's face as he glared at Vesyon's precious bundle. Would the girl remember the old man? Or dismiss him as a stranger? Vesyon couldn't be sure. His eyes traversed the broad lines of the man's face with grave worry, not wanting to throw his old friend into the storm of chaos she would invoke, yet knowing he had few other options.

"You weren't followed?" Peter asked although he knew the answer. Vesyon wouldn't be in his home if he'd been tracked. It didn't mean they were safe, only that they had a little time to discuss details. Vesyon shook his head before setting the young sleeping woman down on the fire-warmed hearth and wrapping fur blankets securely around her shoulders.

The old man's living quarters were nothing more than a single room: kitchen, living room, and bedroom, all scarcely lit by a swinging bulb over the kitchen table and the glowing fire in the corner. Electricity was a luxury in the rundown villages of Aspera, but Sierra Village made do with what it had. Aside from the electric icebox in his butchery, Peter kept his home largely stripped of those technological advancements the wealthier villagers possessed. The old man wasn't one for fancy. He had a simple and functioning home and it was a welcoming stop after Vesyon's long, brutal journey through the wilderness of Aspera.

Above their heads, through the latticework, was an attic large enough for Peter's eight-year-old grandson. Young Lunci's soft snores drifted down to Vesyon's sensitive ears pushing a momentary smile across his stern features. Despite Vesyon's impromptu appearance, the kid slept through the commotion, for which Vesyon was grateful. The details he was about to unload onto Peter wouldn't be well-suited for a young boy's mind.

"You really shouldn't be here," Peter said, his tone strained yet friendly. Trespassers weren't welcome in the village, and Vesyon knew the consequences of being caught inside the grounds by the wrong person.

"I had little choice as my message relayed to you," he replied smoothly. Which was almost true, but he wasn't ready to think over the details of his decision. Few were trusted by Vesyon, and Peter was a hardened man through experience, but his wide-open heart offered unending compassion for those without a leg to stand on. Leaving the girl in Peter's hands was the safest choice imaginable.

Peter's lips parted, his features laced with hesitation. Nodding at the sleeping girl, he asked, "You really think she's ready for this? For what position you're about to put her in?"

It was a substantial question. Vesyon wasn't sure of the answer himself. He sat down on a wicker stool, pulling the heavy fur cloak from his shoulders. The heat billowing from the hearth felt good. He closed his eyes for a moment of peace within the comfort of warmth.

Removing a rusted poker from its hook on the wall, Peter shuffled the coals in the hearth with quick, sharp stabs, stoking the smoldering wood into a soft flame. A smile curled the corners of Vesyon's lips as he observed Peter through the hooded sweep of his sooty lashes. Despite the frailty implied by age-spotted hands and knobby knuckles, the man held his own.

Approving of his freshly stoked fire, Peter nodded once before grabbing a plate of meat slices from the kitchen table and offering them to Vesyon. Politely declining, Vesyon finally replied, "I have no idea."

Pulling a worn pipe from his cloak, Vesyon opened a thin canvas bag filled with the dried leaves of his favorite tobacco. He carefully pressed the delicate bits into the pipe's mouth and stared into the dancing flame in the hearth with a sense of momentary calm that he knew wouldn't last. The second he walked out the door, the chaos would consume him again. It was only a few minute's reprieve—a moment to catch his breath—he told himself even as his legs twitched to be on the move again.

"LeMarc had her locked in his dungeon for the past seven years," Vesyon said, his voice tinged with a hint of vexation as he pulled a knife and flint stone from his pocket.

He ignored Peter's stern glare at the disrespectful use of the High King's first name. Vesyon would never think of LeMarc Lowenhaar as a king, let alone the High King of Aspera. The man was a deceitful, power-hungry monster. Vesyon saw no reason to show the man any sort of respect, whether in his presence or not.

"We honestly can't be certain of anything." Vesyon lit his pipe and puffed three times in quick succession to catch flame on the dried leaves. The sweet tang of tobacco smoke filled Vesyon's lungs, and he sighed in relief at the tingling sensation buzzing through his veins as he exhaled.

Peter's gaze shifted to the bundle of fur by the hearth and landed on the heavy brown boots poking out the bottom. "She looks so fragile. Is there no other option? No one else?"

Vesyon studied the girl's delicate features bronzed by the glow of the fire. Peter was right; despite her age, she looked too young and innocent for battle. She was someone he'd give his life for; Vesyon hated knowing what she was about to endure. "She's all we have. Our rebellion can't wait a second longer—she must be prepared."

"How long will she be here?" Peter whispered, pulling the fur blankets more securely around the young woman. Bitter fall air seeped through a cracked windowpane, and Peter shivered. Vesyon wondered if it was from the weather or the burden he'd just heaped onto the old man's shoulders. "It's going to take time to assess how destructive her induced amnesia is. From what Langhorn expressed to me, she might not remember anything at all."

Vesyon's upper lip twitched at Peter's probing words, a subtle tic of the displeasure he tried to hide. Hopefully, Langhorn had succeeded in obliterating everything the girl had endured over the last seven years. If she was lucky, she'd wake up without recalling the smallest detail of her life before that point. It was cruel to rip away someone's identity, but they'd had no choice. If even an inkling of her memories survived, they'd all pay for the horrible atrocities inflicted on her mind, body, and soul while she'd been locked inside LeMarc's torture chamber.

Peter's eyes studied Vesyon's unshaven face before he lowered his creaky body onto the stool near the fireplace. Bones snapped and popped as he settled into the sagging wicker, reminding Vesyon of the extreme fragility most Asperians developed from lack of proper nutrients over the years. He winced with barely concealed worry, but thankfully Peter didn't notice.

"Tea?" the older man asked, pushing a heavy blackened pot into the heat.

Vesyon nodded, knowing he should leave, but not wanting to be rude or end this rare feeling of comfort. He had asked Peter for an incredible favor. He owed the elderly man a moment of company despite his growing urgency to leave. No one knew he was here; he had time to drink a cup of tea—but only one.

"Do you have an idea of where the High King is?" Peter asked as he handed Vesyon a steaming cup of lavender tea.

Vesyon blew across the rim of the dingy grey mug, watching tendrils of steam curl into the bitter air and disperse like mysterious ghosts. "I don't have a clue," he replied. "Metus—"

"The King Regent," Peter corrected sharply.

"Yes," Vesyon replied, trying to hide the smirk tugging at the corner of his lips. Peter hated the High King and the King Regent as much as anyone else involved with the rebellion, but he believed in respecting the titles of those in power, and Vesyon wasn't one to press that button too hard. "He's still managing the throne and has been since the Praetorian Exile. However, I don't believe for a second that LeMa—the High King—" Vesyon corrected, "is idly sitting by. His absence is worrisome, but more than that, his complete silence over the last seven years proves Langhorn right. The High King is up to something of grand proportions, and I want to ensure I'm ready when he lays out his cards."

Glancing out the frost-riddled window, Vesyon smiled with genuine affection at Neeko, perched like a sentinel on the windowsill, his mouth full of fresh forest mice. Beyond the cat's silhouette, thick clouds were rolling in over the forest canopy. A storm was coming, and it was time to leave. He still had so much to do, and not nearly enough time to do it.

Tipping his mug up, Vesyon took a hefty gulp and almost choked as the scorching heat burned its way down his throat to his belly. He grunted in mild discomfort, prompting an arched brow of bemusement from Peter, but Vesyon waved him off and blew more intently on his tea. "I can't thank you enough for this Peter. I have no possible way to repay you for taking care of her."

Peter shook his head, a tender grin running over his lips. "Consider it a payment repaid to a dear friend—one very much *deserved*, mind you."

Vesyon opened his mouth to protest, but Peter raised a withered hand to ward off even the smallest objection. "I have always hated being in debt to favors, especially when it comes to friends. As I see it now, watching over her is a small contribution toward what you have given me these past years. If my wife were here, or my daughter," Peter said, tears glistening at the corners of his eye, "they would say the same."

A zing of guilt struck deep in Vesyon's chest. Peter's beloved family hadn't escaped the slaughter. Behind closed eyes, their hollowed faces appeared, thick red blood streaming from the gashes in their throats, their twin bodies slumped on the ground, lifeless. Vesyon disagreed with Peter. The man was giving far more than Vesyon had ever returned.

Sipping his only moderately scalding tea, Vesyon's gaze drifted back to the young woman's face. "Knowing she'll be with Neeko *and* you puts my mind at ease."

Peter chuckled, his milky eyes twinkling with mirth. "I might bore that poor cat to tears in this village. The most exciting adventure he'll have is chasing down a rat. Are you sure he is actually *willing* to stay?"

"Willing is a strong word." Vesyon eyed Neeko perched at the window, his stoic haunches barely twitching in the bitter rush of wind snaking down the mountain and through the village grounds. He would miss the little fur ball, but it was the only protection he could provide that would remain at Camille's side. In the coming moon cycles, she would need security and companionship. With a slight smirk Vesyon dumped the ashes from his pipe into the dwindling flames of the fire. "He'll stick by her though, and that's what she'll need."

"Well, as far as Count Jenkin is aware, I have a distant relative staying with me until further notice. He'll meet her as soon as she acclimates to the village. I don't expect a warm welcome," Peter said with a slight frown. Pretending the woman was a distant relative of Peter was the only way to ensure the villagers wouldn't shun or forcibly remove her. Sierra Village wasn't in the practice of being hospitable to strange folk, and despite every excuse Vesyon had fed himself to keep Camille close at hand, this was ultimately the best plan of action. "But they will accept her well enough," Peter assured, assessing Vesyon's pinched expression with obvious concern.

"She's with you Peter. She's in good hands. Teach her everything you know about hunting, trapping, and tracking. She'll be a bit rusty when she wakes."

Peter nodded. "Any idea when you'll come back for her?" he asked, taking the half-empty teacup from Vesyon and placing it on the bare kitchen table with a subtle 'clink.' As the flames in the hearth stretched out their last arms in a dance of withering energy, Vesyon packed away his pipe and tobacco pouch before shrugging into his heavy, fur-lined cloak.

"You have twelve moon cycles. I will come for her then," he said. Their eyes met, and they grasped each other's hand in farewell. Peter's shake was firm, but Vesyon felt the tremble beneath the steel exterior. Vesyon plucked the heavy iron pistol from his belt and placed it on the rickety table beside the door. The smell of gunpowder singed the lining of his nostrils, sharp and bitter, and recognizable to any warrior.

Peter eyed the weapon warily. "Is that necessary?"

"Just in case," Vesyon said with a final glance at the young woman shrouded in fur blankets. "I've given you two bullets. It's all I have left. Hopefully, it's enough for you and Lunci if our plan turns south."

A heavy silence descended. No words were necessary. Peter understood the weight of his role in Vesyon's plan, as well as the consequences. There was no other route, no other option. They had one path: forward.

Peter nodded. "She'll be ready."

"Keep her safe, Peter; keep her hidden from the High Court. No one must know she's here."

Peter stared at him, his wild caterpillar eyebrows dipping over squinted blue triangles before consenting with a curt nod.

"I need to get back to Romeo Village before the High Court realizes what I took from them—I can't leave Phillip alone with the mess they're in right now. The poor man hasn't yet recovered from what happened in Charlie Town."

Peter raised an impatient hand. "I know. No need to explain."

With a quick nod of appreciation, Vesyon ducked out the wooden door and disappeared into the dark forest, not once looking back.

***

The woman's eyes fluttered open, and she shied away from the intruding light and heat that assaulted her fragile senses. She couldn't place her location, and her back ached with stiffness as though she hadn't moved in ages.

"Awake, are you? It's about time. You've been sleeping for days."

The woman sought the source of the voice: an old, scruffy man perched close to the glowing hearth. She didn't consciously snap to attention or shove the fur blankets to the floor. She didn't feel the blade's smooth wooden handle as she yanked it from the old man's belt and didn't hesitate to angle the freshly sharpened metal against his throat.

"Where am I?" she croaked, her throat raw as if scratched with sandpaper. It felt like she hadn't spoken in years. But that couldn't be right, she'd just been—she paused. She couldn't remember *where* she'd last been. "Who are you and what do you want with me?"

"I'm a friend, and I want nothing but to keep you safe," the old man said carefully, holding himself stiffly against the blade. "Do you remember how you got here?"

"No," she snapped in sharp frustration. "Where am I?"

"Sierra Village. In my home," the old man said, keeping his eyes locked on hers. "Hungry? I can make you something." He gestured to the kitchen area, but she refused to look anywhere but at his face while deciding whether he was lying or not.

Keeping him in sight, she surveyed the small room, noting small knick-knacks, a wooden bowl filled with overly ripened apples, and a bedframe near the hearth with a feather mattress and an aged brown quilt. It wasn't a prison or holding cell. It was the old man's home—and a cozy one at that. A small, iron kettle hung over glowing coals, probably boiling water for tea. The comforting aroma of fresh rye bread wafted from the pantry and the scent of smoked turkey wrapped in salted bindings made her mouth water. She briefly eyed the nearby electric icebox. Her stomach growled.

Scowling stubbornly, she retorted, "I want answers. I don't need your food."

"It would seem your stomach says otherwise. I'm not a threat, child. I'm here to help you."

The woman pressed the knife harder against his skin. "'Help me?' You want to *help* me? Then give me answers!"

He stared at her blankly, and she seethed.

"Who are you?" the woman shouted wildly, body shaking in terror. "Help me by telling me who you are!"

"I won't hurt you," he said, raising his hands in a show of peace. "My bones are far too old and fragile." The woman remained steadfast, blade to his throat, and the old man chuckled. "My name is Peter Schroder and you've been in my care for a week. You won't remember me, but we have met before."

His features twitched, and she sensed a deep sadness emanating from his entire being as he spoke. Their last meeting hadn't been a pleasant one, it seemed.

"Where? How do you know me? When did you last see me? *When?!*" The woman's words tumbled out in rapid fire, but Peter remained calm and collected.

"I don't have all the answers to your questions, child. But I promise you're safe in my care."

His response failed to temper her racing heart, but she removed

9

the blade and stepped back. She remembered nothing about herself, not even her own name. Where had she been born? Who were her parents, and where were they? This man wasn't familiar in any way.

"I'm sorry," she mumbled, sitting on the bed and placing the knife beside her. She gathered the furs that had pooled around her worn leather boots and pulled them tightly around her shoulders, shaking her head. She'd *smelled* that knife, its hard steel tang, before visually locating it on Peter's belt. She'd identified every entrance and possible exit in the tiny home before her fingers had even reached the blade—they amounted to four if she counted the little window above her head. She even heard the soft rush of breath from a sleeping child overhead in a makeshift bedroom loft—all of these skills, and yet she couldn't recall anything before the moment she'd opened her eyes.

Peter appeared to understand her fright and confusion and busied himself with stoking the fire into a decent flame as she angrily wiped moisture from her eyes. "Your name is Camille Scipio," he said, "and you were brought to me eight nights ago by a close friend. I'm to care for you until he returns."

"Cam-EE-ill," she said, rolling the syllables of her first name around her tongue but feeling no familiarity.

"I have no doubt you're wary of your surroundings right now, but in due time, things will come back to you," Peter added with a small smile.

Camille looked up at him with curious, searching eyes, before staring at the skinny black and brown cat by her feet. "That's all you have to say?" Camille asked, furtively reaching down to scratch the cat's furry head.

How curious, she thought with each stroke, *that this cat's presence makes me feel—calmer.*

"I'm afraid so. I'm to care for you until it's no longer needed. That's all I know."

"That doesn't tell me anything," Camille countered. "Who left me here? You said it was a 'friend.' Who are they, and how do they know me?" Her bottom lip poked out with indignant frustration as she turned an icy glare on the man, hoping it would force loose a sliver of information. The man was like a new gravestone, unyielding and aloof, hiding the depth of its secrets far beneath the surface.

"I can't say any more, child. I apologize. But I *can* assure you that you're safe and most welcome in my home," Peter said, moving slowly to pour Camille a steaming cup of tea.

She accepted the chipped stone-ware mug and sniffed at the purple-tinged liquid inside. It smelled flowery. "What's this? Some sort of draught to knock me out?" Her stomach gurgled again in a desperate plea that she indulge despite her misgivings.

Peter glanced at her with a comical expression. "It's just a cup of lavender tea."

Camille couldn't muster the energy to question him further. Sudden heaviness weighted her eyelids, dragging her down with more insistence than her stomach's hunger pangs. She sipped the warm liquid that tasted of lavender and mint and set the cup down as the cat jumped up beside her. Petting the cat as he cuddled against her hip, Camille slid down on the flat feather pillow and drifted back into a heavy sleep.

***

The wind picked up, whipping against the ancient trees of the Dun L'er Forest like a hungry monster, every branch alive in the dance of early Fall. Despite the pounding sense of danger riding every wind wisp, Peter was relieved. The uprising was finally underway—a whisper of reckless abandon hummed through the bitter air—and this time they'd be ready.

Peter shuffled from the kitchen counter to the whistling kettle to pour himself a fresh cup of tea before he settled down across from the sleeping Camille with a plate of turkey and cheese. Neeko was curled into a ball against her stomach, purring contently. The pair of them appeared at ease in slumber, short-lived but much needed. It had been so long since he'd last seen her, but even to his old and frail eyes she hadn't changed in the least.

He recalled the first time he'd seen her face, seven years before on a night chilled by the oncoming of winter. Her eyes had blazed a deadly black, and her entire body had been slathered in blood—she'd worn it like a token of achievement.

He *should* fear having her there after witnessing what she'd done to the ones he loved. Almost his entire family had been slaughtered right before his eyes, one after the next, in swift slashes of metal. Whoever hadn't escaped his village when she'd arrived had died—

11

yet she'd left him and his grandson untouched. Not a word had been expressed, not a single sound had crossed her lips, as she stared down at them, eyes ablaze with ballistic rage, before she turned and walked away.

He didn't know then, or now, why she'd kept them alive, but it was enough of a reason to allow her into his home. Peter believed Vesyon—Camille was the key to their rebellion, and her past was not a reflection of who she was, but what she was capable of being. Aspera had suffered enough under the strong arm of the High King. Allowing this woman to sleep under his own roof was the least he could do to aid the rebellion if it kept their weapon safe from the High Court's greedy fingers.

He'd made a promise to Vesyon, an honest vow to keep her protected and hidden no matter the consequences. Despite the truth of his word to lay down his life to protect Camille, his grandfatherly worry for the small child sleeping above their heads prickled at his conscience. But, without her help in the rebel movement, Aspera would fall, and there'd be nothing left to fight for: no viable future for his grandson, Lunci.

"Please, Mother Ma'Nada, giver of life and protector of this land—please guard my family against evil," Peter whispered as he brought his palms together before his chest. He repeated the prayer over and over again, his words a steady stream of faith and devotion. The Mother Ma'Nada, though fierce and powerful in the many stories of his faith, had always bestowed good fortune on Peter. The loving goddess had never abandoned him through his many battles, and he held tight to his faith with white-knuckled determination.

The storm began its rhythmic song as the wind whistled through the empty grounds of Sierra Village, picking up speed and rattling the fragile windowpanes in Peter's kitchen. His eyes flicked back over to where Camille slept, her vivid red hair cascading over her shoulders in wild curls. Though he couldn't see them now, he'd been utterly surprised earlier to learn she possessed green irises identical to her mother's. She looked so much like a normal girl of seventeen: lithe and gawky, with muscled biceps, curls that flowed halfway down her back, and a spray of freckles over her petite nose—but he knew better.

She was their only weapon against High King LeMarc. But, if she failed to learn to control the monster living inside her, no one would be able to survive her next explosion.

"Ad Astra per Aspera," he whispered, sipping his tea. "To the stars through difficulty, Camille."

CHAPTER TWO
HIDE AND SEEK

ELEVEN MOONS LATER...

The sun hung low in the distant clouds, the branches above Camille's head heavy with the multicolored leaves of early Fall. Camille was easily concealed behind an ancient trunk covered in sickly grey moss, yet her heart pounded all the same. A small, piercing ache to broke between her lungs. How long had she been running for *this* time? She heard soft steps closing in on her and knew her hiding spot wouldn't last long. A twig snapped in the distance and her stomach twisted; it was time to relocate.

She could smell the tangy scent of his sweat; he was beginning to tire, but his footsteps were nearing. She racked her brain for a plan as she pressed aside a wayward branch, crouching in a hunting stance.

Her instincts told her to act first and think on her feet, and that innate, animalistic sense of battle preparation still startled her. How did she know these things? The storm flowing in over the Iron Mountains visible just north between the treetops and the valley twenty feet to the west had a fourteen-degree downward slope. Slight, yes—but enough to enhance her speed by fifteen percent if she really pushed herself. She never could figure out how she was able to make these automatic calculations, but they were useful in her hunting process nonetheless. Mainly when *she* was the one being hunted.

Camille leaped from her temporary sanctuary and dove toward the heavy brush five feet to her left, swiftly running down the sloping valley deeper into the woods. She heard his soft footfalls turn to heavy thudding as he crashed through the dense forest, speeding like a raging bull in her direction.

Ducking behind another large aspen trunk, Camille held her breath, forcing herself to remain silent as she dug her nails into the thick tree bark. She heard the assailant stop just behind her new hiding spot, and her heart slammed against the confines of her ribs.

Camille closed her eyes and prayed the forest would grant her a reprieve; that some branch might fall to the earth and create a diversion, or some bird might fly past so she could sneak away.

"Ah ha!" the little boy screamed as he jumped around the wide tree trunk followed by a mewling Neeko. "That's three for me. I found you in less than forty minutes this time, and *without* any help from my handy hunting partner," Lunci exclaimed happily, before performing a little victory dance.

"You are a worthy opponent in this game of hide-and-seek," Camille said, unable to restrain the enormous smile streaking across her face. They'd been playing all day, and still, he wasn't tired of it. Nor was she, in all honesty. Camille loved the moments she shared with Lunci, even though she was almost ten years his senior. He reminded her of what it was like to be a kid again, and considering she couldn't remember her own childhood, Camille welcomed the chance to live vicariously through Lunci whenever possible.

Lunci was unusual for a nine-year-old. He never wanted to hunt with boys his own age, and girls who glanced at him with innocent flirtation received nothing more than a sweet smile and a passing glance. Peter passed it off as nothing more than a young state of mind, but as much as Camille loved Lunci's penchant for fun, she felt his childlike demeanor stemmed from something deeper; perhaps even something traumatic.

"Round four?" Lunci asked with a grin, one that Camille knew would disappear when she informed him it was getting too late to play in the deepness of the forest they'd migrated to.

Although they were still within the gated confines of Sierra Village, they were far enough away to cause Peter to worry. "It's getting pretty late there, mister. I think we should start heading back. Your grandfather will have my head if I keep you in the forest past sundown."

"Awww—come on!" Lunci whined. She feigned toying with the idea of refusing him, loving the way he stamped his feet and kept repeating, "Please, please, please!" with his hands clasped.

"Okay, one last time. But after that we are going home," Camille said sternly, making a mental note to pick a secure hiding spot that was within sight of the village grounds. Lunci broke out into another little jig before slumping to the ground, hands over his eyes as he began to count backward from thirty.

She ran a medium distance away, making sure to keep Lunci within earshot, taking heavy steps so he could detect her path more easily. She never dared go too far from him and held her hunting knife with her just in case any real predators decided to join the game. Despite the fact it was her day off from hunting, Camille wouldn't pass up the opportunity to bring fresh game home for Peter to sell.

"All right, ready or not, here I come!" Lunci yelled into the thick foliage.

Camille smiled when she heard him rustle through the same bush she'd just passed a few moments earlier. He usually spent a few moments trying to decide which direction she'd gone in, but apparently, he'd conveniently forgotten to close his eyes this time. She took extreme pride in his growing abilities to track prey. It was a small lesson she carefully explained over their months of weekly playtime, but she would let this little cheat slide under the radar.

Camille made a quiet trek back up the sloping valley toward Sierra Village, ensuring she heard Lunci's footsteps close behind her. Her stomach growled at the idea of dinner filling her to near-bursting, but tonight's offering would only be a small plate of food despite the fact she lived with the village butcher.

It was two days before the Moon Tax was due, and only the wealthy didn't dread the offering. The rest of the village scrounged for food to meet the High Court's demands, but luckily Camille's hunting skills and market trades kept Peter's table filled through most of the month.

At the end of every moon cycle the buffoon Grenswald, a foul-mouthed, grubby man thicker than he was tall, came to town in a cloud of stale whiskey and body odor. He would barrel his way from door to door, collecting items he deemed "presentable" to the High King's court. Even though Camille had only lived in Sierra Village for a year, she clearly understood what it meant to hate the

High King, his cruel Moon Tax, and the disgusting people he kept readily at his beck and call to maintain total sovereignty.

Camille led Lunci further up the hill toward the heart of the village, snapping twigs and rustling leaves as she did so. Ducking around a relatively large boulder and scurrying through a thick bush, she hid, waiting for Lunci to reach her spot. She hunched down and slowed her breath to an inaudible pace, but after a few moments realized she no longer heard Lunci in the distance.

Her stomach clenched, a searing jolt of panic zipping through her system at the sudden silence of her surroundings. What if Lunci was hurt? Would she have heard Lunci if he screamed? Camille bounded out of the underbrush and still heard nothing but her own ragged breaths—not even a distant bird call. Something was wrong. She felt the unleashed gallop of her heart pounding out a thunderous tempo inside her chest. Usually, Neeko would bounce back and forth between her and Lunci, his tracking senses far superior to any human's. But she didn't even see his bushy black tail anywhere amongst the darkening forest terrain.

No need to panic, she reminded herself, trying to calm the erratic burst of fear crashing through her body. Last week, Lunci had gotten distracted by a small family of squirrels in the trees, but Camille had been high up on the hill and observed him the entire time. This was different. She couldn't hear him at all, couldn't see him, and the forest's ever-present cacophony of twitters had stilled.

The eerie silence cut into her calm reserve, grating against her skin with unrelenting harshness, and just like when she slipped into hunting mode, a tingling, unnatural heat grew beneath her eye sockets.

She grasped her hunting knife tightly before racing back through the forest along the path she'd just taken. This time she was silent, shifting through the damp leaves and twigs beneath her feet without the slightest sound. In the distance were heavy footfalls pounding against the earth directly north of where she'd last heard Lunci.

"Please don't be hurt; please be ok," she whispered on repeat under her breath as she moved. There was no way she would allow the what ifs to cloud her focus. Lunci *had* to be ok, she wouldn't be able to live with herself if anything happened to him.

Rounding a tree she'd passed earlier, Camille stopped dead in her tracks to listen. She heard distant voices from the village, a subtle hum of wind whistling through the trees, but no sign of the boy.

"Lunci?" Camille said evenly, trying to keep her voice neutral. "Lunci, it's time to get home now." Nothing.

"Lunci! Neeko!" Camille repeated, not caring any longer whether she sounded worried.

What if he was on the ground bleeding from an attack? What if she'd overestimated her ability to keep him protected from such a distance?

An internal flood of dread permeated her system making it almost impossible to think—and that's when she saw them through a thick bramble bush: heavy-lidded, blood-red eyes the size of her fists and oddly human in appearance.

Fear invaded her senses, leaving her frozen on the spot. She'd heard of a shadow beast, a monster roaming Aspera in the dead of night: The Chimera.

Soft footsteps came treading up the path behind her, and Camille's back went rigid; Lunci had found her.

"Lunci! Don't come any closer," she instructed, keeping her focus on the stark red eyes. Her tear ducts began to water in her desperation to keep the red eyes in sight, but the moment she blinked, the gleaming red stare was gone. She held stiff and silent, counting the seconds before the monster decided to attack.

"A little jumpy there, sweetheart?"

Camille leaped a foot in the air as a sultry voice assaulted her tender, overly aware ears. Whipping around with her knife at the ready, she careened off-focus when she located the man who'd addressed her. "Who are you?"

Leaning against an ancient tree, arms casually folded across his chest, stood a young man not much older than she. Blonde wavy hair fell back from his angular face, with both sides shaved and the top left long. The man dragged a hand through his thick strands, gaze never leaving her. His irises were the strangest hue Camille had ever seen: a bleached blue, almost devoid of color; like the bright tinge of the sky at high noon.

"Well hello to you too," he responded, pushing away from the trunk to saunter closer, a broad grin spanning his face. He glanced at the dagger she still held and chuckled. "You thinking of stabbing me? Or do I get a proper hello?"

Camille kept the knife raised, a slight tremor in her hand. "Stay back stranger, who are you?"

She fought to keep the raging monster coiling inside her from surging to the forefront. She'd spent the past eleven moons working to keep her inner beast on a tight leash. It had taken several moon cycles living under Peter's roof to understand that her wild range of emotions didn't have a specified direction or focus. When she was happy, she was ecstatic; when Camille was annoyed, she became unreachable; fear turned into unimaginable terror, and anger transformed into explosive fury. Nothing was at equilibrium within Camille, raging out of control at the tiniest shift.

The stranger's brows knit together with apparent confusion, his lips pursing in contemplation. "Do you not recognize me?" he asked softly, all form of humor dissipating.

"No," Camille snapped. "*Should* I?"

"How long have you lived in this village?" he said, ignoring her question.

"That's none of your business."

He shook his head. "Can't have been more than a few months; maybe a year. Sweet Mother Ma'Nada, I can't believe it. It is you, Camille?"

How does he know my name? Camille narrowed her eyes, taking in his appearance. She noticed three hefty throwing daggers and a short-nosed sword with an ample blade. His clothes were well-fitted and made for travel; a loose cotton shirt and black vest were layered beneath a brown leather coat, and black pants tucked into dirty black leather boots. She could smell the bag of coin hanging on his hip filled with copper duggars, silver rubles, and golden gilders—enough money to buy a year's worth of food for Peter and Lunci.

"Who are you?" Camille insisted, glancing around for any sign of the boy.

"A drifter. I have no name," he said sarcastically, flinging his arms out like he was presenting himself to the royal court.

"What do people *call* you then?" Camille retorted.

He smiled. "You can call me anything you like, sweetheart." He wiggled his eyebrows suggestively at her, drawing closer.

"What are you doing in my woods then, Drifter? And how do you know who I am?" Camille asked, instinctively stepping back. She continued to scan the forest in a slight panic, still unable to detect Lunci or Neeko nearby.

"*Your* woods?" he said, the corners of his lips quirking. He was annoyingly easy to look at, and Camille found it very distracting. His left cheek boasted a soft dimple with every smirk and smile—an uneven flaw in most but endearing on him. "I didn't realize these trees were spoken for."

"You're in Sierra Village. You aren't one of us. So, who are you? And how did you get past the guard tower?"

"Your 'guards' are quite seriously the most moronic Asperians I've ever seen. Those lazy bastards wouldn't know how to guard their dinner against a pack of puppies, let alone an entire village against a Chimera attack. I mean, *honestly*," the drifter continued, ignoring Camille's incredulous expression as he took another step toward her. "Now—are you planning on putting down that little toy of yours?"

"No!" Camille shot back, lifting her dagger more prominently in front of her. "Not until I know whether you did anything to Lunci."

"Ah, I see," the stranger cooed, looking to his right and left in a conspiratorial fashion. "You're looking for the little blonde boy, yes?"

"If you hurt him, so help me—"

"Whoa, whoa...easy there, sweetheart. He's fine. The boy's about fifty yards south of us." The drifter rubbed at the back of his neck, and Camille was immediately drawn to the flexing of his muscles.

Every facet of the stranger seemed slightly *familiar* to her: his mannerisms, his movements, his voice. The man's scent, especially: it was one of oak and pine, soap and musk, and it sent her pulse galloping.

"How do you know where he is?" she growled, trying to keep her anger from building further.

"Ease up Cam, your temper isn't necessary."

She felt a pinch embarrassed but wasn't ready to let down her guard. The stranger seemed to understand this and sighed loudly, his shoulders slipping with apparent perplexity. "Perhaps if you dialed back that temper, you would've been able to deduce his location yourself," he snapped, looking to a spot just over Camille's shoulder.

Camille didn't want to glance away from the drifter for even a second, but Lunci's careless steps were approaching. She took one more step away from the man before spinning to face the rustling leaves on her left.

Lunci broke through the bushes in a childlike gallop. "I got you! Thought you could hide from me, but none can escape the power of the incredible Lunci!"

Lunci leaped at her with careless abandon. Camille twisted away to avoid stabbing him, causing the silver amulet she always kept hidden under her clothing to swing free, pinging loudly against the flat side of the blade.

"What's wrong?" Lunci rasped, eyes going wide at the sight of the knife.

Neeko picked that moment to join them, a low and menacing hiss escaping his throat as he stared at the spot where the red-eyed beast had been.

Camille whipped about, searching the now-vacant spot where the drifter had stood. "Neeko, do you smell something?" Camille whispered. Neeko hissed in response, the fur bunching up around his neck as his tail swished back and forth.

"Camille, what's going on?" Lunci's voice shook as he edged closer to her, looking in the direction Neeko hissed.

"*Where were you?*" Camille said, grabbing Lunci's hand as her emerald eyes scanned the bushes for a pair of blood-red ones. She led them quickly around fallen trees and piles of dead leaves, constantly scanning their surroundings as they followed the slope of the hill toward the village.

"Where was I?" Lunci said, sounding confused. "I was looking for you! Why'd you quit hiding?"

Camille didn't answer. Instead, she continued to drag Lunci toward the safety of the village. As they left the tree line, Camille stole one more glance into the forest edge searching for the truth of what she'd seen. Without warning, Lunci's hand slipped from her grasp, and the side of her face smacked into a solid, hairy body that reeked of stale fish and week-old perspiration.

CHAPTER THREE
AYYA SISTERS

"Watch it, idiot—oh, it's *you*," Grenswald rumbled, sneering down at Camille with cracked dirty lips and blackened rotting teeth. Camille despised him out of principal being a hired hand of the High Court, but her distaste for his proximity was more profound than his presence alone. His muddy brown eyes lit up at the sight of her, and Camille was positive he recalled the first time they'd met.

She hadn't been in Sierra Village long, and most of the villagers kept their distance but for fake pleasantries when they saw her behind the butcher's counter.

Grenswald hadn't been too keen on making her feel welcome, and when she'd tried to hide a small apple away for Lunci during her first Moon Tax, the fat oaf had dragged her outside to make an example of her disobedience. He'd bellowed to the townspeople about the foul, beastly nature of those who stole from the High Kingdom, screaming that no crime would go unpunished. He'd gotten seventeen lashes in before the head guard stepped in, and Camille still couldn't believe she'd restrained herself from throttling the man.

"Grenswald," Camille nodded curtly, scanning the wagon he'd filled to the brim with cartons of meats, bread, and vegetables: the best Sierra Village had to offer.

Before she could get around the behemoth, Grenswald grabbed her upper arm with his grubby sausage fingers. "What do you have for the Moon Tax today? It's two cartons this month, and you *better* not be hidin' goods from the High Court again."

"You're here two days early," Camille said, breathing through her mouth as wave upon wave of his stench assaulted her nose. As politely as she could manage, Camille removed his grotesque hand and looked up into his beady brown eyes, making sure to keep the hatred writhing in her body under control. Neeko sidled in front of her and hissed, and Grenswald took a few clumsy steps away.

"If you pardon me, sir, I'll go collect a hearty payment for you right now," Camille said through clenched teeth.

His eyes roved her body crudely, before landing just below the cavity of her neckline. "That's a pretty trinket you got there," Grenswald said, reaching for the slim silver amulet hanging from her neck.

There was no thought to her motion as Camille's flat palm surged up into Grenswald's nose, the flat expanse of her hand connecting with a sickening crunch of cartilage. He stumbled back a few steps away from her, his eyes now streaming with tears of pain.

"Yow bw-ok muh noh," Grenswald mumbled through a gurgle of blood and mucus.

"You've been warned," Camille roared with fierce intent. An explosion of anger burst out of her throat as she watched the man's pathetic retreat. Her entire body tingled with power, her muscles coiled and primed for attack.

"Don't *ever* touch my necklace. Don't even *look at it.*" She grabbed the amulet with one hand as the warm rush of blood pooled behind her eyes, her gaze becoming sharper and ready for any unexpected movement. He would not be allowed to lay a hand on her again, consequences be damned.

Grenswald's eyes widened, a mixture of fear and surprise spreading like wildfire across his features. "You're a...a..." he said, stumbling back to slam into his wagon with a loud thump.

"Keep your distance from me, understand?" Camille snapped at him as he clutched at his nose with one hand. He nodded slightly, wincing at the pain of movement, but he didn't advance on her.

"Oh dear," Peter said just behind Camille's shoulder. She tensed at the sound of his voice, uncertain how he would react to what had just happened. There weren't a lot of bystanders, but enough for Grenswald to have witnesses of her attack. The sharp surge of anger that had taken over eased slightly as a fissure of worry crept through the barrier of her walled-in emotion. "Did you slip and fall Grenswald?"

Camille eyed the bleeding oaf through squinted lashes. The hefty weight of his body pressed against his cart as though his legs no longer worked. She silently dared him to speak. Staring Camille straight in the eye, he nodded his head, the jowls of his neck shaking with the effort of movement.

"Well that won't do, so sorry to have kept you waiting! I have a hearty payment for you, nothing so inconsequential as a trinket of little value," Peter said, his chin angling toward Camille still gripping her necklace with stern ferocity. "It's just a piece of tin and painted glass, anyways—no worthy value to you or the High King." The old butcher shoved two cartons filled with bread, vegetables, and a bag of fresh meat into Grenswald's cart before handing him a slightly tattered handkerchief from his pocket.

"For the mishap," Peter said with a heartwarming smile, as though offering a token of good will to a man in need. He then took Camille by the shirtsleeve and steered her home.

Camille fingered the amulet as they walked, tracing her thumb over the single red ruby it held. Soldered into the metal were branches bent to create a perfect circle, while the back of amulet was stamped with undefined ancient symbols. She kept anticipating Peter's reprimand for losing her temper with the king's henchman, but it never came. Instead, Peter silently ushered Camille and Lunci inside his cabin and set a pot of water boiling as Camille slumped into a chair.

"Camille!" Lunci shouted, dancing in front of the hearth. "Guess what?"

Camille quirked a brow at him, dropping the amulet back beneath her shirt front. "What?"

"Papa said we get to celebrate Fómhair!"

"What's 'Fómhair?'" Camille asked, massaging her aching temples. It had been an eventful afternoon, more than she'd anticipated, and her body was paying for it.

"It's the best holiday ever!" Lunci exclaimed, practically swooning. "So much food!"

"And when was *this* decided?" Camille asked, peering at Peter.

"After all these years, the only thing you remember is the *food*," Peter chuckled, disregarding Camille's question. "That isn't all there is to Fómhair, my dear boy."

Peter disappeared down the short hall to the adjoining butchery, no doubt to grab whatever little options he'd set aside for them that evening.

"It's truly the best holiday," Lunci continued. "There's mountains of food, as well as dancing and singing."

"In truth, it's a *heathen's* celebration," Peter said from the kitchen. "But we allow the Katolites their interpretation of our holiday. For true Daeites and followers of Ma'Nada, Fómhair is a day of celebration of the end. The end of long days and warm nights, the end of our harvesting season, and the celebration of those we've lost. It is a day of dancing, drinking, singing, and eating; but all together, it is to be a day of reflection and honoring of what is now past."

"*Oh,*" Camille said in wonder. "That does sound delightful."

"Tomorrow marks the thirtieth day of Deireadh Fómhair, which will end the harvesting season before the onset of winter," Peter continued as he busied himself around the kitchen.

"Count Jenkins has been storing apples for us this year, can you believe it?" Lunci said, his little body literally shaking with excitement. "We get to eat *apples*! And I heard Betty Anne is going to make her famous gingerbread loaf. Isn't that great?"

"Yeah, sure." Camille said with a small, wavering smile. It all sounded incredible, but she couldn't help feeling a pang of guilt. The Moon Tax was harsh, and many suffered through the season without much in their winter storage. Eating and drinking in such excess felt wrong.

"Don't worry yourself," Peter said from the doorway, eyes alight with mischief as he held a small plate of meat and cheese out for her. "The count and some of the wealthier villagers stored away additional food in the last couple months of harvesting. We've been lucky this year, my dear—far more than the last. No need to fret. Mother Ma'Nada has been kind with her blessings this year, and many want to share in the giving."

"I don't want to take what I haven't earned," Camille said, picking at her fingernails to avoid the kindness in Peter's expression. "I don't want to owe anyone anything." As much as she knew the offer of food was an open invitation, she still felt as though she didn't deserve to be a part of the treat. Despite her ability to be amongst the inner circle of Sierra Village, she still felt undeserving of its benefits, yet she couldn't pinpoint why.

"You just might have to join the hunt the week, then. Fresh meat is more than enough of a contribution," Peter answered with a sly smile, reading her expression keenly. "Perhaps even Lunci can join."

"Join I will!" Lunci cried. "I will slay every last enemy and bring home food for twenty families!"

Both Peter and Camille laughed at the nine-year-old, but Camille couldn't discount the shadow of worry that darkened Peter's face as he watched his grandson.

She considered sharing her earlier encounters in the forest with Peter, but something about the interaction with the strange blue-eyed man made her want to keep it to herself. Also, a large part of her felt incredibly embarrassed about how close Lunci had gotten to danger under her protection, and there was no doubt he'd never be allowed to play in the woods again if she said anything.

They went about their nightly routine, picking through the oldest meat in the butchery that was still edible and stoking the fire to cook it. Peter reached for a loaf of bread and carefully picked off the staleness forming over the top, placing three thin slices on the rack beside the dancing flames. Lunci pulled a ripened tomato from the pantry store and sliced a couple of juicy sections off before handing them to Peter to roast over the fire.

It was a routine Camille cherished: huddling by the hearth to keep warm, clasping hands to pray to Mother Ma'Nada, and enjoying their meal together. Everything about their life felt natural to her, a comfortable sweater she'd worn many times before. It was in those moments that she felt like one of them, just as much as she felt like a complete and total outsider the rest of the time. Their routines and rituals weren't hers; they were utterly foreign. Yet she pretended not to care that none of it belonged to her, instead smiling and giving thanks for the blessings bestowed upon her that day.

"Can we have a story tonight?" Lunci begged, plucking a small piece of mold from the edge of his bread before he took a hearty bite.

Peter smiled as he lowered himself on his weathered wicker stool stoking the flames into a steady crackling burn. "A story? I guess we can manage that," he said with a jovial wink in Camille's direction. "But only if you agree to the terms."

Lunci beamed, his mouth splitting wide with an infectious smile. "Of course, I agree to the terms!"

"Which are?" Peter prompted, the stoker in hand resting the metal tip against the stone hearth like a cane.

Puffing up his chest with importance, Lunci lifted a single finger into the air. "Never repeat these stories outside of our home."

"Yes," Peter said with a nod as Lunci held up a second finger.

"Never discuss these stories with others outside of our family," he said as a third finger popped up. "And never tell anyone of my love for the mother, Ma'Nada."

Peter turned a severe eye on Camille, his blue eyes narrowed with intent.

"I won't tell a soul, Peter," she said without hesitation. She may not devoutly believe in the mother Ma'Nada as Peter and Lunci did, but she understood Peter's reasoning for keeping his beliefs to himself. His faith in the mother was strictly forbidden within the borders of Aspera by order of the High King. Camille found she enjoyed Peter's stories and didn't want to jeopardize their tradition just because she didn't believe it to be true.

"Which would you like to hear?" Peter asked as he returned to poking and prodding the coals into a dancing flame.

"Have you heard the story about the Ayya Sisters, Camille?" Lunci asked, bouncing up and down on his haunches like a puppy in anticipation of a meal.

"I don't believe so," Camille replied, taking a piece of sliced turkey and a chunk of cheese before settling down next to Neeko by the fireplace. She stroked the top of Neeko's soft furry head as Peter began.

"Ma'Nada, the great mother of this world, has, since the birth of time, loved all living things. She did, however, form a tremendous kindred love for the moon and stars, the sun and knowledge of the world, and the many plush wonders within the Realm of the Five Shores. With her love for these elements, Ma'Nada gave life to three lovely Daughters: Buvona, Joanna, and Nimeha.

"Buvona was the protector of the night sky and those crossing into Cydonia, the land of everlasting life. Her hair raven black, her skin a warm honey brown, and eyes a fierce grey, Buvona was a dark Goddess and a brilliant light to behold. Joanna, the protector of the Sun and all organic life, had hair of fiery copper like a torching blaze on her head with eyes green as grass."

"Like Camille!" Lunci pipped in.

"Yes, just like Camille," Peter said with a smile.

"Then there was Nimeha, eldest of them all, the protector of time, wisdom, and fate. Right, Papa?" Lunci asked, his exuberance and enjoyment of the story infectious to Camille's normal reserved state.

"Correct, my boy. Nimeha had the most beautiful hair, cascading down the length of her back, neither white nor blond, but a mix of the two slipping from tones of honey to the white iridescence of pearl. Her eyes were of the lightest amber, soft and inviting."

Camille eased the stone pillar against her back, slipping into the story with ease as Peter's slow rumbling voice continued. She enjoyed the stark tales of love and adventure, of loss and good fortune. Each story came with a strong message or warning, all she felt were slightly recognizable, but she could never place her finger on when she had heard the tale.

"The Daughters were often referred to as the Ayya, the three forms of life joined together in a circle of infinite growth and cycle of nature. Soon after enjoying the gift of new life and the exploration of their surroundings, it wasn't long before the pang of loneliness struck them.

"Nimeha, understanding the workings of fate, had it in her mind that Ma'Nada wouldn't leave them to suffer in longing. She patiently waited for her true love to find her. Joanna, walking the flat plains, grassy knolls, and rocky terrain of her lands, lived for the exploration and nurturing of life all around. She didn't much mind the longing for human interaction as she had the animals and the trees to converse with. She kept a peace of mind, if not a slow yearning, knowing that her time would come. Buvona, fierce in stature and pressed into the darkness of their world, felt the sting of loneliness the most. She cared for those in passing and nurtured all who crossed the gates into Cydonia, but she could neither save them nor ease their pain. Buvona, youngest of the three sisters, felt cheated."

Peter pulled the steaming kettle from the hook inside the hearth and went about pouring three cups of his specialty lavender mint tea. The earthy sweetness filled Camille's nostrils, and she grabbed a slim slice of bread off the plate as Peter offered her the steaming cup. "Thank you," she said quickly, not wanting to interrupt his story, but Peter continued with a mere nod of his head as he blew methodically on his own steaming cup of liquid.

"One night, Buvona begged for mercy from Ma'Nada, asking for the gift of man to bring her some sense of warmth and bond of family. Ma'Nada agreed, wanting love in her daughters' lives. From the seeds of Ma'Nada's womb, she gifted her daughters with three handsome men: Edis, Gideon, and Fotrix.

"Edis, a proud man with a penchant for the sea, took to Joanna, their mix of land and sea melting together as one. Their love true and bond secure, together they nurtured and protected not just their domains but also each other. Gideon, finding his passion in the craft of writing song and poetry, soothed his heart in the arms of Nimeha and her infinite knowledge. Fotrix was a sly trickster. Though joyous and bubbly at heart, he wasn't honest or truthful. His passion was to manipulate, to trick, to deceive. His falsities and lies tricked Buvona, who was desperate for light and love in her life and fell deeply for the silver-haired fox.

"As Joanna and Nimeha explored the joys of love and blossoming family, Buvona remained sadly alone. Despite Fotrix's expressed desire to love and cherish her, and his promise to build a family, Buvona walked the silvery nights alone and without any children to soften the harshness of being alone. In a spur of great cunning, Buvona devised a plan to trap Fotrix in the darkness of the underworld, allowing him only to roam the lands at the brightest of all full moons for her to easily find him."

"I've always thought Fotrix deserved to be tricked," Lunci spoke up, his lips pursed with intent thought.

"Oh?" Peter said, taking the pause in storytelling to sneak a bit of turkey between his lips. "Why is that?"

Lunci scrunched his tiny nose in thought, his sharp blue eyes watering with focused intensity. "Well, because he is mean. Buvona loves him and she is a caring, beautiful person, but he brings out the worst in her. He makes her look evil, even though she isn't."

"Keen observation," Peter replied, nodding once in agreement.

"Please continue," Camille spoke up, now profoundly intrigued with the tale.

With one quick gulp of tea, Peter quirked up an eyebrow in thought as though searching for the words rolling around somewhere in the confines of his brain. His lips pressed together, his eyes scrunched before his mouth popped open into an 'o' as though locating his mental bookmark and he continued the story.

"Fotrix didn't like to be the center of a trick and loathed Buvona for succeeding in trapping him in the dark depth of the underground. He was allowed out into the open air once at every moon cycle when the fullness of its light could grace the lands with a bright silvery glow. It was on these nights that Buvona expected him to come to her, but that he did not. He instead enchanted the rocks, the trees, and the late-night animals to charm her while he planned a devious trick against her. Fotrix schemed to give a child to both Joanna and Nimeha, shielding their eyes for them to believe they lay with their lovers. Buvona, enchanted as well by Fotrix's charm, thought herself to be full with child.

"In the following months, two beautiful girls were born: one to Joana, and one to Nimeha. The pair of the girls were clear images of Fotrix. The mothers didn't want to forsake their newborn babes, but they realized at once what had happened. They waited for Buvona to step out of her underground home into the evening air that night and shared the news with her. Buvona, heartsick and anxious for her own child she was supposed to have birthed, looked upon these two baby girls and realized that her own pregnancy had also been a falsity.

"The girls were supposed to have been hers and Buvona, hating what Fotrix had done to her, snatched the newborn girls and pulled them down into the darkness of afterlife with both Nimeha and Joana helpless to stop her. Buvona, desperate to make Fotrix pay for his deceit, plagued the lovely daughters with an eternal curse of life and death. Eliza, born to Nimeha, was cursed to birth many children many times over in preparation of all battles. She alone would have the gift to birth an army of mass proportions. Morrighan, daughter of Joanna, was cursed with a touch of death to all living things. Buvona wanted nothing more than to end the life of her most hated enemy, and she spent her life using both Morrighan and Eliza to destroy Fotrix and kill him once and for all."

Camille frowned, but Peter winked at her. "Not all of our sacred stories are happy ones, Camille."

"Yes but, don't you think it's incredibly unfair for Buvona to have suffered so much when everyone around her was barely affected by the pain of loss and loneliness?"

Peter quirked a questioning brow at her. "You think she was the only one to suffer? The center of a storm isn't typically where the damage happens, it's only where the chaos begins, no?"

"Yes. Does she ever get him back for what he did to her?" Camille asked, her tea now completely gone, her hands gripping the empty mug with a bit more force than necessary.

Peter glared at her for a long and arduous moment, his milky eyes a depth of sorrow she couldn't even begin to untangle. His face, though devoid of emotion, ripped a cavernous hole inside Camille, and yet she was unable to pinpoint its origin digging against the lining of her flesh.

"Lunci, my boy, go wash up. It's time for bed."

Lunci's face crumpled into a heap of disappointment before Peter's stern eye found him, and the little boy scurried down the dividing hall toward the washroom.

Camille remained where she sat, back straight as an arrow, her heart thudding in her chest. She couldn't be sure where the impending sense of foreboding came from, but as Peter cleared away the plates and took a seat across from her once again, she knew without a doubt that Peter had a history she wanted no part of. It was evident in the broad lines of worry and stress running the length of his face, the downward angle of his lips and the heavy tinge of sadness that sat on his shoulders like a well-worn shroud.

"The stories aren't all good you know—the scriptures of our gods. They capture an embodiment of holiness, morality and wellbeing, but in truth, the stories are an outline of the death and cruelty to one another. They point out the truth of man and our many flaws."

Camille remained silent as Peter pushed the iron kettle onto the counter instead of back into the fire for another round of tea and headed to the shelves lining the right side of the kitchen wall. Reaching into the topmost shelf, Peter extracted a stone bottle corked with a waxed and wooden stopper. He grabbed two glasses from the sideboard and poured several inches of a thick caramel colored liquid into each cup.

Taking the glass he handed to her, Camille could smell the smoky notes of whiskey mixed with a woodsy tang of oak.

"Buvona spent her entire existence trying her best to defeat the trickster. Unfortunately," Peter said with a sad smile, "some monsters can't be killed, no matter how hard you try."

"Do you believe the stories, these scriptures of your faith?"

31

Camille asked, taking a small sip from her cup and enjoying the sharp burn as the whiskey traveled down her throat.

"Oh, I do," Peter said, a resigned sigh escaping from between his lips. "Buvona may never see the end of her own internal torture, but she did give rise to another power, perhaps a stronger one."

Taking another sip of whiskey, Camille coughed slightly, the hint of burn sizzling the lining of her throat in a somewhat uncomfortable and yet pleasing fashion. "You think the High King is that stronger power fated to rule by the Gods?"

Peter laughed then, a deep belly laugh that brought a fluttering grin to Camille's lips. "No," Peter said with a certain finality. "Definitely not."

"Then what?"

"Hope," Peter replied easily, as though the single word had been resting on his tongue throughout the entire evening. "The Mother and her three daughters gave us hope."

Camille snorted in response. "Oh, come on, you can't be serious."

"I'm dead serious my dear. Buvona may have cursed her nieces but she left Aspera with two incredible protectors. A giver of unending life and an unstoppable warrior able to kill even the deadliest of all evils. She may not have saved her own life, but she sought the answers to help Aspera in need of protection against the trickster."

She couldn't tell if he was being completely serious or pulling her leg, but felt it best to remain silent, uncertain of what Peter was trying to say to her. If the sharp glint in his eye was anything to consider, Camille felt Peter was unloading a dark secret he thought it wasn't his place to keep any longer.

If she was truly honest with herself, she might admit that as much as Camille *wanted* answers from Peter about who she was and her past, there was an immense amount of fear surrounding what the truth might be. Perhaps the past and its many stories were best left alone, untouched and disintegrating with time.

CHAPTER FOUR

CAPTURED PREY

Wafts of steam billowed up from his mug, but he wasn't ready to drink from it. The taste he knew well, light in sweetness with an earthy after note. This morning felt different, though he couldn't be sure why. Langhorn stared idly at the slow dance of steam as it curved upwards into the rafters of his study. He didn't want to drink the tea even though he knew there was little choice about it. Getting old wasn't easy. Today, his stomach clenched inside the cavern of his body, closed off from invasion. Drinking any beverage seemed an impossible ask.

"Doctor?" A timid voice called from the doorway.

Langhorn looked up to see a young girl, her black hair cropped level with her chin and sharp, onyx eyes gleaming. One would expect the depths to be stern, yet they held a bounty of kindness most would find refreshing. Maggie was indeed unique.

"Yes, my dear?"

She smiled at his welcoming tone, and entered his study with more purpose, her black hair swinging as she walked. He had known the young woman all her life, but just recently began to see promise in her future. At sixteen years, Maggie was a quick study in the medical world, already taking tasks from him like a well-established assistant. It was difficult to find decent help; not many were made for the dirty work. Finding a stern minded individual with a steady hand and a strong stomach had seemed an impossible task. Maggie had been sent by Ma'Nada herself, of that he had no doubt.

Maggie was so much more to him than an assistant. She was like a daughter and it made him happy to see her in such high spirits. The young girl's energy reminded him of his daughter Jesabelle, a quick-witted woman who had always kept him on the tips of his toes.

Maggie approached, lifting the dreaded teacup from the saucer with delicate hands. She spooned in a dollop of honey and stirred the dark brown liquid before tucking the china cup and saucer in his wrinkled hand.

"Thank you, dear," Langhorn said with a slight grimace. He didn't have a choice; he would drink the tea even if it made him sick.

"There is someone here to see you, Doctor," Maggie said as she walked toward the door. "Would you like for him to come in or would you rather meet him in the breezeway?"

Smoking his favorite pipe weed on the breezeway did sound delightful, but he knew a long conversation awaited. Glancing at the tea cooling in his hand, he scrunched his nose, and took a bitter sip, forcing it down with an audible gulp. "Here is quite fine."

Boots thudded down the stone hallway as Langhorn waited. A man entered wearing a heavy blue cloak, the hood pulled low over his face. His boots were rough brown leather, the heavyweight made for long journeys, and yet his clothing seemed untouched by the rugged terrain surrounding White Wall.

"It's good to see you again," Langhorn said, making no move to get up or even welcome the guest by name. Their meetings were most often short, and impersonal. They weren't friends, but they were indeed on the same side of the war, and in the end, that was all that mattered.

"I came as quick as I could; I don't have long," the man replied as he pulled the hood away from his face and sat across from Langhorn, his legs and muscles bunched tight.

Langhorn set down his tea and leaned forward, elbows resting atop his knees. "I got your message this morning. What's the problem?"

"He found her. He knows where she is, and he's sent a pack of Chimera to collect."

Silence filled the room. Langhorn hadn't thought it possible, they had put in so much effort to keep Camille's location under the radar. If he were honest with himself though, they had found much luck in the past year regarding Camille. It was impossible to hide someone as infamous as she for long. "How?"

"I received a raven from Grenswald. He said he found a red-haired woman whose eyes turned black as ink when he tried to steal her medallion. It's her. Langhorn, I know it is, and so will the High King. We need to send for her."

Langhorn let out a long sigh, a breath of air he hadn't known he'd been holding.

"They would be coming from Charlie Town heading south through Dun L'er forest. We have three days at most."

"Maggie!" Langhorn called out, knowing the girl would be close at hand.

"Yes, Doctor?" She walked through the door with a book in her hand and a teacup poised at her lips.

Langhorn smiled gently at her, not wanting to alarm her despite the pounding urgency rushing through his system. "Please send word to the Raven Ward. I will need to be sending out some letters post haste."

She nodded in response and took off down the hall.

"Langhorn, that is not the worst of it I'm afraid," the cloaked man said, his eyes heavy with the weight of his news.

"LeMarc is on the hunt for Ephidra Lily."

"Does he know where it grows?" Langhorn said, pacing to the open window overlooking the distant West Iron mountain range and sighing with the additional weight pressing down on his shoulders. The autumn season hadn't yet fallen into the gloom of winter, leaving the lower ranged peaks still visible beneath the clouds a soft and brilliant green. It was a beautiful sight, as was most of Aspera, but soon the distant mountains would be covered in winter white. Cold, bitter air would slip through the lands, bringing a storm of terror. Idly, he ran a gentle finger over the neck of his brown and white speckled hawk, Archimedes, sleeping on the ledge of the open window. As stark yellow eyes befitting a hunter turned toward Langhorn in pleasant surprise, Langhorn began to formulate a plan of what must be done.

"He is making plans to head south," the man spoke up from behind him. He remained in his chair, back straight and features stern.

Langhorn nodded, giving Archimedes one last pet of attention before turning back toward his guest. "From where exactly?"

"That I cannot say," the man replied tersely as though surprised Langhorn would even ask. Langhorn hummed with an air of annoyance, but his face remained stoically blank of emotion as the man continued. "I can give you details of his movements and actions. I'm not able to tell you where the High King is located now. Few know. Therefore, *few* he could pinpoint to slaughter if word got out of his whereabouts."

Langhorn nodded but remained silent as he began to pace the length of his office, head down in contemplation as the fabric of his robes swished around his legs.

"You don't trust me," the man said, his voice low and sharp.

"Of course, I trust you," Langhorn snapped back. "That doesn't mean I don't second guess the information given to me. You think you have all the details? Do you honestly think the High King tells you everything?"

The man snorted loudly, his limbs jerking with a constant jitter as though he was anxious to be on his way. "No, of course not."

"Well then," Langhorn replied with a sardonic grin, "I can trust you and also not trust you are telling me everything."

The man nodded, though his thin lips pursed together in grim irritation. "He will be sending a portion of his Equestrian troops from Alpha Quarter by foot, but most will arrive by ATS."

"He's sending his air fleet?"

The man nodded silently.

"This is dire," Langhorn whispered.

Archimedes screeched from his perch as though in shock, to which Langhorn nodded as though in silent agreement with the bird.

"I don't know how much time we have, but I do know he is sending out a full battle line of Equestrian soldiers."

"Where?" Langhorn asked, hoping that the man wouldn't be able to give a definite answer.

"He plans on passing through Whiskey Wharf first in the effort to appear they are prepping for mass trade at the waterfront. The Equestrian units will hit Romeo next."

Langhorn's legs almost collapsed beneath him at the mention of his home village. "He's found the Sanctuary?"

The man nodded, his eyes downcast. "He knows. I'm certain he doesn't know where the other sanctuaries are located. Only that they exist, and they are the key to what he has been searching for."

Langhorn nodded, the billowing lengths of his robes swishing across the stone floor as he moved toward the towering piles of books laid out over his desk. He found the ink pot he was looking for and sat down to write the one message he hoped never to write.

"There is one more thing of note," the man said, almost as an afterthought though Langhorn knew better. The man's tone had shifted downward, leaving room for Langhorn's own interpretation.

"Oh?" Langhorn inquired politely as he scribbled out the words banging around in his head.

"Something Vesyon will most certainly want to be aware of," the man said lightly as though uncertain of how to unpack the thoughts spinning through the confinement of his mind.

"Spit it out," Langhorn said, growing impatient.

"The Praetorians within Aspera must remain on high alert. Camille's name, as well as others, have been whispered amongst many in the deeper corners of Aspera now that the rebellion has begun to expand. She isn't safe to wander, and neither is he."

Langhorn nodded, watching the man with intense curiosity as his gaze shifted anxiously about the room. "Noted," Langhorn finally replied, his pen hovering over the piece of parchment.

The man silently excused himself, disappearing through the open office door as though he'd never been there. Archimedes squawked, his feathers ruffling up in the way of conversation.

"I agree my dear friend," Langhorn responded to the puffed-up bird as he dipped his feathered pen in ink and made to write out his messages. He wrote three identical letters, sealed them with the White Wall crest against melted red wax, before turning to back to Archimedes now staring out the arched window.

"This needs to get to Vesyon right away. I'll send these last two via raven," he explained his needs to Archimedes as he would any messenger. Even though the Count of White Wall preferred to send all messages via raven, Langhorn always sent his urgent letters via Archimedes. He'd never thought of the hawk as a pet, but more an extension of himself.

Archimedes cocked his head at Langhorn's request and shifted his weight to extend his leg toward the old man.

"If you are unable to find Vesyon," Langhorn began before Archimedes' feathers ruffled in warning of a sharp bite. "Not that you won't find him dear friend! You are the best tracker in all Aspera; I have no doubts in you. But if a problem should arise, please go straight to Theo." With a sharp nod, Archimedes extended his leg more prominently, his feathers pulled against his body with his beak extended upwards in public preening of the offered compliment. Langhorn inwardly chuckled as he tied off the final note.

He watched the beautiful spread of wings as Archimedes took flight to the east. The words of his message played on an unending loop in his mind: *He's found her. They know.*

CHAPTER FIVE
UNDISCOVERED SECRETS

The morning of Fómhair came quickly, causing Lunci to squirm with anticipation all through breakfast. After promising to bring home a sweet prize that night, Camille dashed out the front door with her bow slung over her shoulder and two hunting knives attached to either hip.

The sun peeked its shiny face over the eastern edges of the Iron Mountains, spreading light across the azure sky. Warmth did not accompany it, and Camille pulled on her fingerless gloves in quick, jerky motions. She jogged effortlessly through the ramshackle cabins and measly vegetable gardens toward the edge of town, where a small group of men bantered loudly to waken their groggy minds.

Marcus Flint, the Head Guard of Sierra Village, was waiting in a small clearing as Camille joined the men. Marcus pulled out a slew of daggers from his hunting pack, handing them to the unarmed villagers who'd decided to join the morning hunt.

"Morning Camille," Marcus said as he approached her. He wore a worn leather vest marked with the Sierra Village crest: an owl in flight over a standing pine tree. Most guards wore their hunting doublets to showcase their power and authority, but not Marcus. He wore his out of necessity. His pockets were packed to the brim in preparation for the hunt.

Mumbling a groggy good morning in Marcus's direction, Camille passed by him debating if she should tell him about the

Chimera. It would be smart to warn him, as the Chimera were a serious threat to the village. If she did, she'd not only lose her playtime with Lunci but her hunting time as well. She'd need to be extra vigilant in watching the nine-year-old, never letting him out of her sight in the forest from now on.

"Brian and Jacob—head along the west path with Camille," Marcus said to two younger boys standing next to Camille. "I was told yesterday that a pack of wild turkeys was spotted there, and I'm hoping to get one on our menu tonight. Watch each other's backs and make sure to report to me immediately if you see anything outside of the norm."

All three nodded, and Camille led the way.

"See what you can do, our little golden hunter," Marcus murmured as she brushed past. He'd quickly recognized her as one of the best hunters in the village when she arrived, and treated her with respect when they were alone amongst the trees. In *public*, however, he ignored her often and had barely smirked a few times when they crossed paths, regarding her as if she were a homeless beggar asking for a bite to eat. It bothered her more than she cared to admit. She took extra precaution when in his presence not to allow her inner turmoil to seep through the wall holding in her wild range of emotions.

"Any wagers this morning, gentlemen?" Camille asked, peering closely at her hunting companions coming up behind her.

"Wagers? Against *you*?" Jacob said incredulously. His black hair shined an almost vivid blue in the early morning light, hanging shaggily over his amber-hued eyes. He leaned down to gather his hunting gear, which was all frayed and rundown despite his best efforts to maintain it. Jacob's parents were both blacksmiths but weren't considered well off within the village. They got by like the rest of them—just barely, with several pounds lost after the winter chill snuck in.

It wasn't easy to get on his nice side, and at first, Camille hadn't cared to try. She'd ignored the men, hunting by herself until these teenagers had seen her for what she was: a great ally. They'd reported her skills to Marcus one evening after a particularly great hunt, and her popularity on the trails had increased overnight.

Jacob no longer shot verbal daggers at her as he'd done their first few months of hunting. Instead of harping on her short stature and female qualities, he now regularly asked her for pointers on her pristine hunting tactics. There was obvious curiosity surrounding Camille, a stranger in their home village explained away as a long-lost relative of Peter's, but she deflected all questions about her origin.

"The only wager I'd take against you would be if you shot with your eyes closed, Camille, and even then, I bet you'd still shoot down more game than little Brian here." Jacob elbowed Brian, a lanky, mousy-haired boy not much older than thirteen.

Even though Brian Bower was three years his junior, Jacob only stood a mere three inches taller than him. Brian was kinder, though, with wide blue eyes the color of the evening sky and a shy smile Camille had immediately taken to.

"I doubt I could hit anything smaller than a deer with my eyes closed," Camille said to Brian. "So you might obliterate my record."

"Uh huh, you're just humble," Brian replied, his face breaking into a wide smile. "You'd miss on purpose to give me the upper hand in a competition, Cammy. Don't even try to argue with me on that."

It was hard not to like the two boys who'd taken her in. They teased her, swapped goods after hunting, and shared stories about their experiences in the village growing up together. Brian was sweet and good-natured but followed the crowd, and he hadn't really befriended Camille until Jacob decided to. Jacob, at first, had treated her like Marcus had, but, in the last few moon cycles, his attitude toward her had drastically changed. He sought out her attention and praise, not just in a crowd but also when they found themselves alone. She valued their friendships regardless of their past behaviors, and it felt good to have something constant in her life. Something she could pretend had always been a part of her past.

The three of them laughed freely as they went up to their usual path, enjoying the brisk autumn air along the western trail through Dun L'er. Camille led the way, pointing directions instead of voicing them when she heard game rustling in the leaves of the forest floor. Brian was the first to shoot down a rabbit and smiled widely when Camille lied and said she hadn't even seen it.

"Hey Cammy, how's the hand?" Brian asked. He carefully pulled the arrow from the rabbit's neck as Camille had taught him, making sure not to break the arrow's tip off in the process.

She removed her glove and held out her palm. "Totally fine. I told you it'd heal fast."

Brian's eyes bugged out as he took in her smooth skin, absent of any mark. She'd cut it severely two days ago chasing down a deer, but the surface layer had grown back within a few hours. "You'd never even know..."

"How's that possible?" Jacob asked, one thick, black eyebrow quirking up as he grabbed her bare hand to inspect up close. "If I cut my hand like that it would've taken weeks to heal." Camille merely smiled as she gently pulled her hand from his grasp and shoved her glove back on.

"It's obvious, isn't it?" Brian said from a few feet away, now collecting a cluster of mushrooms that were growing in the thick grass. "Cammy's one of those super soldiers."

"Careful Brian!" Jacob said quickly, searching the area for eavesdroppers. "I wouldn't tell that to anyone else, Camille. They might get the wrong impression, and you're already an outsider."

"What do you mean?" Camille glanced from Brian's expression of pure awe to Jacob's, which was now pinched with worry.

"You never heard about the rebellion? The Chimera outbreaks? The mass exiles?" Jacob asked, voice barely over a whisper.

Camille shook her head, a black hole of apprehension growing in her stomach.

"The whole reason Marcus and the entirety of the guards are afraid of infiltration is the mass outbreak that happened eight years ago in Charlie Town."

"Outbreak of what? The shadow beasts?" Camille asked warily.

Brian hushed her quickly, his eyes snapping left and right in quick succession. "They're called Chimera," Brian whispered.

"One and the same. Charlie Town was overtaken with the fever, and the whole lot of 'em turned," Jacob said, his mouth turning up in a weird, menacing sort of grin. "No amount of praying to our Holy Father would save them."

Camille removed her dagger from its holster and studied the forest floor for possible dinner options. She wanted answers; she wanted to know the truth. However, something about the way Jacob's eyes lit up told Camille she might regret learning about the past.

"Your god Faeder?"

Brian eyed her suspiciously out of the corner of his eye as he came up close beside her. "Of course, I mean Faeder, *our* Holy

Father, Camille. He's the *only* God."

She nodded in reply, unwilling to start the conversation of beliefs with them when she was desperate to hear other, *more critical* information. Picking up her pace, she stepped over a wayward tree that had fallen many years prior, the wood rotted and frayed splaying out its innards across the main path.

As Jacob and Brian trailed behind, Camille pressed her luck as she pulled out an arrow in slow preparation. "What do you mean by 'turned?' They all got sick with a fever?"

"Chimera aren't only huge monsters; they were humans before they got infected. Once you get bitten by a Chimera and the fever sets in, you're a goner. You either die or you turn. I imagine most would choose to die first," Jacob said, chuckling.

"How would you know? You've never even seen a Chimera before," Brian pointed out.

Jacob kicked at a loose rock, shrugging his shoulders in an offhanded way. "I've heard the stories. It's enough to know I'd never want to turn into one of those monsters."

Brian elbowed Jacob in the ribs. "We aren't really supposed to talk about this. It's not a good idea to speak ill of those who've turned to shadow."

"Just a little more? Please?" Camille pressed, trying not to appear desperate.

"Yeah, okay," Brian said under his breath. "Most of the people in Charlie Town succumbed to the fever. But before they turned, the High King sent in one of his special guards to protect those who were still alive. It didn't quite go the way the High King had planned. The guard went crazy and ended up slaughtering the entire town, leaving half of the Chimera horde to run wild into the neighboring villages of Aspera. We think they might have even extended past the Kingdom borders into other territories. It would explain why the High King closed the borders after the infection spread."

Camille didn't know why, but her mouth had begun to go dry at Brian's words. No wonder Sierra Village was always on guard. Fear of such a fever would surely keep them wary against anyone they didn't know firsthand.

"What happened to this special guard?" Camille asked as she notched an arrow to take aim at a distant squirrel. The fluffy animal saw her movement and dashed behind a branch before she could

43

fire.

"Oh," Jacob said, "he wasn't just a guard—he was a Praetorian. One of the High King's lead soldiers. His blood-lust and destruction of Charlie Town was the start of the Praetorian rebellion. They were tired of being slaves to a king who forced them to kill at his command, and this Praetorian slaughtered an entire village to send a message. They were done fighting for the crown. After the slaughter, the High King exiled all his Praetorian guards, but they didn't go quietly."

Jacob's nonchalance seemed to appease Brian's cautious nature, and he chimed in more freely. "The High King stated to all of Aspera that Praetorians were unfit for duty and no longer followed the laws of the Aspera Munera."

"What's the 'Aspera Munera?'" Camille asked, blowing wisps of flyaway hair from her perspiring face.

"It's the Asperian Duty, laws we have to follow, like the Moon Tax. This Praetorian broke the law, so the High King exiled them all. The battles that followed were a bloodbath at first—a lot of Asperians died trying to rid the kingdom of the rebel Praetorian soldiers."

The story sounded familiar to Camille, but it was like a dream or a half-buried memory. There was the sensation of recognition, but no concrete details Camille could cling to.

Huffing in frustration, Camille angled away from her friends. She had to be careful. It was one thing to show curiosity and intrigue, but it was another to show rage at their words. She couldn't be sure, but something boiling in her gut told her the Praetorians had never been an enemy of Aspera.

It took everything she had not to lash out in frustration over her amnesia about the past. Each new story of Aspera or the High King or the mistreatment of the villages reminded her of how little she really knew. How many memories and stories had been ripped from her mind? Who had she lost, or forgotten? It was unfair.

"What's so different about these Praetorians?" Camille asked, now fully invested in uncovering the truth.

Jacob narrowed his eyes, seeming to debate whether to respond. "They are superior. They have special abilities. But like Brian said, we really shouldn't be talking about them. It's forbidden."

Camille nodded slowly, trying to appear unaffected as her head spun with the new information.

Jacob gathered his pack in the sudden lull of conversation, and together they agreed to head back to town. "I bet you can understand now why our village is wary about outsiders and those who seem a bit *unusual*."

Camille ducked her head, immediately self-conscious. Her rapid healing abilities, magnified senses of smell, direction, and sound as much as Peter kept waving them away as "special talents," Camille had begun to realize how much deeper they went than that.

"You okay there?" Brian said as he quickly shoved a handful of berries into his pack. Juice seeped from between his fingers, running red down his bare arm. She stared at it, transfixed by sight. It looked like blood, a small trickle sliding along the surface of his skin before plopping onto a dried leaf with a loud *plunk*.

"Yep," Camille replied, snapping out of her trance. "Let's head a bit north. The hill will give us an advance on scouting those turkeys Marcus was talking about."

Brian eyed her as they headed out, leaving their earlier conversation behind.

The morning faded quickly into the afternoon, and, within five hours, heavy clouds had moved in overhead to shower them in cold, fat drops.

"I think we have enough," Jacob said, his pack now brimming with three short and chubby turkeys.

"I agree," Camille said, pulling an arrow from a small rabbit. After stuffing the fluffy brown animal into her hunting bag, she stood up and turned her face to the cloudy sky. A spray of mist chilled her heated cheeks and a shiver of uncertainty settled into her bones. Tonight's festival wasn't going to be enjoyable for her, not with all she'd just learned.

Camille never stopped examining the shady underbrush on the trek home, looking for a pair of red eyes as they exited the forest line.

"Hey Cammy, I set aside some arrow tips at my parent's shop. Care to join?" Jacob asked, motioning toward her right hand full of lifeless rabbits. "I need to drop off a few things before we head into town for lunch."

"Yeah, I could use some new ones. I need to stop by the bakery too, so I might as well head into town with you guys. Are you working today?" Camille asked Brian, who helped with the day-to-day errands at his mother's bakery.

"Naw, we're helping to set up for the festival tonight. Count Jenkins said he needed some strapping young men," Brian joked, pounding on his chest with a free hand.

"Looks like you might be left out of this one then, Jacob," Camille said, unable to control the laughter that followed. It felt good to laugh, to put their earlier conversation behind them.

They carried on with their lighthearted wisecracks until reaching the blacksmith shop, when Camille's jubilance promptly melted away. Jacob's parents gave Brian and their son a warm welcome, their tone turning frosty with bitter contempt when they asked Camille what it was that she needed.

"A bit of the usual, girl?" Mr. Welsh bellowed, eying Camille with beady brown eyes down a slightly bulbous nose. His thick mop of curling black hair sprang up in wild tufts over his head, a stark contrast to Mrs. Welsh. Her grey hair and waif appearance gave her the weakened look of most in the village: malnourished. Both of Jacob's parents were thin and hollowed in the cheeks. Despite their obvious distaste of her, Camille still felt terrible that they had so little to spare in the way of goods. Camille had gotten quite used to the blatant dislike of her presence and felt bringing attention to it was the worst possible idea imaginable.

"Yes, please," Camille replied as politely as she could manage, handing over five pounds of game as usual. She received ten bodkin iron arrow tips in exchange. They were the cheapest kind of iron but the easiest to acquire, and there was little point in trading for better quality. She only needed a sharp point and a flat piece to fly true; the quality of the metal was of little consequence. "Thank you kindly," Camille chirped as she shoved the linen-wrapped purchase into her pack, but the Welsh couple didn't feel the need to reply.

"See ya tonight!" Jacob said with a quick wave over his shoulder to his parents as they embarked, walking to the bakery next. Brian's mother was a sweet, good-natured woman who looked as gentle as a daisy. Her name was Jyllel, but everyone in town called her Mama J.

"What would you like today, my dear?" Mama J asked as Camille walked up to the rough-hewn wooden counter. The entire right side of the store leaned heavily against an old pine tree, the curved walls sagging into the massive trunk as though exhausted from the weight of time. Dull straw roofing and creaking pine floors gave the whole structure a homey and comfortable appearance. A black stone oven kept the front of the store warm during the winter and was often used to make hearty loaves of bread, cookies, and buns, while a crumbling brick fireplace in the back heated warm beverages and kept the back rooms livable for the Bowers' family of three.

"Just one loaf of bread and a small cookie for Lunci please," Camille said, opening the pack to give Mama J her pick of the loot.

"I think a rabbit this round, dear. I'm afraid the festival tonight has me baking up a frenzy. I won't have time to skin anything beyond one ruddy rabbit." Mama J smiled gently, and Camille appreciated the friendliness even if it was forced.

Waving their goodbyes after collecting a few baked goods, they made for the northwest section of the village where Camille did her daily trading. The market didn't look like much at first, but a closer glance behind the shabby structures revealed baubles, clothes, food products, and finery that nobody there would've been able to get ahold of without the underbelly of the trade network.

The whole of Sierra Village was laid out like a large cross, with the inner cross-section holding the great hall, Count Jenkins' home, an everyday church, and the town jail—one usually full of drunkards. The rest of the local market stores spread out from the square center including the blacksmith, the baker, the linen and leather ward, and the primary food market. The outer "arms" of the large cross were comprised of small, mostly shabby homes.

The best part of Sierra Village was the many items available in the slinky narrow walkways of the market. It was kept furthest away from prying eyes in a dodgy bit of town populated by those less fortunate. But the joke was on the outsiders and the High King's guards, for it was those beggars and gypsies who ran the black-market trade in and out of Sierra Village.

With a bag still full of game and Brian and Jacob in tow, Camille weaved casually in and out of the narrow streets, ducking behind a worn-down door before slipping into the side alley of her second-favorite place in town. The tiny shop windows all held small fortunes, and many more boasted large amounts of unique products easily affordable to the everyday trader. Camille passed by a cart filled with freshwater fish smuggled back from Black Bottom Lake. Fresh fish was hard to come by in Sierra Village, and only those willing to leave the safety of the village would travel in search of such fare.

Camille moved on toward a well-lit window showing off a massive case of high-end netting, a common trade in Whiskey Wharf, which bordered the Roseus Sea. Sauntering by a few darker displays of fine silk, linen, and heavy furs, Camille ran her fingertips along the soft materials, promising to purchase a fur wrap in the future when she had the means to do so.

Camille's eyes flitted over a large display of silver gems and beautifully constructed weapons—a trade found predominantly in Alpha Quarter. Those items were always the costliest, and few in the town could afford them. Occasionally, there was a tempting item amongst the glittering jewels and baubles, but Camille never indulged in frivolous purchases. She had very little money and mostly meat to barter. An ornament wasn't something she needed, or could afford, but a substantial meal would always be welcome.

Brian's stomach rumbled as they squeezed through the crowded streets. "I'm so hungry my innards are eating me from inside out. Let's go eat."

Camille nodded as they passed under a tattered white banner featuring the prominent pine tree and brown owl marker of Sierra Villages crest. She could smell the delightful scent of cooking meat and the heaviness of old ale as they slipped through the narrow wooden doorway into the Broken Goat to catch a bit of trade and some decent grub.

Betty Anne, the owner of the Broken Goat, always had a taste for fresh game, and in turn, offered food and drink as payment. Camille rarely gave in to the desire to drink the hearty mead or sour ale Betty Anne served, but she never turned down the meal of the day. *Jacob*, however, overcompensated, usually throwing back two glasses of mead and asking for Camille's.

"Will it be the usual you three?" Betty Anne asked as they approached the dingy countertop.

Camille lifted three large rabbits and a fox from her pack and handed them over to an enthusiastic Betty Anne.

"Oh, the delicious concoctions I can make with this lot!" she said, beginning to mutter to herself as she set out cutlery for Camille and the guys. "...Cook until they reek with deliciousness...truffle oil, no, maybe a wine reduction, demi-glaze? Or braised? That would be fitting, or maybe stuffed..."

"What masterpieces are you bringing to the Fómhair

celebration? I look forward to your recipes every year!" Brian said with large, hopeful eyes. Brian had a soft spot for cooking, but his father was a village guard and would sooner disown his son than allow him to bake a pie.

Betty Anne smiled at Brian's ploy to have her reveal her secrets. "You know I like you three, but nobody will know a single thing until the amazing concoction touches their taste buds tonight! I *do* have a special treat for you, though, thanks to your fine hunting skills the other day."

She disappeared behind the flapping wooden doors that led into her kitchen, her waist-long, raven black hair swinging as she moved. She returned a few minutes later with a heap of steaming food, and Camille's stomach growled.

"You out-do yourself every day," Jacob said as he dove into his pile of mashed potatoes and cut a bite from his turkey slab.

"You're ever the charmer, Mr. Welsh," Betty Anne said sweetly, before moving down the bar to a group of surly-looking men who'd apparently had a few too many ales so far.

"Is your dad going to make it tonight?" Jacob asked Brian, shoving another forkful of food into his mouth.

Camille moved at a much slower pace, ensuring to savor each bite. She usually had one large meal at the Broken Goat every other week and tried to bring home half her meals to Lunci and Peter. But that day was different—since they had the Fómhair celebration, she felt absolutely no guilt in eating every bite Betty Anne had to offer.

"No, he's out on patrol tonight. I think he might show up later, after his shift change," Brian said in an overtly neutral tone. Camille could tell that Brian missed his father, but never complained about it aloud—not wanting to be scolded for being a "sissy."

"Al'ri, gentlemen," Betty Anne barked at the group of men nearby. "I think yeh've had plenty of my finest mead for the moment. Sober up before I toss yeh on your arses out the door!" She was never serious about tossing anyone out—unless they criticized her cooking, and then they were shamed by the whole of Sierra Village and never allowed back.

"You gonna sic a Praetorian on us, Betty Anne?" one of the men cajoled, his lips splitting into a lopsided grin.

"Aye! Watch yeh backs, or I'll fetch my Praetorian," Betty Anne teased, before ambling back to Camille's side of the bar. The group of rowdy men clapped and yelled, but it quickly subsided into murmurs and slurred repartee. They were completely harmless, but Camille still had no doubt she'd see them leaving the prison the following morning. For those on the rundown side of town, it was easier to drink themselves into a stupor and hunker down in the jail than to freeze out in the open air.

Camille's ears had perked up at the mention of a Praetorian, and she squinted as Betty Anne wiped down the counter.

"Looks like somethin' cookin' away in that there lil' head of yours, dearie. Care to share?" Betty Anne prodded, sidling closer to Camille. Her raven hair shifted attractively over her shoulder, and despite the spider web of lines edging her eyes, Betty Anne was quite the attractive woman. Camille placed her somewhere in her mid-forties but couldn't be sure. Her sharp hazel eyes retained the most youth. Through a shroud of sprouting grey hair and blooming wrinkles, Betty Anne was a very young and vivacious woman at heart.

Camille swallowed an unusually large bite of food before her tongue was able to form the words on her mind. "How many Praetorians lived here in Sierra Village?"

Betty Anne stopped her circular rhythmic cleaning, her brow quirking into a sharp arch. "That's a hard one to answer."

"Why?"

Betty Anne inspected a tiny stain on her polished wood countertop, rubbing the spot repeatedly with quick circular motions. "To be honest, it's all speculation. They weren't the easiest to pick out o' a crowd. They were once Asperians, yeh know—looked just like yeh and me. There were a few signs, though—a few ways to see through their shield."

"How?" Jacob asked.

Betty Anne winked at him conspiratorially. "They never age. It's one way to tell."

"They don't *age*?" Camille repeated, a little shocked.

"From the day they turn, their bodies are frozen in time. They can neither age, nor be killed 'less someone *really* tries. I'd like to see someone come back from the dead once their head has been chopped off!" Betty Anne said, a rumbling boisterous laugh bubbling from between her cracked pink lips.

"Have you ever seen one before?" Brian continued.

"Oh yes," Betty Anne replied, clearly enjoying their rapt

attention. "Once yeh recognize their patterns, they're hard to miss. There's speculation that some are still around, a few at least. Hungry eaters they are, wouldn't mind them stoppin' in for a heavy plate or three of food!"

"I can't believe it. Praetorians were here in Sierra Village," Brian said, face alight with awe.

"Absolutely. The High King needed to ensure a strong army against the intruders. I'm surprised your parents haven't told yeh. Not long ago, they were everywhere." Betty Anne shook her head wistfully and wove her long raven hair into a loose braid.

Red eyes and black, matted fur swam to the forefront of Camille's mind at the mention of intruders. She knew very well that Betty Anne spoke of the shadow beasts, and the question remained: why would the High King exile an entire army of unbeatable soldiers if those creatures were still roaming Aspera?

One of the villagers down the bar hailed Betty Anne away, but Camille's brain continued to speculate.

"I see the thoughts rolling around in your head," Jacob said with a frown. "Out with it."

"Would you turn away an elite group of protectors if there were threats of an intruder?" Camille asked, her focus on both the boys sitting on either side of her. Jacob shoved a hefty chunk of meat into his mouth followed by a thick pile of potatoes. His cheeks bulged out like a chipmunk hoarding his winter storage of nuts. He shrugged noncommittally and lifted his glass of mead to wash down the mash of food in his mouth.

"Well," Brian chirped up. "It depends on how dangerous the protectors were, no? Perhaps the Praetorians are the threat."

"Listening to Betty Anne talk about them that doesn't seem likely. I mean, to the everyday observer they would have looked like you and me. Why remove them? Doesn't it sound strange?" Camille huffed as her mind whirled with questions. "It doesn't seem like the Praetorians were the problem," Camille mused, stabbing a chunk of potato with her fork.

"It wasn't all of them that caused the exile; it was just one. That *one* Praetorian started the rift, and it rippled throughout the entirety of Aspera. Like a bad apple, you know?" Jacob said, licking the grease and butter from his fingers.

Camille scrunched her nose in distaste at the visual image of a crumpled rotting apple in a barrel of freshly picked red ones. Betty

Anne's potatoes usually tasted delicious, but Camille's edginess began to make all her food taste like a thick paste. She choked the current bite down, then went to work on the fatty meat, hating the idea of wasting food. Jacob shifted in his seat as he peered at her from his peripherals. She could feel the heat of his glare, and it made her feel uncomfortable—asking too many questions must've been against their Asperian rules.

"Rules are rules," Brian chimed in. "We follow the law of our Holy King, Faeder. The High King was appointed by our Lord and carries out his teachings. It doesn't matter if just one person broke the law—they all had to be exiled. It's just how it's done."

"I hope you realize how ludicrous that sounds," Camille said with an unladylike snort.

Jacob shrugged, one shoulder lifting slightly higher than the other as he grabbed his half-empty mead glass and drained it effectively in two loud gulps. "Yes, perhaps. I'm not one to follow the teaching of this oh so holy lord," Jacob said with a twitch as though his words didn't quite fit with the teachings of his youth. "In my opinion, The High King had to prepare for the backlash of his actions, no? You make the martyr of one, the rest will follow."

"What do you mean?" Camille asked, dropping her fork full of meat to pay closer attention.

"Well," Jacob said as he shoved a hefty amount of buttered bread between his lips. "Wouldn't you be afraid of a Praetorian's retribution if you banished one of their own? And not just *a* Praetorian, but from the stories I've heard, one of the *best*."

He has a point, Camille thought with blooming intrigue. "What is this law exactly?" Camille asked between small bites of bread.

"The Aspera Munera," Brian stated in an official air.

Jacob reached into his pocket and slammed a crusted, grimy piece of paper down next to Camille's plate. "She lives with Peter, nuthead. She's not going to know what the rules are."

"Why not?" Brian asked blankly, staring at Camille as though she were a rare bug to be examined.

"Yes, why not?" Camille asked with slight hesitation.

"Peter was *part* of the rebellion," Jacob said matter-of-factly. "And he doesn't follow the teachings of our Holy King. Peter is a follower of the old ways."

Camille's jaw dropped wide open. "He *what*?"

"Yeah," Jacob continued, shoving a sturdy piece of meat into his mouth and slowly chewing. Camille inwardly squirmed with impatience, but she waited in silence for him to continue, not wanting to miss a single detail of what he said. "Peter isn't just a butcher Camille; he was Rogue, one of the head resistors in the rebellion against the Praetorian exile. Most Daeites were resistors to the High Kings law."

Camille felt her chest contract at Jacob's words. Peter was a follower of Ma'Nada. Every story he'd ever told had been from the sacred text of Daeism, but he'd never showed her the written word. He knew it all by heart, every story and every line. It was only now Camille understood why. Everything he'd taught her about his belief wasn't just a secret between them but a crime against the crown.

Brian seemed to be just as surprised as Camille but didn't look so taken aback by it that it affected his appetite. How did she not know this about Peter and yet Jacob did? Not that Peter would have told her, but in all her time with him, how did she not *see* it on him? It was true that he never spoke of the High King in great favor, but he'd never voiced a passionate dislike for the ruler of Aspera either.

"I've never heard him talk about these things," Camille said as she reached for her mug to take a small sip to wet the dryness of her throat.

"No, I can imagine not. Peter isn't one for sharing stories of his past, but my parents know. They told me when I met you to 'beware of the old man's heathen teachings,'" he said with a chuckle. "Don't worry Cam, I don't care what Peter believes in or who he prays to."

Brian's mouth fell open at Jacob's harsh tone. "You don't mean that."

"I do," Jacob said without flinching. "Peter isn't the only 'heathen' in Sierra Village. Just because the High King tells us to follow in step doesn't mean that we must. Peter fought against the High King's rule of Aspera. There's no way he'd want to talk about the rules of Aspera, let alone follow the demands some absent king enforces on his kingdom." He then leaned toward Brian in open jest and elbowed him in the ribs. "Next thing you know she will start asking about the Lowenhaar prophecy," Jacob snickered openly. "It's all hogwash if you ask me."

Camille's gaze flew to Jacob's face, focusing on one single word.

"Absent?"

The soft amber of Jacob's eyes hardened as he stared at Camille with a slight note of bewilderment. He nodded then with a small shrug of his shoulders as though accepting her complete ignorance without question. "Yeah. The High King hasn't been seen since the fall of the rebellion; it's been a little over eight years now. Once the heat of battle died down, he vanished, and King Regent Metus took over."

"Jacob," Brian said in a hushed whisper. "We aren't supposed to talk about the prophecy. Someone might hear us. You remember what happened to the last person to talk about it?"

"Oh, shove off, it's not like anyone believes in it anyway," Jacob replied on a scoffing note.

The idea of a prophecy meant little to her. It was as realistic as the stories Peter told her and Lunci before bedtime. But the realization of the High King's absence from the throne at that very moment was like a gold mine. Camille was no longer listening to the back and forth banter between Jacob and Brian as her mind struggled to retrieve any details in the depths of her memory that would solidify what they were telling her.

Instead of finding a correlation in memory, her mind felt ready to burst with Jacob's words. It was overwhelming to hear all of this in one day, but she needed to push through it—she wasn't sure when she might get another chance. "Tell me more about the Aspera Munera."

Jacob traced his finger along the worn sheet of paper that appeared to have been folded and unfolded over one-thousand times. The edges were frayed and brown and curled at the corners. Camille was a little nervous to breathe on its surface, for fear it would crumble into dust as both Jacob and Brian recited the paper's content by memory.

Most of the rules seemed straight forward and palpable. *All Asperians must follow in the teachings of Katolism.* It was the religion of the High King and therefore the religion of the people. The Moon Tax, devotion to the Holy King Faeder, and absolute fealty to the High King himself all appeared straight forward. However, as she continued through the daunting list of laws, her eyes widened as she skimmed over the word *Praetorian*.

VI. All Asperians must submit their lives to compete in the Praetorian

Munera Trials if they are chosen to enlist. To abandon this order is punishable by death, including the end of one's own family.

    a. *All chosen Asperians must submit their lives to the Praetorian Guard and live out their remaining years as an enlisted soldier to the High King.*

    b. *If one is not a high-ranking competitor in the tournament, one is required to submit one's skills to the High King's Equestrian Guard. If one is deemed unworthy of the Equestrian Guard, one will be sentenced to trade work by order of the High King.*

    c. *If one is deemed unworthy of trade work, one will be sentenced to life in a designated section of the High Court grounds by order of the High King.*

"What's this one?" Camille said, pointing to the smeared ink of number six. "Is this still in effect?"

Jacob shrugged casually as he shoved a large hunk of bread into his mouth. He elbowed Brian to speak up.

"We aren't supposed to talk about it," Brian hissed back at Jacob, who rolled his eyes upward and forcefully swallowed the bread he'd been chewing.

After taking a quick gulp of ale, he turned back to Camille. "The quick answer is yes, but it hasn't been put into effect for a while. The last Praetorian Trial enforced happened..." he paused, nose scrunching in deep thought as he soundlessly counted through the years. "Eight years ago? It'll be eight years this Yule festival."

"Isn't that a long time? Why wasn't there another trial afterward?" Camille slid the tattered paper toward Jacob's greased hands after reading the document twice over.

"The High King went into hiding. There's no reason to build a guard in his absence," Jacob said with conviction.

Camille stared at him in shock, but he didn't appear to take notice. *No reason to build a guard.* The red eyes in the forest slipped across her thoughts again, and Camille shuddered in fear. Dark creatures roaming freely through their lands was an excellent reason to enlist an army, Camille thought.

The boys kept eating, unruffled, while her thoughts galloped into full speed. How was it possible that a single Praetorian could cause such an uproar? Was the High King so afraid of this single Praetorian that he removed himself from the spotlight of his own subjects? Perhaps the drifting away from a Praetorian Trial was the outcome of his fear.

With her appetite sufficiently ruined, Camille began to pack up her few belongings. She wondered what caused the Praetorian to commit such horrible crimes knowing the consequences of his actions. Had he known what the outcome would be for the others? Why would the High King just up and vanish after exiling the offender? None of it made sense to her; it didn't fit. There was more to the story, and she wanted answers.

Camille pushed away her plate, having wrapped up the few remaining bits of bread and meat. She slid off her chair offering a clipped goodbye to Jacob and Brian as she waved to Betty Anne before heading back to the butchery.

The rain went from a light drizzle to a steady downpour as she snaked her way back toward the tiny cabin, a hand raised to protect her eyes. Each falling drop of water dimpled the puddles with significant force, creating a cadence of musical pings and plops against the tin roofs of the village. Her boots sloshed through the mud, squelching with every step. She picked up her speed, not wanting the rain to soak clear through to her skin before she reached Peter's home.

As she rounded the corner along the outskirts of the village, she focused on a single thought. Being a Rogue and fighting against the sovereign rule, Peter knew more than he let on. There were apparent connections to her past and the Praetorians; the timing was just too coincidental. She could feel the answers thrumming beneath the surface of her skin. After listening to the dark paths taken that ended in the Praetorian exile, she couldn't help but liken herself to them in several ways—and the more she ruminated on it, the more she was desperate for answers.

CHAPTER SIX

IN THE DEPTH OF SHADOWS

The townsfolk of Sierra Village had decorated the great hall grounds with green, yellow, and red apples alongside colorful gourds from the vegetable patch. A large turkey that Camille herself had shot rotated on a giant spit above the roaring fireplace at the end of the hall, and every table had several bowls filled with nuts and dried berries from the summer season.

The harvest that year had flourished in Sierra Village, making Fómhair even more elaborate and decadent than previous years. Even with a Moon Tax under their belt, they still had plenty of food for the festivities.

The town center's great hall was looking its absolute best. Stubby candles sat on every table, with soft leaves of orange, red, and yellow strewn about. There was a large fireplace the width of Peter's home at the end of the sitting area, and a tiny table laden with copper mugs for red wine and mead. Though the hall was mainly used for town meetings, weddings, and funerals, for Fómhair the space had been transformed into a rare sight of warmth and beauty.

After filling her mug with a sixth helping of sweet red wine, Camille walked along the outskirts of the growing group of villagers. She felt nothing more than a warming buzz in her body as she watched the evening unfold. Count Jenkins had pushed most of the tables and chairs to the outer part of the hall to provide room for dancing, and a small group of grubby-looking men

Camille recognized as crop tenders formed a string quartet band near the fireplace. Before she knew it, she was dancing with Lunci in a circle of villagers to a lively tune.

The celebration was better than she could have imagined, effectively pushing Camille's troubles away with each sip of wine and dance move Lunci came up with.

"Come on Camille, no sitting!" Lunci cried the moment he saw her backing away from the festive frivolity to perch on a nearby stool, her feet aching, stomach full of cinnamon apple pie and wine.

"You dance, I'll watch and try to learn," Camille said with a huge smile. Lunci fake-pouted but gave up quickly when a small blond girl caught his attention.

"Have you heard from the Rogues?" A rough voice whispered just in front of Camille. "The inner-city gates have been breached."

Glancing up, she noticed that Peter and Marcus were huddled together at a table a foot away, facing the other direction and unaware of her proximity. She was tempted to duck away, hating the idea of eavesdropping, but with Betty Anne's voice still lingering in Camille's mind, she couldn't help but remain where she sat. She hoped she appeared inconspicuous to anyone who glanced her direction.

"Breached? Where?" Peter asked, calm and collected.

"In the mountain regions of Echo Town. The border wall was breached by a pack of twenty."

"The Rogue Resistance has gone silent; I've received no updates," Peter murmured. "Albeit a message of warning from the Doctor, but nothing so much as that."

"Where *is* he? Vesyon said twelve moons, did he not?" Marcus fidgeted in a way Camille had never seen him do before, his boots tapping out a rapid beat that wasn't in time to the music.

"Do not question him, Marcus. If he isn't here, it's for a good reason. He's asked us to wait, and that's what we'll do until further instruction is given. Until then, we will double our security on the wall. It won't be long now."

Marcus leaned forward. "They're closing in on us, and there's no doubt we'll have to reinforce our regiment yet again by the end of the week. I'm not the only one who's sighted one of the beasts. It's just like before; they won't rest until they have what they want. We can't continue like this."

"Do we have enough soldiers for the rounds tonight?" Peter asked, ruffling his hair nonchalantly when a pair of giggling dancers spun within earshot.

"Barely," Marcus scoffed. "We also just got word from our contact at Alpha Quarter."

Peter's hand froze. "*Inside* the High Court?"

Marcus chose that moment to drink his wine in slow gulps—a power move and one Camille could tell irked Peter based on the hunched arching of his shoulders. "Don't sound so surprised. I have many eyes and ears in this Kingdom; my reach has no limits."

Peter tilted his head, wordlessly inviting him to continue.

"LeMarc will be sending out invites for a new guard to join the High Court at the beginning of the next moon cycle," Marcus stated.

"*Impossible,*" Peter gasped. "He's been absent for eight years, not to mention the exile. The Praetorian Munera is dead."

Marcus shook his head vehemently. "He is going to form a *new* regiment for Aspera. This isn't a Praetorian Munera, Peter; it's the dawn of a new era. It's starting again, and this time we will need to be ready."

"Yes—but this time the High Court knows about the Chimera. Neither High King nor King Regent has done anything to halt progress. Despite the High King's absence, the crown isn't forming this new regiment to *help* us."

"Wake up, old man! He isn't in *hiding*—the High King's been planning. If he's building an army, then we need to find a way to protect ourselves. We need to finish what the Rogue Resistance started," Marcus said, draining the remaining liquid in his glass in three swift gulps.

"Last time, our main weapon against the High King was compromised in Charlie Town," Peter snapped. "It's difficult to finish something without any tools. He took our last line of defense that night. The war in the East wasn't an accident. The High King had a hand in that too. He isn't just fighting for his own lands anymore; he is pushing to gain more."

"It won't be like it was then. We won't allow the High Court to take what is ours."

Peter shook his head in seeming disbelief, gripping Marcus's shoulder with an old hand. "It's not that easy. If the High King is building an army, we'll be on our own when the border kingdoms fight back."

Marcus sighed audibly, before grabbing a hunk of buttered bread from the plate before him and gnawing off a huge bite. He chewed methodically, his jaw muscles bunching with fierce effort along the sharp angle of his cheekbone. Turning to Peter, Marcus leaned in, his voice barely audible above the tumbling lilt of music coming from the head of the hall. "The time is coming for us to find allies, regroup our rebellion and fight back. We know war is coming, and we must stand our ground no matter which side attacks first. We *must*."

"With who to back us up? The Rogues are all we have right now. There's no one else to help us this time. We don't have enough time to assemble a stronger defense."

"There isn't really much choice, now is there?" Marcus insisted. "We can't fall like before; I won't become a pawn of the High Court. The King Regent doesn't fight for us—he fights for glory, for a place in the holy hall at the feet of his one true king: Faeder. There's no reason to stay hidden in the shadows anymore. We have our own army and the mother Ma'Nada will protect us."

"I wouldn't speak so loudly of your views tonight, Marcus. We aren't with like-minded people even at Fómhair. The followers of his holy lord are in every corner of Aspera. Sierra hasn't been known to fight against the crown no matter how high the taxes increase. There are loyalists here Marcus, and we must tread carefully. Things are changing, yes, and we need to prepare, but it would be advisable to keep any opinions on the matter of reform to yourself until Vesyon tells us otherwise. Do you want to be exiled and sent to Olin with the rest of the deserters, heathens, and criminals?"

Marcus silently shook his head.

"Good. So, for now, we must remain silent and on our guard."

"You can't deny you feel the same as I do," Marcus said with grave intention.

"No," Peter huffed in slight defeat. "I can't."

The music picked up once more, carrying Peter's next words away with the melody. Camille was suddenly itching to vacate the hall and craved a serene sanctuary away from the claustrophobic space to dissect all that she'd just heard. She twisted out of her chair and marched toward the exit, aching to feel a cool breeze against her cheeks.

Just as she crossed the threshold, a loud and shrill scream echoed from her left, alongside the thick bramble and rose bushes. Camille blinked and spun, pushing past a few horrified villagers to locate the source of such commotion.

A young person's body was splayed upon the muddied ground, his chest and face drenched in ruby-hued blood. Camille bent down beside the source of the cries—a blond girl, and the one Lunci had been dancing with not fifteen minutes before.

Camille reeled and nearly fell backward as she identified the bloodied boy as her beloved Lunci, his form unmoving and lips an ashen blue. "Oh, dear mother Ma'Nada—"

"We were dancing in the garden because the rain felt so good— it was so fast...I only saw it for a second—dark fur, a beast of some kind with red eyes—" the blond girl blubbered, snot bubbles forming under each nostril as she coughed and wailed.

"What's going on?" Peter yelled from the great hall's entrance, stumbling over the uneven ground.

"Peter, no—"

"*Lunci?!*" Peter bent down and picked his grandson up without difficulty, then turned to Marcus, whose mouth was agape in horror. "Send word to Romeo Village and White Wall. The beasts have come for her. Make sure to send out a rider to Vesyon, but no written message. We can't have any lost notes getting back to the King Regent."

"Yes, a-all right," Marcus stuttered, running back to the great hall with instructions for everyone to go back to their homes and remain there.

"What can I do?" Camille asked in a haze of panic as Peter took off in the direction of his cabin. Her voice wobbled and her knees crunched against one another as she stumbled after him.

"If we drain the poison in time, we might be able to save him," Peter called out over the rain.

"Drain the what? *Poison?*"

"Quick—to the house! The Chimera will be back soon!"

The square was chaotic, a rolling sea of bodies desperate for sanctuary. In the far distance, Camille heard loud metallic clangs so deafening that they vibrated in her bones: it was a warning that meant another Chimera had been sighted. The clanging bells strained for attention over the wild cries of panic as the villagers clamored into the closest buildings they could reach.

Camille didn't ask any more questions; instead, she followed closely on Peter's heel as he raced down the frenzied street toward their cabin. His eyes roved down every side street, and Neeko was pacing frantically outside his front door when they arrived.

As soon as they were inside, Peter set Lunci down on the wooden table before yanking supplies from his chest drawers, scattering bowls, plates, and cups in the process. "Get a fire going, we need to keep him warm. I'm not sure we got to him in time."

"What do you mean?" Camille asked, shoving heavy logs into the fireplace and desperately trying to make a spark burst to life. Her hands were steady as a rock, but her focus kept pulling her back to Lunci's greying skin and the gruesome gashes across his chest. After seven strikes against the flint stone, she was finally able to coax a spark into a rolling flame. Heat billowed against her cold skin, but she barely felt it.

"You said there was poison," Camille said, striding to the table. "From what?"

Peter turned around, a large bowl in one hand and dagger in the other. "Lunci's been bitten by a Chimera. If we don't clean the wound and drain the poison, he'll..." Peter trailed off and lifted Lunci's arm, dragging the sharp dagger along his delicate skin until blood flowed in a steady stream onto the floor.

"What're you doing!" Camille asked as Peter moved to the other arm and did the same thing.

"I'm draining him as much as I can. Now go to the butchery— in a small ice box you'll find five containers filled with blood and a red case next to it. Grab those and set the kettle over the stove."

Camille did as he instructed, soon depositing the items beside Peter and checking the kettle for steam. Peter moved around Lunci's limp form like a trained doctor, cutting the blood-stained shirt from Lunci's body to reveal several puss-filled puncture wounds. Peter wiped each boil with a cloth and lanced them with a small silver dagger. "Water! Pour it into a cup for me!"

Camille did so, and Peter poured the steaming water on Lunci's infected chest, dousing the wounds until they ran clear.

"I'm so sorry—I should've been watching him," Camille mumbled, her throat nearly as tight as her fists.

Peter's eyes flicked up to hers for a moment. "Camille, there are a lot of things I haven't been able to tell you—to prepare you for. But I can tell you right now that this *isn't* your fault."

As Camille opened her mouth to respond, a medley of terrifying howls rang through the village. At the eerie call, Lunci burst to life, echoing their sound through a gargle of mucus. Peter grasped the red box and pulled out a silk, tube-shaped bag attached to what appeared to be a snake fang with twine and beeswax.

"Hold this," he barked, handing her a small glass bottle of clear liquid as well as a bag full of blood. "I need you to slowly pour the liquid into this bag." He held out the device with a drawstring closure at the top requesting she pour the blood inside. It reminded Camille of the icing tubes Jyllel used on her decorative cakes. This contraption, in contrast, had a nasty looking fang jutting out the end.

"Get the next one ready," Peter said as he yanked the wax stopper off the fang end and jammed it into the crook of Lunci's arm. He gently squeezed the bag of blood forcing it through the hollowness of the fang into Lunci's body at an alarming speed.

When the first bag was almost empty, Lunci sat straight up with a piercing scream, his yellowed eyes wild and completely bloodshot.

"Quick! Camille, hold him down!"

She dashed over to Lunci and grabbed him by the shoulders, trying to pin the nine-year-old to the table. He thrashed against her, bellowing a garbled stream of cries and slamming his head repeatedly on the table's wooden planks.

"Keep his arm steady!" Peter screamed, replacing the empty bag with the second sack filled with blood.

"How will this help?!" Camille yelled over Lunci. "He's *so strong* right now!"

"I'm replacing his blood and injecting an antidote!"

The second bag of blood seemed to help, as Lunci ceased his thrashing and howls to instead dissolve into a whimpering, twitching mess.

Camille's arms ached from the strain of holding Lunci down. "Will he be all right?"

Peter prepared the third bag for use, filling it with the clear antidote before sliding the fang tip into Lunci's arm and squeezing the liquid into his body. "We'll have to wait and see. If the fever sets in, it's over." Despite Peter's calm tone, Camille could see how his fingers shook.

A soft, persistent scratching against the front door pulled her attention away from the dying boy on the table. Before either of them could peek out the peephole, the door burst open in a whirl of frigid wind and sleet.

"Is he all right?!" A voice growled gruffly from underneath a heaping coat of bear fur. A massive black hood kept the man's face obscured in shadow as he moved into the small quarters of the house and slammed the door behind him. His hands brushed over Lunci's tiny face and narrow neck, moving as gently as if Lunci were a trampled baby bird.

"I believe I got most of the poison out, but I just don't know. I don't know if I made it in time. The boy is so little," Peter said, voice hitching at the end.

"How long's it been?"

"Twenty minutes, maybe less."

The stranger removed some of his heavy furs and pulled back the hood to reveal a man not much older than twenty. His face, though tanned and lightly bearded, held a boyish youthful quality. Long black hair tumbled in a mess of tangles hitting just above the shoulders, but it was his grey irises that caught Camille's attention the most. She *knew* those eyes.

"Where did it happen?" the man asked, seemingly unaware of Camille's presence near the fireplace. She'd backed away from the table when the stranger burst into the room.

"The town square, just outside the main hall. Vesyon—the entire village could have been slaughtered. Thank Mother Ma'Nada that didn't happen," Peter ground out, wiping at the wetness in the corners of his eyes.

"The pack moved south from Charlie Town. I was in Whiskey Wharf when I received word from Langhorn," Vesyon said as he handed Peter a strip of crumpled paper. "I came as quick as I could, but they moved south toward Dun L'er faster than I imagined was possible."

"How'd you know about the attack?" Peter asked, squeezing the blood bag to hasten its absorption.

Peter shook his head but kept his focus on Lunci.

Vesyon paused, watching the old man as he worked. "On my way here, Neeko found me," he continued. "I'd warned him to locate me as soon as he saw the Chimera closing in. He found me this morning enroute to you."

"Neeko? But he was out yesterday afternoon with..." Peter

blanched, his brow furrowing with sudden understanding. He aimed a questioning glare at Camille, and she promptly looked down at her feet in shame. "It's starting, then. The Chimera is on the move, and they found what the high court's been looking for. It won't be long before the King Regent hears about this."

"Someone must've aided the beasts in their search. I believe more than one is behind it," Vesyon said to Peter, before turning to regard Camille with indifference. "Have you followed my orders, Peter?"

"I have. She's been training."

Vesyon nodded and ambled toward her. "Do you know who I am?" He leaned toward her, his dominating stature causing her instincts to prickle in defense. Her fists unwillingly clenched at her sides as a tingle of acute awareness flooded her system.

"No," Camille said, standing to her full height and remaining a good half-foot shorter than the man. "*Should* I?"

Another echoing call pierced through the air, this one much closer than before. Neeko's fur stood on end, and he growled deep in his chest; Camille had never seen him so unnerved.

"There isn't time to explain what's happening. We need to leave. *Now.*" The man moved deftly away from her, collecting his fur cloak and wrapping it about his shoulders before marching toward the front door.

"Absolutely not! I'm not leaving Lunci like this," Camille refused, crossing her arms and backing away from the hulking man. "Peter needs me."

Camille looked to the old man and her heart fissured—there was a shift swirling behind those blue eyes— a tremor of mistrust. It was then that she knew she was mistaken. He no longer *wanted* her to stay. She should've told him about the Chimera, should've known that the beast would come back and destroy everything she held dear.

"Where are her things?" Vesyon asked, oblivious to Camille's mounting despair.

She opened her mouth to snap that she didn't own a damn thing, but Peter responded for her. "Outside, north wall, under the house."

She wanted to scream, to utter words that would blast away any chance she'd have of ever being welcomed back. The monster inside her chest bellowed in rage, begging to be released, but something about Vesyon's austerity stopped her dead in her tracks. Whether it was his familiar eyes or his powerful aura, she held her tongue as he moved toward the door.

"I don't know if I'll make it back," Vesyon said to Peter, jerking open the front door.

"Just get across the river," Peter replied. "I'll handle my part of the deal if you handle yours."

Camille cocked her head at their cryptic exchange, but Vesyon was already moving through the doorway before she could question his intentions.

"Grab only what you can carry," Vesyon commanded over his shoulder as he left. Neeko followed in quick pursuit, the front door slamming behind the man and cat in a whirl of sleet and bitter wind.

Camille's eyes tore away from the door to land sharply on Peter's soft blue irises. "Please don't make me leave. I didn't mean to keep the Chimera I saw a secret; I didn't mean to betray you."

"There's nothing you can say to change the course of the evening," Peter said, turning to face Lunci before she could read his expression. "You need to grab your things and leave."

"Why? I can stay. I can *protect* you," Camille pleaded, her hand outstretched in desperation as tears slipped from the corners of her eyes unwillingly.

"I'm sorry, but you can't stay here. It's not safe. Vesyon will take you to the next village."

Camille sighed, her hand filled with the weight of understanding falling back to her side. She grabbed her hunting gear, her cloak lined in thick black fur, and her favorite dagger, shuddering all the while. In her broken memories, Camille only ever remembered Peter and Lunci, but she *recognized* the feeling of complete loss. She grasped the doorknob and steadied herself, stealing one final glance at Lunci sprawled on the table, his skin a healthier shade of peach and his chest softly rising and falling.

"Ad Astra per Aspera, Camille. Always remember that," Peter said from his grandson's side, unable to look away from her. "Go now, while you still can." His expression, though sharp and determined, seemingly brimmed with heartache as she watched several tears slip down his weather cheeks.

They stared at each other for a long, silent moment before Camille walked out into the black depths of the night.

CHAPTER SEVEN
STRANGERS IN THE FOREST

Camille collided with Neeko the moment she stepped out of Peter's home, and the ordinarily sleek cat puffed with annoyance at her delay in leaving.

"I had to say goodbye," Camille bit out, blaming her tingling nasal cavity on the brisk chill and not the tears threatening to fall in rapid succession. Neeko wasn't moved by her excuse in the least. He mewled sharply and disappeared around the side of the cabin, apparently expecting her to accompany him.

Camille squelched her way over, the mud sucking at her boots with each step. A blast of rain pounded against her hood, running down her shoulders and arms in icy rivulets. The worsening storm's barrage muted the sounds of the village, but she felt just as vulnerable and open to the shadows of the forest as she felt removed from it.

"Took you long enough," Vesyon said from the shadows. He stepped into view from an open gap beneath Peter's home, snug and removed beneath bright green shrubbery skirting the edges of the foundation.

"I had to say goodbye," Camille snapped back, unable to keep the sharp sting of abandonment from her voice. Despite the unavoidable turn of the evening, and the clear understanding that she was no longer *able* to stay with Peter, she still felt as though she had been deserted. She had lived in happy comfort with Peter for over eleven moons and in a single night she had not only lost her home but also the only two people she had known as family.

Glancing up through her downcast lashes, she noticed Vesyon surveying her with sharp, glinting eyes. His lips twitched, appearing as though he wanted to say something, but remained silent. He hastily handed her a sheathed sword, several glinting daggers, a worn leather belt, and a pack filled with supplies.

"These aren't mine," Camille said as she fingered the intricate weapons in awe. Vesyon grunted in reply as he bent down to right his boots and adjust the many weapons he had clipped to his belt. "Well thanks, I guess," Camille said almost to herself as she inspected the weapons more carefully before wrapping the belt around her hips, securely holstering the sword and daggers and pulling the pack tightly against her back.

"We need to go," he said, rain droplets catching on the fur coat draped over his shoulders like little glossy bugs, running the length of his upper body before losing their grip and crashing into the mud. The massive hood hung low over his hair, protecting his face from an onslaught of water. His silhouette appeared bearish in contrast to the sleek form beneath the layers of fur.

"Where are we going?" Camille asked, trying to engage him, but his stoic stature remained coolly silent. She was gliding her hand appreciatively over the shiny silver hilt of the sword, inlaid with fiery red rubies, when she heard the warning howls of an impending attack and froze in place. Her face snapped to Vesyon in apprehension but he remained calm, detached and void of emotion as the storm raged above them.

"They're here. Let's move."

"The Chimera?"

A second growl rumbled even closer, and Vesyon took off at a clipped run south toward the Dun L'er forest edge.

"Where are we going?" Camille bellowed as she vaulted over a fallen tree trunk and lurched into the maze of the forest—*her* forest.

"We need to get over the river!"

An overwhelming sense of desperation took over, and she felt her steps slowing, slipping out of rhythm. She craved a moment, just a single *second*, to offer her goodbyes to the life she'd had.

"And what about after that?!" Camille shot back, trying to keep her annoyance in check.

"Out of Sierra Village," he grunted over his shoulder as he

continued to move in swift, even strides. "You brought far too much attention to yourself here. I thought someone of your stature would've been more careful."

"*Excuse* me? You have no right to treat me like a child—you don't even know me! And how are you so sure the Chimera are following us? We might've outrun them!"

As they entered a small clearing, Vesyon suddenly spun and growled at her mere inches from her face. "You've always been a hothead, Camille, but right now I need you to shut your mouth and follow my lead! You're either with *me*, or you're supper for them. Decide!"

The sharp spark in his slate stare made her stumble backward a few steps. Her back rammed into a rough trunk of a pine halting her movements and jarring her senses. His words came without sugar or tenderness; his meaning punched her straight in the gut. She had to make a choice, and there was no time to catch her bearings: leave with Vesyon and abandon Sierra Village or stay and find herself without a home.

Her eyes met his in resignation, a quick breath of understanding puffing from between her lips. "*Fine.*"

Vesyon turned toward Neeko, sitting patiently at their feet. He whispered a short message to the sleek feline, and the cat sped away into the night as Vesyon faced west.

"Where's he going?" Camille snapped, feeling suddenly abandoned by the only friend she had left.

"To warn Romeo Village of what's coming." He said, ignoring Camille's obvious discomfort, before moving west into the dark depths of the forest. Camille followed without question, uncertain of what else she could do.

"He'll never forgive me," Camille mumbled as they marched at a swift pace through the underbrush. Immediately, she wished she could take back the unexpected words of vulnerability. Her eyes snapped up to Vesyon, seeing only a portion of his profile— assessing his reaction but he seemed as neutral as ever.

Together they moved, their boots a bare whisper through the layer of wet leaves. Camille walked in sync behind him through the thick growth of trees for almost a half mile before he responded to her. "Perhaps Peter isn't the one you need forgiveness from."

"What's *that* supposed to mean?" Camille snapped back at him, unable to control her reaction.

Vesyon sighed and stopped to face her again. The barrier holding back his emotion faltered, and for a mere moment, she registered sympathy swimming in the grey of his stony expression. He stood only a few feet from her but closed the distance as he reached a bare hand up to her cheek and pushed a flyaway curl behind her ear, his warm breath feathering across her cold cheeks. "I can see you're feeling guilty, Camille. You're searching for forgiveness, but you won't find it in Sierra Village."

Camille's mouth fell open in shock at his tender words and actions. She may not have recognized the stranger, but *he* apparently knew her very well. His hand cupped her cheek for a mere second, a smile twitching his lips with what she thought might be compassion before he stepped away, putting a substantial amount of distance between them, and slipping his glove back in place.

At first, the man had appeared young, the look of a boy growing into a man. Now, however, in the dead of night and on the run from Chimera, he appeared ages older than herself.

"Who *are* you?" Camille asked, unable to keep the question tumbling from her lips.

"I'm an old friend Camille; you don't need to be afraid of me."

"I'm not afraid," she replied, her voice confident—unlike the subtle shake in her hands.

He nodded once in apparent agreement. Without wasting another second, Vesyon headed up a path through the hills and Camille trailed behind in a tangle of astonishment.

The air tasted different the higher they went, filled with the bitter fragrance of wet pine needles instead of the soggy sweetness of rotting leaves at the end of autumn. Snow lay in icy piles along the tree roots and over the tops of bushes, a chilly blanket draped over the forest grounds. They moved in sync, one foot in front of the other. It was like a mesmerizing dance to Camille—one she'd done many times before and yet couldn't remember until she was already doing it.

Vesyon slowed his pace as they headed toward a snow-filled meadow, one too expansive for Camille's liking. She felt a cold tingle run the length of her spine. Something wasn't right. "Are we crossing?"

Vesyon nodded curtly, glancing around the widespread clearing. The meadow extended almost a quarter mile in front of them, a sea of weeds and waist-high grass dusted with white.

"We're no longer in Sierra Village, are we?" Camille whispered. She sensed his urgency to keep moving, but he remained still as a statue.

"We're much further south than I believe you'd remember. Just through that forest and beyond the hillside is the northern end of the Red River. We need to cross here to make our way into Romeo Village," he said in a bare whisper. The rain had slowed considerably. Water droplets slipped through the air, gentle and calm against the naked plains of Camille's face. Vesyon's hood was now pushed back. She could see the sharp angles of his face, and his features, though striking, were not conspicuously handsome. His black, shoulder-length hair lay in stringy cords, wet and glistening like the coat of a seal. His eyes were the color of early dawn, a whisper of unknown horrors hiding in the shadowy depths. She wasn't afraid of him, but she could see why anyone in their right mind would be.

Weighed down with a handful of weapons, a downward angle tugging on his lips in a perma-frown, and a stoic expression cemented in place, Vesyon was incredibly intimidating—as a much as a full-grown grizzly could be.

"What are we waiting for?"

It was as though the whole earth hushed at her words. The rain trickled to a complete stop. Milky fog obscured their view of the meadow's grass, rising upward as though the ground itself had exhaled its warm breath into the frigid air. Slowly, Camille noticed bright red eyes winking like rubies amongst the fog.

"They can't see us yet, but they will once we enter the meadow. The beasts *can* smell us. They know we're here," Vesyon said.

"How many?" She only saw two pairs of eyes glaring in her direction, but the heavy mist billowing above the powdered snow was misleading. There was no telling how many Chimera were out there, and Camille's instincts warned her to prepare for the worst.

"Don't know. Let's move," Vesyon mouthed, motioning for Camille to follow his path. He crept along the edges of the meadow, skirting along the tree line, and within seconds the moon emerged to light up the ground with its silvery rays.

Camille gasped. The field was absolutely *crawling* with beasts.

Together they edged forward as quietly as possible through the crackling, icy grass, but it was impossible not to make a sound.

More eyes appeared at their right, pair after pair, and Vesyon tugged on Camille's hand.

"*Run!*"

Camille bolted toward the opposite side of the meadow as Vesyon kept pace beside her, the dense trees looming ahead.

"To the left, head for the docks!" Vesyon bellowed, leading Camille through the forest terrain toward the wide belly of the Red River. They dove between the trees and down a rocky hillside. Camille slipped and fell before shoving herself up to maintain speed with Vesyon. The Chimera were closing in on them—she could hear their thunderous steps and smell their foul, reeking breath. It was an incredible feat not to vomit on the spot with them so close.

"They'll catch us!" Camille shouted.

"No, they won't! Keep moving!"

A small boat sat on the edge of the dock, bobbing in the river's current. Vesyon reached it first and yanked the tether free as Camille bounded inside, spinning to stare down the dozens of Chimera emerging from the trees.

They were at least seven feet tall, with matted black fur covering their massive wolf like heads. Multicolored scales glistened like oil down their backs and neck as they moved, hugging the bulky weight of their body. Claws the length of Camille's forearm gripped at the earth, stamping in frustration, their muddied legs a mess of matted fur and dried blood. Ghastly red eyes watched as Vesyon and Camille drifted along the water, their mouths splitting open to reveal several rows of sharp teeth.

"They don't swim, do they?" Camille asked apprehensively.

"No—Chimera are really only great at doing one thing in the water: drowning."

A nervous flutter gripped Camille's insides. "So they can't follow us?"

"Of course, they can. Chimera know how to use a bridge," Vesyon said, steering the tiny boat through the swiftly moving current.

"Where's the next bridge?" Camille asked, panting as she massaged an aching stitch in her side.

"About half a day's ride on a horse, but we'll be long gone at that point. We're going to cross here and head the remaining distance to Romeo Village on foot."

Camille didn't question his authority. After barely escaping a pack of Chimera, she was more than happy to listen to Vesyon's instructions. They quickly docked along the grassy banks on the opposite side of the Red River before taking off into the trees.

After several more hours of intense running, Vesyon finally slowed enough for Camille to catch her breath and take in her surroundings. The rain from Sierra Village had stopped completely, but a slight dusting of snow dogged their movement through Aspera.

Vesyon dropped his bag onto the hard-packed earth with a thud and thrust a small blanket into Camille's shivering hands. "You need to rest a bit; there's a boulder over there you can sleep under. I'd build a fire to keep you warm, but we can't risk it."

"Can't risk what?" Camille asked through chattering teeth.

"They'll eventually find a way over the bridge, and I need you well rested when they do."

Her mouth fell open as he began to walk away. "Wait—you're just going to leave me here alone?"

He stared at her for a moment with an expression that could only be described as bewilderment, before disappearing into the shadows.

This man is crazy, Camille thought as she shook out the musty blanket and curled up beside the massive boulder. How could she possibly sleep knowing there was a pack of bloodthirsty Chimera on the way?

Camille groaned as her exhausted muscles welcomed the little warmth of the blanket, and the moment her eyes closed, she was out.

***

Blurry images of unknown people swayed in front of her eyes: half-starving, gloomy in presence, and white as death. Bloodshot eyes stared at her ominously, their mouths hanging slack as an oozing black substance drained from their lips to turn their skin into fur and scales.

They advanced on her, hordes of them, their eyes a deep-set red, glowing like embers. It was terrifying, but the person walking shakily at the front of the crowd kept her feet locked in place. It was Lunci, and his skin was transforming before her eyes into black fur and scales, eyes fiercely red and trained on her. He wasn't Asperian anymore—he was a beast, and one that thirsted for the dark red liquid coursing through the meat of her body.

"Lunci," Camille blurted out weakly, but there was no verbal response from the boy, only a menacing growl as he fell to all fours, reaching for her with razor-sharp claws that clenched down on her windpipe—

"Lunci!" Camille gasped as she jerked awake, drenched in a cold sweat.

Soft dawn light filtered through the damp leaves overhead, and Camille felt a distorted fuzziness cloud her mind while she tried to process what she'd just seen.

It'd only been a dream, but was so intensely real that it burned her to the core all the same. Not until she shook her head to rid herself of the images did she realize that she was clasping her hunting knife, ready for an attack.

Soft footsteps crunched against the rocky ground nearby, and her head snapped toward the intrusion. "Good, you're awake," Vesyon said, eying the sharp hunting blade briefly. His expression was pinched and slightly worn with fatigue, and he seemed instantly older to her. "We need to be on the move again—by mid-morning this hillside will be swarming with Chimera."

"Now wait for just a second," Camille said shoving the frost dampened blankets off her legs before standing to face him. "Is it really a good idea to keep running from these beasts only to lead them into another village?"

"We aren't running *from* anything—we're leading them toward us," Vesyon replied briskly.

"I'm sorry—what?!" Camille asked. "Why would we do that?"

"You're the most infuriating woman!" Vesyon burst out, leaning so close she could've punched him square in the jaw if the mood struck her. "We don't have time for this! We need to be on the move." He immediately regained control and stood back, though his eyes continued to storm wildly.

"But why'd we leave Sierra Village alone? Shouldn't we have stayed there to protect them?" Camille asked. "What if they didn't all come after us—what if some stayed to take out the whole village?"

"We *are* protecting Sierra Village," Vesyon huffed. "We're taking what they want most as far away from that village as possible."

"Which *is?*"

"Isn't it obvious by now?"

Camille snorted as she shoved her belongings in her pack. "I can assure you it isn't."

"They want *you*, Camille. They were coming for you."

"*Me?*" Camille nearly dropped her pack. "Lunci had been attacked because of me?"

"Yes. So, keeping you out of Sierra Village is the best way we can protect the people there."

His words rang in her ears and Camille fell against the boulder, overcome with guilt. Without warning, Vesyon reached out with a gloved hand pulling her upright and into his arms. "I'm sorry Camille. I left you there too long." His arms tightened around her, gentle and yet firm as though he were trying to press his apologies into her skin. She felt the raking brush of stubble scratch against her cheek as he shook his head. "I'm so very sorry for what I've done."

His intimacy caught her off guard as much as it fascinated her. She couldn't be sure, but she could swear that he looked at her the same way Jacob had stolen glances at her a few times during their hunts: deep longing so beyond a simple desire that it was almost painful. Camille had never brought it up with Jacob. She hadn't wanted to embarrass him, but every time she caught the sideways glances or desperate longing in his stare, she had smiled gently in a show of blissful ignorance, not wanting to stoke the fire with encouragement.

With Vesyon, the piercing looks felt incredibly different. It not only caught her off guard, but it also confused her. She didn't look at Vesyon like a friend or a hunting partner; she saw him as a stranger. Albeit a very present and intense stranger currently pressed against her and holding her close. He was a fierce and intimidating man, but he was incredibly warm, and for the first time in her life she felt completely safe.

Disentangling himself from her, he kept his eyes averted, putting several feet of distance between them. The chill crept back in, and she more than regretted his sudden distance.

"The pack that followed us to the river will be here soon. We must cross into Romeo Village before nightfall," Vesyon said, his eyes looking everywhere but at her. She nodded, clutching her cloak tightly around her shoulders as they trekked deeper south into the trees, her skin still tingling where he'd touched her.

It was well into the afternoon before they crossed into the outer arms of Romeo Village, and by then Camille's stomach was roaring for sustenance.

"We can stop here," Vesyon said, glancing around the area. "I'm going to collect some wood for a small fire—see if you can find some food."

Camille studied the frosty ground and came up empty plant-wise; she'd have to do some hunting. Dropping her pack to the ground, she dug around and found some thin but heavy-duty rope that was perfect for trapping.

She set about tying off looping circles and knots for her tree traps, keeping a circular loop on the ground and devising a weighted pulley system by wrapping the remaining rope over a tall branch and under a rock at the base of the tree. The loose and tight knots felt so familiar under her small fingers that she found herself smiling at the memory of Peter teaching her how to hunt. A pang of worry stung her chest as thoughts of Lunci swam to the forefront, but she batted them away like flies, concentrating on the matter at hand: she was hungry and needed food. It was a problem she *could* solve.

With one trap done, she set about starting a second one. Camille knelt in front of a new length of rope, continuing to knot and loop the way she'd learned.

"What's this? A hunter off her guard?" A silky voice remarked from behind her as a blade pressed into her back.

Camille's fingers instantly froze, her heart speeding into triple overtime. The voice was familiar, but deeper in timbre than Vesyon's.

She leaned slightly forward and spun, kicking out her right leg to throw him off balance. He leaped away, and Camille pursued him, throwing another kick that landed successfully against his left shoulder. "Ow—hey!" he shouted, glacier-blue eyes dancing with playfulness.

He arced the sword in her direction, and Camille ducked, yelling as it whooshed mere inches over her head. "It's *you*!" Camille burst out, shoving the blond drifter she'd seen in Sierra Village against a nearby tree so hard that his sword flew into some nearby bushes. "You—you just tried to stab me!"

"Oh, I knew you'd dodge it," the man said smugly. "And don't look so happy to see me. A genuine 'hello Theo Shaehy, so good to see you again' would've been fantastic, but alas."

"First—I don't know you. 'Theo,' is it? Well, it's not nice to say hello with a sword at my back," Camille retorted.

"Oh?" he said in a challenging tone. "A welcoming knife is better, is it?"

Camille blushed at the memory of seeing him in the woods, her small hunting dagger her only weapon at the time. Now she was properly weighed down with tools of protection, but there was little use in grabbing one. The sparkling bubble of humor swimming in the ocean depths of his eyes let her know that he was merely teasing her.

"Perhaps a sharp blade and a curt word or two is the best and only way to greet a man such as yourself."

"Is that so?" Theo replied, his eyebrows shooting up toward his hairline. "I can think of a better way." His smile, though incredibly alluring, caused Camille's entire body to stiffen. He moved toward her, arms stretched out to either side in a motion of embrace, but she quickly backed away, her hand jutting in front of her to hold him off.

"What are you doing?" Camille said, her voice curt and sharp, crackling through the brisk air like a leather whip.

He stopped, faltering for a moment, and then stared at her. His eyes narrowed into slits and then relaxed again in open assessment of her. It was quite unnerving and yet she didn't turn away from it. She, in turn, glared back at him with just as much attention, her eyes roving his body to place him in the unknown empty memories of her past life. *Who was he to her?* Just like Vesyon, Theo knew her, and it bothered her to no end to not recognize him in the slightest.

The sides of his head appeared freshly trimmed almost down to his skull, but the top blond mop of his hair curled charmingly over the back of his head as though he had just run his fingers through the wavy silken strands. His crescent moon eyebrows were full, hunkering over nomad-blue, almond-shaped eyes sparkling in the late afternoon like rays of light on cresting ocean waves. He was taller than she remembered, just a hair shorter than Vesyon if she had to guess, but his build appeared stockier. His shoulders pressed outward against the muddied black linen shirt he wore as though it were almost a second skin, and yet his waist trimmed down into a very dramatic "V" leaving the shirt loose and waving in the wind beneath a dark brown leather vest.

A sharp nose and angular cheekbones gave his face a stone-like visage, but the scar running the length from his temple down past the corner of his left eye destroyed any perfect symmetry he perhaps had at one time. He quirked a cocky smile, apparently loving her silent perusal of his body.

"Are you done?" Theo said, one brow tilting upwards in obvious amusement.

Camille tensed at his expression. Shaking her head with annoyance, she felt ready to slap the stupid grin off his gorgeous face when it miraculously melted away. He went rigid, staring at a spot just over her shoulder.

"Don't. Move," Theo said slowly, bending to reach for his discarded blade. "Move very carefully toward me, Cam."

"Which is it? Move or don't?" Camille hissed.

"Keep your mouth shut, Cam, and just inch toward me. Trust me."

Camille opened her mouth to question him further when she smelled it: the stench of rotting flesh, followed by a deep and guttural growl. *The Chimera had found her.*

CHAPTER EIGHT

ILLUSIONS REVEALED

"Cam, *jump*!" Theo screamed. Her muscles catapulted into action as she dove into a roll, narrowly missing a deathly swipe from the Chimera's claws. Just before the Chimera's enormous fangs could clamp down on her calf, the rope of Camille's trap wrapped tightly around the monster's left hind leg, yanking it up into the trees.

The branches Camille had used for her trap wouldn't hold long. They were only slightly thicker than the Chimera's enormous neck and would be ripped down in a matter of minutes. Both Camille and Theo stood their ground in front of the Chimera, tense and ready for the fight to come.

"Aim for the neck but keep away from its claws. And *whatever* you do, don't let it bite you. It will be the last thing you ever feel," Theo said.

Panic gripped her insides like a vicious snake, coiling and uncoiling, seeping its venom into her extremities and causing her to tingle uncomfortably. She had never fought such a beast before; she wasn't even sure she knew how. Doubt clouded her senses for barely a moment before a rush of warmth slipped throughout her body just beneath the skin, filling her with strength. The soothing heat tingled at her fingertips and radiated around her eyes.

Camille glanced at Theo, and her jaw dropped at the sudden change in his appearance. His eyes were completely black. The irises had lost all their color, the coal hue expanding past the skin of his brow line. Theo had turned from a mysterious and comical stranger into a demonic monster.

"What *are* you?" Camille asked, her shock freezing her momentarily in place.

"I think you should ask yourself the same question," Theo said, smiling as roguishly as if he hadn't just turned into a creature of the afterlife before her eyes.

The Chimera ripped it's leg from the restraints in one last angry thrash before it fell to the ground in a heap. The beast didn't wait to advance; it charged forward, with Camille as its priority target.

Her body responded instinctively, slipping into a seemingly familiar dance. She didn't pause or hesitate as she lurched forward, raking one of her blades across its belly. The seven-foot-long tail of the Chimera swished with menace, each spike along its length glinting with poison.

Camille battled wildly with the creature, bringing her blade down on the tail to cleave it cleanly from the body in one slash of metal. The beast cried out, its vocal cords releasing a strangled yelp. In frustrated pain, it turned on her in a fit of rage.

"Oh crap," she mumbled as she careened backward, slightly off balance.

The Chimera took that moment to pounce on her. One front paw slammed heavily on top of her right arm, the other smashing against the hard-packed ground close to her head. Sharp yellow fangs grinned down at her, and its putrid, sickly stench washed over her face in a whirl of breath. Camille felt its massive paw crushing her upper arm, *daring* the bones to break, but she wouldn't give in so quickly.

Whipping out a short-nosed dagger from her belt she jammed it into the paw still holding her captive. Just as the Chimera pulled back with a nasty hiss, its foreleg now oozing a sickly black, Theo slashed his blade under the beast's thick neck, spraying the cold ground with a waterfall of blood.

Theo let out a battle cry of victory over the whimpering Chimera as Camille drove her blade into its neck. It fell to the ground in a heap of dead flesh, thick, black blood oozing from its wounds.

"That was an easy kill, eh?" Theo said.

Camille pulled her trampled arm against her body as she stood, trying to ignore the bitter ache of bruising spreading across her flesh. "*That's* what you have to say?"

Theo shrugged. "Next time you should follow my lead. Maybe then you won't get trampled."

"So, are you going to tell me who and *what* you are now?" Camille blurted out, rubbing her arm.

Theo didn't respond right away. Instead, he began to clean his bloody sword on the black hide of the dead Chimera. "You really don't remember me?" he said finally, sounding almost *troubled*.

"There are a lot of things I don't remember," Camille replied defensively. She felt her hackles rising at his question, desperate to prove that she wasn't strange despite her inability to explain her past.

"Not even a glimmer, eh? That's a bummer," he said casually, trying to make light of the situation, but Camille saw the murky depths of his expression. He wasn't just hurt by the realization that she didn't know who he was, he appeared to be downright devastated.

"Vesyon—" Camille started, but stopped suddenly as Theo jerked to attention.

"He's here?" Theo barked, his eyes sparkling with fervor as they flitted around the forest. "I have a few words for him."

"Yes—he was here before you attacked me."

He whirled on her, his smile so devastatingly brilliant that it almost blinded her into shocked silence. "I didn't *attack* you," he replied matter-of-factly. "I merely caught you off guard. You're the one who attacked *me*."

"What?!" Camille shot back, no longer lost in a stupor of awe. "I was defending myself against a stranger. You put your sword to my back!"

"Always overreacting, Cam. It's not like I would've done anything."

"Not even in each other's company for twenty minutes and you're already bickering. I believe that's a record for you two," Vesyon said, appearing through the mist of the chilly forest with an armful of dry wood.

It didn't pass Camille's notice that he looked worse than when he'd left; his hair was tousled and dirty, his shirt torn at the shoulder to reveal a fresh wound.

"Didn't realize collecting wood was such a battle. What happened?" Camille asked, unsure of whether she wanted to hear the answer.

"Vee!" Theo shouted.

"It's good to see you Theo—glad you found us," Vesyon said, setting the wood down to embrace the blond man. "I wasn't sure Neeko would get to you in time. He stayed back in the village, yes?"

"Yeah, still there guarding the grounds and awaiting your next orders. He's as welcoming and friendly as a pine-cone, that one. Makes me think he only has affection for two Praetorians—and I didn't make the cut," Theo said, glancing at Camille.

Camille swallowed, her blood running cold at his words. "W-what?"

Theo shook his head, chuckling as he did so. "You haven't told her yet, Vee?"

"I'm sorry—you're mistaken," Camille replied, vigorously shaking her head. "I'm *not* a Praetorian. I'm not one of those traitors."

Silence filled their surroundings for several beats before Theo chuckled softly, his expression kind if not slightly sympathetic. "Please, you've got to tell her. It's not fair to lie to someone like this!"

"How dare you laugh at me," Camille snapped at Theo, causing his gentle laugh to cease abruptly. Vesyon ignored them both, kneeling to build a fire. "Vesyon, explain to him who I am."

"He's aware of who you are," Vesyon said. "He's known you almost as long as I have."

Camille huffed in frustration. "I don't care if he knows my name, he doesn't know *who* I am. I'm not a Praetorian, not one of those exiled hack soldiers."

Her words were intended to harm, but Vesyon didn't appear to care. Theo, however, went silent and turned to attend his muddied weapons. Both men avoided her glare, which only enraged her further.

She waited for Vesyon to defend her, to deny Theo's statement, but as the seconds ticked by, her desire to hear him say such a thing began to waver. If she *was* a Praetorian, she could go back and protect Lunci—she could keep the boy and his grandfather safe.

"What the hell are you doing?" She finally burst out in a mounting explosion of annoyance.

"Building a fire. What does it look like I'm doing?" Vesyon

answered, keeping his gaze on the task at hand.

"You're a complete imbecile, you know that?" Theo snickered in Vesyon's direction, his eyes rolling with disbelief. There was a slight pause from Vesyon, but other than that he didn't appear to be affected by Theo's prodding comments.

"There's no need to worry for the moment, Camille. We are good to make camp for a bit before moving on." Vesyon nodded at the dead Chimera less than thirty feet away from them and continued to strip kindling from the pile of wood he'd collected.

Camille stood in a numb haze as she waited for Vesyon to explain, but he remained silent. "What do you mean 'we don't need to worry?'" she said as slowly as possible. "We have been running from those things for a full sun cycle. Killing one Chimera doesn't make me feel any safer!"

"We weren't running from them, as I told you before. We were leading the Chimera away from Sierra Village. And as for the rest," he said with a heavy grunt. "They've been handled."

A subtle buzzing began inside her head, and Camille felt almost dizzy from the flood of irritation pouring into her system. This time she recognized the wave of warmth shifting through her body and understood what it meant. Her face grew hot, and she knew without a doubt that she appeared as Theo had: solid black eyes radiating with pure rage.

She most definitely was a Praetorian.

"You have to understand," Vesyon said without looking at her, "I needed you out of Sierra Village. There was no safety in keeping you there any longer. If the Chimera attack hadn't occurred, I would've requested you leave on different orders. You might be angry at me for not explaining to you what you are, or that we could've defeated those beasts on our own. The truth is, you still protect those people by *not* being in that village. I hope you can understand and trust that I know what's best for you, as well as them."

The last year of her life flashed in front of her eyes with a stark and unavoidable truth. She could run faster than anyone in her village, hunt better than men who'd been hunting their entire lives, her body could heal in a matter of hours, and now—glancing back at the Chimera carcass—she could battle like the best of them. Vesyon hadn't told her the truth because she *would* have stayed in Sierra Village. She never would've left Lunci behind if she'd known how capable she was of protecting him.

"I think she's starting to come around," Theo said with gentle ease, shifting an inch or two further away from Camille, leaving Vesyon as an easier target to reach when she felt inclined to strangle one of them. "It's not that bad, Cam. Us Praetorians have a great life once you get used to the blatant disgust the High King harbors for us, the way we must slink in the shadows amongst most of upper-level society, and how we can drink gallons of ale without feeling a damn thing! It's quite magnificent."

"Ignore him," Vesyon said, slashing his dagger against a flint stone and sending sparks into the kindling. "I didn't tell you what you are because if you knew, you'd never have left that boy's side."

She wanted to hit Vesyon directly across his bearded jaw. "You lied to me! I should be protecting them right now!"

"I did what was necessary," Vesyon countered, finally looking at her directly. His irises flashed, a myriad of steel-grey stone and frigid ice, emotionless and unapologetic.

A stinging wetness gathered at the corners of Camille's eyes, but she blinked it away. "They were all I had," she said shakily, her anger crumbling into crippling grief.

"No, they weren't," Vesyon said simply. "Peter and Lunci are safe now; that's all that matters."

"We don't *know* that Lunci is safe! He could be dead!" Camille snapped.

"You will understand my reasons in time, Camille."

Camille fisted her hands and stalked around the two men, avoiding the patches of mud as she searched for a place to sit. "How many Chimera did you kill?"

Vesyon didn't even hesitate in answering. "Twenty-six."

It didn't surprise her. They hadn't been running because Vesyon was unable to handle the beasts alone.

"So, I *am* a Praetorian?" she confirmed, rolling the syllables around and trying to make sense of their meaning.

He waited an achingly long thirty seconds, allowing the fire to grow, before facing her. "Yes, you are. As am I," Vesyon said, reaching into the neck of his shirt pulling out a silver medallion with a single black stone inlaid in the center of the interweaving metal branches and roots—one just like Camille's.

"You hardly look old enough," Camille spat.

He gifted her with a small smirk before shaking his head. "No, you're right about that. I don't *look* old enough."

His offhanded response piqued her interest, and Camille scrutinized Vesyon's face and body with a more critical eye.

"Trying to assess my actual age?" Vesyon asked.

"No!" Camille shot back, though her eyes kept roving over his features. She was unable to see how he could possibly be any older than he looked, and it was then that she heard Betty Anne's voice lingering in the back of her thoughts: *They never grow old—from the day they turn, their bodies are frozen in time. They can neither age, nor be injured without intensely great effort.*

"It can't be true," she whispered. "I can't possibly be older than eighteen."

"But you are. Your flawless complexion, however, will remain forever young," Theo said with a saucy wink.

She ignored him and continued to stare at Vesyon, who was now regarding her with equal fervor.

"Twenty-five," Camille said in quick succession.

Vesyon silently shook his head.

"Thirty?"

Another silent shake.

"I can't possibly be forty," Camille said.

"Forty-*six*, to be exact," Vesyon said coolly, continuing to stoke the flames.

Camille studied her hands—the smooth, unmarked look of them. She had no visible scars running the lengths of her arms, legs, or hands; even the extremely painful whipping at the hands of Grenswald hadn't permanently marred her perfect skin. Theo was right; she was the embodiment of youth, forever captured in the body of an eighteen-year-old woman.

"You aren't alone, sweetheart. I'm one year older than you are. Vesyon is the grandpa," Theo said nonchalantly, moving even further away from where Camille stood.

"You need grandchildren to be a grandpa," Vesyon said in Theo's direction, his eyes never leaving Camille's. "I'm sixty-four."

Camille's jaw dropped wide open. "But you can't—that's not..." Camille said, her mouth flopping like a fish to speak.

"Possible?" Vesyon asked with a smirk. "Many things are possible."

She waited in silence, staring at one and then the other, hoping their mouths would split into a smile, bursting into laughter at the joke they were playing on her. They didn't speak, nor did they laugh.

"And in being a Praetorian, you're a protector of *what*, exactly? The crown?" Camille blurted out, desperate to learn more about this strange new world she was apparently a part of.

Vesyon seemed bothered by Camille's question, based on the way he squinted as he cleaned and sheathed each of his daggers. "We aren't here to protect the High Court—we're here to protect the people of Aspera. We were *never* created to protect the High King, Camille. You should know that first and foremost."

"And you're a Praetorian as well?" Camille accused Theo. There was something about him that put her on edge, but she couldn't place what. It might've been his cocky air, or the way he walked, fierce confidence and surety that she had never seen someone carry quite as well as he did. Perhaps it was the fact that even though the fighting had stopped, Camille's pulse kept kicking into overdrive whenever he looked at her.

"Yep. I'm the Praetorian protecting Romeo Village now," Theo said quickly, lifting a small silver medallion from under his shirt that held a single dark sapphire in the middle. He casually dropped the silver piece back under his shirt before glancing back at Vesyon and picking up a long skinny stick to poke the fire aimlessly. "I thought you were lying to me. Playing a trick on my soft emotions," he said, blinking rapidly and clearing his throat as he jabbed one of the larger logs sending loose a spray of sparks into the darkening lavender sky. "She really doesn't remember a thing."

"Don't talk about me like I'm not here, *Theo*. I don't take kindly to rudeness," Camille snapped.

Vesyon laughed softly at her retort, arranging the additional kindling near the fire pit. "Just because *she* can't remember you doesn't mean her intuition doesn't. I guarantee Camille will be just as sweet toward you as she always was."

"*Great,*" Theo mumbled.

Camille ignored his response and pulled out some hunting gear from her pack. "Can I go?"

Vesyon nodded wryly, while Theo simply glared at the dancing flames.

She hastened away, needing distance and a silent moment alone. Her entire world had been dumped upside down in a matter of days, and she needed to understand what was left of it.

***

Stomping through the underbrush, Camille made a show of her irritation by kicking every fallen stump and punching as many low-hanging leaves and branches as she could. Despite the torrent of things to be frustrated with, her buzzing anger seemed to zero in on Theo.

How *dare* that man point his sword at her back and then battle alongside her, expecting them to be *chummy friends* afterward! He was the most arrogant and overly confident man she had ever met.

The worst part was he was right. Camille couldn't remember a single thing about him; there was nothing but a fleeting sense of familiarity floating in the deepest narrows of her past. It irked her. How could she possibly not remember him? Who was she? More importantly, *what* was she? Where had she come from?

It hadn't escaped her that these two strangers had all the answers to her questions, and it made sense to remain at their sides for now. They not only knew about her past, they knew and understood what she was.

She raised her bow just as the first tasty option crossed her path, letting fly the sturdy arrow directly through the rabbit's eye: a direct kill shot. Camille shook her head in bewilderment—even after everything she'd been through, her instincts were still spot on. It was a little eerie.

Why had Vesyon come for her just after the Chimera attacked Lunci? Why not sooner? She stopped dead in her tracks at the thought of Lunci running free through the woods, a smile shining on his jubilant face. It didn't fit the image of that same little boy she'd seen on the table, ashen-faced and dying. *I should've protected him.*

She kicked at another pile of dead leaves as guilt washed over her, which sent several squirrels scampering across the damp ground. Her arrows flew straight and true, downing two meaty squirrels. It was strangely comforting to methodically yank the arrows free, clean them, and shove them back in their holster; it was a small moment of understanding in a world blown severely off course.

It took everything Camille had not to turn tail and head back to Sierra Village. If the threat had been neutralized, was there any reason *not* to go home? It made no sense to keep running from home unless it was safer for her to keep her distance, but why? Sierra Village held no danger to her, did it?

Strangely enough, the notion of returning to Peter's home rubbed Camille the wrong way. It wasn't just that she'd left, Peter had made it very clear she was no longer welcome to stay. Perhaps the deal between Peter and Vesyon had run its course, or worse — she'd run out her welcome. She knew her part in Vesyon's plan, whatever it had be originally, was now far off course. She wouldn't be returning to Sierra Village, there was more to it all than the Chimera, more to it than her lost history as a Praetorian.

After an hour of hunting, she made her way back with one rabbit and three squirrels, annoyed with such a small takeaway. The soft leaves and grass beneath her feet muffled her steps, and she crept silently over to the camp, listening in on Vesyon's and Theo's conversation as their voices floated through the open space between the bare frigid trees.

"It's good to see you Theo, but I gave you strict orders to stay in the village. The borders of Aspera are wide open, and there is unrest in the East, making our patrols important. We have no idea what to expect from the outside kingdoms," Vesyon said, pushing the kindling back and forth with a stick.

"Yeah, I know, but the second Neeko showed up, I knew she'd be with you. You couldn't have expected me *not* to come," Theo said pointedly.

"Oh, and I guess I'm just supposed to believe you 'happened' upon her in the forest a few days ago? Don't try to con me, Theo. I know you better than that," Vesyon said.

Theo kept quiet for a moment, staring idly into the dancing flames. He seemed so young and weary for a sliver of a second, his shoulders drooping forward as though they couldn't withstand the pressure of his internal torture. What was troubling him? Camille felt a sort of tenderness and desire to comfort him—but then he straightened with aggressive bravado, and it disintegrated into nothing.

Vesyon hadn't noticed the transition of Theo's body language and continued as though Theo was listening. "I expect you to do what you're told. If the High Court found us—"

"I don't care about the High King or his Regent. I'm sick of hiding Vee! Besides—" Theo interrupted, picking at a wayward pine-cone and tossing it into the crackling flames, "nobody has seen the King since the massacre. We're fighting against an enemy that no longer exists! The border kingdoms are pushing back against foreign invaders, which is its own new beast." Theo tossed a handful of brush and twigs into the fire, and the flames danced and sparked wildly. "There's also this new problem we hadn't planned for," Theo said, his head tilting in the direction Camille had entered the brush. "I doubt you'll be able to keep her whereabouts secret much longer."

Vesyon sighed. "I'm sure he already knows she's fled Sierra Village. Peter said the Moon Tax collector saw her blood medallion, and it's only a matter of time before someone else recognizes her. Despite his absence from the throne, LeMarc will learn of her whereabouts. I'm sure of it. *He* sent the Chimera after her, I've no doubt."

"Why does he want her so badly?"

"I don't know why. We have no knowledge of what happened to her after the destruction of Charlie Town, but he obviously wants her back."

Camille found it interesting that Vesyon habitually referred to the High King without his title. He knew a lot more than he was willing to discuss, and by the stern look of determination blazing across his darkened features, she had a hunch that pulling her from Sierra Village was the beginning of a plan set in place long ago.

"Does she remember *anything*?" Theo asked, sounding fragile once more.

"This is not the place to discuss her past."

Theo heeded Vesyon's harsh tone, albeit begrudgingly. "So, let me get this straight," he said as he poked the stick he held into the belly of the dancing flames. "The High King has sent bloodthirsty monsters after a Praetorian everyone thought was dead or exiled to Olin because of one glimpse of her medallion? Do I have that right?"

Vesyon scoffed before flipping open a pouch filled with shelled nuts. "LeMarc knew she was alive and within the Asperian Kingdom. He's known since I rescued her that she didn't miraculously 'disappear.' *Now*, because of that oaf, Grenswald, he found where I hid her. It's only going to get worse from here."

Camille couldn't keep herself in the shadows any longer. "How could this *possibly* get any worse?" she asked, ignoring the look of annoyance on Vesyon's face and shoving the game into Theo's hands. "I'm not going anywhere with you until you tell me what's going on—Chimera or not."

"It's not so easy to explain," Vesyon said.

"Try me," she shot back.

Theo got to work on skinning the game as Camille settled onto a round stone near the fire.

"You already know what the plan is. We're leading the Chimera away," Vesyon said, cracking a nut and popping the salty insides into his mouth.

"And we killed those Chimera—all twenty-seven of them," Camille said. "So why are we still on the move, and why is *he* here?"

Theo smirked at this but continued his work on the game.

"Theo's presence here is inconsequential. He disregarded his orders to stay behind and will be reprimanded once we get back to Romeo Village," Vesyon explained.

Theo grunted as he chucked a skinned squirrel back at Camille. "Like you could keep me away, Vee. Besides, you know as well as I do that my duty is to be here with you. I'm tired of staying under the radar and playing 'lead babysitter' of Romeo Village."

"Duty? What duty?" Camille asked.

"The duty of being a Praetorian. Theo should've stayed in Romeo Village, until we arrived, to guard the people, but he apparently wants to do things his own way," Vesyon said, grabbing a portion of the squirrel meat and wrapping it around a skinned branch to dangle over the fire.

"If my duty is to the people, why am I here with you?" Camille asked.

"I'd watch that mouth of yours, Cam. The sharp attitude is completely ineffective with him. You can't ruffle his feathers; I've seen you try and fail many times," Theo said while attacking a particularly stubborn piece of blackened meat with his front teeth.

Camille and Vesyon each stared venomous daggers at Theo.

"Well, it's true!" Theo burst out, his lips covered in shiny squirrel grease. "You know she's good at weaseling her way under someone's skin." Theo shook the animal's bone in Vesyon's direction.

"You might know something about that, hmm?" Vesyon said under his breath.

"You can shut your trap, 'mister high and mighty.' Just because you have the personality of a rock doesn't mean you're better than me!" Theo shouted. "I have feelings, you know. I'm a sensitive man."

"'Better than,' did you say? I can't argue with your logic."

Theo opened his mouth to shoot another snide comment in Vesyon's direction, but Camille wasn't in the mood to listen to a wordplay cockfight. "Enough! Please," she said with a huff, doing her best not to release the burning frustration boiling in the pit of her belly. "Just answer the question."

Vesyon gave Theo one last look before wearily turning his attention toward Camille. "There are a lot of things I can't explain," Vesyon began. "You understand the importance of that, right? That it's for your own good?"

She took a minute to register his words, the same ones Peter had said the first day she woke up. "Whether it's for my own good or not, I'd like to have the choice to decide my own fate." Camille finished eating her squirrel meat and tossed the bone onto the ground. "So no, I don't understand the point of keeping valuable information from me. I just want to know where I come from. I want to know what I am. I want to know who I was before I woke up in Peter's home. Is that so much to ask?"

Vesyon's heart appeared to break a little at her words. His face scrunched in what looked like pain, but the emotions vanished as quickly as they'd appeared, and his visage was once again impenetrable.

"I'm sorry man, but I'm with her. She deserves to know," Theo said, his eyes hooded with defiance. "*I* should be allowed to tell her—"

"No!" Vesyon roared. "Camille—we aren't *keeping* information from you. We're protecting you from an uncertain *reaction*. We want you to remember your past at the *right* time, when you're ready."

"And if I don't remember things on my own?"

"You'll know everything you need to when the time is right," Vesyon cut back. His voice didn't carry an ounce of emotion, but his eyes were filled with concern saying everything his words couldn't. Despite the harsh, dry tone, Camille saw an undercurrent of tenderness there.

Vesyon cared about her, and despite his use of manipulation to pull her away from Peter and Lunci, she trusted him. Perhaps it was the way he looked at her, those grey, storming eyes filled to the brim with honest concern, or maybe her intuition was feeding her a long-forgotten memory.

"A year ago, *you* brought me to Peter's. Right?" Camille asked.

Vesyon's lips pressed into a hard line as he nodded, his hesitance igniting Camille's curiosity that much more.

"Why?"

"The why isn't important; it had to be done. You are extremely vital, Camille, in ways I can't even begin to explain. Peter was the only one I could trust to watch over you while I solidified our plans. Few people know anything about what happened to you back in—"

Without warning, Vesyon's head snapped up in attention. An intense, primal awareness slipped over his features as he crouched, ready to attack with a blade in his grip. "We need to leave. Now," he ordered, tossing his pack over his shoulder. He kicked dirt and wet leaves over the fire, causing the flames to plume into a swirl of white smoke.

Camille saw it then, a lazy swirl of ashy smoke twirling up into the stars, the signal of life undone. The bitter stench of burnt flesh filled her nostrils. It smashed into her system like a tidal wave, vibrant reds and flickering orange, a tapestry of horror laid out before her like a grotesque masterpiece. She shook her head, pinched her eyes closed as hard as she could but the smell of death increased.

"Camille!" Theo barked at her.

Opening her eyes again, she looked up to see the swirling trails of smoke had vanished, the bitter stench and canvas of endless red having disappeared from sight.

"Grab your things," Theo commanded, while Camille remained sitting in a haze. He tossed her a bag and several loose belongings, and she fumbled with them, hands shaking at the men's urgency.

"Camille," Vesyon barked from the distant tree line. "Let's move, they're gaining on us!"

Glancing up across the misty wooded expanse, she saw a group of soldiers charging toward them through the foggy haze dressed in full black from head to toe. Their armor shone dully in the evening atmosphere, a chinking tune of impending doom sounding out with their horses' every gallop. Strips of red leather in two straight lines encircled their right bicep: the mark of a High King Equestrian.

"The High King's Guard?" Theo snarled. "They're far away from home."

Vesyon pulled his sword free of its scabbard, and it appeared to Camille that running was no longer an option. They didn't have time; they would have to stand and fight. Camille had never engaged in hand-to-hand combat against a person before. The idea of killing another Asperian bothered her, but she had no other choice. She wasn't a murderer—she was a Praetorian protecting herself. *Wasn't that something different?*

As the men swarmed around them, Camille waited for the warmth to fill her, for the energy to flood her system, but nothing happened. In her moment of hesitation, her Praetorian abilities failed her. Doubt crept in, a horribly cold and debilitating feeling that rendered her arms and legs useless.

Vesyon moved first, slicing his blade swiftly across the torso of the first soldier to arrive. The man fell with a thunderous crash just as Theo angled in front of Camille, taking on three more soldiers at once. She was quickly left to her own devices, cowering on the ground, hands still gripping her pack, unable to move.

"Hello, little girl," one of the soldiers mocked, entwining his fingers in her long red hair. He yanked her head back so that she was forced to look up at him. The sour stench seeping through his leather chest guard hit her in the face like a charging predator, harsh and unyielding. His heart was pounding, every thud ringing like a battle call in her ears. He wasn't a weak man by any means, and his hands alone looked as though they could crush a man's skull.

She screamed inwardly at herself to move, to act, but her body steadily ignored her. *What was going on?!* She was Praetorian for Ma'Nada sake, and yet her instincts refused to react.

A second soldier lunged at her, sword in one hand and a dagger in the other, angling to slice right through her. Her body jolted awake at the imminent threat, and she pivoted away, the motion tearing out a chunk of her hair. Her scalp bloomed with pain and tears pricked her eyes as she swayed on her feet, feeling a sense of powerlessness at the mercy of these men.

"Have some training, do you?" the first soldier said with a crooked grin, shaking her loose strands from his meaty fingers. His teeth were pearly white and straight, his face, though possibly considered pleasant, contorted with a nasty sneer of disgust making

Camille shiver.

He didn't give her a chance to respond before slamming her head against the tree trunk behind her. She slumped to the ground, her vision swimming as her skull pricked with the rushed urgency to heal itself. Blood crept down the side of her neck, warm and wet, as both soldiers standing in front of her laughed, discussing what to do next.

"You grab her feet, I'll get the top," the first soldier said as he reached for her hands.

"That would be a mistake," Camille gasped, desperately trying to regain her equilibrium. "You should run while you still have a chance."

"Camille!" Vesyon roared a mere ten feet away. "Get away from her, you filthy dogs!"

She should've been able to fight them off, to protect herself, but as one man took her ankles and the other reached under her armpits, Camille's instincts barely flinched.

They pulled her just out of eyesight behind a sizeable flowering bush, dropping her carelessly on the mossy, mud-slicked ground. One man gripped her waist and began to tug aggressively at her pants, his dirt-riddled nails digging into her skin.

"Cam, where are you!" Theo screamed, voice brimming with terror.

She squirmed at the soldiers' efforts, scrambling to get away as one soldier managed to slip a hand inside her pants while the other groped at her breasts.

"It's been far too long since I've touched a woman. Fight all you want, little girl—no one is coming to save you," the first soldier said, grabbing greedily at her naked hips.

He groaned and shuddered with excitement as he pinched her flesh, telling his comrade to hold her down. "This one has some meat on her, and I want to see it!"

The second soldier ripped her shirt and vest wide open as he grappled to press her arms into the mud. One hand cinched down her windpipe to hold her in place as Camille heard the first soldier's pants hit the ground by her feet.

A small voice, piercing and unrelenting, broke free from the depths of her soul. There was no way she was going to let this happen. She would fight to the death if she had to; fear be damned. Camille slammed her boot heel against the first soldier's crotch.

"Agh!" he wailed, slumping over her. Camille felt the familiar rush of blood flow through the tiny veins around her eyes, and she practically whimpered in relief. Her Praetorian instincts took over, and she lost herself to the motions, no longer crippled by panic or pain.

Punching upwards, her fist struck the chin of the soldier holding her down. As his comrade fell forward, they collided into each other with enough force that she was able to pull up her pants and scoot away from them both. With the flood of Praetorian instinct surging through her veins, she allowed a tiny smile to flit across her face as she righted her clothing the best she could.

"Got a little fight in you, eh? Think this is fun?" the second soldier growled, spitting blood on the ground and wiping at his busted chin. "Good—I like 'em feisty!"

He lunged toward her again, sword in hand. Camille evaded the blade and yanked him into a headlock, twisting his chin with such violent force that she heard the quiet *pop* of his spine snapping. She dropped his dead weight on the forest floor like a heavy sack of grain, then removed a small knife from his belt. The first soldier gawked at her, his pants still down and his hands cradling his groin.

"I told you," Camille said as she wiped the sticky wetness of blood from her cheek, "that attacking me *was a mistake.*"

The guard backed up and tripped over a tree root, crashing over it as Camille pursued him. She pulled his hair as hard as he'd done to her, driving the blade straight into the side of his neck.

The soldier's face went white, his eyes bulging purple as his mouth opened and closed like a beached fish.

"Struggle all you want," she said, throwing his words back at him in a smooth, whispering lilt, "no one is coming to save you."

"Who are you?" he gurgled.

Camille removed the knife from his neck and watched the dying man's crimson blood coat her forearm, trailing into her shirtsleeve. "My name is Camille Scipio, and I'm a Praetorian."

"Camille?"

She spun with a menacing snarl, but it was only Theo jogging through the trees. His blue eyes moved from her bloodied weapon and torn clothing to the dead men beside her and understanding darkened his features.

"They came at me. They almost they pulled my pants down—they were going to—" Camille blubbered, dropping the knife beside the first soldier's slain form as her entire body began to shake. *What have I done?*

"It's okay, you're okay," Theo said as he approached with slow, calculated steps. She shifted warily but didn't move away from him despite her desire to bolt. "I'm not going to hurt you, but I need to see your head. It's bleeding a lot."

"I killed them," Camille said as Theo gathered her close, pulling her head to him to inspect the damage. Her knees buckled, and she fell against the solidity of his frame, horrified with the pool of blood billowing out from the soldiers' lifeless corpses.

The ground was littered with dead bodies, many more than the two soldiers she'd just murdered. A flood of memories invaded her consciousness, dismembered and harsh, vividly bright and unrelenting. "Oh Ma'Nada; I killed them, didn't I?" Camille moaned as the edges of her vision blurred. She was no longer in Romeo Village, but somewhere much different, somewhere full of fire and screaming. She was surrounded by death.

"Camille?" Theo asked, his voice a world away.

"I killed them," she repeated, clinging to Theo and trembling all over. "*I killed them all.*"

CHAPTER NINE
ROMEO VILLAGE

Pinpricks stabbed unrelentingly into Camille's left shoulder, and it felt like her arm had been severed directly at the socket. Her eyes snapped open, wild with attention as images crashed together in front of her. It was worse than waking in Sierra Village because now she *remembered*.

Camille took in her surroundings with quick and swift calculation. She was alone in a simple, unfamiliar bedroom, with Neeko stoically perched on the window ledge above her head. She breathed a heavy sigh of relief in the comfort of otherwise complete solitude.

Her head ached and she reached up to assess the delicate new skin and auburn hair sprouting where it had been torn out. She pulled down her loose cotton shirt to see a smear of fading yellow bruises traveling over her chest and down her arms, many in the outlines of a man's hand.

Blinking away the stinging sleep from her eyes, Camille took in the paneled wood roof above her. The room smelled both earthy and metallic, which was very strange. Fluttering light twitched and danced across the ceiling, moving with the tempo of the wind whipping through the trees outside her window. Squeezing her eyes shut in a moment of hope and desperation, she begged for darkness. Everything hurt within her, down to the marrow of her bones.

Stifling a yawn, Camille pressed the palms of her hands

abrasively against her eyelids, trying to will good thoughts back into her mind. When she stared around the room once more, Camille noticed a shadowed figure in the corner and her heart launched into her throat.

"Cam?" it said, sleepy and barely audible. "You okay?"

"Holy crap, Theo! I thought you were an intruder!" Camille collapsed against the feather pillows, eyes fluttering with unwelcome weariness.

He came over to sit on the edge of her bed. "I'd never attack you," he said with intense seriousness before a gentle smile curved his prominent lips, and a glimmer of humor sparkled in his expression. "Not unless you asked me to." His eyebrows wiggled suggestively over his twinkling blue eyes, and it was difficult for Camille to keep a smile from finding its way onto her lips.

"Lurking in the dark watching someone sleep is nearly as bad as attacking them."

Theo's smirk bloomed into a full smile. "My sincerest apologies, my dearest lady."

Camille snorted as his genial tone, aware of a sudden flutter in the depths of her belly.

"How's the head?" he asked.

She felt around the tender area with her fingertips. "It's healing."

"I should've been there for you," he said, reaching out but stopping when Camille flinched backward into her pillow.

She drew a deep breath, feeling immediate guilt at the hurt in Theo's eyes. But she didn't know him; there was no reason to feel bad for an automatic reaction. She had every right to be uncomfortable, and yet the only emotion bubbling through her system was a growing heat in the pit of her stomach.

Wiggling her toes and readjusting her propped up position, Camille's line of sight slid over the shadowed room to keep from drowning in Theo's blue gaze.

"I handled it," Camille replied, pressing her palms down on the sheets and comforter to make them as smooth as possible.

"That's no excuse. I can't tell you how sorry I am." His head hung, shoulders slumping as he scratched at the back of his neck. "You shouldn't have had to deal with this. It wasn't fair. I'm sorry, Cam."

Camille had no retort; he seemed genuine, despite his previously sarcastic nature. This version of Theo clearly cared about her, maybe even liked her. She grew nervous under his intense gaze but found it was incredibly difficult to keep her eyes averted for any extended period.

"I, um, well, something strange happened when the men attacked, and I don't quite know..." Camille started but felt the words lodging thickly in her throat. The Equestrians had aggressively attacked her, and her Praetorian abilities had failed her. Theo seemed to understand the words burning in her throat by the look of empathy in his expression. His hand slowly moved toward hers, a gentle and silent question, waiting to see if she would pull away from his intention to touch her. She didn't. Linking his fingers with hers, his lips quirked upward for a slight moment before they drew down in apparent distaste. His expression glazed over, his body present but his mind far away in a long-ago memory.

"Being a Praetorian isn't easy Cam. Sometimes it's downright horrible. We experience a constant, wild surge of emotion in every direction. It can feel incredibly impossible, but we trained for years to learn how to restrain it. Fear is just as debilitating as anger can be empowering. If you let the emotion overtake you, you will lose control."

As much as she didn't want to relive or think about what had happened in the forest, she knew precisely what Theo was talking about. She hadn't just felt fear as the Equestrians descended on her, she had been wholly paralyzed with terror. Having spent most of her energy on diffusing the raging monster screaming through her blood in times of anger or frustration while living with Peter, Camille hadn't realized the monster would abandon her in times of absolute terror. Like a blind person relying only on sound, she had put too much stock in what she had no control over. To manage the beast within, she would need to learn how to manipulate it, and not allow the inner monster to manipulate her.

"Where's Vesyon and how long have I been sleeping?" She asked casually, gently pulling her fingers from Theo's grasp and straightening the wild tumbling disarray of her hair. She combed her fingers through the thick strands, untangling and patting down the frizzy curls into a semblance of order and feeling more than a bit self-conscious of her bedraggled state.

"No need to rush, Ace," he said with a pat on her knee covered in a mountain of blankets. "Now that you're awake, things are significantly better. We're in Romeo Village. Vesyon is taking care of a few things up top, and you are to stay in bed and rest. *His* orders." Something about the way his eyes flitted away from hers felt off.

"You're keeping something from me."

Theo appeared shocked as well as annoyed at her deduction. "No!"

"I'm going to find Vesyon," she said in a matter-of-fact tone.

Theo's eyebrows rose. "Of course, you are. Why would you stay put?"

"I've slept long enough," Camille retorted, shrugging off his clipped annoyance.

"It's not about sleeping, Cam. You've been through a lot, and you should take it easy."

"I said I'm fine. Now drop it!" She could feel the rush of blood fill the veins around her eyes, threatening to break free, and there was no doubt the whites of her eyes had begun to darken before she regained control.

Theo huffed, pinching his lips together. Perhaps he was right about her having been through a lot but lying in bed wasn't going to help matters.

Pulling back the covers to prove her strength and determination, Camille instantly regretted her decision when she realized she wore nothing but an over-sized linen shirt and undergarments.

Camille snatched up the crisply folded pants at the foot of her bed and hastily dragged them up her goose fleshed legs. Once she was a little more presentable, she turned her attention back toward Theo, who had occupied himself by attempting to pet Neeko. The black cat wasn't having it and kept moving out of Theo's reach further along the windowsill.

"*Fine.* Stay there like a grouchy porcupine."

Neeko hissed in response to Theo's verbal barbs.

"Watch it! I have no qualms roasting you for dinner one night."

Neeko didn't seem bothered by the threat and turned to begin grooming his hindquarters as Camille went to a side table where a bowl of water sat. She splashed some of the warm liquid on her face, hoping it would help to soothe her fraying nerves. Lifting her eyes up to the small mirror above the water bowl, Camille leaped back in shock at her gruesome reflection. Her face dripped with blackish gore and blood, and her eyes were no longer a vibrant emerald but a deep, obsidian black that bled across the whites of her eye sockets. She looked like a demon from another world.

"Camille?" Theo said softly from behind her, his concern racing through her senses like a cold rush of water.

She dried her face with a rag and shook her head, willing the image to flee. Her complexion had been perfectly clean just a moment before: she had imagined it. It wasn't exactly a calming thought.

Camille peeked through her lashes, absolutely terrified of what she might see. Clean skin, green eyes, and pale cheeks greeted her.

"Everything all right?"

Her eyes narrowed as they met Theo's in the mirror. "I'm fine."

"You just jumped three feet in the air for no reason. I think 'fine' is grossly inaccurate."

"I said I'm—"

"Fine? In my opinion—"

"*Nobody asked for your opinion, Theo!*" Camille shouted, whipping around to face him. The silence that followed filled the void between them. It was deafening. She could hear the heavy thud of her heart pounding out a quick tempo against her ribs, but neither one of them seemed to know what to say next.

"Camille, I..." Theo started as Neeko jumped down from the windowsill to rub against her ankles, purring loudly.

"Let's go," she barked, bending to scratch the cat between the ears before pulling on her boots with rushed, erratic motions. Her hands shook with weariness and embarrassment over her outburst, but she wasn't going to let either of those things distract her. Vesyon was her only source for answers, and she had a mountain of questions to throw in his face.

"Good luck getting up top on your own. It's kind of a maze down here," Theo smirked, all pearly white teeth and sexy bravado. The thin, pinkish scar running from his temple down to his cheekbone stood out against the tanned complexion of his skin. Despite the perceived flaw—it only enhanced his rugged demeanor, which irritated Camille further.

"Neeko will show me the way, won't you sweetheart?" Camille cooed. The cat meowed in response, confirming that his loyalties always lay with Camille. "See, I don't need you."

She grabbed her vest and fur-lined coat from on top of the

dresser, yanking them on as she headed for the bedroom door.

Theo didn't attempt to stop her but followed quickly on her heels. She jerked open the wooden door and stopped immediately when harsh white light flared brightly against her eyes. She stared down an endless hallway from right to left. Gleaming steel plates lined the walls, clinical, white tiles blanketed the floor, and yellow fluorescent bulbs dotted the ceiling every five feet. The thick mahogany door she'd walked through was metal on the other side.

Bizarre, she thought as she stared critically at the sterile-looking hallway. It smelled even more heavily of earth, and the air was dense, as though they were miles underground.

Camille studied the small window just above the bed she'd been sleeping on. Soft dusk light filtered through the glass, and there appeared to be a copse of thick evergreens, ashy aspen trunks bare of leaves, browning bushes and snow-dusted mountains in the distance. "That's not..." Camille stared openly at the window in shock. "Is that fake?"

"It's a reflection panel. It takes the temperature and light refraction from above and transitions that information through the microchip placed in the wall sensor. The panel recreates a similar scene so that it still feels like you are above ground," Theo said smartly, sounding the way Peter had during one of his lessons. Most of his words were nonsense to ·her, but she understood the concept. It was crazy to see such progressive technology in Romeo Village when Sierra Village had been so minimal in its growth and mechanics. They were opposites.

Camille reentered the bedroom and examined it, beginning to see where her first impressions had been completely off. She couldn't smell the pine needles through the seemingly thin pane of glass; she only smelled the sharpness of fertile soil. And the heat she'd felt wasn't emanating from the sun outside, but from the reflection panel across the room. "So, we're under the village?"

"Exactly. The reflection panel is here, so we feel more at home buried underground like gophers. It was Vesyon's idea."

"*Fascinating,*" Camille said moving past him and back into the sterile hallway. "Look—I don't mean to be rude, but I want explanations as to why I'm here, not about whatever 'fancy' stuff Vesyon's come up with in his spare time."

Theo's full lips pulled into a frown at her demeanor. Perhaps she could've been more delicate, but her patience was rapidly dwindling. She turned around, taking his silence as either an inability or lack of desire to help her, and strode down the metal lined hallway.

"You don't even know where you're going," Theo said sharply after her.

Her pace quickened, and she rounded a sharp corner, one that led to a hallway identical to the one she'd just walked down. In fewer seconds than she cared to admit, she was lost. Every hall looked the same. Metal floors and walls with buzzing fluorescents baked bright spots of color into her pupils. The visions wouldn't stop, either—every few minutes she'd peer down at her hands and see blood everywhere, and the next minute they'd be clean. She was losing her mind.

"I really don't think this is a good idea," he said, shaking his head and crossing his arms. "You seriously need to rest."

Camille snorted. "Rest is the last thing I need or want, and I'm doing this whether you help me or not. Though without it, it will take longer." Peter had taught her plenty of useful things, but nothing to do with flirting or using her feminine wiles to manipulate a situation. She'd seen the girls in Sierra Village bat their eyelashes and toss their hair over their shoulders enough to know that it worked if executed successfully.

Trying her best to seem frail, Camille fluttered her lashes as she looked up at Theo.

"Do you have something in your eye?"

"Oh, for Ma'Nada sake!" She turned on her heel and stormed down a new hallway, one that twisted and turned to end in front of an elevator. A small circular button blinked green to the right of the doorway. She pushed it and was instantly rewarded by a rush of cold air as the metal doors slid apart.

Camille charged inside and pressed another glowing button labeled "one" inside the small space, waving at Theo as he rounded a corner and advanced toward her.

"Camille, wait, you don't know where you're going—"

The doors closed, effectively cutting the handsome man off and sending her vaulting upwards. Camille grinned with genuine glee, watching the panel of numbers light up in rapid order from fifteen to one.

Her blurry reflection split apart as the doors soundlessly opened, giving way to a quiet side alley sprinkled with early autumn snow. Crisp air swirled inside the tiny confines of her metal cage, teasing Camille's senses with the promise of home and reminding her of how far away she was from everything she loved. She set out, her boots crunching across the frost-covered ground while her eyes roved the quiet side street.

Stopping suddenly, surveying her immediate surroundings with a scrutinizing eye, she realized her predicament. She was alone in a strange village, without a clue of where to find Vesyon.

"Damn it," she cursed under her breath. Perhaps Theo had been right; she had no idea where she was or where to go.

She poked her head around a building at the end of the alleyway and saw a decrepit-looking village square and a frayed black banner boasting the three interlocking gold circles of the Romeo Village crest. A broken fountain stood in the center, one with a life-sized cement statue of a woman bathing. Snow dusted her upturned face and shoulder, but her right arm was completely missing, and she had deep gouges running up her legs that looked like bullet holes.

There was a light dusting of snow littered across the cobblestone square and a well-worn path of foot traffic from the entrances of the closest buildings, but for the most part, the village appeared almost vacant. There couldn't have been more than twenty people milling about; a blacksmith in the smoky confines of a thatched roof dwelling, a baker covered in flour rolling out fresh dough to rise, a herd of chattering women bundled up in thick shawls and coats, their full dresses and petticoats dancing in the chilly wind. It was strange and didn't fit with the sharp fluorescent hallways and stark white walls of the underground.

Camille stood out like a sore thumb, dressed in green fitted pants, a loose linen shirt, and well-worn leather vest and jacket. She wasn't dressed appropriately to be above ground, and it would only be a matter of time before someone noticed the stranger amongst the village norm.

Two men in green and white uniforms noticed Camille and began heading across the courtyard in her direction. They weren't the High King's Equestrians, and, though they didn't fit into the Romeo Village appearance either, she got the feeling they weren't exactly friendly.

The guards picked up their speed when Camille wheeled back to flee, but she wasn't going to let them catch her. She sprinted down the opposite end of the alleyway and took a sharp right onto another side street, wondering why Vesyon had even brought her here. Every building appeared to be deserted; the pathways were lined with broken bits of brick, wood, and piles of gathered rocks and dust.

The frozen ground recently hit with rain turned the walkway into a mush of muddied snow, making it impossible for Camille to camouflage her path. Who *were* these men, and why were they chasing her? She needed to get back to the elevator to disappear back within the compound.

She banked right, ducking between two cabins and angling back toward the wreckage of the main square. A large group of the townsfolk was just up ahead, and she need only slip between them—but it was too late. Another guard near the group had already spotted her and was pointing her out to his fellow comrades. She immediately spun on her heel, only to find the larger of the two earlier soldiers coming up the pathway toward her.

Camille retreated against the wall of a cabin, searching wildly for a weapon. She saw nothing but a small fist-sized rock and grabbed it as the massive crunch of their boots closed in on her.

The larger man looked down at her with supreme boredom, his shoulders the width of a grizzly bear. He held his gun down and away from Camille in a passive gesture, which confused her. "Are you Camille?"

"Who wants to know?" Camille shot back, raising the rock.

"We aren't here to hurt you; we're trying to help."

Camille's eyes flicked down to the name on his grungy uniform: General Phillip Ballen. *He'd recited the perfect thing,* Camille thought wryly, *just what a soldier of Sierra Village would say before they shackled an intruder and threw them into the unknown wild beyond the Asperian wall.* The men closed in on her, making her entire body scream with a warning. She would die before she let another soldier touch her. "You stay back, don't come any closer!"

Phillip stopped, his eyes scanning her face as he raised his hands in an offer of peace.

The second soldier, a man named Lieutenant Acher Greeves, walked carefully over to join them. He mirrored the General, his hands open and displaying his palms to showcase his intent of kindness. "Camille, we're not your enemies. Vesyon ordered us to collect you and bring you down to operations. It'd be a lot easier if you came willingly."

Hesitating for several long moments, Camille turned her attention to the General. "How do you know Vesyon?"

The burly man sighed in annoyance but seemed to understand her hesitation. "I've known Vesyon for a very long time, long enough to smell like his damn smoking pipe for how often he picks it up in my presence. I'd rather not force him to collect you himself as he is in a rather...serious meeting," Phillip said, his stern glare never wavering from her face. After waiting a few seconds longer, Camille allowed the small rock to drop to the ground at her feet.

Phillip gestured for Camille to follow, and the three of them headed down the muddied path back the way she'd come. Once they reached the elevator, Phillip pulled out a white plastic card from his jacket pocket and swiped it against a metal panel to open the doors.

Phillip and Acher walked inside, dragging Camille with them. She could feel her patience slipping away and her panic rising as they shoved her into the furthest corner, apart from the sliding doors.

"We have her, Captain," Phillip said, pressing a black button on the wall and speaking into an intercom.

After a long pause, Vesyon replied in curt stiffness. "Bring her to operations, please." Though his words were dry, they meant something different to Camille: *We are not safe to speak openly here, so please keep your thoughts to yourself.* She wasn't sure how she knew that, but for once she wanted to listen to him.

The elevator stopped much more abruptly than her ride up and opened to reveal another long hallway with doors labeled by numbers and names. Large green letters spelled out "Romeo Village Operations" just across the top of the metal door at the end of the hall, and the two men made for it with her in tow.

Phillip swiped his card once more, and the panel lit up before the heavy metal door slid open to reveal a substantial, circular room and a surprisingly loud screaming match between two men just inside the doorway.

"I told you to watch her!"

"I told *you* she wouldn't sit still much longer!" Theo yelled, his face flushed and eyes threatening to darken.

"You should carry out my orders no questions asked, soldier," Vesyon said, immediately back in control.

"Tell that to your Praetorian. She obviously doesn't listen very well," Theo snapped under his breath.

Both men went silent and whipped around as Camille was led inside, with Theo zeroing in on Acher's vice-like grip on her left arm. "It isn't wise for you to handle a Praetorian like that," he remarked.

Vesyon also stared at Acher, his expression turbulent. "I requested you *ask* her to come, not force her. There is a huge difference."

Phillip looked slightly perturbed but requested his soldier to release Camille. He instantly dropped her arm.

"Thank you, General. Your help is much appreciated," Vesyon said to Phillip. "We will discuss matters further after the evening meal."

Phillip nodded and exited after the Lieutenant while Camille came to stand mutely at Vesyon's side. Everything about the situation seemed incredibly strange to her. Despite the anger Vesyon clearly displayed, she could tell it wasn't directed at her.

Vesyon waited until the door had closed behind the soldiers before he looked at her. "How are you? Are you feeling weak or tired at all?" His tone soaked into her system like warm butter on freshly toasted bread, and she was equally relieved as much as worried by his calm reaction.

"I'm fine," Camille said swiftly. "Should I not be?"

"Before anyone else interrupts, I need to be clear with you. The King Regent knows you're here—the soldiers who attacked us in the forest were scouts looking for you."

Camille's line of sight zeroed in on Vesyon as her mind whirled with the news. "I don't understand. I'm not the only Praetorian in Aspera," she said, looking from Vesyon to Theo and back again. "Why isn't he after either of you?"

Theo's eyebrows scrunched in discomfort. "Vee—just tell her man, what have you been doing since you rescued her?"

Vesyon glared at Theo. "There hasn't been much time between running from the Chimera, finding you in the forest, and getting attacked by Equestrian Guards."

This threw Camille for another loop. "Why would they be sent so far outside the High Court?"

Vesyon shook his head wearily. "The High King wants you back, Camille. He sent a pack of Chimera after you, and now he's sending his best guards. You must understand that I only left you in Sierra Village because I thought you wouldn't be found. It was my mistake—I should've come for you much sooner."

"What do you mean he wants me *back*?"

"There's a lot I haven't been able to explain to you," Vesyon murmured, gaze downcast.

"Yeah, I can see that. Answers would be nice," Camille retorted.

He blanched; her sarcasm obviously hit home. She could feel that something was off, but no matter how intently she stared into Vesyon's grey, storming expression, she couldn't place what it was. Her stomach felt uneasy, and her intuition set off a warning bell of uncertainty.

Vesyon collapsed into the closest chair, balancing his elbows on his knees as his head fell into his hands. "An army of two thousand Equestrians left Whiskey Wharf this morning. They're headed in our direction as we speak."

"But why? I don't understand," Camille said.

"You aren't the only one," Theo said dryly.

Both Camille and Vesyon turned a sharp eye on the arrogant blond before silence settled in. She could run; she could take her sword and find a way to make do.

"I know what you're thinking, and it's not possible," Vesyon said with a shake of his head.

"Why not? Can't we just leave? *Disappear*." If the High King was after her, she wanted to be as far away from civilization as possible.

"The idea itself isn't horrible, darling—it's just not an actual possibility," Theo said gently. "I'm sure you've noticed this isn't a typical village of Aspera. There are a lot of things we are *protecting* here. We can't just abandon it."

"Theo," Vesyon warned.

Camille looked between the men. "Okay, seriously. What's *really* going on?"

"Just tell her!" Theo said, flinging his arms out in exasperation.

Vesyon glared at him without restraint, a silent argument taking place that still left Camille in the dark.

Theo finally broke the silence, ignoring Vesyon and regarding Camille with frank honesty. "We're hiding a weapon—something we can destroy the High King and his army with."

"Theo!"

"A weapon?"

"Yes, and the High King has sent an army to break down our

efforts to reform, as well as to collect you, apparently," Theo said, completely ignoring the fire blazing in Vesyon's expression. "We've been building this compound for protection from the High King, but it appears even steel walls and cement ceilings can't keep out the rats. So, we didn't stop at protection—we targeted our efforts toward defense."

"Is this true?" Camille asked, turning around to see Vesyon's face slide into a mask of neutrality again.

"I should've brought you here sooner," Vesyon said, ignoring her question and raking his fingers through his shoulder-length black hair. "You have to understand what we've been trying to accomplish, what we've been *working* toward. I should've kept you under lock and key, but I didn't want to keep you from living. I knew once someone recognized you, the King Regent Metus would be close behind," Vesyon said.

The syllables of King Regent Metus's name crashed viciously against Camille's memory, forcing all other questions out, leaving a disgusting taste in her mouth. She'd heard this name again and again in Sierra Village, but always on the tongues of the villagers. Metus was the unyielding King Regent, the right hand to the absent High King, the one enforcing Asperian laws. Yet hearing his name spoken by Vesyon shook loose a recollection long forgotten, and she shivered in response.

Theo squinted, scrutinizing her reaction. "You remember him?"

"I don't *remember* him, no. But something strange *did* happen to me down in my bedroom this morning..."

"What?" Vesyon asked, his voice thick with worry.

Camille blinked against the barrage of images infiltrating her mind. "I saw things that weren't really there. One minute I was fine, and the next I was covered in..." Camille couldn't bring herself to go on. Explaining the entirety of it would bring the memories roaring back, and the last thing she wanted was to see them again. "Words spark a memory that I can't seem to suppress, and then suddenly I'm hallucinating. I don't understand what's happening to me."

Vesyon's steel façade slipped as his shoulders slumped. "The wall in your mind is beginning to crumble, and your past will flash into your vision with incredible realism when you are weak or exhausted. It's my fault; I've pushed you too hard since we left Sierra Village."

"So, everything I've been seeing—it really happened?"

Vesyon nodded his head and began to massage his temples. "Memories will continue to return until the wall blocking your past is completely broken. It's not just you who experiences this—all Praetorians see things in our moments of weakness. It'll get easier with time, and, eventually, it won't catch you so off guard."

"I'm not sure I'm ready for this," Camille said in a rush.

"Unfortunately, you don't have a choice."

"But these flashes, these images—they make me sick. Make me feel like I'm turning into something I'm not."

Vesyon turned away, most likely to avoid meeting her pleading expression. Vesyon was still hiding something from her, and she had a sneaking suspicion he was *afraid* of her memories returning. "You *always* can control who you are, Camille. Being a Praetorian just makes it even more important to control your reactions to situations."

"I'm afraid of what I'll become."

Theo grasped Camille's hand, a gentle, soothing motion that sent a rocket of heat up her arm to fill the empty pit of her stomach. It was unnerving that a single touch could cause such a reaction, but she didn't pull away.

"The virus we were infected with when we became Praetorians has several side effects and reliving disturbing images from our past is one of them. The doctor calls them 'Praecollection.' As you gain more strength, they won't be so debilitating," Theo said softly, brushing his thumb back and forth across her knuckles.

"We need to stay on task here," Vesyon said, his tone curt and crisp, once again causing Theo to pull away and cross his arms against his chest. "Metus is on his way, and we need to prepare. Camille, I'm sorry to say this, but it would be best if you stayed out of the main fight. You aren't strong enough—"

"Says you!" Camille burst out against her better judgment. Vesyon was right; she still felt weak, and her entire body ached to climb back into bed. But this wasn't something Camille wanted to run away from, either. She wanted to know why the High King was after her, and when the King Regent arrived, she wanted to be front and center to fight him off. "I'm *not* hiding from him."

Theo chuckled appreciatively. "That's our Cam, blazing into battle on all cylinders." His confident smile lifted Camille's spirits. Even though he was as overprotective as Vesyon, he still seemed to appreciate her desperate need to prove she could handle herself.

The room fell silent between the three of them, each lost in their own whirl of thoughts.

Vesyon eventually spoke first. "Take Camille up to the kitchens, Theo. She needs to eat and regain some strength. Make sure she gets to bed afterward. She needs rest."

Although she wasn't even close to understanding everything, the mention of food had Camille's mouth involuntarily watering. A huge pang of homesickness throbbed in her stomach when she thought about Betty Anne and a nice warm meal at the Broken Goat.

Reminiscing would have to take a back seat, though; Camille was starving, and a piping hot meal was more than deserved after the week she'd been having.

CHAPTER TEN
SECRETS IN THE NIGHT

Camille sat back against her chair; her stomach distended blissfully with the pressure of food she just devoured. The small red plate of rosemary chicken and tomato salad with cured cheese had been so delicious she was tempted to grab her plate and lick off the remaining flavor left behind.

"Another one?" Theo said, handing her a fourth goblet filled-to-the-brim with a drink Theo called "Scotties." It was the most delightful thing she'd ever tasted, a smooth and savory concoction of buttery caramel and cream.

"Oh yes, please!" she said as she happily accepted the silver glass out of his hand, her fingers barely grazing against his. A spark of electricity zipped down her spine at the slight skin contact. "Thank you," she said, her body clamming up with a sense of shy apprehension.

Why does he make me feel so on edge? she thought as she sipped at the warm beverage in her hands.

He smiled at her enthusiasm, his expression tender as he watched her.

"You're doing that thing again," Camille said, keeping her eyes glued to the glass in her hand, slowly drinking and savoring the buttery sweetness rolling over her taste buds.

"What thing?"

"Staring at me."

He didn't reply as he continued to stare, his gaze boring into the side of her face with unrelenting heat.

"This is quite an impressive kitchen," Camille said conversationally to break the tension she felt thrumming between them. She pulled her focus away from his attention, desperate to calm the erratic beating of her heart.

Romeo Village appeared poor and rundown with neglect topside. However, the inner workings of the compound were downright glamorous by comparison. The kitchen hall was lined with reflection panels circulating the entire room and making it feel as though she were sitting on top of a tower over-looking the mountains and trees of the village. It was incredible, and unlike anything she had ever seen before. The pinewood paneled floors were shiny and clean, not a dust mite in sight or errant cobweb through the weaving of exposed wooden rafters expanding the width of the hall. Everything was alive with the glow of a soft rising moon.

"I'm sorry that I keep staring," Theo said finally as he pushed his empty plates away, scooting closer to her on the bench. His left thigh pressed against hers, sending a fiery spark of electricity up and down her spine. "I just can't believe you're here with me."

The grin plastered on his face was almost comical. She wasn't certain if she wanted more of his attention, or if she wanted to run and hide from it, either option made her insides squirm uncomfortably. "I think I'm ready to go to sleep," Camille said, unable to look him in the eyes.

"Sure," he replied, his tone slightly less enthusiastic than before.

Their scuffed and muddy boots echoed down the dimmed hallways as Theo walked her back to her room. She knew she wouldn't have been able to find her way without him.

"Here we are," Theo said on a sigh as though he didn't want to leave her alone just yet. It was endearing and made Camille smile in response. They stood silently for a moment in front of a door Camille never would've placed as hers.

"Thank you for walking me back to my room; it really wasn't necessary," Camille lied.

He smirked in response, then took her hand and brought it to his lips. He brushed a feather-light kiss across her knuckles, sending a flutter of nervous butterflies through her bloodstream. She could feel the heat radiating off his body, and it made her desperate to draw nearer. It was weird to handle such a strong pull toward a man she barely knew. Even after what had happened in the forest with the Equestrians, Camille felt safe and intrigued by Theo's subtle advances. She craved them and wanted more.

"We both know," he said, looking into the depths of her eyes with a sparkling hint of mischief, "that you never would've made it back without my help."

Her gaze pulled away from the intensity of his expression down to his full lips, ones which she couldn't help but linger on. Her sense of modesty disappeared whenever he looked at her, and it made her lips form into a smile without even thinking.

"I can't even begin to tell you how good it is to see you again," he said, allowing his free hand to wander the sides of her waist. His fingers splayed wide against the small of her back, pulling her forward with the tiniest bit of pressure against her spine.

Despite her effort to recall his face, his aromatic, woodsy scent and the barely contained look of lust he was giving her, she still couldn't place him in her memories. She sighed with frustration, longingly staring at his face. "I'm sorry," Camille said, pulling away. "But I don't remember you."

Without warning, Theo's hands caged her face, and he dragged her to his lips, pressing with such intensity that she could barely breathe. Her entire body froze with delightful surprise as wave after wave of desire shot through her system like a roaring fire. His mouth moved with purpose, nipping at her bottom lip sending a sharp tingle of excitement zipping down her spine. His fingers threaded through her hair to yank her closer, sending jolts of electricity over her skin. His every move, each fervent touch, the heat of his body pressing against her—it all filled her like a drug she didn't know she'd been craving.

Theo pulled back for a second but remained close enough that their breaths mingled and danced in circles. "Mother Ma'Nada, I've missed these lips, your smell, your taste; I've missed you."

Her stomach dropped like a sinking stone into an open pit of nothing. Immense frustration boiled within her and she jerked back, breaking the spell Theo had cast with his mouth. "No, stop it. I can't do this. I don't remember you."

Theo hung there; his arms still outstretched as his face pinched with massive confusion. "What do you mean you can't? We are." He tried to pull her close again, and she automatically shied away, hitting the door behind her. Theo's expression crumpled with the understanding of sudden loss.

"You are a stranger to me, Theo. I'm not going to remember no matter what you try. A kiss won't bring her back—this girl you think I am. I don't know you, and you shouldn't be entertaining some fantasy you've had."

"'Fantasy?'" he croaked, his voice low and unsteady. "Our lives, our memories—those aren't fake Cam. They're more real than anything else in the world; you just have to try to remember."

"Well, I don't remember, okay?! Whoever it was that you knew before is no longer here. She's gone!" Camille shouted, shoving him away.

He stood there, mouth agape. "I can help you, Cam. I can show you," he said, his hand outstretched in an offering of peace and vulnerability. It didn't soothe the burn of discomfort boiling inside of her as she stared at his proffered extension of friendship. His bare hand, smudged with dirt, reminded her of the attack in the forest, of the Equestrian guards that pressed on her weakness to gain her submission. She took a small step backward, fists clenched at her side as a wave of nausea rolled over her.

"Cam," Theo said in a whisper. "I'd never hurt you. You know that."

"How could I possibly know that? I have no idea who I am, let alone your intentions. There's nothing past the last year—no memories, no family—nothing. You're nothing!" The words tumbled out of her mouth in a rush, jabbing at him like a blade of ice.

Theo wore his emotions like a crown, the swirling moods and sharp mental pivots visible to see in his physical stature. Knowing him less than a few days, she could read his emotion like an open book. His entire body tensed as her words crashed into him, the warmth of his tender offer sizzling beneath his frozen, cobalt glare. In the span of a sentence, she'd unknowingly torn away his glowing crown, the agonizing effects consuming him whole.

"You're right about one thing," he said taking a massive step away from her. "You're not the Camille I used to know. She'd know that no amount of time or distance could ever come between us."

His words slapped her across the face like acid, sharp and stinging. She had no response, nothing that could heal the injury she'd just caused. And yet she stood her ground, unmoving in her resolve. The gap between them grew into a broad valley of disenchantment as Theo turned and stomped away from her.

"Sleep well, Camille. Breakfast is two hours past dawn," he bit out over his shoulder, not bothering to look at her.

"Theo, wait—" Camille clipped, clinging to her doorframe. "I'm s-sorry..."

He either ignored her or didn't hear what she'd said. Either way, she felt the air zip out of her chest, and a familiar chill slipping into her bones. She was left to stand by herself in a dark pit of regret she had no idea how to escape from.

***

Vesyon pressed the stubborn tobacco more securely into his pipe with his finger. He enjoyed his small rituals, the mindlessness of them; they allowed him a reprieve from the chaos his life was usually comprised of. A little moment of control and silence amidst all the noise.

The calming snap and pop of breaking logs in the fireplace before him filled the room with a soothing ambiance, and Vesyon leaned into the high back wing of his chair. Phillip's office was sparsely decorated yet felt completely comfortable. A long oak table across the room held a lamp, a pen, and a pad of paper. No mess, just basic necessities—that was the way of the General. It was the reason Vesyon had grown so attached to the man in the last twenty years he'd known him; he reminded Vesyon of himself. The pain in Phillip's eyes undoubtedly mirrored what Vesyon carried in his own, and sometimes they'd catch one another in a moment of vulnerable reminiscing when verbal explanations weren't necessary. They would nod in understanding and walk the opposite direction—it was the common courtesy of men who knew what it felt like to lose someone they'd truly loved.

Tonight, however, Phillip wasn't in the mood to leave Vesyon alone. Their problems had exploded overnight with Camille's arrival. It hadn't been a part of their plan, and as usual, things had gotten a little out of control.

Once Vesyon was satisfied with the amount of tobacco wedged into his pipe, he pulled out a small match and flicked the end along the edge of his flint stone. He then dragged in a satisfying amount of smoke, hoping it might ease the turmoil broiling inside him.

"You should've left her there or had Neeko take her back," Phillip said, pacing over the shaggy blue rug he kept dead center in his office. "There was no reason to bring her here."

"I didn't have a choice." He braced himself for the sharp response he knew he'd receive from Phillip. They both knew that statement was a lie. Instead of making the smarter choice he'd made a selfish one.

Phillip shook his head vehemently in response. "No, Captain. You had a choice. You should've sent her back!"

He couldn't help but smile at Phillip's name for him; he never could call him Vesyon in front of their own Rogues. *It's demeaning; you are above them in rank, it must be noted,* he would say whenever Vesyon asked he call him by his first name. Vesyon would always ask him if the Rogues thought it strange their General would take orders from a mere Captain, but Phillip would shrug off the question as though it wasn't a matter to bother with.

"Sending her back would have made things worse, not to mention more difficult on Peter. I had to take her with me. Then there's Grenswald, whowould have notified Alpha Quarter that he found a Praetorian in Sierra Village. It doesn't matter that he didn't know *who* she was—the Equestrians would've found her there, and I wouldn't have been able to protect her. Not with what we have coming our way. Now that she's here, we will have to improvise."

The shaggy rug's tufts of blue cotton shifted beneath Phillip's feet, victim to his endless pacing. The poor blue carpet was now tattered and browning around the edges. It'd seen better days. As it were, it endured Phillip's rapid stomping with the relaxed ease only a worn carpet could manage.

"Fine," Phillip finally conceded, halting in his movement. "You brought her here, so now what? Keep her in her room to make sure no one sees her?"

"That's impossible; she's more stubborn than her mother ever was," Vesyon said, the ghost of a smile flitting across his lips at such a mention. Thinking of Jesabelle was like listening to the wild rush of the forest during a storm. At times it was quiet and enabled him to think clearly. The winds would dip through the hanging boughs of pine, willow, and birch like a mournful whisper. The ache in his chest pressing on him like a bruise, making it impossible to breathe. Other times, it would rip through the canopy in a crescendo, the cadence of fury bursting out of him in a vicious rage.

In this moment, the storm ceased. He cherished these moments as much as they caused him to recoil. In seeing Jesabelle, he always inevitably turned his thoughts toward Camille. She was every bit her mother, so much so that he could swear she was Jesabelle at times. The auburn hair, emerald eyes, alabaster skin—it was almost impossible to separate the two of them in his mind. If Vesyon were honest with himself, he'd admit to bringing Camille along not because he thought it was safer for her, it was because he needed her.

Pulling his mind away from the longing he felt for Jesabelle, and the similarities Camille embodied, Vesyon packed another round of tobacco into his pipe and repeated the drugging ritual he so desperately needed.

"You're pretty transparent when you think about her, you know," Phillip said, staring Vesyon straight in the face.

"I don't know what you're talking about."

"Lie to me all you want, Captain, just as long as you're not lying to yourself. They're practically twins."

Vesyon blinked, willing his features to remain impassive. "Yeah, sure. They do look similar, but I know Camille isn't her mother. I brought her to Romeo because I made a promise to keep her safe. That's it," he said in a tone that clearly meant the topic was no longer up for discussion.

"What'd you tell her?" Phillip asked, tracking a new path across the cement floor.

Vesyon quirked a brow in irritation at the General before lighting the blackened embers of his overstuffed pipe. "She believes the Equestrians are only coming for her."

Palpable pressure filled the room. "Wow, Captain. I believe you've outdone yourself."

"I can't very well tell her the truth! Camille and many others would think it all incredibly ill-advised."

Phillip grunted in response, his head bobbing like a cork in a barrel of water. "They wouldn't exactly be wrong. It's a terrible plan."

Vesyon's glare sharpened in exasperation. "You agreed to it."

"Aye, I did. Doesn't mean it isn't bloody idiotic."

"Look," Vesyon huffed, "it's simple. We know that LeMarc is in search of Ephidra Lily."

"Yes, you've told me. Though I don't know where you got that information."

"From Langhorn, the royal physician."

"I know who Langhorn is you dolt," Phillip said under his breath. Vesyon ignored the obvious jab and continued.

"He told me LeMarc would be moving forward with his plan when he sent out for Ephidra Lily."

"What plan?" Phillip replied, his eyes narrowing with suspicion.

Vesyon hadn't exactly shared his entire vault of information with Phillip, and he was beginning to see it hadn't been such a great idea to keep him in the dark. "We don't know yet." Vesyon kept his eyes latched on the sparking flames of the hearth, anything to keep from meeting Phillip's fiery stare. "I spent the last year sending out thinly veiled clues to other villages and soldiers that we had an underground vault filled to the brim with the plant."

"Why would you do that?" Phillip interjected. "That isn't true."

Vesyon snorted. "Of course it's not true, but LeMarc doesn't know that. And neither does the spy who told him. The goal was to make them believe we had it. I don't need to know *what* he plans on doing; I only need to know *when* he plans on doing it."

The fire crackled loudly as Phillip absorbed Vesyon's words. "What is it about this plant—this Ephidra Lily—that he wants so badly? What's he going to do with it?"

Vesyon inhaled a massive breath of smoke and blew the flavorful tobacco out between pursed lips. "All I know is that LeMarc is willing to send his entire army and a fleet of ships our direction because he believes we have some in our possession. That alone tells me the stuff is hazardous."

Even though Vesyon understood the basic concept of why LeMarc and even Langhorn coveted the precious plant, he had no idea why the High King was so desperate for it now. Ephidra Lily extract was a strong bonding agent used to create the Praetorians. It was their primary source of stability, the only thing that kept the Praetorian virus at a manageable level within their systems. Very few knew about the plant at all, and even fewer knew how the plant was effectively used in any such capacity. As far as Vesyon saw it, only Langhorn and LeMarc himself understood what Ephidra Lily was truly capable of.

"Let me see if I understand. We plan to pull the High King out of hiding by luring him here with the promise of Ephidra Lily that he no longer has stock of. Delay his plans, whatever they might be, and lead his troops and soldiers into the maze of the compound and blow them all to smithereens," Phillip recited. "Do I have that right?"

"Correct," Vesyon replied. "None of that included *her*, however."

Phillip had the gall to laugh. "Thank you, Captain, but I'd figured that out for myself."

Vesyon ignored his dry tone and continued. "This upcoming battle that I told her about is only meant to distract LeMarc's attention; I don't need her standing in the middle of it making a stance for the rebellion."

Phillip stopped his rhythmic pacing to fall into the high-backed chair across from Vesyon. "You will surely pull the High King's attention if the King Regent sees her in your possession. Not to mention the reformation of the Rogue Rebellion. They've been looking for Camille. For an entire year. Any reason to attack the Rogues, they'll attack, and they will do so in the name of protecting the kingdom from rebels. All the while planning to yank her back into the hands of the High King."

"They won't see her," Vesyon assured.

"Oh no?"

Vesyon didn't respond. Instead, he dumped out the burnt embers of his pipe into the fireplace before beginning to clean it. "I'll make sure she's out of sight."

Even as the words left his mouth, he knew they weren't entirely truthful. He had told Camille a half-truth, and now she wanted to help their cause. Phillip was right; he shouldn't have brought her to Romeo Village, not now. Taking her to White Wall to be in the security of Langhorn would have been a smarter plan of action. Currently, however, he couldn't be more at ease knowing she was only a few floors away from him.

"And the leak? You better have a plan to fix this. I never agreed to this, and I definitely don't do well lying for you when asked about it."

"It's not a problem. I created it purposefully, and so far, it's worked."

"There are over one thousand people within this compound, Captain. How are we supposed to deduce who's feeding our secrets to the other side?"

"Don't worry," Vesyon said, focusing on the flames in the fireplace. "I'll figure that one out too."

"Right. And if we figure out that issue, how are we going to evacuate those not able and willing to help us in the fight? My people not only don't have a clue of what is coming—as you requested, we kept them blissfully unaware—they also have no idea what you are asking of them when the battle is at our doorstep. This is their home, Captain. I hope you remember that and take it to heart."

Vesyon refilled his pipe with a wad of tobacco leaves, their scent sharp and inviting to the rush of nerves fluttering through his system. "They will deal with it in the same way as we did, General. They will accept it for what it is."

"And what is that exactly?"

His eyes rose, staring at the General, his arms crossing in stark defiance of what was heading their direction. "Survival," Vesyon replied, stone-faced and determined to make his point seen. "I told you years ago after we rebuilt this compound that every bit of this sanctuary was temporary. You knew then that this homestead would never last. My plans from then haven't changed."

Phillip nodded, though Vesyon was sure it wasn't from actual agreement so much as it was acquiescing to the forward motion of the plan set in place. There was no stopping its trajectory now. For several minutes, the only sound in the room was the pop and crackle of the fire as they both fell into a trance, watching the sporadic display of light and smoke swirl in an endless dance.

Finally, Vesyon felt Phillip's gaze returned to him. "You have to tell Camille, Captain. You can't keep this a secret much longer. If she's already experiencing Praecollection, it's only a matter of time before she remembers what she did. Who she is."

"It's not an easy thing to tell her," Vesyon replied. "She's a ticking time bomb. I have no idea if or when she might lose control again like she did back in Charlie Town. I need to ease her into it."

Phillip shook his head, knowing full well the weight Vesyon carried. "What does the doc say about Camille? About her condition?"

Vesyon chuckled at Phillip's choice of words. "I'm not sure Langhorn would call it a *condition*, per se. The term he used was 'blood rage.'"

"What happened still makes no sense to me, even after all this time," Phillip said, shifting in his seat.

"I've heard the story; it's not your fault. You wouldn't have been able to stop Camille even if you knew what was about to happen," Vesyon said, knowing the weight of guilt Phillip still carried.

"I'm telling you; she'd been normal that day. She came into Charlie Town when I was on patrol. The sun had barely gone down and then there she was, charging into town like an army of warriors was on her heels. She seemed half-crazed with worry, but her eyes were green—that I know for certain. I remember thinking how much she looked like her mother, red hair flying every direction and a sense of purpose blazing across her face. Jesabelle had been my best Lieutenant, you know—she wasn't afraid of anything. Camille came looking for her that night, told me it was an emergency. Apparently, her mother had sent word of a Chimera attack just inside the village. It crushed me to tell her, but I hadn't seen her mother in over two months since LeMarc requested her presence at Alpha Quarter. She knew her mother hadn't made it, that Jesabelle had gone missing and no one had heard from her. Not to mention that there'd been no Chimera attack to be spoken of. She screamed at me, told me I was an ass of a soldier, and took off toward Alpha Quarter. Tough Praetorian, that one."

"You sure she was in her right mind?" Vesyon asked, aware of the fact he'd asked Phillip the same question over a hundred times already. He knew the story, knew the details. Knew Camille had returned to Charlie Town the next day just after dusk, less than one full sun cycle after talking to Phillip. In that short amount of time, something had happened to her. There was no explanation for it, no logical reasoning behind her fierce change of attitude.

Phillip had always explained it as the coming of the end, a princess of fire blazing through the village with a thirst for death. It had only taken two hours for Camille to slaughter almost every citizen of Charlie Town, Phillip's wife included. Vesyon had been too late to extract Camille after the attack. Chimera rushed in on the heels of her destruction, laying waste to remaining dregs of the city. It was seven years after the massacre of Charlie Town that Phillip finally saw her again after Vesyon rescued her from LeMarc.

"How am I supposed to tell her she brutally murdered an entire village? How am I supposed to break it to her that the whole reason Praetorians were exiled is because of what she did?" Vesyon continued, wishing he had more tobacco to smoke.

Phillip shook his head. "You know that's not entirely true; the High King exiled Praetorians because of what he wanted. She was a pawn in his game, and we both know she never would've destroyed Charlie Town of her own free will. If I can forgive her for what she's done to my family, then she'll be able to see it that way too."

"Yes, but *he* didn't kill them. Camille did. Innocent men, women, and children. I can't tell her that. It'll break her heart. Not just your wife, but also Peter's wife and their daughter. Telling her the truth will destroy her no matter how you or Peter have been able to cope. I have no idea what really set her off the first time and Ma'Nada knows what might flip that switch a second time."

"You do know what set her off, Captain. Her mother had gone missing two months prior, and Camille had received a message that night from Jesabelle written in her own hand."

Vesyon vehemently shook his head. "Jessie didn't send that message." He paused after uttering his favorite nickname, his mouth going dry. It wasn't like him to talk about Jesabelle, or to reminisce about his long-gone beloved.

Phillip stood and went to a crystal decanter, filling a small glass with ruby red wine and offering some to Vesyon.

Though he would typically abstain, Vesyon accepted the wine and greedily gulped it down.

"She thinks the King Regent is heading here on the High King's request for her and that's it?" Phillip asked, his voice taking on a note of business. They'd known each other long enough to understand the violent effects of their past, and how it was never good to dwell there for too long.

"That's right."

Phillip's eyebrows rose toward the short brown hair he kept impeccably well-groomed at all hours of the day. "You've obviously become a better liar these days, Captain—but you need to tell her what the King Regent is actually coming here for. What he intends to collect."

"There's no need because he won't find it."

"Perhaps. But Metus doesn't know that, and neither does she."

Vesyon looked at Phillip square in the eyes, the deep tones of the General's ebony features angled with contrast in the flickering light. "Camille doesn't need to know. The less she knows, the safer we are around her. We have twelve days until the army is at our doorstep; that gives me some time to figure out a backup plan."

Phillip drained his glass before pouring himself another round. "Your plans will backfire on you one of these days. I hope you realize that."

Vesyon shrugged, but Phillip was undeterred.

"You tell her, Captain, or I will."

It would be idiotic not to acquiesce to the General, and Vesyon nodded his head in agreement as a sigh escaped his lips; he could only keep Camille in the dark for so long, no matter the consequences.

***

Camille woke in a haze of delicious warmth, blankets cocooning her body like a perfectly conformed second skin. For several disorienting moments, she couldn't figure out where she was, or what had startled her awake. Moonlight filtered in through the slivered window above her head, a subtle blinking haze of bluish light casting patterns across her green bedspread.

It was quiet, the kind of quiescence that pressed into her eardrums with unrelenting force. She usually woke to the soft rumbling snore of Lunci, a gentle press of Neeko's paws as he stretched at the end of her bed, or the tender song of early birds rising for breakfast; but now there was nothing. Silence enveloped her ears as the sleepy stupor cleared and a sharp pang of loneliness struck her chest without warning. Her mind raced with the recollection of Theo, his lips pressing against hers with such heat and wanton desire. There was no sense lying about it; she wanted more. Her stomach flipped at the thought of him being in her room again. She groaned and rolled onto her side.

According to the reflection panel just above her bed, dinner had been several hours ago based on the moon's placement through her window. The "sky" outside was bright, with wisps of clouds that obscured the moon's rays from time to time.

Camille rubbed at her eyes, and the second her lids closed she saw the image of her hand gripping a sword drenched in blood. Her breathing rose to a rapid staccato, and Camille blinked into the darkness, willing the hallucination to cease.

"Neeko?" Camille whispered to the shadows, trying to slow the galloping beat of her heart. There were a lot of places a black cat could disappear, and a room lit dully by a technologically generated moon didn't offer many clues about the animal's location.

Soft padding from the end of the bed crept up the blankets toward her, followed by a gentle purring. Neeko walked straight up to Camille and nuzzled at her fingers, before gently tugging on her hand in a request that she accompany him. She didn't even think twice; it had become a sort of ritual between them. Neeko had always pulled Camille into the woods at night, a kind of training of a different caliber. It had never been clear to Camille *what* Neeko was, but she'd always known he wasn't just a cat dead-set on killing mice—though he played the role well when necessary. He had a bright light of intelligence beaming from his yellowed gaze and she never doubted that he understood her every word.

Camille obediently peeled the heavy blankets away from her half-dressed form and fell prey to a case of the shivers. The wooden floors against her feet shot sparks of bitterness into her bare toes as she shuffled toward the side table drawers to retrieve an extra shirt, fluffy white socks, and freshly laundered pants.

She quickly glanced in the mirror above the side table and ran her fingers through her mess of tangled hair, opting to leave it loose down her back.

Neeko purred loudly from the doorway, urging Camille to follow without further delay. "All right, I'm coming," Camille murmured back, smiling as she opened the door and followed him into the main hall. Despite their one-sided conversations, Neeko always gave her a sense of ease when he was in her presence.

Walking up four flights of stairs and tiptoeing down endless amounts of hallways, Camille couldn't help but wonder where they were going. She was utterly lost yet again. If she ever needed to find her way back to her own room, she'd be hard-pressed to do it without a map. She prided herself on her expertise in tracking, but the metal, cement, and plastic compound appeared insanely upside down and backward in her tracking mind.

Neeko gave no purr or meowed response to her queries of where they were going, just continuing at a clipped pace up another flight of stairs and down a long corridor much less stark in color and appearance than the others.

The walls there were lined with heavy red panels of smooth cherry wood, and Camille's boots were soundless on the weathered cobblestone floor. There were no harsh fluorescent lights here, but soft glowing lamps emitting a gentle orange glow every twenty paces. It felt as though they had been transported into a completely different compound; the starkness was gone, and for the first time since arriving at Romeo Village, Camille felt a fondness for her surroundings.

The hallway abruptly ended at a metal spiral staircase shooting straight up through the ceiling. Neeko didn't even pause; he alighted on the first step and bounded higher, disappearing from Camille's view in moments. She approached the spiral staircase and looked up into what appeared to be the hollowed insides of a huge redwood. Camille's jaw dropped, and she was no longer worried about what she would find at the top.

She bounded up the steps two at a time, anxious to see what might be waiting for her. The last step up the winding stairs opened to a small landing stretched out from one of the topmost branches of the tree. An inlay of beams, netting, and foliage kept their perch well out of sight. Outside of a small open viewpoint along the far edge, they were well hidden from both intruders on foot and from the air.

There, Vesyon stood, silently staring into the stillness of their surroundings, leaning casually against a support beam. Dragging on a worn wooden pipe, he glanced at Camille before motioning for her to come closer.

"We're here in Romeo Village for a particular purpose, and I'm sorry I haven't yet explained to you why we must stay," Vesyon said after a long drag on his pipe.

He had a way of starting a conversation without any pretenses, which would typically catch Camille off guard. With Vesyon, it felt natural; there was never any fuss when he was trying to make a point.

He focused once more on his pipe, occupying his hands with the loose tobacco poking out the top of the opening.

"It would be nice to be in the know," Camille said, trying to keep her yawns at bay. "And I take it Neeko's loyalties lie with you? Ever since I first saw you, he's been quite attached."

Vesyon smiled at Neeko where he was standing guard at the top of the stairs. "Yes, he's a longtime companion. I requested he stay with you at Sierra Village."

"As a spy?" Camille said with a wry smile which caught Neeko's attention. He peered over at her, eyes wide with hurt, and she immediately felt terrible, offering him a hand for scratching his back against which he quickly accepted.

Vesyon didn't even pause before responding as he watched the black and brown cat cuddle against Camille's feet. "As a *protector*," he corrected. "He's a Felius Metamorphi: a shapeshifter and a gift from an old friend."

Vesyon brought his pipe to his lips and pulled in a hefty amount of smoke. Camille watched as the tendrils rushed out his aquiline nose, trailing upwards into the night sky before dissipating into nothing.

"Are there many of those that you know of?" Camille asked, her amazement of the furry friend she'd had for almost a year expanding quite drastically.

"Only one other that I am aware of, but that discussion is for another time," he said quickly, effectively stubbing out the conversation before changing directions. "Have you had any flashes of the rebellion? Memories of the Praetorian exile? Anything from before your imprisonment with LeMarc?"

Camille shook her head, afraid of what her voice might reveal. Vesyon eyed her curiously from a distance, making her feel as though he saw right through her.

"Nothing at all?"

She bit her lip, uncertain of how to express the random, incoherent visions she'd seen so far. Vesyon nodded once as though understanding her hesitancy.

"The rebellion didn't begin suddenly; it started slowly, a steady beast growing in strength over time," he said as his stare clouded over. "About seventy years ago, just before LeMarc became High King, the gates to the outer kingdoms were open. There were lines between the Kingdoms, but the trade routes were open and the understanding of peace was strong. Five Kingdoms, fives shores, and peace in our realm.

"LeMarc's father, High King Lucas, ruled with a sure and strong hand but understood the value of compromise and strong trade routes. It was he who bartered with the outer kingdoms for treaties of peace. His reign in the early years was fraught with battle, the struggle between Aspera and Dai'Cia Kingdom constant. The Dai'Cian Queen was greedy and power hungry. After the Queen was usurped by one of her own, High King Lucas drafted a treaty of peace with the new Queen of Dai'Cia. There were almost fifty years of peace between our lands." Vesyon sighed, exhaling a hefty amount of smoke in the process. "That was a very long time ago."

A ghost of a smile tugged at the edges of his lips, and Camille realized that Vesyon himself had been there during the time of High King Lucas. She didn't know much about Vesyon, let alone his history, but she recognized a look of wistful remembrance when she saw it.

"High King Lucas died one summer. It was a quick death; I was just a child. LeMarc stepped into power, and our kingdom turned a different direction. The change didn't take long, a couple years at most, and suddenly our kingdom's bliss was thrown into complete and total chaos." He focused momentarily on his pipe again, pressing more tobacco down the opening even though it was full. "LeMarc had been the High King for just over seven years when the Chimera virus broke out. Thousands of people and entire villages were wiped out in the blink of an eye. It was terrifying. There was no cure, no clue you were infected until it was too late to try to save you. Families, friends, and entire villages were burned to the ground for fear of spreading the virus across Aspera. Most gave up or gave in before it even got to them."

His eyes sparkled softly in the dim starlight and held a tenderness Camille was confident he didn't often show. "Out of the blue LeMarc offered a cure—a solution," he continued. "Asperians took to it like bees to honey. He was the High King, after all, so no one questioned him.

"His first order was to close the Asperian gates and divide the remaining people into quarantined villages to rid us of any residual viruses. This, of course, seemed like a brilliant idea to those afraid of it spreading. Most didn't realize that those already infected didn't get to take part in this—they were removed entirely, never to be seen again. What was worse, those quarantined had little chance of traveling."

It wasn't hard to see where the story was going, and Camille felt a rumbling unease settle in the pit of her stomach as Vesyon continued.

"His second order was a request for an elite army to push the boundaries of Aspera in search of more land and loyal subjects to the crown. On the surface his message was sincere, but the route was severe. Those loyal to the crown pushed north, east and south of our borders, spreading the word of the High King and preaching his devout faith in Faeder to anyone willing to listen. He gained land and some willing subjects, but his style of conquering put a sour taste in the mouths of those unwilling to conform.

"I thought the northerners were devout Daeites? Believers in Ma'Nada like Peter."

"You're correct. Not many took well to LeMarc's demands that they believe in his god. Those in Dai'Cia and Dwaa are firm believers in Ma'Nada, the old ways and the many gods of her kingdom. The Dai'Cian are proud people and active in their faith. LeMarc's pressure into their lands caused a massive rift against their peace treaties. Being the power-hungry king that he is, LeMarc was never one to ask; he demanded fealty. If one didn't fall to their knees in honor of him and his god-given righteousness, he killed them. Without a second thought and without care. In the early years, his goals were land, loyal subjects, and the spreading of his faith in the Holy King.

"Several years after the external fighting began, the Chimera virus broke out in multiple villages across Aspera once more, and we needed another solution. A *stronger* solution."

The wind picked up across Romeo, pushing a dense fog in from the eastern shore. It blanketed the snow-dusted treetops before them like a bath of milk, allowing only the tallest of trees to remain in sight. Those still viewable stood fiercely defiant, solitary soldiers in a silent sea running up the vast hillside and distant mountains bordering the Dwaa Kingdom.

Vesyon coughed gently to clear the smoke from his lungs before taking another swift puff. "It was then that LeMarc installed the Praetorian Guard," Vesyon continued. "Offering protection to the people while he distributed an antidote and continued his crusade. To many, this would be a new beginning. Praetorians were the protectors of the people," he shrugged as though trying to rid himself of an annoying overcoat. His brow hung low over his deep-set grey eyes, and he appeared almost angry.

"At least, that's what we were told," he bit out, shoving new leaves into his pipe despite the smoking embers smoldering a deep red in the depths of the pipe end.

"LeMarc created the Praetorians and *also* distributed the antidote for the virus?" Camille asked in shock.

"He had a hand in it," Vesyon replied in an offhanded way. His eyes scanned the horizon line as though searching for a better explanation, but his mouth remained firmly closed.

"That didn't seem strange?"

"A lot of things back then were strange," Vesyon said, a haunting smile gracing his lips for a mere second before sliding away. "But no one was willing to question his motives. He took control of the southern lands, the Kingdom of Dwaa conquered. Their lands and goods owned by the High King and his righteously holy rule."

"The mountain lands belong to the High King?"

Vesyon grunted, pulling deeply on his pipe and expelling the smoke in a quick exhalation. "More or less, when his rule was strong."

"And his rule isn't as strong now?" She picked up the bag of pipe tobacco and lifted it to her nose. The earthy spice slipped up her nose and filled her lungs. It struck a chord in her memory, but she couldn't place the time or the location. He was there though, in her history, in the back of her mind where she'd lost everything and everyone.

While living in Sierra Village, she hadn't minded the absence of *self*. The lost memories and blank history had become a part of her. Now, however, the lack of history felt like a disease, like there were holes in her body that she was desperate to fill.

"Those against LeMarc are pushing back."

"Why now?" Camille asked, tucking the edges of the tobacco bag closed again.

"The Kingdom isn't as strong as it once was—before LeMarc went into hiding," Vesyon said as he watched Camille drop the tobacco back on the wooden plank between them.

"Just like the glory of this kingdom, the beauty of being a Praetorian didn't last. Before long it was rubbed away. The cold hard truth remained: we weren't royal subjects or high breed socialites. We were nothing but glorified slaves to the crown, his trained assassins pressed to attend to his every command."

"You were forced to kill Asperians?"

"Asperians, Dwaans, Dai'Cian, all of them. No one was safe, and no Praetorian was pure," Vesyon said.

Camille gulped, immediately understanding what he was implying. *She'd* killed innocents too, and this realization made her insides squirm uneasily.

"We were required to kill our chosen targets, no questions asked. We were told they were infected, and infected people were to be removed from society. We sincerely thought we were doing God's work at the time," Vesyon said as his shoulders sloped downward with the heavy weight of his past.

Camille felt the urge to comfort him but wasn't sure how to achieve it. The words slipping between his lips felt like a downpour of history he'd been unwilling to share, but there was no stopping him now that the flow had begun. Every syllable appeared to crush him and yet he continued in a hurry to be done with the pain.

He laughed then, a sharp, bitter sound that pulled at his features, forming dark shadows over his eyes. "Fools is what we were."

"You didn't know any better," Camille offered, but he shook his head.

"We did know better. We were created to *protect,* not destroy. To be a Praetorian was to be the High King's property, but after years of killing, after countless unquestioned assassinations of people we didn't even know the names of, we began to question the morality of our duty to Aspera."

He stood then, the energy of his words strumming through his body like a sudden bolt of lightning surging from the center of his chest and outward to every extremity. Camille's eyes swiveled to follow his movement back and forth across the platform, his boots clapping across the planks with every step.

"I'm not sure telling you everything is such a great idea." Stopping in the middle of the cramped space, Vesyon stared down at Camille as though assessing her.

"Well I won't argue with you, but I have to admit it's getting bloody exhausting not knowing the details of my own life."

His mouth parted momentarily before pressing back together, his eyes narrowing into sharp grey slits followed by an almost imperceptible nod.

"I was at Sierra Village with Langhorn," he spoke up before retaking a seat next to her. Instead of looking Camille in the eyes, he glanced out over the stillness of the night, watching the shifting, slow swim of fog slipping between the treetops.

"Who's that?"

"White Wall's physician."

Nodding in understanding, Camille felt her brows scrunched together, wanting to place the name in her memory but came back with nothing so much as a fluttering feeling of familiarity. "Do I know him?"

"You've met," Vesyon said, his gaze slipping over to her for a mere moment before retreating.

"I received an urgent message from Phillip," Vesyon continued. "At the time he was the Count of Charlie Town. I headed there straight away. The message said the entire village was under attack and to send *additional* help. It made no sense; there hadn't been a word of a mass Chimera outbreak, so there was no reason why a Praetorian would already be there. When I finally arrived at Charlie Town I understood Phillip's meaning."

His words were heavy like molasses in her ears, pushing their way through her memories to bring everything back to the surface. Her vision swayed with blurry images of her sword slashing through the air, laying waste to screaming people, and blood—so much blood it made her sick.

"I can't explain all the details." His hand reached toward her, his fingers a bare whisper of heat along the back of her hand. It jarred her out of the sluggish pool of her past, and she blinked away the images fighting to take control.

"Yes, you can," she said without thinking. "I need to hear it."

With a small twitch of his lips, he pulled back slightly. A heavyweight of indecision slipping over his features, weighing down his already torn expression.

"I'm not sure knowing everything is best."

She nodded then, knowing that the secrets he held weren't all secrets of his own making. "Please, Vesyon," she pleaded, her voice surprisingly strong even to her own ears. "I only need to know what I did. Right now, that is enough."

She couldn't look at him anymore. Instead, her eyes slipped toward the distant mountains lining the southern border between Aspera and Dwaa. It was bitter cold on their perch, the icy chill seeping into the thin layers of her sleeping wear, and she wished she'd thought to bring a coat. Appearing to notice her chill, Vesyon slipped an arm over her shoulders pulling her in close against his side as he wrapped her in his heavy fur cloak. The gesture, though simple, made her smile despite the horror of what she knew she was about to hear.

"Charlie Town was a military base, a holding unit of weapons and our only barricade along the northern border between Aspera and the Dai'Cian Kingdom. Some of the leaders of the village, including Phillip, started to see the fissures in LeMarc's rule. Charlie Town had become a home base for the rebels, a strong fort against a tyrannical king. Once our plans to fight back were laid out, he caught wind of our treachery, and he sent in a weapon to destroy the beginnings of our rebellion."

"A weapon?" Camille echoed.

"The slaughter wasn't your fault," Vesyon said leaning into her, squeezing her shoulders. She felt the wariness in his movement, his slight hesitancy but he didn't pull away. She suddenly felt desperate to hear the truth and didn't move or pull away in fear of knocking him off his path. "LeMarc wanted to wipe out Charlie Town to send a message to the Rogues, and he needed a Praetorian to be the one to do it."

Camille lost control of her limbs as Vesyon spoke, slouching against him on the smooth surface of the wooden platform. It felt like all the air in the world had disappeared, and she was left to gasp in a gaping void. The Praecollection that assaulted her as he spoke wasn't gentle; image after image of screaming, bleeding Asperians flipped through her memory like a running marathon of gore as the words slipped into the air.

"Something happened after LeMarc set you loose on Charlie Town. Something I still don't understand and can't explain. I doubt LeMarc knew what would happen. The entirety of Charlie Town was destroyed, and when I finally found you, you were..."

Camille gasped on a sharp intake of breath, barely able to keep down her dinner as the images took over and she was lost to them. "I was *what*?" She pressed her eyes closed as tightly as they would go and still the past assaulted her. Vesyon wrapped both arms around her, rocking her back and forth as he spoke.

"You were kneeling in the town square covered in blood. You were holding the hand of a little boy; he must've died only minutes prior."

Camille clutched at her chest as an aching cry escaped her throat. She could see it as though she was transported back in time. The little boy, his face ashen against the red splotches dotting his cheeks and neck. Eyes wide in fear and horror, the last moments of his short life having slipped through the wide gash in his throat. Hot tears streamed down her face as she stared at the lifeless body trying to understand what she'd done.

"How? Why?" Camille said struggling to find her way back to

the present. "I don't understand how I could have done this?"

Vesyon cupped her face in his warm, calloused hands, a river of tears running down her cheeks. She blinked several times as Vesyon's face came into clear focus. "It's not your fault Camille," he said with stern determination. The pad of his thumb ran over her cheekbone moving back and forth in a line of heat. "It's *not* your fault," he repeated, his voice soft and tender.

His fingers found their way into her hair, brushing the flyaway back familiarly and soothingly. Her tears began to slow, and the flashes of Charlie Town lessened as she focused on the warmth of his touch against her skin, the gentle way he kneaded at the tightening knots in her neck and shoulders, and the soothing notes of his voice.

"Despite the tragedy of Charlie Town, you uncovered a truth that changed everything," Vesyon continued, kissing the crown of her head multiple times.

Her heart fluttered madly to change directions, to comprehend Vesyon's explanation, but it was slow, trudging work.

"LeMarc never wanted to destroy the Chimera virus. He was the distributor. He used Praetorians to remove those that would challenge his right to retain power. It was never his intention to protect the people and give them a future of growth and rebuilding. His desire has always been to rule not just Aspera but all five shores, all Kingdoms. He was going to use us Praetorians to make his desire a reality. The Chimera virus was a means to an end. Instill fear in your subjects, and they will follow you blindly without question."

"This tyranny can't continue," she stated simply.

Vesyon smiled slightly, a ghostlike action that dwindled away as quickly as it surfaced. Everything about the conversation ripped at Camille's conscience, and her hands gripped tight to Vesyon's as the past threatened to take over again. She focused on the image of their fingers intertwined and the strange reassurance she felt in running her thumb in a small circle over his knuckles. She wasn't alone in her struggle to push the past away; she could hear the depth of pain in his voice as he spoke. She wasn't the only one to experience something horrible that long-ago night. Vesyon was battling his own swarm of demons.

"The Chimera and Charlie Town, how do they fit in with *this* rebellion?" Camille questioned.

Vesyon took another deep breath and leaned his head against hers. It felt comfortable and secure, unlike the storm of nerves and emotion that bloomed in her stomach when Theo got too close. She didn't back away but instead embraced it.

"In following LeMarc's orders, you discovered the truth of his plan, the lies and deceit he'd spread. The rebellion began because you allowed us to see the ugly truth of his intentions. LeMarc has never been, nor will he ever be for the people. His actions are to further his agenda, nothing more."

Camille rolled this new information around, filling in the gaps of her memory with facts instead of shifting flashes. It helped her regain some control over the raw red welts of pain inflicted on her overly sensitive emotions.

"Camille—you have to understand what it is we're dealing with. LeMarc demands power, control, and he's convinced he has the divine right to rule the five shores and the five Kingdoms within them. He singlehandedly destroyed more than half of Aspera's population to gain balance over those against his rule and those willing to fight for his cause. The problem has never been his determination to grow his power, it was that he murdered hundreds of innocents to achieve it, and no one was willing to step forward and accuse him of his crimes. Fear has run this kingdom for far too long and it's time we fight to take it back."

Vesyon readjusted his shoulders, causing Camille to lift her head. Their faces were a breath apart as his stare glided from her eyes to her hair, and finally her lips. He leaned in close, so close that she could smell the rich musk of his skin, the salty cedar, smoky tobacco, and sweet pine. His forehead connected with hers in a light tap of needed contact before he pulled away, grabbing his pipe and putting significant distance between them.

He prepped the pipe end again, appearing desperate for a reason not to look at her as he spoke. "Fear is what kept Asperians blind to the truth," he went on. "They didn't want to see what was truly there, and they didn't want to fight an enemy who'd cause more pain and destruction."

He seemed flustered and agitated, but she wasn't sure if it stemmed from what he was telling her or because of the intimacy they'd just shared. For some reason, she didn't feel troubled or uncomfortable, only intrigued by the difference in how his closeness affected her compared to the riot of emotion Theo caused.

"When LeMarc realized our intentions after the fall of Charlie Town, he spread the rumor that Praetorians were dangerous. The slaughter was blamed on uncontrollable anger, a symptom of being a Praetorian: blood rage. Of course, it's ridiculous," Vesyon snorted in annoyance. "We knew LeMarc forced you to kill those innocent people. But unfortunately, Praetorians aren't immune to human emotion, and when something like grief, anger, or love is strong, it can be crippling to the point of insanity."

"Praetorians feel emotion differently?"

Again, Vesyon smirked, his glance slicing back up to her face to assess her features as though trying to figure her out. "It's not my expertise, but from what I understand it's a chemical imbalance within our Praetorian system. We don't feel it *differently*, just more intensely. The Praetorian virus we were given when chosen by the High King stripped our brains of specific regulating hormones, so we have no controlled base level of emotion. When we're sad, we're crippled with depression, when we're happy, we're ecstatic, and when we're angry, we're filled with rage. We're taught to accept and handle these emotions in our preliminary training when becoming a Praetorian, but there's always a breaking point. Somehow, LeMarc was able to find yours."

"Which was what?" Camille asked, uncertain of whether Vesyon would tell her.

His grey eyes found hers, the depths brimming with wariness before he spoke. "Your mother," he said, glancing away toward the misty treetops. "He told you your mother had been murdered by a riot in Charlie Town."

Camille's insides coiled sharply at his mention of a woman she couldn't remember, a face she couldn't place. "Everything that happened in Charlie Town was a reaction to extreme emotion?"

"Not necessarily," Vesyon said with a sharp shake of his head. "You would've been able to control basic emotional turmoil, but you were compromised. You should've never been allowed to go to Charlie Town alone in search of your mother, and LeMarc knew this. He used the absence of her against you, using the immense pain to manipulate you into wanting to obliterate that village and every Asperian living there," Vesyon said vehemently.

Camille knew he was trying to make her see that the destruction she'd caused wasn't solely her fault, but it was hard to believe.

"After LeMarc spread the word of this blood rage, what happened to the Praetorians?"

"We were exiled, deemed unworthy of protection and dangerous to all Asperians. It was a load of shiat; we'd been trained from day one to control our emotions. Most Praetorians fled to the western lands, the Kingdom of Olin, but some stayed to fight back. Chimera ran rampant in the villages, and LeMarc wasn't about to abandon his desire for continued growth throughout the kingdoms."

Camille glanced up, searching through the impenetrable façade plastered on Vesyon's face. It was evident he hadn't stayed solely to fight against the High King; he had ulterior motives. His eyes remained clouded, the truth hidden behind his many walls of protection. It was impossible not to feel intrigued by him despite the tremor of hesitancy regarding what she'd find if she dug deep enough.

His eyes cut back to her, aware that she was staring at him. "That's what started the rebellion," he said, his eyes seemingly unable to leave her face. "It's time we fight back. We've slowly been building a Rogue army to take back what's ours."

Her brows lifted quizzically. "And what is that?"

Vesyon smiled genuinely for the first time all night, his lips pulling apart with pure happiness. "Freedom for Aspera and those who want to live as we once did. Returning to the peaceful existence we had *before* LeMarc destroyed it. We're fighting for our right to live."

She couldn't help but return the smile; it was an infectious thought. "Sounds nice. Are we just going to walk out there and kill the High King?"

Vesyon laughed at this, a happy, bubbling sound. He was quite attractive when the light of humor touched the grey of his eyes Camille thought with absolute wonder. "No, no we can't do that. That's why we're building an army. We need numbers more than anything. We need strong fighters, and this compound has helped us build our strength over the years."

Camille eyed him with interest; something in his tone suggested he was about to tell her something she didn't want to hear. "I have a feeling I'm not going to like where you are going with this."

Vesyon kept going as though she hadn't said a word. "It's been made clear to us that LeMarc is sending his King Regent and an army of Equestrians our way. They will be here in twelve days. I need to make sure you *understand* the situation."

For a fraction of a second, Camille's body betrayed her with panic. She felt a swarming buzz fill her body, *the terror of the Equestrian soldiers* grabbing at her body so real in her mind that she could almost feel their rough hands against her skin.

"Camille?" Vesyon said, his eye filling with concern and dropping to his knees in front of her. "Are you ok?"

He didn't touch her, didn't move to hold her, and she at once felt the desire to be held and yet didn't want to be touched. Shaking her head to push the memories out, Camille grasped Vesyon's outstretched hand and pulled his palm flush against her cheek.

"What exactly is the situation?" Camille asked, finding her strength again in his touch.

Vesyon's other hand found purchase against her bare cheek, and he pulled her face closer to his. "LeMarc can't win this time, Camille. I won't let him take you from me. The King Regent will rip you away from me if he gets the chance."

Camille moved her chin imperceptibly, unable to pull her gaze away from the fire in Vesyon's stare. "I don't want to hide; I want to be by your side. If the King Regent is coming to collect me, he'll leave empty handed—if he can even walk after I'm done with him."

His eyes slipped away from hers toward the foggy mountain horizon as his hands fell back to his sides and he stood, putting distance between them again. "He won't hesitate to take you as a prisoner if the opportunity allows it, and I can't let him do that. You're far too valuable and important. You understand?"

Camille held her tongue for a moment, picking invisible lint off her white shirt. "You don't want me to stand and fight?"

"I want you to be safe," he replied without pause. "You aren't ready for a full-blown attack against the Equestrians. If they get a hold of you, the game's over."

Camille's eyebrows scrunched as she struggled to maintain control. She had almost failed herself in the forest when the Equestrians had attacked them. Vesyon had a right to worry. His doubt pulled at her emotions and adrenaline, but she was able to stem the flow, pushing it back down to a manageable level. He was *testing* her.

"I feel like I have something to offer. I can fight; you've seen me do it," Camille urged as her fists bunched at her sides.

Vesyon smirked, seemingly unaffected by the raw passion in her tone. "I know you can. But I'm not sure how you'll react once you see Metus."

"I'm *not* weak!"

"I never said you were. Right now, I need you to understand that there's a plan you must go along with, no questions asked," Vesyon said evenly.

Camille wanted to argue with his logic more than anything, but kept herself in check. "Why do I have the feeling I'll be sitting in my room twiddling my thumbs while the whole compound goes to battle?"

"You won't," he responded with a shrug.

"I won't?"

"No. I have full faith you'll do what I need you to do—even if it *isn't* using a sword."

"What exactly will that be?"

Vesyon went from jovial to serious in less than a second, his emotions flipping so quickly that she almost lost the balance of the conversation. "There's a leak in the compound. Someone is feeding information to LeMarc, and I need you to figure out who it is."

He *hadn't* been kidding when he'd said he was placing his full faith in her. "How am I supposed to do that?" Camille asked incredulously.

"Stealthily," Vesyon said, scooting closer to her side again.

"Thank you for being so incredibly obvious, but I need a little more help than that," she replied, extending a finger to poke him in the chest as he sat next to her.

He grabbed her hand before she could withdraw it, holding it comfortably in his own. "Right now, I think you need to return to your room. Breakfast is in three hours, and then you'll be training with Theo. We'll discuss more after dinner."

Neeko mewled from behind them, having waited patiently on the staircase during their conversation.

Camille wasn't ready to leave yet—she wasn't prepared to shut off the valve of information and comfort that Vesyon provided. "You want me to train with Theo? Why?" She gently pulled her fingers from his grasp, not wanting him to feel the flutter of excitement zipping through her system at the mention of Theo's name.

"Because I asked you to." He returned his focus to his pipe, removing any remaining tobacco before tucking it inside his worn leather pouch. It was a silent dismissal, but clear all the same.

"Okay..." Camille said, dragging out the syllables while trying not to sound uneasy. She suddenly felt torn between the two of them. Theo made her feel electric, desirable and wanted. He brought a wildfire of intensity with him—every touch, every *look* sent her body into a dizzying haze.

Vesyon made her feel calm, collected, and comfortably at ease with herself. He didn't press her to remember things; in fact, he seemed desperate to keep her from the memories he knew would be too painful. His closeness was a breath of fresh air, and she craved more of it. Vesyon shook his head as a smile brightened his face. "Camille my dear, I've missed you more than you could possibly imagine."

He stood and extended a hand to help her up, his eyes never leaving hers. She glowed instinctively as she slipped her arms around his middle, burying her face into the crook of his neck. His arms wrapped around her slim form as he pulled her close, molding her body to his. His sturdiness felt good, and his strength made her feel protected.

"I want..." Camille started, uncertain of her own intentions as she pulled away. Their eyes clashed as she peered up toward his rugged face. His cheeks and chin were sternly defined, covered by a short spray of dark facial hair. Shoulder-length raven hair framed his features most handsomely, and she felt the urge to kiss him, to explore a depth of closeness she craved.

"What do you want?" he asked, voice husky with restraint.

She continued to stare in silence, watching his pupils dilate with indecisiveness. Internally, he appeared to be at war, uncertain of whether he wanted to pull her closer or push her firmly away. He slowly tipped forward, surprising her, and came to a stop mere millimeters from her mouth. She stilled, lips parting in anticipation as she dug her fingers into the linen of his shirt. He moaned so softly she wasn't sure she'd heard the sound at all until he ripped himself away, putting several feet between them.

"No," he said, breathing heavily and leaning against the platform's railing. "I can't do that."

Camille frowned, suddenly much too vulnerable for her liking. Guilt slid like a blade of ice through her stomach, chilling and deeply unsettling. She opened her mouth to question him, maybe even to apologize, but he placed a finger to her lips and pulled her close once more.

"No, no, don't do that. Please don't apologize," Vesyon said, clutching her against his chest as though he would press the insecurities from her body. "I care a lot about you, Camille. More than you will ever know. We just can't walk down that path. You understand?"

She searched his features for a sign of discomfort or regret but saw none, and she nodded. He, too, seemed to feel a sense of comfort around her, and it put her mind at ease even though he was refusing her.

He leaned forward and kissed her cheek before putting several steps of distance between them. "I'll see you later today."

"Yes, later," she echoed, uncertain of her own emotions as her fingers gently explored the skin his lips had grazed.

Camille backed away on unsteady legs and descended the stairs after Neeko, leaving Vesyon with only the misty morning and softly swaying trees as his companions.

J. MCSPADDEN

CHAPTER ELEVEN
INTO THE STORM

Camille left her bedroom, ascending two floors before gliding between the artfully frosted glass doors of the kitchen hall. It was barely two hours past sunrise, and the circular room's entirety was packed with the roaring hum of aimless chatter. Shoving her hands into her pockets, she glanced around the expansive room, immediately recognizing Theo sitting at a table to her left. After their interaction the previous evening she wasn't sure how prepared she was to eat with him, but Vesyon *had* told her she'd be training with him later that day. There wasn't much choice; she'd have to face him eventually. Might as well be sooner rather than later.

Gathering her courage, she headed into the center of the hall to take whatever food was being offered. She selected a ceramic plate from the stack and maneuvered her way to the table laid out with oven-warmed toast, butter, a bowl of very ripe fruit, and a pile of greyish-looking eggs. It was a meager offering of sustenance, but Camille felt like royalty.

Asperians didn't even attempt to hide their obvious ogling as she shifted through the spread of tables, passing men in basic cotton shirts and pants as well as Rogues in full Romeo green uniforms. The women dressed in an array of homespun long dresses and thick petticoats, the clothing appearing worn and well-used yet hearty and ready to combat the weather topside. There was a smattering of women in Romeo uniform, the green pants and stark white shirt covered by a bulky green coat—a complete contrast to the women in feminine wear.

As Camille smiled casually at the gawking strangers, she felt a warm sense of familiarity having experienced just the same response walking in the main square after her first week in Sierra Village. It seemed Sierra Village wasn't the only wary group within Aspera. Apparently, all villages would look at her like a strange bug creeping into their status quo.

Despite the turn of the head, and the quick hush of conversation, as soon as Camille passed each table, they reverted to their morning routine of breakfast and gossip. It was very ritualistic, a rhythm the entire village appeared to enjoy. She wondered what the reasoning was behind hiding everyone underground. It was against her nature to live beneath the ground, but everyone there seemed to enjoy the safety—the knowledge that the High King and his many soldiers couldn't touch them.

Having only spent a day in the compound, it was hard to tell how many villagers lived in Romeo Village, but those present were apparently healthy. It perturbed her to think of all the struggling Asperians back in Sierra Village, ones who didn't have the benefit of a hot, free meal three times a day. Her lips thinned in distaste as she set her tray down across from Theo on the smooth pine table with an unforgiving thud.

"Hello, Camille. Surprised to see you here," Theo said, his voice an odd mix of astonishment and guilty pleasure. Despite the slight tinge of pain in his expression, she didn't notice an ounce of anger in his natural state as she'd expected. It was the first time he'd used her full name without reason to, however, and it immediately irked her.

Camille opened her mouth to respond with something biting but only then noticed a beautiful chestnut-haired woman, her smooth complexion a dark caramel gold, seated next to Theo. Her elegant hand was casually draped over his forearm like a mark of ownership. The woman's eyes were a sharp amber, bright and direct like a hawk's, her long brown hair falling in perfect waves down the middle of her back.

"Hi, there!" the woman said, grinning to reveal a line of straight white teeth.

"Uh—hey, hello," Camille responded, wondering if it was too late to grab her tray and make up a lie that she had someone else to sit with. She glanced around, but the remaining seats in the hall didn't appear to be all that welcoming. Biting her lip, she resigned herself to stay where she was.

"Oh, forgive me," Theo started, his cheeks pinking with a defused blush. As he reached for her tin mug taking a quick sip of tea. "This is Charles Ballen. The General's daughter."

"I'm sorry?" Camille squeaked. "Your name's *Charles*?"

The woman laughed like a tinkling bell. Camille's shoulders cinched in response, the sound jabbing into her like tiny needles dancing across her eardrums. Charles smiled coyly at Theo, her eyelashes batting in that perfect flirty fashion that Camille couldn't have replicated if she tried. Charles's hand plastered itself back onto Theo's forearm as she leaned into him as though sharing a private joke with him. *Was there anything not perfect about her?*

"Well, actually," Charlie said matter-of-factly, not even looking at Camille as she continued to admire the side of Theo's face. "Everyone calls me Charlie, but yes. My official name is Charles." She grinned like a lovesick puppy and poked Theo in the side, her eyes twinkling with admiration. There was no stopping the roaring flood of the girl's infatuation with Theo. "My father desperately wanted a boy, and when a girl popped out, he wasn't about to change his mind on the name he'd chosen. I would say it's always a good idea to prepare with a backup plan no matter how stubborn you are."

At this, Charlie giggled and pressed her body against Theo's side dipping her head to nuzzle into his shoulder. Theo unsuccessfully tried to disentangle himself from her grip with a plastered smile and a mumbled excuse of being hungry. Theo and Camille had put a hefty dent in their newfound friendship, but after what he'd expressed to her last night, she didn't think he was the type to run off and dump his anger into another female. She didn't know him well, but his sense of honor and pride was as easy to see as his anger. And yet here he sat, less than twenty-four hours after he'd kissed her passionately, with another woman on his arm.

Camille wasn't ignorant. He was using Charlie. Unfortunately, by the look on Charlie's face as she held a fork-full of sausage in front of his lips, there was a reason for her puppy love. Theo tossed a smirk in Camille's direction pulling the fork from Charlie's fingers, setting the sausage down on his plate. In his effort to torture Camille for her cruel words the night before, he'd pulled an innocent girl between them, a girl gushing over his every move.

Despite her own immediate dislike of Charlie, Camille felt terrible for her. Charlie's actions blared the truth of her innocence as well as her intentions. For her it was natural to flirt, touch, and tease Theo; perhaps alone they did it all the time. Charlie had no inkling of what Camille meant to Theo; even Camille had no damn clue.

If she could tell anything by the flush of pink blotting the edges of Theo's ears, she could guess his feelings on the immediate situation had turned a bit sour. What she knew for sure: she abhorred the idea of Theo being with anyone else. The thought of Theo kissing Charlie the way he'd kissed her last night had her fingers clenching into stern fists beneath the table top.

"Vee said I need to see where your skill level is," Theo said, interrupting her thoughts of lunging across the table and slapping Charlie's hand off his bicep. "Are you listening to me?"

Camille felt a crackling surge of frustration zip through her system, but she effectively smacked it away like an annoying bug. She wasn't going to let the idea of Charlie and Theo being an item bother her, not today. She patted at her unruly auburn locks self-consciously, desperately trying to soothe them down into a semblance of order as she picked at the food on her plate.

"We need to make sure you know how to handle yourself," Theo continued, his confident tone of intimacy toward her like a hot poker in the gut. She wasn't sure if it was the way he looked at her or the immense depth of his azure stare, but she felt a sizzling bubble of heat brewing in the pit of her stomach as she glared at him from beneath her lashes. *Did Charlie notice? Was she aware of the spark igniting?*

She shook her head and ducked her eyes to focus on the greyish eggs on her plate. At least Vesyon made her feel a sense of comfort, like he was there to help her through the confusion of remembering who she was, how she felt, and what she wanted. Theo's familiarity with her felt *too* close, and it unnerved her more than she wanted to admit even to herself.

"What do you think, Camille?"

Her eyes popped up to his face, her expression a blank slate hiding the tumble of emotions beneath the surface. "I'm sorry, what?"

"Did you not sleep well last night?" Theo said, waving his hand in front of her glazed eyes. This made Charlie giggle, but Camille was pretty sure the brunette would find Theo hilarious even if he were reciting the Aspera Munera twenty-four-seven.

"Um, no." Camille retorted, shoving a large pile of eggs in her mouth to keep the rising embarrassment from taking over her facial features. She didn't want to admit to the reasons why she'd gotten so little sleep that night before. After her meeting with Vesyon, Camille had tossed and turned as her mind warped images of Vesyon and Theo together in a myriad of brilliant pleasure and frustrating dead-ends. She hadn't woken that morning so much as given up on the idea of finding sleep in the first place.

Theo's lips parted in a knowing smile. He was getting under her skin, and he liked it. "I asked," he said with slow focus on each syllable, "what do you think?"

"About what?" she shot back, caring little for his cocky expression as she jammed her fork through a piece of sausage. Her mind unwillingly zeroed in on the memory of his hand slipping around her hip and cinching her body against his, and her throat seized. The memory made her choke, sending her into a spasm of coughs, spewing pieces of sausage all over her plate.

"You ok?" Charlie asked, her face pinched with slight disgust.

Camille coughed and hacked the bits of sausage still lodged in her throat but nodded in response, not trusting her vocal cords to form a single syllable without sending her back into a fit of coughs. Grabbing for Theo's glass of water, she chugged it quickly, downing the contents in four large gulps.

"I was drinking that," Theo said dryly with a frown, but Camille ignored him. "Anyway," he said, staring at Camille to gain her attention. She glanced up and nodded once, encouraging him to continue before she lowered her face to keep the blazing heat of her embarrassment to herself. "There isn't a great place to train down here at the moment, so we're going to head up top," Theo continued, moving subtly away from Charlie's thigh casually pressed against his.

"You sure that's a great idea?" Camille replied after a hefty gulp of steaming coffee she pulled from Theo's side of the table. He didn't argue but snatched the cup back the second she placed it back on the table.

"Why wouldn't it be?"

Camille shook her head, thinking of what Vesyon had told her the night before of the Equestrians coming to Romeo Village. Camille felt her cheeks flush yet again remembering the warmth of Vesyon's breath against her lips, a single breath away from making contact. Compared to the natural comfort of Vesyon, Theo's touch had been a roaring blaze burning her straight to the bone. She began to lose focus when her thoughts slipped toward how her dreams had contorted the events of her evening.

"You positive you're alright?" Theo asked, his brows knitted together over his penetrating stare. "What's wrong with you?"

"Nothing!" Camille shot back. "I'm fine."

His brows shot upward into his hairline, the softer features melting away into a hard line of assessment.

"I can guarantee you going up top isn't a problem," Charlie piped up, weaving a delicate arm around Theo's. He seemed unsurprised by her action and didn't make a motion to distance himself. "Acher Greeves assured us this morning that we could head to the north flats to train today,"

"You've already seen me fight," Camille said, glaring at Theo. She shrugged casually hoping he didn't hear the jealousy in her voice. "I'm not sure it's necessary." The last thing she wanted was to spend more time with him when Charlie was so obviously desperate for his attention.

"It's absolutely necessary. I need to see you in full combat to test your skills," Theo said with a wink in Charlie's direction, puffing out his chest in a show of bravado. Charlie sighed audibly looking like she might faint with desire.

Camille rolled her eyes and went back to her plate, both surprised and disappointed to find it empty. "I fail to see how fighting you will showcase my expertise in protecting myself. I'm supposed to go up against the best to prove I'm better, am I not?" she said, snatching a piece of bread off Theo's plate.

His mouth popped open in surprise, watching as she shoved the entire piece into her mouth, chewing with satisfaction at his dismay.

"There's no way I'm missing this," Charlie mumbled, nibbling on the edge of an apple.

Theo quirked an eyebrow at Camille, allowing a tiny smirk to flash across his features before returning his full attention to the last bit of eggs and toast on his plate.

In the span of a meal, his mood had gone from icy arrogance to sizzling excitement. His eyes rarely left Camille's face, staring at her as though everything between them was back to normal. The flip and sway of his emotions were disorienting, and despite nausea creeping in, Camille's stomach felt distended in bliss. It was the first time she'd been full in several days. A pang of guilt slid across her conscious thinking of Sierra Village and those she'd left behind. They'd never had such filling meals day after day. If they were lucky, they'd have one full meal per moon cycle. She surveyed the nearest villagers' plates in awe.

"How do you have the ability to feed everyone here?"

"You saw topside, didn't you?" Charlie answered as Theo chewed on a huge chunk of buttered bread. His cheeks bulged out on either side making him look like a squirrel hoarding nuts.

Camille nodded, doing everything she could to avoid looking at Charlie's gorgeous heart-shaped face and pearly white teeth. The girl was insanely beautiful, not much older than seventeen and very aware of how everyone in the vicinity saw her. Charlie didn't just sit at the table as Camille was, she perched almost regally, her back straight and her chin held high. Confidence oozed off her like a perfume, a scent not to be ignored.

"The High King doesn't know about the compound; he assumes what we have topside is all there is, but there's actually a large farm beneath our kitchens. Giving the Moon Tax collector our 'best goods' is quite a fun game to play." Charlie chuckled to herself, convinced she'd made the most amusing joke.

Eggs, sausage, and toast curdled in her stomach as she glared at Charlie. "'Game?'" Camille spat. "You think giving everything you have to the High King is a *game*?"

"She didn't mean it like that, Camille," Theo jumped in after finally swallowing the bread he'd been chewing.

"Oh?" Camille challenged, her eye line zipping between their faces.

Theo didn't give into Camille's sharpness. "Just because we've found a way around the High King's demands doesn't mean we're not suffering down here too. And, don't take it out on Charlie; she's endured plenty."

Camille snorted in disgust. "Oh, yeah, it's hilarious to dupe the High King and leave your compound filled to the brim with food that other starving villages would kill for. So. Very. Funny."

"Cam," Theo said, his voice tender with concern. "It's not like that."

Camille squinted at him, her anger boiling beneath the surface. Not wanting to face the truth of why she felt so much frustration when she looked at him, Camille instead zeroed in on a large breadcrumb clinging to Theo's bottom lip. She grasped her napkin and tossed it in his face.

"You should wipe your face off, not that it would really help matters," Camille snapped out, in hopes of lightening the mood and pulling it away from the sharp edge of her words.

Theo clutched the napkin she tossed at him before deftly wiping his face clean. He didn't give her the satisfaction of laughing at her off-hand joke; in fact, he ignored it completely.

"Romeo Village isn't the bad guy here Cam, it's not their fault that—" Theo started, but Camille cut him off with a penetrating glare. She knew Romeo Village wasn't to blame for the poor, decrepit quality of life the Sierra Villagers suffered through, but it felt wrong not to speak up about the injustice.

"Is this seat taken?" sounded out a familiar voice just behind Camille, cutting through the tension. She turned to see General Phillip beside their table, a food tray in his hands, his eyes locked on Charlie's display of intimacy toward Theo. Theo coughed, shifting in his seat away from Charlie before shaking her hands off his person. Camille immediately felt her body relax at the purposeful motion and made note that despite what was going on between Theo and Charlie, the General obviously disapproved.

The General resembled a medium-sized mountain bear, with close-cropped brown hair and eyes the color of liquid chocolate. Despite the thick cords of muscle in his arms and his stern expression, he exuded a kindness that Camille trusted. His skin tone was darker than Charlie's, yet still a warm caramel that made the dark depths of his eyes pop out in sharp contrast. She wondered what Charlie's mother looked like—Phillip and Charlie's complexions and appearances being so similar and yet completely different.

"By all means, General," Camille said, indicating to the spot beside her.

"Hi Daddy," Charlie said, her lip pouting slightly at Theo's divisive separation.

"General," Theo said in welcome, averting his eyes and slowly shifting further away from Charlie.

"Daughter, Theodore, Camille," Phillip said in turn, never taking his eyes from Theo's obviously purposeful blank expression. "I don't mean to intrude on your conversation, but I feel we have some topics to discuss."

Camille smiled mischievously and mouthed the name 'Theodore' to Theo in jest. He glared daggers back at her, obviously annoyed the General had used his first name in front of her. She hadn't known his name *wasn't* Theo but was glad for the nugget of knowledge. Anything that annoyed Theo she would tuck into her back pocket for future use.

"It's Theo, General, if you don't mind."

"I do mind," Phillip replied smartly as he took a seat next to Camille. Theo swallowed audibly, scooting still further away from Charlie.

The General faced Camille then, seemingly satisfied with Theo's reaction and immediate response. "I see you've met my daughter and Second Lieutenant of Romeo Village; that's good. I apologize for being so short with you yesterday, but we were under orders to retrieve you as quickly as possible."

Phillip glanced around the hall, appearing to assess his surroundings. It was a bizarre thing to do within the comfort of his own home; if this beast of a man and leader of the compound was uneasy, that wasn't a good sign. "Obviously we all know what's headed our way because of a rat in the compound."

"Do the Asperians here know about the leak?" Camille asked her whispered tone poignant and direct. "Are they getting prepared for the Equestrian attack?"

Phillip shook his head. "No—they'll only be notified when absolutely necessary."

"They don't know?" Camille asked, her mouth hanging open in shock. The General didn't seem the type to omit truths from anyone. "That seems a bit unorthodox. Why the secrecy?"

"That information is classified," Phillip replied, his voice sharp and filled with authority. "It's for their protection *and* yours."

Camille was sure this was Vesyon's doing—and it meant there was more to the story than what he'd told her.

"I would never pretend to understand the ways of a Praetorian, and I'd hope you could do the same in regard to my responsibilities." Phillip kept his eyes on Camille's, and a sense of uneasiness bloomed in his irises. "I can see why Vesyon believes you to be different, but to the villagers here you're just another Rogue soldier who will leave when the time comes. I prefer that their perception of you remains that way. I'm a friend of Vesyon's, and therefore a friend of all Praetorians—but please understand that we, for the moment, must continue to believe Aspera is no place for a Praetorian anymore."

She *did* understand then, with crystal clarity. Vesyon was a captain, Theo, a soldier. Even in the safety of Romeo Village, they weren't Praetorians, at least not openly. She'd need to play along as well.

"I'm surprised you were able to stay in one place for so long without being noticed for what you are," Phillip said, his eyes squinted to see past the illusion of her Asperian front. He appeared satisfied with her straight spine and soldier's clothing—having only clean Romeo garb to wear—but his eyes narrowed as he assessed her face and hair. He not only seemed perturbed by the glowing radiance of her auburn locks, but appeared to detest its existence, full and flowing in wild waves down her back. "Your secrets will not be your own for long, here or anywhere else, I'm afraid. You, my dear, have quite the target on your back with the Equestrian army on their way, and unless you're willing to face your demons, you'll always be running from them."

"You think I should leave?" Camille snapped much more harshly than she'd intended.

Phillip's expression didn't change, though his eyes softened slightly. "No, no. Leaving is not the option; I meant only to find a way to blend in with your fellow Asperians. Peter is a known rebel against the crown, but also considered a heathen for his beliefs. Despite what some say, I, too, believe in the old ways, but prefer this knowledge to remain private. Following in the practice of the holy King Faeder isn't just a *belief* within Aspera, but a law—one that must be followed to the letter."

Nodding in understanding, Camille bit her lower lip, keeping her tongue from spilling the words sliding around her mouth. Peter wasn't the only one she knew that followed the teaching of Ma'Nada. For the first time, Camille saw how dangerous it was to admit one's belief if it challenged the Munera. Phillip didn't just appear serious in stature, his expression said it all. There was fear wrapped around his beliefs having spent a lifetime in the spotlight of his peers.

"I say this as a warning—be careful who you trust," Phillip continued. "Once word gets out of *who* you are, and who you are connected to, there aren't many who'll be your friend."

"Thank you for your concern, General," Camille responded tightly.

Phillip bobbed his head up and down. "I hope Vesyon knows what he was doing bringing you here." After finishing his last bit of eggs and downing the dregs of his tea, the General stood with his tray and left, walking toward the kitchens as though he'd never joined them to begin with.

"Don't mind his brusque nature, Camille," Charlie said, buttering a piece of toast and taking a hefty bite before placing it on Theo's plate. "He worries the most out of all of us, but it's only because he cares so much. Sometimes he gets a little carried away with his sense of responsibilities."

"He isn't wrong to worry. It's my fault the High King is sending his troops here in the first place," Camille said quietly, scanning the Asperians seated nearby. *All these innocent men, women, and children could be in danger because of her.* The weight of this understanding pressed down on her, making it hard to breathe.

"Cam, don't think like that. Vesyon's no amateur; if he brought you here, it's for a good reason," Theo said with finality. "Let's head up top. Vee wants to make sure you can handle yourself, and we need to take advantage of the daylight while we can."

"Mind if I tag along?" Charlie asked politely, lifting her wide golden eyes in Theo's direction.

Theo quirked an eyebrow in Camille's direction, the jagged scar running down the side of his face twitching pink against his otherwise unmarred skin. The blatant pass of Charlie's question into Camille's court made her want to slap him across the face. He could tell Charlie no and make it easy on Camille, but he didn't. His polite smile and casual shrug was a sign of his desire to make Camille squirm. "Not a bad idea," he said, adding a heaping dose of casual sweetness to his words. "I'd love for you to join—if it's alright with Camille."

Camille sighed; she couldn't very well say no to the bubbliest girl in all Aspera and not appear like a jealous brat. "I guess," Camille conceded as she grabbed her tray and headed toward the dish receptacle at the end of the hall. "It's not like I care either way."

Unfortunately, she did care. Camille held her tongue all the way down the hall, up two flights of stairs, and through several doorways to the weapons room with Theo and Charlie leading the way. Watching them walk practically hand in hand in front of her, she realized how much it bothered her. *What was Theo's game plan here?* It was painfully apparent, as she watched them, that Charlie was the main instigator to their flirtation. She couldn't keep her hands away from Theo, no matter how many times he smiled and shrugged her off. Always with a smirk or joke, but he didn't tell her to stop.

Together they pushed through the iron door of the weapons room, Theo jumping through first before Charlie giggled and ambled after him.

"Ugh," Camille sighed as she pressed a hand to the door and followed the couple into the room. Her breath caught in her throat when she took in the surroundings of the weapon's hold. There were swords, knives, daggers, bows and arrows, spears, shields, guns, bombs, chains, and ropes covering every inch of the walls and floor space. Several long tables displayed the weapons for easier access, but even more guns and blades stood at attention against the walls, as though waiting for an invasion. She mutely picked up several different weapons at random, uncertain of what she could use. Everything at her fingertips and yet she couldn't decide.

The brilliant smile that lit her features immediately crumbled as Charlie picked at a few items, brushing her fingers against Theo's whenever possible. They bumped against each other as Charlie hovered in his space, seemingly desperate to touch him at any cost. There was a sense of normalcy to their interaction, and it was as if Camille's presence made it uncomfortable, which dug under her skin like a sharpened knife.

Zipping over to a table laden with swords and daggers, Camille grasped several choice weapons and loaded up her belt before locating the travel packs for outdoor use. "Can we go?" Camille barked roughly when she was done, tapping her toe with impatience.

"That anxious to fight with me, hmm?" Theo teased, sauntering across the expansive room toward her as he perused the array of weapons at his fingertips.

A loud and very unladylike snort escaped Camille's throat.

"Let's just get this over with. I'd rather be with Vesyon, anyways." The second the words escaped her lips, she regretted it. Camille felt the blazing heat of embarrassment bloom through her cheeks and spread across her skin like a flesh-eating disease, hungry to envelop the entirety of her.

Theo's head whipped toward her so fast she thought his head might snap off. "Is that so?" he said, eyes narrowing with suspicion. "Why?"

Her mouth popped open, her lips unwilling to say the words burning against the lining of her tongue. She wasn't sure what made her say those words, but she knew being with Vesyon was easier. The erratic jump of her heart and spike of nerve endings along the sensitive membranes of her skin didn't seem so acutely aware of Vesyon as opposed to Theo. Theo's presence came with a hefty dose of molten flame, burning through her veins at a mere glance in her direction.

"I'm dying to know, Cam. *Tell me* why you'd rather be with him than me," Theo growled, prowling closer. She instinctively backed away from him, and he paused his stalking motion, the ocean depths of his eyes searching for truth in the blank, passive expanse of her cemented features.

"Because he's hot," Charlie said plainly from across the room. "Honestly, look at the guy, all dark and mysterious. You'd be blind not to notice."

Theo snorted, his eyes rolling skyward at the comment, but Camille noticed a hardened line grace his lips. He didn't like the idea of Camille being attracted to Vesyon, and the realization made her lips split into a wide smile.

"You misunderstand me," Camille whispered under her breath for only Theo to hear, eager to change the current dynamic in the room. "I only meant that if I had to choose between training with you or him, it'd be him."

Theo's expression went dark, teeth bared in a malicious grin. "What if Charlie wasn't here? Would you still want to be with him *then?*"

"I don't understand you, Theo," Camille snapped back. "Last night you stomped away from me in a huff and today you're using Charlie to get under my skin—no, don't deny it." Theo's mouth popped open as though to reply, but Camille's quick words efficiently cut him off. "What's your game here?"

"There's no game, Cam," he said taking a step closer. His glance flicked over to Charlie, but the gentle softness sliding over his features was angled at Camille. "I'm sorry I got angry with you last night. I didn't intend to. It's just..." he paused. When the azure blue of his stare peeked up at her from beneath the sweep of his sooty lashes, Camille saw a tenderness she hadn't been expecting. "Camille, I waited for you, for eight years. Every day I waited. When I heard you were alive and in Sierra Village, I *had* to see you. It was a shock at first, but not so much a shock as when I realized you didn't remember me. I was determined to fix that. I thought maybe I could bring your memories back."

The words were tender, his eyes gentle, but his actions throughout the morning didn't match up. "So, after one night, you turn to someone else?"

Tucking his chin and slouching inward on himself, it appeared as though she'd stabbed him in the gut, her words cutting into him viciously. "That wasn't my intention. At least not entirely," he conceded. "Though it was worth it to see you get a little jealous."

"I'm not jealous!" Camille harshly whispered as Charlie bounced across the room toward them.

Theo's eyebrows shot skyward. "Oh? Could have fooled me."

"She's going to hear you, you know," Camille snorted in response, taking several purposeful steps away from him.

"Her hearing is no match to ours. She can't hear us, and you didn't answer my question," Theo said with a casual air directly into her ear. Charlie was across from them picking up a few daggers and rolling the handles in her hand to assess their weight. Camille's voice caught in her throat as Theo pressed slightly into her, the heat of his body searing into her back as though urging her to speak the words he so desperately craved.

Her stomach flipped unwillingly as she struggled to reign in control of her heart banging like a drum against the lining of her ribcage. Images of the previous night swirled through her mind, and she found herself imagining him grabbing her and kissing her like he'd done in the hall by her room, fingers threading through her hair and lips sealed to hers.

Clamping her eyes shut and pressing the images of Theo out of her mind, Camille scooted past him and moved toward the opposite side of the table.

"I think we have better things to do right now than discuss my personal preferences," Camille replied flatly when she was a good distance away. She plucked a menacing looking silver dagger from the wall and slipped it through the front holster of her belt, adding it to her repertoire. "What do you care anyway? You got what you want, no?" Camille's chin angled in Charlie's direction, busy fluffing her hair in the reflection of a perfectly shined glass case.

"Cheeky," Theo said, lips twitching with humor, and she would have believed the good-natured motion if not for the dark swirl of black shifting through the icy blue. With pinched lips and squared off shoulders he was inches from her face in less than two strides.

"You know what I want, and it has nothing to do with anyone else but *you*." He said it inches from her face, his breath fanning against her cheeks with the heat of his words.

"Theo, I—" Camille started, her tongue locking uncomfortably to the roof of her mouth. What did she want to say, *she was sorry?* She wasn't, not really. There *was* something between them, undeniably, but her gut feeling wasn't enough. It wasn't fair to assume she would start where they'd left off, especially having no clue where that'd be for him. Forcing her feelings to catch up to his felt not just wrong but unnatural. She didn't want someone else telling her how to think or feel.

"Are we going to do this or not?" Charlie asked, coming up behind Theo, her smile dazzling with white brilliance as she held up two nasty looking daggers in either hand.

Theo stared at Camille with deliberate eyes that made her heart skip a painful beat before he turned on his heel and marched out of the room. "Let's go!"

Camille had no choice but to follow, telling her heart to slow down and get a grip. She hadn't felt the heat of his fury sizzle over her skin as she had the night before, but Camille couldn't be sure if he'd forgiven her for everything she'd said. The fire blazing across his features when their eyes clashed was proof enough; there was an avalanche of emotion beneath the surface waiting to crush her.

After two flights of stairs and one prolonged hand-crank elevator ride, the three of them were out in the open of the desolate village square. This time, Camille felt prepared: she wore her thick fur-lined vest to ward off the fall chill, a long-sleeve linen shirt, a heavy fur wrap that clasped at the neck with an elegant green and silver beetle pin, and thick green pants tucked into her favorite brown leather boots. With a sword at her side, a bow with metal-tipped arrows, and a hefty dagger sheathed against her hip, she felt more than prepared for battle.

Theo led them west out of Romeo Village, before turning further north toward the outer edge of the town's barriers. Snow crunched loudly under their boots, each step like a gunshot piercing the bitter silence.

Camille's breath snaked out of her mouth in jolts, blasting her cheeks with momentary heat before dispersing into the canopy of bare branches above their heads. The distance they were putting between themselves and the compound made her more than a little jumpy; it felt too far from the warm embrace of security. She kept glancing over her shoulder to gauge the amount of time it would take to sprint back, but soon realized she couldn't even see the tall towers of the outer village square through the thickness of the surrounding forest.

It was strange to be enclosed by a landscape so familiar yet so foreign to her. Sierra Village had been warmer and filled with maples, oak, willow, and aspen trees. In Romeo Village, the air tasted crisp with notes of pine, burr oak, green ash, and hackberry, their branches weighed down with fresh snow or bare-limbed and draped in delicate ice. She felt caged inside a dome of endless white.

"Are you sure it's a good idea to be out this far?" Camille asked as a gust of chilly air whipped her ears. She yanked back the heavy weight of her hair into a thick knot of loose curls on top of her head, not wanting the long strands to get in the way of her practice.

"Yeah, it's fine. Acher told me this was the best place to spar and remain within view of the village. We'll be fine," Charlie assured her, walking several feet in front of her. The woman's long hair curled invitingly down the length of her back, swishing from side to side, the light brown highlights shimmering like honey against darker brown curls. It came to rest just where her waist dipped inward before her display of full hips. Camille tried not to feel the stab of jealousy in her gut but found it hard to press the emotion away. Charlie was so perfect in every way. It made Camille second guess herself, looking at her stature and physicality and seeing the vastness of her inadequacies. It gnawed at her, raking its sharp teeth against the tender lining of her confidence.

They walked fifteen more minutes before Theo abruptly halted several feet in front of Camille and Charlie. "I think it'll work just fine," he said, gesturing to the slightly open area nestled between a wall of trees and a steep, rocky hillside.

Charlie moved to the edge of the clearing and found a comfortable place to perch. Even in the frigid weather, her skin glowed golden, highlighting the yellow depths of her eyes and hair in the prettiest, most aggravating way.

Does she have to be perfect all the time? Camille thought, rubbing absently at the run of snot slipping from her red-tipped, icy nose.

Turning in circles away from the prim perfection of Charlie, Camille assessed their surroundings with a sharp hunter's eye. "We're pretty far from the village. You sure Vesyon's okay with this?" Camille asked, glancing back toward the foggy trail they'd taken. She shivered with a prickling sense of warning, but Theo didn't seem to share her feelings of apprehension.

"We'll be fine," he said with a confident shrug.

It took everything Camille had not to punch the smugness right off his face, but instead of giving in to her immediate and more violent tendencies, she merely rolled her eyes and swore under her breath. "Fine then," she said, removing the day pack from her shoulders and tossing it on the ground.

"I can take that for you," Charlie offered, taking a step toward Camille from her perched position.

"I've got it—"

"She's got it—"

Both Praetorians stopped to glare at one another, Theo's stoic stance sparking with intrigue as Camille's facial muscles twitched with ire.

"Fine—just thought I'd offer a hand," Charlie said with a slight tinge of exasperation. That made Camille smile; apparently, they were both feeling slightly perturbed with the events of the morning.

Everything slowed to a slug's pace as her bow slipped from her grasp, warning bells pinging through every cell of her body. Before she could process her Praetorian reaction, Camille grasped the dagger looped on her belt and her sword attached at the hip, ready before the bow even hit the ground. Her entire body tensed for action, eyes homing in on the target: Theo, who was charging at her with black eyes sparkling with vicious intent.

He was all muscle and force where Camille was grace and sophistication. Her shuffling side steps and casual leaps barely made a sound, each step dominated with pristine precision. Theo swept a leg out to take Camille down, but she rolled into a backward flip as though planned. The longer they fought, the more their tango became a graceful dance of war: a dirty, sweat-riddled battle of the best.

"Looks like you remember all right," Theo barked, finding his footing in the cold ground as he deflected Camille's forward slash.

"Such a tone of surprise," Camille shot back, raising her sword again as her legs coiled in preparation.

Their eyes continued to darken with each missed blow, the black spreading further up their foreheads and down their cheeks. Camille no longer looked like an Asperian; she radiated fierce dominance and rage and wasn't slowing down in the least.

"You're starting to resemble a real Praetorian," Theo said, angling his chin toward her face.

"Stop trying to distract me," Camille replied, spinning away from his blade as it sliced through the air in front of her nose.

He echoed her movement, bringing his sword against Camille's to form a "T."

"No—what I meant is that you look like *you*," Theo said longingly. He removed a hand from the sword's leather grip with ease to caress Camille's neck. "Don't you feel it? You trust your senses, even if you don't remember. I'm begging you, please, open your eyes to me."

"My eyes *are* open!" Camille spat through her clenched jaw, wrenching away from Theo's grasp. She glanced at Charlie, who didn't appear to have heard their conversation even though her eyes were glued to Theo's every move. "Why can't you just let it go, let me just be *me*?"

"Because you aren't you, not the girl *I* remember! I won't just let it go, Cam, I need to see her again. That girl you were, the girl I fell in love with. How's it possible in the deepest depths of your heart that you don't remember me?" Theo continued, unaware of the effect he was having on her.

Her stomach tied itself in a series of knots, and it felt impossible to move, to take a step away from his intoxicating proximity.

"Did they take so much of your memory away that I'm no longer there?" Theo continued.

The gentleness of his tone struck a chord in her chest, blinding her with a memory she hadn't been prepared for. Deep in the recesses of her mind, she saw him: a very young boy chasing her through the whitewashed hallways of their childhood home. She felt the steadiness of his hand against her cheek as a young man, tasted the sweetness of his innocent kiss in the middle of the night. She smelled musky pine, fresh and clean, as she nuzzled against his chest in the early dawn of the morning. She heard him whisper her nickname, "Cam, my Cam," as they fell asleep in each other's arms. A routine so well-traveled, moments so well known. His hands and face were a map of memories guiding her through an entire life spent by his side.

Theo's bitterly cold fingers brushed against her cheek, and Camille slammed back to the present. "Cam, you okay?"

No, she wasn't okay. A surge of emotions crashed down on her with force, and she could do nothing but push them solidly away. She was suffocating beneath them, desperately gasping for breath. The Praecollection exploded inside her mind, cracking through the barriers to spill into every corner of her consciousness. As much as she wanted to remember her past, this wasn't the way to do it. Forcing the decades of information through a narrow crack to the forefront of her memory was like trying to shove the entire five shores into one drinking cup. It wasn't just impossible, it was agonizing.

"No, stop it!" she shouted, shoving Theo away. She gulped down cold air, begging for relief from the onslaught of memories hammering at her skull.

"We can slow down, try this again," he said, hands raised in surrender.

"I don't want to!" She charged him, desperate for a distraction, aching to flush out the memories surging through her body with physical exertion. She raised her sword and squared off for an attack.

Theo responded, swiping his blade through the frosty air and barely missing Camille's neck. She staggered back, flinging a look of disbelief at her attacker.

"I don't believe you," he said with a winking smirk. "Besides, I *always* get what I want."

A slow and steady growl rumbled from the back of her throat as she regained her faculties, pulling her focus into order. She dipped away and went into a backflip, kicking Theo under the chin with one steel-toed boot. His neck snapped back violently, and he

160

staggered a few yards back, while Camille landed gracefully on the balls of her feet.

She pursued him, jamming a knee into his chest to send him sprawling to the icy ground. Retrieving her dagger, she held it to Theo's throat, knee pegging him in place. "As do I."

Laughter bubbled from Theo's lips, and his eyes glittered with flecks of silver, azure, and cobalt as the swirl of black receded from his facial features. "That's my girl!"

Camille cracked a small smile, the blade's edge balanced against Theo's throat a moment longer than necessary. "Shut up," she retorted, retracting her sword, though not caring enough to correct his demands of ownership.

"And here I thought you'd be a little rusty!" Theo rolled into a sitting position and began wiping mud, leaves, and crusted snow from his backside. "Vee wasn't kidding when he said you've been training."

"You both look as though you've done that before," Charlie spoke up from the tree line. Camille had completely forgotten she was there.

"We used to, but it's been a while," Theo called. "Needed to see if she still had what it took."

"Looks like she's *more* than prepared to hand it to you," Charlie replied with evident appreciation.

Camille whipped around, starting with shock and surprise at the brunette's words. "Thanks, Charlie."

"Well, you bested him in under five minutes, Camille. I think that deserves some acknowledgment," Charlie said, making her way over to them with a flip of her hair and an upward turn of her chin.

Camille wasn't sure whether Charlie was *impressed* or just wanted to stick a thorn in Theo's side, pretending girl allegiance with Camille. Either way, it felt victorious.

"I look forward to reconvening," Theo hissed while Charlie remained a considerable distance back. He glanced at Camille from beneath his lashes close enough for her to feel a rush of heat spark from their proximity.

"Oh? To lose again?"

He snorted, a sharp grunting noise emerging from the depths of his throat. "Not likely. But if sparring with me lets loose memories in the process," he said with a casual shrug, "then I wouldn't say no to this outcome every time."

Ignoring him, Camille slid her blade back into her hip holster and made slow work of tucking away her dagger and righting her own clothing, slapping mud and crusted ice from her long white shirt sleeves. He took another step toward her, effectively turning his back on Charlie approaching them to keep their conversation private. "There's so much you don't know, so many things I want to tell you..." Theo trailed off, the words dying in his throat. The brilliance in his eyes flickered black as his head whipped toward the western tree line. Camille also tensed, a thick buzzing in the air like an electric current shooting through her bones.

"Shiat, this can't be possible. I was told we had more time," Theo bit out harshly in Charlie's direction as she approached them, the black spilling like a river of ink beneath the surface of his skin. "You fed us false information!"

"What are you talking about?" Charlie asked, stopping suddenly in shocked bewilderment.

With his features flooding black and his sword in hand, Theo wasn't just a Praetorian, but a formidable warrior prepared for battle. "I'm talking about the horde of Chimera charging our direction! We're out here in the middle of nowhere. You said it'd be safe!"

The wind whipped with building force against Camille's face and she smelled the familiar stench of Chimera mixed with the sharp, brisk crackle of an oncoming downpour. Overhead the sky darkened with bloated purple clouds, threatening to dump its entire contents straight onto their heads.

"No, I didn't! I told you Lieutenant Acher gave me the approval!" Charlie shot back, her fists bunched at her sides in obvious annoyance of his accusation.

Theo whirled away from her with a menacing snarl and pulled Camille closer to his side.

"We shouldn't have come here," Camille said, voice shaking with apprehension.

"Stick by me, Cam, as close as you can. If you see the King Regent though, you run and find Vesyon, do you hear me?"

She began to shake her head in disagreement, but Theo gripped her upper arm and yanked her to his chest. Before she could process the warmth of his body enveloping her, he kissed her, his lips bruising hers with the fierce demand of his pressure. Pulling back to speak into her ear, Camille reeled, her body spinning.

"Please, you must listen to me. I will *not* lose you again."

"No," Camille replied fervently. "We can outrun them."

She made to move back down the path they'd come, but Theo's hand snaked out, clamping Camille's wrist in a vice grip. "It's a little late for that, sweetheart," he said nudging his chin toward the trees just behind the rock Charlie had been perched on.

A line of Chimera edged toward them, their footsteps silenced by the snow-covered terrain. Energy raged through Camille's system, setting her body on fire with anticipation.

"Are you sure we can handle this? I'm down to run," Charlie said, drawing closer to the pair. She neither appeared afraid nor worried about the incoming attack. Despite a steady line of sweat breaking across her brow, the beads like spots of dew on a flower at dawn, she appeared formidable. For the first time, Camille saw the soldier in Charlie. She held her sword like it was a well-known friend, her grip solid yet at ease.

Theo's boots crunched on the hardened snow as he drew his sword, moving a slight pace in front of Camille and Charlie. It was meant as a protective gesture, she knew that, but she proceeded to step beside him in kind. His attention flicked to her face for a mere moment, and she could swear his lips flickered with the hint of a smile.

"Never doubt a Praetorian, Charlie. We were made for this," Theo said in a low warning growl. "But as an Asperian, you need to watch your bare skin. Don't get bitten—that's an order, soldier."

"You have no authority to give me an order," Charlie snapped back.

"Just don't get bitten Charlie, got it."

She huffed an exaggerated breath before acknowledging his request.

Camille's face warmed with blood, and she focused her Praetorian-enhanced vision to the forest. The beasts crept through the crosshatch of trees, their muscles bunched and ready to pounce. They appeared slowly through the chilly mist one and then another, a slow wave of monsters dusted in snow edging toward the trio.

Her gaze floated up toward the massive purple clouds and she cringed at their ominous appearance. It looked as though a million buckets of water hurtled toward them as the sky broke into a violent storm. The three of them were soaked in seconds.

With one last glance at Theo, Camille adjusted her stance before peering into the distance toward the pack of monsters anxious to attack. There was a slight shift in the atmosphere—like the silence in the eye of a storm crackling with energy before breaking into complete chaos—and then the Chimera charged.

.

CHAPTER TWELVE

THE GREEN-EYED MAN

"Brace yourself!" Theo bellowed over the sheets of water separating them. Nothing could have prepared her—Camille had never fought in such conditions against so many predators at once. Each step and turn were taken with as much care as she could manage, but it was difficult to focus her attention on the swift movements of the Chimera while maintaining her footing on the frozen ground.

The monsters attacked randomly and in jerky motions, which was troublesome to fight yet easy to evade. Just as Camille was beginning to gain confidence in her strength, she stumbled over a jutting rock. Camille's body crashed to the icy ground, her arms lifting her sword just in time to slay a Chimera seconds before it clamped down on her bicep.

"Ugh," Camille snorted when the dead Chimera slumped on top of her, covering her chest with blackish blood and gore. The weight of the beast pressed into her chest bone, making it difficult to breathe. She wiggled like a flopping fish out of the water, desperate to escape the insurmountable pressure.

"Camille?" Theo cried out, sounding much further away than Camille expected. Between the sudden downpour and intensity of the attack, she'd completely lost track of the others.

"I'm here!" she yelled back in a wheeze, shoving with increased urgency at the downed Chimera.

With a hefty shove, she wriggled free of the matted, bloody

165

mess. Her legs and chest were now a sickly black, her clothing soaked through. Spotting Theo in the distance, she took a step toward him but was immediately headed off by another Chimera. The beast snapped its menacing jaws at her, its lips curling upward as it growled. It didn't attack her. Instead, the creature herded her backward away from everyone else. Once she'd retreated considerably, he left her alone, keeping her stationary with a steady growl any time she tried to make a run for it.

"Cam, where are you?!" Theo barked across the distant expanse crawling with beasts.

Camille opened her mouth to yell a response, but her body froze as her Praetorian awareness crackled with sharp attention. Tiny jagged knives of apprehension zipped like lightning through her system. She whipped around to face the dense shadows of the forest, unsure of what lurked in its depths. The heavy clouds cloaked her surroundings in shadow, with the heavy blanket of rain camouflaging everything that lay beyond her line of sight.

"I'm not here to fight you, little dove," a voice said clearly, ringing out from the shadowy trees.

"Who's there?" Camille yelled back, blinking rapidly against the downpour. Icy rivulets ran down her face and neck like pricking needles, but it didn't chill her blood as much as the silky voice drifting to her ears from the shadowed forest line. "Show yourself!"

"Camille, honestly—I'm not here to fight," the voice went on, this time a little softer. A man emerged from the misty shadows, his face obscured by a cloak and hood. "I'm here to talk, that's all." His gloved hands stretch out before him in an honest invitation to converse, but Camille noted the sword at his waist and remained on guard.

"You've picked a hell of a time to want to talk. Who. Are. You?"

The man chuckled, a jingling sound that would have implied merriment if it wasn't for the grating needle-like effect it had on her eardrums. "Always with the attitude. So much spark, my little dove."

Camille's mouth filled with bile at the sickly-sweet way he said, *my little dove*. She felt as though she could practically breathe fire at this man. He radiated evil; she could smell the pungent scent of malevolence billowing from his every pore. "I am not your *anything*."

"I always said you had more personality than you knew what to do with." The man edged closer, bringing his overtly pale skin into view. His rounded yet firm jawline, the color of fresh snow, blended perfectly upwards to the shockingly white hair slicked down over his skull. A thin sloping nose angled over wide full lips, tinged slightly purple around the edges, giving him the look of a dead man walking. He squinted at her through the sleeted downpour, the minty green orbs ringed in brilliant silver. They twinkled as he looked her up and down with a sharp gleam like that of a tiger stalking its prey. "You wound me little dove. How could you ever forget this handsome face?" he said, his voice tender and seemingly genuine as though Camille had forgotten a dear friend.

"I don't know you," Camille hissed, glancing behind her to locate Theo and Charlie. She could barely make out their distant shapes, as they lunged and twisted wildly against the growing number of Chimera surrounding them.

She had a nagging desire to run in the opposite direction of the stranger standing coolly in front of her, but she held her ground. She wouldn't give in to her fear; Theo could hold his ground a little longer, and Camille was sure Charlie could too.

"I assure you we most definitely *have* met. You haven't fully recovered your memories yet, have you?" The man peered at her with a sharp intensity that went to the depths of her bones, grating against her calm reserve unrelentingly.

Camille couldn't help but return his stare through the heavy rain, desperately trying to push away the images now clawing to the front of her mind. His voice she *did* remember. A slow serpentine memory slithered from the depths of her past to the forefront of her mind, and she pressed it away with sharp distaste. "You know nothing about me!" Camille said, her tone clipped and unyielding.

"The memories we share will return in time, sweet dove," he said slowly, looking her up and down with bemusement.

"Wait..." Camille said with sudden recollection, though not from her past. "You're Metus Craven," Camille snarled. Jacob and Brian had talked about the green-eyed King Regent, the man in charge of the throne in the High King's absence. She couldn't remember a single memory, but she did know *who* he was, and her stomach coiled like a mass of slithering eels at the realization.

"Ah yes, so you do know me. Bravo—I knew you would. I do prefer King Regent though, my dear, if you don't mind," he said, pausing for dramatic effect. "I'd hope a person like myself would make an impact on your memories," Metus said with a satisfied grin. His confident tone struck an irate nerve in her body, and any weakness his surprise appearance had inflicted on her extinguished instantly. "It's been a year and some moons since I last saw you, yet so little has changed. You look *so* much like her, you know. Even after the grueling lessons, I put you through. You have her eyes."

Camille went into a Praecollection so fierce and charged with pain and agony that her knees almost buckled beneath her. A sharp ache surged from her neck to her extremities, and she felt the floating sensation of death just out of reach. She begged for it, longing for the pain to be over.

Grasping at her neckline, she searched for the source of pain but felt only her rain-slicked skin and heated blood pumping furiously beneath the surface. Another tiny fissure opened through the wall of her mind, and a surge of memories spilled forth, as fresh and vivid as though they'd happened the day before.

She glared at the man now standing just a few feet away from her. Crippling images assaulted her: gleaming metal tables laden with sharp needles, blades, and surgical tools, the entire room sterile in its whiteness, nothing out of place. The cold bite of metal resting against her neck, draining almost every ounce of life she had. She could practically smell the bitter stench of disinfectant—it had been her prison, her tomb, her own personal hell.

"It was *you*," she choked out. "You helped the High King keep me captive in Alpha Quarter!"

She barely noticed the flush of blood racing beneath her cheeks and neck, the tingling pricks of heightened energy emitting from her fingertips down to her toes. Every molecule within her sizzled with rage at a capacity she'd never felt before. It was addicting, intoxicating—and she didn't want it to end.

"Captive? Such a strong word," Metus said, his lips turned downward with a slight shake of his head as though bewildered by her reaction. "I *saved* you from imminent death. And look at us now: swords at the ready and preparing for battle," Metus crowed over the screaming wind.

"I was nothing more than an experiment to you. You stole me from my Praetorian duty; you *tortured* me!"

"I was trying to help you control your power, Camille! You misunderstand me, even now. I only want to *help* you."

"*Help me?!* You're sick—you and that vile monster you call a King!"

He shook his blond head, hair slicked back to the curves of his skull by the torrential downpour. To many, Metus would appear an attractive man, his face pleasantly round but not overly so, his brow line straight, his nose a little slope into a slight upward turn at the end. His posture was stern like he had a steel rod for a backbone, his shoulders yanked into place, emitting an air of confidence Camille wasn't sure he had the right to demand. A slight smirk lifted the corners of his lips, but she felt it was an act: he was afraid of her.

"Let's just calm down first," Metus said, voice brimming with fake sweetness. "It's good to see the rumors of your location are true, obviously, as you're standing here before me."

"You've seen me, so I suggest you leave before I add your carcass to the growing pile of dead Chimera." Camille pointed the end of her sword straight at Metus's chest to support her threat.

His eyes widened at Camille's deadly display of anger. "You think you're the only reason I'm here?"

"Camille!" rang out a deep voice, one like molten steel—*Vesyon*. She immediately felt safe, and the deathly black ink slowly receded from her limbs as quickly as it'd spread. She was safe; she was no longer alone.

"Big surprise, Vesyon Vestra to the rescue," Metus bit out sharply. His eyes, which had been pleasant and almost shockingly radiant in color, turned black and menacing in less than a second.

"*You're* a Praetorian," Camille said in a slight state of shock.

"Keen observation," Metus snapped back. "Obviously your *protector* doesn't watch over you all that well."

"He doesn't keep me imprisoned to experiment on either," Camille snorted, her anger capped at a manageable level now that Vesyon was within yelling distance. It was startling to experience the immediate calm Vesyon's presence had on her, like a balm to her scattered nerves.

Despite her reaction to Metus's closeness and her desperation to get away, she wanted to know why he'd gone to such lengths to separate from the rest of her group.

"He treats you like a sheltered dog, keeping information from you that you rightly deserve to know. I never kept anything from you, Camille," Metus said venomously. "I'm certain Vesyon knew where to find you in the seven years we shared together—so why'd it take so long to show up?"

Camille paused, unsure of what to say. She still had no idea why she'd been sent to live with Peter, nor what Vesyon had been doing in the time beforehand. The memories she'd recovered were few and far between, mere snippets, and she couldn't be sure of their authenticity.

"Do you even know what happened to your mother, or *why* your memories were removed?" He snapped, waiting for a response from her, but when nothing surfaced, he smiled at her. "Your blank expression tells me no." Metus glanced from Camille's face to the dwindling group of Chimera keeping Vesyon, Theo, and Charlie just out of reach. "Looks like our reunion is about to be cut short, but do yourself a favor, little dove, and ask questions. They're keeping information from you. Despite what they say about me or your past, it's detrimental to you to be kept in the dark. You deserve to know the truth, no matter the cost."

"Not that it's any of your concern, but Vesyon's told me everything I need to know."

Metus shook his head, grimacing with what appeared to be pity. "You sure about that?"

She narrowed her eyes. "You're a liar," she said, her voice finding more strength as she glared at his twisted smirk. "You're the *last* person I'd trust in the whole damn kingdom."

"Then you're a fool, Camille. Vesyon can't protect you—not from what's going to happen to Aspera. The High King has plans for you; I suggest you prepare for what's to come."

"I don't care about what the High King has planned, and I *sure as shiat* don't need your advice."

A soft chuckle erupted from between Metus's lips as he shook his head. "Naiveté is not so attractive on you, little dove. I highly suggest you leave this pathetic village before it's too late; there'll be a fleet of Equestrians here in two hours. They don't plan on leaving survivors."

"A fleet?" Camille asked with a growing sense of panic as a swarming image of the men that attacked her slipped into her mind. She batted it away with disgust, hoping that she would be strong enough when the time came to fight off not just two soldiers, but an entire fleet of the High King's Equestrians.

"Heed my warning: the High King isn't a tolerant man. You

have two hours to leave." His eyes quickly changed back to their crisp, vibrant green before he bowed his head and turned to walk away.

"So you can capture me as soon as I'm away from Vesyon? Not happening!" Camille shouted as Metus sauntered into the veil of darkness.

He stopped abruptly, barely visible among the bare trees. "I didn't come here to collect you, little dove. Didn't Vesyon tell you?" He chuckled again, and the humorless tone left a spread of gooseflesh across her arms and legs. "There are more pressing matters at hand. Besides, when the High King demands your presence, there'll be no avoiding it. You can't outrun his rule, though you're welcome to try." He turned without another word and slipped into the shadows, disappearing. The Chimera appeared to follow, edging away from the battlefield as though marching in line to his silent command. Camille was in too much shock to process his retreat or his words and stood frozen until the clearing roared with the sound of rain battering the ground with unrelenting force.

"Camille!" Vesyon yelled again, this time his voice just behind her right shoulder.

She spun, squinting against the sleet as it pounded against her naked cheeks. "I'm here," she uttered softly, before the adrenaline that'd been holding her up dissipated.

Camille sank to her knees on the icy ground as memories swarmed her vision: warm blood soaking through her clothes, running down her arms and splashing against her face. It knocked the raging energy entirely out of her. She couldn't shake them and was hard-pressed to even *want* to process any of it. Closing her eyes only made it worse. She saw a woman ducking down in fear as Camille's sword curved toward her collarbone. Children cried and begged Camille not to hurt their mothers, their sisters, their brothers—but they were all eventually silenced by the sharp edge of her blade.

"H-how could I," Camille gagged, clutching her head and keeling over into the mud.

It was Charlie Town; she was seeing the massacre and destruction dealt out by her own hands. The memories rammed into her, one gory second after the next pounding into her skull like a battering ram.

"Camille, look at me!" Vesyon called over the howl. "What happened?! Tell me!"

The shaking began from deep within her chest before radiating outwards through her limbs. She felt powerless to stop it, and fright choked her into silence. The intensity of her Praecollection pressed against her eyes and temples with immense force, digging its fiery fingers into her skull.

"*What's happening to me?*" Camille burst out before raking her fingers against her eyelids, praying the current vision would end:

She was running through a village, through the rain of blood and gore. Fire surrounded her on all sides, but she pushed on; she felt like a machine on overdrive. She slowed at the sight of a particularly familiar man and a young, brunette woman. Both clung to one another, the mark of family. It sickened her, their embrace and their joy of life, and her insides began to boil.

She was standing in a dark room surrounded by decrepit-looking Asperians all dressed in black. It was to hide their wounds; their blood. Nobody saw the darkness of pain inflicted on a body covered in black. She raised her blade and slaughtered them, without thought, without hesitation. There was a sharp jolt at her neck, signifying it was time to move to the next target.

"Again," the voice said without emotion.

She was in a room of cold stone, huddling in the corner farthest away from the door she'd learned to dread. Her entire body ached with the struggle of continuous pain, yet in the silence of her stone seclusion, she had a glimmer of peace: solitude.

The door opened, and she cringed, body recoiling over what they'd make her do next. "No," she mumbled between cracked and bleeding lips. "Please, I can't anymore."

"Camille," a heavy voice said in her ear, soft and determined. "It's me, Vesyon. I'm here to take you home."

Her mind had clung to his name, sifting through the endless folds of memories for recognition. He was there, somewhere. She knew his smell: dark cedar and heavy smoking tobacco. He lifted her away from the cold stone room, and the lights in her mind blinked out.

"It's okay, Camille, I'm here. Everything is all right; you're all right."

Camille heard Vesyon's voice, felt the firm grip of his arms

172

cradling her against his chest, and felt the warm fur of Neeko at her side, but her mind remained in the past.

"Make...it...stop!" Camille sobbed, clutching at Vesyon's shirt as she buried her face in the crook of his neck. "Please, make it stop!"

Vesyon pulled her shaking body close, pressing her ear to the place his heart-beat loudest. "Listen, Camille. Focus on my breath. Listen to my heart and try to emulate it. You must calm down, you must resurface."

She heard it, the steady thump of blood pulsing through his system, and focused on the regular rise and fall of his chest. Her hands pressed into him wanting to absorb the heat moving beneath the surface of his skin. With every breath, she heard the rush of movement through his lungs, the thud of his heart, and it rolled in her ear like the comfort of a sheltering cocoon.

"That's it," Vesyon whispered. "Calm down."

The images disappeared in a cloud of wispy thoughts until all she heard was the siren whistle of the wind through the trees.

"Camille," Vesyon spoke slowly, allowing her mind to wrap around his words. "I need you to tell me what happened."

What happened? She had no idea what happened. One minute she was talking to Metus, and the next she was on the ground being attacked by a torrential storm of memories she never wanted to remember. Worst of all, Metus had given her news that awakened a new sense of terror in her: they only had two hours to escape.

Her voice felt trapped in her throat, and a constricting pull against her vocal cords kept her silent longer than she meant to be. "It was him," Camille finally mumbled. "The King Regent."

"You saw Metus?" he asked quickly, lifting her into his arms with ease as he walked.

"Yes."

Vesyon led the small group of soldiers he had arrived with, alongside Theo and Charlie, back toward the compound with Neeko bringing up the rear. The rain continued as they trampled through the icy ground, their heads bent downward.

"What'd he tell you?" Vesyon asked as he stepped into the main square of Romeo Village.

Camille's head collapsed against his shoulder. "We have two hours before the Royal Fleet attacks."

CHAPTER THIRTEEN
EPHIDRA LILY

The elevator raced past the first ten underground floors of the compound, depositing the weary, blood-soaked group into a brightly lit hallway. Neeko escaped immediately, scurrying down the white tiles without making a sound, his little mud riddled paws prints the only marker of his direction.

Vesyon set Camille down on shaky knees, pulling her gently along by the elbow. Despite his thoughtful touch and outward demeanor, Camille felt a radiating heat of anger sizzle in the pit of her stomach. It wrenched at her insides, the haunting words of Metus like a buzzing fly in her inner ear. *They're keeping information from you, and despite what they say about me or your past, you deserve to know the truth, no matter the cost.*

Her skin tingled with the absence of Vesyon's grip as he walked ahead of her to meet Phillip at the end of the hallway. She recognized the door they entered as operations, and this time the room buzzed with energy. Every person except for Vesyon, Theo, and Camille flitted around the room like a horde of determined yet fretful bees, yelling loudly across the crowded space and motioning with their hands until they were red in the face.

It looked exactly the way Camille felt inside: full of chaos escalating with every passing minute. She felt as though she'd just run twenty miles in a flat-out sprint, yet at the same time, her muscles were charged with fresh energy.

Phillip barreled toward the group, his face pinched with concern as he grasped Charlie in a quick yet heartfelt embrace. "Are you all right?!"

Charlie allowed a few seconds of hugging before shaking him off. "Daddy, I'm fine. See? Nothing to worry about."

Once he'd made sure any blood on her clothes had come from an outside source, Phillip turned to Camille. "What happened? Are *you* okay?"

With a flap of his hands, he ushered them as a unit into a private room just off the main floor of headquarters, and they followed in silence. Phillip glared at her as they crowded into the small quarters, shut off from the buzz and panic of operations. Camille felt her mouth go dry at his direction attention. He didn't press Camille for a response. He appeared aware that she was still processing what had just occurred. She opened her mouth to speak, but the words sat heavily against her tongue. *Was she okay?* Her physical well-being wasn't the issue, yet it was impossible to explain what she was feeling. Camille's eyes glistened at the memory that had crashed to the forefront of her mind in the absence of Metus: a woman's face framed in a curling wave of chestnut locks, her dark skin bleached of its natural sunny glow. A river of tears tracked down the woman's cheeks, and Camille knew who she'd been—Charlie was the spitting image of her. The realization of it made Camille's stomach turn over in disgust.

Theo stepped forward to respond to the General. "Chimera. At least thirty of them."

"What were you doing so far outside of Romeo Village?" Vesyon asked sharply, his eyes swimming with hints of black as he surveyed the trio. With arms crossed, his fists buried beneath his fur cloak, Vesyon radiated fury, and she felt a prickling sense of infuriation at his attitude.

"It wasn't my idea to train her, *Captain*."

Camille blanched at Theo's tone but felt the words had been well deserved. It had been Vesyon's idea for them to train.

Vesyon didn't acknowledge Theo's jab as his eyes returned to their usual steel hue. "You were outside the main gates. Why?"

Taking an almost imperceptibly small step toward Charlie, Theo eyes never left Vesyon's face. "We were told it would be safe."

"By whom?" Vesyon challenged, his sharp stare flicking from Theo's flat, expressionless face to Charlie's downcast eyes.

"Charlie?" Theo said softly, taking another small step toward her.

She glanced up to her father, eyes pleading before they snapped to Vesyon's and finally landed on Theo. "Acher told me it'd be ok," Charlie squeaked out before shifting her line of sight to Vesyon. "He told me it would be the best place to train well outside the Asperian line of sight."

Theo snorted audibly; his icy irises bitterly sharp at the mention of Acher. "Remote and difficult to call for help, more like." His attention shifted over to Vesyon's grave expression. "How'd you know we needed back up?"

"The guard on duty rang the alarm. He'd received word of an incoming surge from our scouts along the Romeo border," Vesyon said.

"Wait a minute, back up. You said *Acher,* my First Lieutenant, told you to go outside the main gate and thus beyond our protection?" Phillip asked skeptically, glancing from Charlie to Theo.

Theo's eyes narrowed at Phillip. "Yes, he did. And if that's a surprise to you, sir, we have even bigger problems." His tone was clipped, challenging Phillip to admit what he knew.

"What are you implying, soldier?"

"A little convenient, don't you think? Acher saw us arrive with Camille, and less than two days later the King Regent is on our doorstep." Theo took several steps toward the General, his tone low and direct. "Was Acher's request that we train so far away in line with *your* orders?"

The implication was clear, and Phillip's hickory eyes widened from the impact of Theo's word before slicing into mere slits of cinnamon and fire. Camille could see his fists clenching at his sides, obviously more than perturbed with Theo's direct accusation. "I'd be careful who you accuse of treachery, soldier. I don't take slander lightly."

The room sparked with anger, wrapping a tight vice around its inhabitants, inducing a tremulous silence. Vesyon pushed his way between the quarreling men, breaking the tension with a wave of his arms. "At ease, both of you." He glanced once at Phillip before swinging around to stare at Theo. "We need to work together instead of slinging unfounded accusations back and forth. And we need to find the Lieutenant."

Theo nodded once but kept his attention on Phillip's face.

"Where is the slimy bastard?"

"I'll give you one guess," Phillip replied gravely, his expression turning sour with absolute disgust. It was the only signal Camille needed as proof of Phillip's innocence. Acher had been running on his own, and the blatant misconduct of his position was apparently a knife in the General's gut.

"The vault," Theo and Vesyon echoed.

"If he doesn't show face, we have our traitor, Captain." Phillip moved from the room without another word, heading straight for a trio of soldiers to send word for his Second Lieutenant.

Turning away from the crowded room, Camille mindlessly watched the bustle within central control. The mad dash of a Village under imminent attack swelled like a bubble of worry in her chest. She shuddered inwardly as Metus's words slithered through the inner lining of her thoughts: *you think you're the only reason I'm here?*

"The King Regent isn't here for me," Camille said bluntly, the words bursting from her lips in sharp demand of attention. Vesyon, Theo, and Charlie whirled to face her. "He was quite surprised to see me."

Theo appeared sheepish for a moment, caught in the act of deception. Charlie's face went blank, but Vesyon's didn't; his expression remained cool and collected, his stern stature unwaveringly calm.

Camille's lips quirked upward in response, a humorless action bringing no light or laughter to her fierce glare. "Thought so," she said, confirming her suspicions. "He suggested I leave within the next two hours. That doesn't sound like someone who's *actively* seeking my capture," she growled, aiming her bitterness at Vesyon, fire practically spitting from her eyes.

"No, you're correct," he replied with stoic simplicity, crossing his arms defiantly across his chest.

"The High King didn't send his Royal Air Fleet to collect me. He didn't even know I was here! He's after something else. Why didn't you tell me last night?"

"When would he have time to tell you that Camille after I took you to your room?" Theo said in quick response.

"She was with me afterwards, Theo," Vesyon replied, causing Theo's eyes to widen in confusion.

"But I took her to her room after dinner, we...we said

goodnight," he said, his voice becoming slightly sheepish in tone. They hadn't quite said goodnight, Camille thought, remembering the way they'd parted.

"What does it matter where I was and who I saw when? The point I am trying to get at is that you *lied* to me! Again!"

"You're damn right I did!" Vesyon shouted throwing his hands up in the air in obvious frustration. His cheeks blazed red as his eyes spit black Praetorian anger. Camille's body surged forward, hands balling into fists as she barreled into his personal space, readying herself for a fight. She felt the heat radiating off him, the black flushing through his stare in a stark show of warning. "I know what the High King sent his men here for because I fed the lies to his spies myself." His fingers clenched tightly at his sides as he glared at her. "He doesn't know you're here, and we'll be long gone before Metus has the chance to tell him otherwise. There is *no way* I am going to risk you getting swept up in a battle we've been planning the past seven years. The rebellion will happen, but you won't be a part of it. You weren't even supposed to be here!"

"Well, I sure as shiat didn't ask to come here! You made me, damn you!" They were inches apart from each other. Their collective anger almost burned her skin, but Camille held her stance. "Why?" she croaked, her voice low and breaking with frustration. "Why did you abandon me in the first place?"

His brows furrowed over slivered grey orbs in slight confusion. "I didn't abandon you in Sierra Village, I—"

"No," Camille snapped, cutting him off. "In Charlie Town."

He grunted tersely, a strange noise emitting from his throat conveying massive frustration. "I told you," he began again, but Camille wasn't willing to listen.

"Don't," she said, her voice curt and direct, raising her hand in command of silence. "I don't need to hear your lies. Tell me why you left me to rot in the hands of the High King and the King Regent for seven years. You knew I was there. You said yourself you were there when the King Regent took me after Charlie Town fell. You were the *only* one who knew where to find me. Yet you waited to rescue me—why?"

Theo shifted toward her, his hand outstretched as though to offer a comforting embrace. "No," she snapped at him, her tone locking his feet to the ground.

"Cam, he isn't trying to be an ass. The situation is—" Theo said, his eyes wide and pleading for her to listen to him.

She shook her head, vehemently cutting him off as she'd done to Vesyon. "No, this doesn't concern you, though I'm certain you've played your part," she said, a frowning line creasing heavily between her brow.

Theo's shoulders slumped in partial defeat as well as possible embarrassment. Vesyon wasn't alone in the game of secrets, it was more than evident by Theo's shifting stance and avoiding stare that he felt some of her words slung at Vesyon hit him square in the chest.

Her glance shifted from Vesyon to Theo and back again, the clarity of their difference so blatantly obvious she almost couldn't believe she'd never seen it before. Theo looked at her with empathy and understanding, while Vesyon stared her down with frustration and inner panic.

"Obviously, I had no choice in coming here, but I have a right to know what happened in my past. I am asking you to tell me the truth." The depth of her pleading spilled from her eyes in hopes he'd see reason, understanding her desperation to know what was happening and why. It went beyond his deceitful actions. She needed to know the truth of her surroundings and her history to keep from going insane. Every minute Praecollection controlled her, it was like an ax to the skull. It split her sanity in half, chopping her identity into pieces. "Please, Vesyon."

"I'm sorry," he said automatically with a shake of his head before putting several feet of distance between them. "I'm trying to keep you safe, and I know you won't understand, but I can't tell you all of the truth Camille. Not now."

He'd kept her in the dark purposefully, regardless of what she wanted or needed. Amazingly, she didn't hate Vesyon for his selfish, controlling actions but she did feel a rolling surge of anger building inside her chest. Despite a sliver of understanding for what he was doing, Camille didn't agree with his tactics.

Phillip's head popped through the doorway, his attention gliding over the occupants in the room to direct his message at Vesyon. "We just received word that the High King's Royal Air Fleet is descending. We have little time on our side. We have to move now with our plan, Captain."

Vesyon nodded once, pulling away from Camille and focusing his attention on Phillip.

"There's no possibility of waiting," Phillip continued, his eyes sliding over to Camille for the barest of seconds. "I'm going to sound the alarm to evacuate the villagers to White Wall. That should give us enough time to gather our troops for the invasion."

Vesyon grunted in acknowledgment before turning his attention back to Camille as Phillip exited the small quarters. "You're right; you didn't ask to be pulled into this."

"And these villagers? You're now demanding they leave their homes? What about them?"

"They may not have been prepped for a last-minute evacuation, but they knew what they signed up for remaining here after the rebellion began," he snapped back at her. "You're right; you don't have all the answers, Camille, and there's a reason for it."

"Not everything is up to you and what you think people should and shouldn't know! They have a right to understand what is happening just as much as I do! You just can't keep us all in the dark!" The burn in her chest fumed, sending fiery heat to every extremity as she closed the distance between her and Vesyon once again. He didn't shy away from her glare; he met her toe-to-toe, ready to take the flaming acid she was preparing to hurl at him.

"I made a promise, Camille," Vesyon said quickly, ripping the reigns of her anger out from underneath her, his tone soft and incredibly intimate. "I made a vow to keep you protected at all cost. You must believe me when I tell you that *everything* I have done has been to ensure your safety."

An alarm suddenly screamed through headquarters, and everyone in the room stood to attention. "That's the evacuation; we need to go," Theo said from the back of the room, his voice terse and hollow.

Vesyon extended a hand toward Camille but seemed to think twice of his actions and pulled it back to his side. He huffed once, looking almost uncertain and yet at the same time decided. "Understand me, Camille, everything I do, I do out of concern for those I care about. I didn't haphazardly pull you from Sierra Village. I decided it was the best option."

"That's my point exactly: *you* decided. I didn't have a choice!" Camille screamed with every ounce of energy she had pounding through her system.

He stared at her, his twin orbs a reflecting pool of icy grey. He didn't appear sorry nor did he seem regretful, only disappointed she didn't understand the depth of his devotion to her. "We don't get to choose the paths we're given, Camille. We can only decide on the direction our new path will take us."

It was then she saw it, the buried pain behind the protective wall he'd been hiding behind since she first met him. His expression didn't denote friendship or the compassion of a mentor; he looked at her with longing and undying devotion. The desperation spilling from every surface of his body begged for her to see the truth of it, to accept his actions as loving and not deceptive. It was apparent now that he didn't just want her to be safe; he wanted her to be with him.

"Vesyon, I—" Camille started but couldn't seem to finish the thought. Her body seized with a sense of urgency to tell him that as much as she was hurt and vexed by his deception, she also understood it. He was right. She may not have chosen to be standing where she was, but in the face of an oncoming attack she had a choice: fight or flee. She'd never abandon those in need, never leave someone to die to save herself. If she had a choice in the matter, she'd sacrifice everything to ensure the safety of even one Asperian soul.

"We need to move, the fleet is closing in," Phillip said from the doorway. "Captain, take the Rogues and head up top. We need to get our men in place before the ground attack passes the outer wall."

Without pause, Camille's focus flew to Vesyon's face, fierce determination spreading across her features. "What can I do?"

Vesyon smiled, appearing proud of her.

"When this is over, I expect answers. I won't let this one lie, you understand?" Camille said with predetermination.

His smile grew, spreading across his features like the glowing mark of sunlight at dawn. The intoxicating radiance in the depths of his expression blossomed as his bare hand touched the side of her face, tender and warm. "You don't even realize it, but you look so much like her."

Theo coughed from the corner of the room, jolting both Camille and Vesyon out of the trance they'd fallen into. Vesyon jerked his hand back to his side as though her face were an open flame. He cleared his throat and took several steps away from her before turning his attention to Theo, the screen guarding his emotions dropped securely back in place.

"Take Camille and head down to the vault through the sanctuary. Acher will believe the product is located there. You'll need to detain him. There can be no chance of him getting back to the High King with his findings. Be quick in getting out, you won't have much time."

"How long?" Theo asked, clearly understanding more about what was to come than Camille.

"The plan will commence in two hours. It's all we can spare of our troops and weapons. Listen for the warning horn—once you hear its call, you'll have fifteen minutes to get out of the Romeo Village grounds."

Theo nodded once in understanding, his face a stone wall, eyes darkened with a flush of inky black.

Vesyon didn't look Camille in the eye as he headed toward the door. "Charlie? You coming?"

Charlie peered over at Vesyon, her face piqued with alarm, having not moved an inch from her silent perch. "Y-yes, just one sec..." She looked shaken and distraught turning toward Theo, chin trembling, and Camille turned away as Charlie wrapped her blood-soaked arms around Theo in a tight embrace. "Stay safe Theo, please."

Theo didn't verbally respond, but Camille heard the rustle of clothing as Theo's arms wrapped around Charlie's small form and hugged her back. A soft sound of lips brushing against skin pricked the inner lining of Camille's tender eardrums, and then Charlie strode from the small quarters, her head held high, a poster of authority and calm control.

Grabbing Camille's hand in a vice grip, Theo pulled her out of the room past Vesyon toward the main hall outside of headquarters. "Take Neeko with you," Vesyon instructed from behind their retreating forms. Theo nodded once, keeping his eyes forward as they moved, Neeko trailing behind sleek as a shadow.

"Theo," Vesyon called out just before they turned the corner. Theo stopped and turned, his shoulders tight, his brow creased in apparent tension. "Once you get through the vault exit, I'll meet you at the foothills east of the village, if it's not too late. If you get to the horses before I do, take Camille to White Wall."

"I will, Vee. I won't leave her side," Theo assured him.

Camille's gaze lingered on Vesyon's haunted expression, making a silent promise that it wouldn't be the last time she saw him.

Her knuckles were crushed in Theo's tight grip as they moved down the hall. She didn't mind the sharp pinch of his steel grasp as he rushed past the others in the compound; it allowed her to focus on something other than the chaos around them. Asperians pressed against them on all sides as the piercing alarm to evacuate wailed above them like a dying bird.

"Shouldn't we be helping them?" Camille asked.

"No, we don't have time."

"Well," Camille said in a flustered state. "We don't seem to be going the right way."

Theo didn't glance back as he ducked between two oncoming Rogues and headed down another long hallway. "We are. They're leaving, and we are going to the vault as Vesyon instructed," Theo replied, his voice dry and unemotional. She frowned at his profile, uncertain of his brusque attitude and if it was directed at her.

"Theo, wait." He didn't even turn to glance at her, his boots pounding out a cadence of rushed fervor against the tiled floor.

"Damn it, Theo, *stop*!" she finally said, yanking her hand out of his grasp. "I need to know what is going on! Please," she pleaded. "Vesyon might not trust me enough to tell me what's about to happen, but I need to know what I'm walking into. The King Regent showed up with more soldiers than we were prepared for, so I understand the confusion, but why in the name of Ma'Nada," she said in a rush, but Theo pulled her to the side of the flow of bodies before she could finish her sentence.

"Don't you get it, Camille? You and the villagers being here *wasn't* part of the plan. Vesyon screwed up, and Phillip ordered an emergency evacuation to get them out of here before...well, to get them to safety."

Camille scrutinized his expression, not wanting to believe what she was hearing. "Are you going to tell me what's actually going on then, or are you just going to jerk me around like a child? Like Vesyon does?"

"I'm not Vesyon," he growled.

"Oh? Could have fooled me."

"We don't have time for this," Theo snapped, his arms cinched against his chest in a wall of impenetrable frustration.

"I don't really care," Camille shot back at him standing her ground. "What isn't Vesyon telling me?"

Theo's lips pressed together, firm and unyielding as he glared at a spot just over her head.

"Not you too," Camille went on, her voice so incredibly soft that his eyes immediately snapped to hers in automatic apology. "Please don't keep me in the dark. You're right. You aren't Vesyon; you know you can trust me."

He didn't look away, but his mouth remained closed. It was Camille's undoing. Her chin dropped, a heavy sigh of exhaustion spilling out from between her lips. Looking down at her blood-slicked arms, covered in dirt and Chimera guts, Camille impulsively moved with the crowd of Asperians away from Theo. She didn't care if the evacuation was in order, didn't care how much or how little time they had to find Acher. She needed to get to her own room, needed silence, needed a moment to herself, needed a place to figure out what she was going to do.

Her feet carried her at a quick pace with the bustling flow of bodies toward the hall leading to her bedroom. Moving of its own accord, without her mind demanding the movement, her body felt unable to stop.

"Camille!" Theo barked, trying to keep up with her, pressing through the mash of bodies moving in behind her. "Come back!"

She shook her head, uncaring if he saw it or not, and continued to move. Her skin felt on fire with the desire to be clean. The weight of the past few days pressed into her flesh unyielding, crushing, and unstoppable; it was too much. And she was sick of it.

She ripped off her coat, vest, and shirt as she moved, uncaring that everyone in the hall could see her exposed upper body stark and naked through the thin undergarments she wore.

She careened into her door, slamming the metal with her bare fist, forcing the weight to swing on its hinges before it smashed against the inner wall with a dull *thunk*. She clawed at the blood-soaked undershirt, wrestling it away from her skin before tossing it onto the floor in a heap of blood and sweat with the rest of her discarded clothing. Her fingers shook with a burst of adrenaline as she yanked off her blood soaked pants, socks, and underwear. She felt tears stream down her cheeks unchecked and fiercely aggressive, though she couldn't be sure why she didn't try to stop them.

A sharp pang of desolation gripped her, stealing her breath and choking all warmth from her body. Homesickness, and the crash of adrenaline from seeing Metus blasted through her, causing her to double over, panting with the effort to breathe. Her blood felt thick, slugging through her system at a snail's pace.

How had this happened? One minute she was playing hide and seek in Sierra Village with the only friend she had ever known, and now she was preparing for battle as a Praetorian warrior? It was too much: the visions, the memories attacking her in all moments of weakness, the lies and deception, and to top it all off, the emotional tornado of both Theo and Vesyon.

She headed straight for the shower, her limbs slick with blood and dirt, her entire body weighed down with uncertainty. Vesyon's stern expression filtered in front of her eyes. It aggravated her to no end. He wasn't just keeping secrets from her, he'd been lying to her. If Metus had given her anything it was a seed of doubt. How was she supposed to trust Vesyon with her life if he couldn't even trust her with her own past?

Pressing her palms into the cavity of her eye sockets, she ground any image lingering in the black depths of her eyelids away. Seeing the swirl and mix of random color was preferable to everything she'd seen that day. Her head bent as she ducked into the shower, the spray of water a blissful balm. She moaned a sigh of relief as the heated pellets of water struck her tender flesh. Every fiber of her being hummed and yet her body began to tremble in the aftermath.

Methodically, she scrubbed at the blood and dirt until her skin was bright pink and raw, her fingers moving in quick motions to keep the shaking at bay. The kaleidoscope of gore from the past couple days melted off her body before slipping down the drain at her feet. She had no clue what to do, no desire to run or flee, and no understanding of what she was about to walk into. There was no clear sense of her emotional status concerning Vesyon or Theo, and to top it off, she had no damn soap.

Camille sighed, comforted in the small luxury of being alone as tears slipped down her reddened cheeks in a river of heat. Despite the chaotic wail of voices zooming past her door, the ever-approaching army just beyond the village gates, and the looming knowledge that she should be rushing to flee the compound, she didn't move. Or rather, Camille couldn't move. There was no purpose to her stationary reaction, but she couldn't, for the life of her, find the energy to leave the fiery hot spray of water. Instead of forcing herself back into the rush of the compound, she gave into the emotions bubbling up inside her, allowing the salty streams of water to flow freely down her cheeks.

***

Theo skidded to a halt at the end of the hall leading to Camille's room. The tiled floor was a mess of strewn items left behind by those rushing to evacuate, but Camille was nowhere to be seen in the mix of bodies racing out of their quarters. She had to be in her room, but he was uncertain he would be welcome.

The scorching expression of longing Vesyon had given her hadn't gone under Theo's radar; something had happened between the two of them. He couldn't be sure of what or when that exchange had occurred, but the current of suppressed emotion had surged between them with Theo being nothing but a bystander. He would never admit it aloud, but Camille's heated anger toward Vesyon made him feel slightly better about his own standing with her.

The previous night hadn't precisely ended in the way he had hoped. He'd curtly dismissed her, not wanting to open the door to the emotions he'd shoved away so long ago. He'd had no right to push her though, to force their past on her assuming they'd jump back to where they'd left off. It had been *eight* years since he last saw her, but it didn't matter, not to him. It made no difference. She couldn't remember him or what they'd once been.

His mind flashed with the memories of their last night together in Whiskey Wharf before the massacre of Charlie Town. She had been in his arms, her wild copper hair draped over his forearm like fire upon his skin. He watched the crackle and burn of the tendrils glowing with a life of their own in the firelight of her room. It hadn't been the first night they'd found themselves in each other's arms into the early hours of the morning, but it had been the first time he'd ever voiced aloud his full desire for her.

"Cam, I love you," he'd said. It was so simple, almost effortless, the words forming on his lips most naturally.

She had smiled—the wide-open smile that made his heart ache with the need to press his lips to hers. "I know you do," she responded before burying her head back into the crook of his neck.

It was dangerous, what they were doing, not just physically but also emotionally. Camille and Theo had never made love but had come close, always stepping right up to the forbidden line between being Asperian and being an honorable Praetorian. It was against Praetorian law to give one's body over to another unless by order of the High King. The idea of procreation wasn't the problem; Praetorians were created sterile. It was the devotion, adoration, and physical desire for anything or anyone outside of the High King himself. Praetorians were designed to love, protect, and serve the kingdom. To do any of those things with another was considered treason.

The High King had his pick when it came to physical interaction with Praetorians. He could take as he pleased without any consequences. The control didn't stop there, however. Theo had been asked not just to kill innocent Asperians, but he had also been forced to lay with them, using his station and skills to extract information from them. It sickened Theo to the core, made worse in the moments he was alone with Camille. It was in her arms and wrapped in the emotional bonds of their love that he felt a deep surge of resentment for what the High King forced him to do.

Kissing her, holding her, even just touching Camille would be considered treason, but the realization of this didn't stop them. It was the only time they willingly gave affection to one another, the only time they denied the High King a say in their lives. Neither of them admitted it, but Theo felt the spark of their love ignite his own desperate need for freedom. He didn't just want to be free of the Crown, he needed to be open to love Camille in every way.

"It's not enough to just love you though," Theo had whispered in her ear. She hummed in response but kept her cheek pressed against his chest, unwilling to move, the chill of the room pressing them together, creating a cocoon of warmth. "I want more than words, Cam; I want you to be mine. I want to also be yours."

Her head lifted then, a flash of confusion running through the green of her irises, a soft pout playing on her still swollen lips. "I am yours," she replied quietly, not understanding his meaning.

Smiling, he kissed her forehead and pulled her back down to his chest. He knew if he waited to ask the moment would pass him by, and he'd never get the courage to ask her again. Despite the fire in Camille's heart for Aspera, he knew deep down she struggled with what the High King asked her to do. She followed her orders with strict adherence. He doubted aside of their nights lying next to one another that she did anything outside the lines of her Praetorian restrictions—even if she desperately wanted to.

"Marry me?" he said in a rush, his words running together in a jumble of sound. "Marry me and be all mine—mind, body, and soul?"

She giggled, turning her head again to face him. Bringing her lips to his, she kissed him soundly. Her hand lightly stroked his cheek, and he noticed the glossy wetness forming in her eyes.

"I'd love nothing more," she finally replied, her voice husky with emotion.

He had woken several hours later, his bed cold with her absence, a note scrawled in an apparent rush pinned to the pillow beside him.

I'm sorry, I think she's alive. I must find her. I love you, my darling.

He sighed, recalling the memory, his steps echoing on the tile floor as he walked to her room. That night had been the last time he'd seen her, the last time he'd held her and felt the reassurance of her heated skin against his.

He felt incredibly idiotic thinking about such things with Metus practically on their doorstep. He stood outside her door with a mere two hours to escape the compound. His focus needed to be on the present, not sliding into the past of long ago wishes and once real desires.

Neeko was waiting just outside her room, staring at the door jamb as though he could open it with the power of his mind. The cat's tail swished back and forth across the ground, his feline body a picture of impatient stillness.

"She in there?" Theo asked, almost expecting a verbal response.

Neeko peered up at him with a look of feigned patience. The yellowed irises narrowed with annoyance at having been shut out of her room, something Theo was sure he wasn't used to. The cat raised a single paw to scratch at the door, but nothing happened. He meowed and scratched at the door a second time with increasing insistence.

Theo opened the door cautiously, uncertain of what he was about to walk into. Neeko pressed into the room before the door was fully open, jauntily bouncing across the wooden floor to the empty bed.

"Cam?" Theo called out. Her clothing was strewn all over the floor, but she was nowhere in sight. The room wasn't just quiet; it felt still as though even the air had halted in movement.

A heavy sigh resonated from the bathroom as water pummeled the tile flooring within the shower. Theo's entire body seized up with guilty intrigue. It's not like he'd never seen her naked, but it had been quite a while, and his body responded in kind. The bathroom door was pushed closed, but not completely shut, leaving a full five inches of open space for him to peer into the hazy warmth.

It was wrong—he knew it was—but he couldn't deny the pull of holding her against him again. Feeling the spread of warmth as they clutched each other skin to skin. He took two steps towards the door, and Neeko meowed loudly from his perch on the bed.

"What?" Theo asked the stoic cat, whose tail swished madly against the comforter. The cat tilted its head to one side as Theo spoke, as though taking in his words and organizing them in his cat brain to understand Theo's meaning. "We are in a bit of a rush you know."

Neeko continued to stare silently, the yellow depths sharp with accusation.

"I just want to make sure she's ok," Theo whispered. He lifted his foot to move toward the door again, but Neeko meowed even louder, making Theo instead take several steps backward. The water in the shower turned off, and both of their heads snapped to the door frame.

The door to the bathroom slammed open making Theo jump in response. Steam billowed around her towel wrapped body, wild wet hair a tumble of fire about her bare milky white shoulders.

"Speak," she said without preamble. Theo knew what she wanted but had no clue how to begin. "I need answers, or I'm not going anywhere." Her cheeks were red, as were the rims of her eyes, but the storm of fierce determination whirled with menacing force in the mossy depths of her stare.

His mouth gaped open, then closed again, before opening a second time, only to remain wide without emitting a single sound.

"Would you mind?" Camille asked, motioning for him to turn around, which he obliged. His own cheeks flamed red, his body's deceiving nature showcasing his physical desire for her. She wasn't just wearing a towel, but a tiny one, barely skimming the tops of her thighs. Thankfully, he had a moment to collect himself.

"I'm sorry, I didn't mean..." he blubbered, wildly groping for what to say to her. His mouth suddenly went dry, and he felt an overwhelming urge to slap himself in the face. What was wrong with him? He wasn't some love-sick puppy; he was a Praetorian for Ma'Nada sake!

She padded softly across the floor gathering her own freshly washed clothing from the bed. A gentle whoosh of cotton rushed through his ears and his skin prickled with goosebumps as he realized that she had just dropped the towel to the floor. It took every fiber in his body not to turn around and ravage her, throw her on the bed and be damned with the two hours they had left within the compound. Through all their Praetorian duties, the restrictive laws, and the High King's demands, they'd never made love. Praetorians had been given no say over their own bodies. Neither of them was pure, but, more than anything, he'd wanted to share that moment with her. He would die a happy and thoroughly satiated Praetorian if he could have her that close to him just one time. Maybe twice.

"Talk," she clipped, as he heard her pull up her pants and button them closed. He shook his head aggressively to keep the images running through his mind from taking over.

"I'm not sure where to start."

She moved again, slipping a shirt over her shoulders. Theo heard the rustle of fabric as it shifted over her hair and across her skin. Feeling a pang of ridiculous jealousy, he suddenly felt desperate to *be* that piece of linen. He wanted to touch her, to feel the heat of her skin beneath his hand.

"Tell me why I'm here for starters."

He snorted, "I don't have the answer to that. Vesyon picked you up from Sierra Village; I had nothing to do with it."

Footsteps moved across the worn wooden planks, a whisper of motion stopping just behind him. A gentle hand pressed against the middle of his back between the shoulder blades and he tensed, not wanting to reveal the tornado of emotion raging just beneath the surface of his skin. He felt warmth flood the soft tissues around his eyes as blood pumped thickly through the heat of his veins. *Dear Ma'Nada, I will toss her on the bed and rip off all her damn clothes*, he thought, gripping his good intentions with tight desperation and mentally shaking himself of the thought.

"I deserve to know what's going on," she said, her voice strong yet gentle as her hand slipped down his spine to rest on the lower curve of his back. Her touch was soft yet burned him to the core, sending his body into overdrive, and the emotion bubbled out of him in a fit of rage.

"It's not fair to push me like this, Cam! There are some things I just can't tell you!"

She did, of course, deserve to know. Theo *wanted* to tell her everything. Unfortunately, a web of lies surrounded her reasons for being at Romeo Village and Theo had no idea what he could say and what he shouldn't. Vesyon had warned him, *she could break at any moment, just a single word could send her back into the manic craze of blood rage.*

"You think it was fair to keep me in Sierra Village for a full year without knowing who I was? *What* I was? I was abandoned there after seven years of being a prisoner to the High King. Not just by Vesyon but also by you."

He whirled on her then, his frustration bursting past the limits of his restraints. The heat of black flooded his eyes and ran down the lengths of his cheeks. "I had no idea you were alive!"

She snorted in response, not acknowledging his Praetorian reaction. "I don't believe that for a second. Talk, or I walk out of here, and you can handle this traitor on your own."

Neeko hissed softly from the bed, his yellow gaze fixed on Camille's back. The sound caused both to jump, but not out of fear: it was as if Neeko were warning Theo to keep quiet. Theo didn't believe her, she wouldn't walk away from the compound and leave hundreds of Rogues and Asperians behind to suffer, nor would she allow Acher to run free of his traitorous actions. However, he wasn't so sure he knew her mindset now. It went without saying that she had surprised him with her efforts on more than one occasion.

Theo grasped the wayward hair fanning over his brow and yanked it out of his face with a bloodstained hand as he turned to face her, avoiding the cat's stare. "Obviously, you aren't the reason they're here," he responded.

"That's a start," she replied coolly, turning to pick up her discarded shoes from the corner of the room.

She glanced up at him as she righted her leather coat with a flattened expression he had never seen directed at him before. It was unnerving. She stared at him as though he weren't just a stranger, but a man who had betrayed her. It sent an unwelcome chill down his spine, pooling in the pit of his stomach like a bucket of ice.

Would Vesyon know if he told her everything he knew? Of course he would—Camille would be sure to make that fact known. Would he be able to live with himself if he kept the truth from her? That, he couldn't be confident of.

"Do you know what your amulet's for?" he finally blurted out as she was tightening the laces of her shoes. He became increasingly aware of the time they were wasting, his foot tapping out a cadence of impatience against the wood floor.

"What?" she said, standing to face him.

"Praetorians aren't natural, Cam. You understand that, right? We were created by LeMarc's physician."

She flinched at Theo's use of the High King's first name; he'd never said it so brazenly before in her presence. He silently wondered why it bothered her to hear it now.

"Praetorians are created with an injection of Ephidra Lily serum that's been bonded with the Praetorian virus. Ephidra Lily is a carrier of whatever it's been infused with—it contains the virus, and then deposits and controls it within our systems. Once we go through the change from Asperian to Praetorian, our bodies are transformed inside: we're stronger, faster, and able to withstand almost all destructive forces. We can run longer, see and hear on a level perhaps only dogs and cats can, and can fight off the weakness Asperians are restrained by in basic everyday life. We heal in days, we can withstand hunger for months at a time if we must, and we no longer age. The key to our enhanced performance is the Praetorian virus, but we wouldn't be able to maintain cordial functionality without the restraints of Ephidra Lily."

She screwed her face up as she listened, her brow creasing across her forehead and her eyes narrowing into tiny green slits of color. It was cute, and Theo wanted to touch the furrowed lines of her brow with his thumb to soften the skin back out. He felt desperate to give her a moment of ease and tenderness before the storm of chaos they were about to walk into, but he knew it wouldn't be well received. She was a ticking time bomb; ready to explode at any moment.

He hated what she was going through and wasn't even sure he wanted to know what she had been through in the last eight years of her absence. Would he ever be able to smooth out the broad lines of worry, terror, and hopelessness he was sure had grooved heavy lines into her soul?

"This," Theo said, picking up the silver amulet around his own neck, "is called a Blood Bond. It keeps the virus from fully taking over our bodies. The necklace is infused with Ephidra Lily, and we are unable to remove it, despite how hard we've tried when curiosity struck." A whisper of a smile moved across his lips, but he quickly stamped it down. He saw a flicker of understanding dance across her features; she must have tried to remove it recently without knowing the consequences. Why hadn't Vesyon told her what she was? Why hadn't Peter?

"If we're separated from the Ephidra Lily," Theo continued, starting to pace the confined area of the room. "The virus will take control of our emotions. The black you've seen spreading just under our skin is the virus, pumping through our veins in moments of intense emotion. We're unable to stop its appearance, but the Ephidra Lily keeps us sane and allows us to maintain control when the virus enhances our physical abilities."

"The black eyes—the ink beneath our skin? That's the virus?"

"A visible aspect of it."

"Okay," she said, exhaling. "I still don't see what this has to do with tonight."

"I'm getting there," Theo said anxiously as well as with a sense of excitement. He was relieved to get something off his chest but also in a slight panic over the time they were wasting. "LeMarc is after Ephidra Lily. He hungers for it and is willing to do anything to get it—clearly since he's sent the royal fleet our way."

He grabbed Camille by the shoulders then, intent on making his point clear without guiding her down a path of endless questions. "He can't get his hands on it, Camille. You must understand *that* above everything. Our freedom from his grasp, from his control, goes hand-in-hand with Ephidra Lily. We can't let him have it."

Camille was starting to understand, as she nodded slowly in response her eyes never leaving his. "Where exactly *is* it?"

"Vesyon orchestrated a leak about three months ago that we were storing some here in our underground vault. It took a while for the information to take hold, but several weeks ago we heard the King Regent was on his way to collect what we had with a handful of Equestrians. We assumed this invasion would be small and quietly contained."

"Obviously you were misinformed."

"Yeah," Theo snorted.

Camille scrunched her eyes in thought as she watched Theo pace the length of the room. "What happens when he finds the Ephidra Lily?"

"Oh, he won't," Theo said, stopping his march to regard her.

"He won't? How can you be so sure?"

"Well, to be honest, he *can't*," he replied with a wry grin. "We don't actually have any Ephidra Lily here; that was the whole point. We only needed to know *when* he was searching for it, and, now that we know, we will make our move to combat his efforts. The rebellion begins again tonight. The King Regent will arrive with an army, most of which will immediately infiltrate the compound. When he sends his troops down into the depths of the vault looking for the product, we're going to set off the fuses we've placed throughout the underground and blow the entire place to smithereens."

Her mouth fell open in complete shock. "You're going to blow it up?! The entire compound? But...but you can't do that!"

"Of course we can. And we will. Vesyon said we have two hours once the bell horn of the evacuation rang, and then we'll need to get out of here."

Neeko appeared to nod in agreement, and Camille hurried to gather her belongings with shaky hands. "Then we need to go! Why didn't you tell me?!"

Theo smiled with his hands out in front of him in a shrugging gesture. "I *have* been trying to tell you, Cam!"

Her traveling bag was packed in minutes, bulging with the few personal items she owned. The three of them headed for the door, but just as Theo moved to open it her chilled fingers grasped his forearm with intensity. "Theo, what happens if there's no Ephidra Lily in our bodies? What happens if someone removes our Blood Bond?"

"Well," he said, twisting the doorknob open, "we'd lose our ability to reason. The virus would take over our system, and there'd be no stopping us from whatever our goal might be. I've heard that our humanity would switch off—or, rather, we would have no way to control our ability to feel emotion."

She nodded in understanding, a question bouncing around

within the confined space of her mind. Her hand slipped over the silver metal piece hanging around her neck, but she remained silent as she stood next to Theo.

"You tried removing it?" Theo asked, nodding to her amulet. She nodded, averting her emerald gaze. "There's only one person that can remove that necklace, Camille, and I assure you, he never would."

"Who?"

"Langhorn, your um, well he's the physician at White Wall," he said, stumbling through a response. She didn't remember Langhorn, by the confused expression on her face. Vesyon had been clear about what to say to Camille: *don't mention a single detail about her past, her previous life, her family, or her friends. She needs to find out who we are as she meets us. Find out where she lived and where she has been as she arrives there.*

It didn't make much sense to Theo. The secrecy and denial of information drove him wholly nuts, but he didn't want to be responsible for a severe mental breakdown on Camille's part. What if he told her one detail too much and she couldn't handle it? Would Charlie Town happen all over again?

The last thing he wanted was to be the one responsible for her breaking, no matter the cost. She'd lost hold of herself before. He'd rather die than lose her to the darkness again.

CHAPTER FOURTEEN
THE VAULT

Not for the first time in the last moon cycle, Camille's head hurt from the amount of information she was trying to shove into it. Metus had warned her about Vesyon's lies, and there were many— why she'd had to leave Sierra Village and come to Romeo Village had both been cloaked in half-truths and omissions. But had Vesyon also known her breakdown in Charlie Town had stemmed from the Blood Bond's removal? There was no doubt in her mind that it had been the cause; she felt the truth of it straight down to her bones. She couldn't have been the only one to think this though. If Vesyon knew the truth, why hadn't he told her that instead of calling it an episode of blood rage?

Unfortunately, her memories from that day in Charlie Town came in short, clipped images, and there was no way to remember whether she'd been wearing her medallion or not. Despite everything, Camille clung to two simple truths burrowed deep within her consciousness: Metus and the High King had spent seven years after the massacre in Charlie Town torturing her, while Vesyon had come to her rescue. *That's* what mattered when it came to where her loyalties would lie.

Then there was Theo: where did her loyalties lie when it came to him? It was apparent he was still hiding information, but she couldn't be sure what. Did she trust him to tell her what she needed to know? *Yes*, she thought, glancing up at him as they walked down the deserted hallway. His gait was quick, purposeful, and confident, and yet she could see the gentleness as clearly as she could see his strength. There was a stern determination set in the hard lines of his shoulders; he wouldn't abandon her and yet he wouldn't give up on what he and Vesyon had started.

When it came to honesty, however, she could read the lies bubbling up on his face. He hadn't told her the whole truth yet, but he *would*. She just needed to push him a little harder, like coaxing a nut out of its shell; she just needed to find the best way to crack him without breaking apart the goods hiding within.

"Are you okay?" Theo prodded gently as they descended an emergency stairwell, Neeko keeping paced beside her. Their boots thudded softly against the cement steps as they moved around a floor platform before descending farther still.

"I'm fine," Camille responded mechanically.

"No need to hold back your thoughts, Cam," Theo said, pulling her from a stair landing into a narrow hall. "I *did* just tell you our surroundings will be on fire in a few hours."

The narrow hall was lit by stand-alone swinging bulbs, their shadows a mirage of dancing figures bouncing along the stone walls as they moved. It was becoming more difficult to breathe as the walls closed in around them, the air pressing down on her lungs the further they burrowed into the depths of the compound.

"You can start by telling me what the point of us being down here is when the entirety of your defense is topside fighting the incoming attack."

He missed a step trying to process her request. His right foot forgot to move, causing him to shuffle before regaining his composure.

"I think you know very well why we're down here," he said in a muffled reply.

"Of course I do," Camille snapped back without restraint. "Vesyon asked you to take me down here, and you listened to him. We should be up there fighting alongside the Rogues, not down here hiding from everyone."

The moment the words flew from her mouth, she slammed into Theo's back, his entire body having jerked to a complete stop.

"Ouch," Camille said, reflexively reaching up to her stinging nose to feel for any oozing drip of blood.

"Sorry," Theo said in a hushed whisper.

"It's ok, I know you didn't mean to..." Camille said, but stopped speaking as Theo's fingertip brushed the end of her nose.

"Are you bleeding?"

"No," Camille replied, her voice sounding small even to herself. Blood rushed thickly in her ears, pounding out a cadence of Praetorian adrenaline. "But even if I were, I doubt it will be the last of it tonight." She tried for a laugh, but the sound came in out a strangled croak.

"He wasn't supposed to collect you until after the invasion, when we were on our way to White Wall. That had been the order," he said softly. "For some reason, Vesyon brought you here after the Chimera attack instead of sending you to White Wall as planned."

He seemed almost as surprised as she was at his sudden explanation. "We should uh...keep moving," Theo said quickly before he grabbed for her hand in the looming dark and continued down the stone hall. They turned left and then right at forks in their path, an unending trail of stone, dim light, and a musty stench of stale air.

"Since I *am* here," Camille chirped up in the silence of their dizzying walk, "perhaps you can enlighten me on a few things."

Theo sighed and shrugged as though resigned to the realization that keeping her in the dark of what was to come was utterly ludicrous. "Sure, what do you want to know?" Neeko meowed somewhere around their feet, his tone one of warning, but Theo ignored it and continued to move.

"What's the Royal Air Fleet?" Camille asked. It would be easier to get answers out of him if she kept it to their present situation and surroundings.

"The High King built a fleet of ships to fly from one village to the next. They're exactly what you'd imagine: huge ships with billowing white sails and wooden decks, but instead of floating on water—they fly."

"I'm sorry—they *fly*? Like a bird?" Camille said, her jaw dropping wide open. It wasn't what she had been expecting, having never seen anyone from the High Court outside of Grenswald and his decrepit wagon of appropriated goods.

Theo glanced back at her, his brows raised. "You've been in one before, an Asperian Transport Ship. Yes, they fly, but less like a bird and more like a swiftly moving cloud."

"I've been in one before?" She scrunched her nose in thought

198

but couldn't bring a single memory to the surface.

"Yeah," Theo said, his voice tight with a hint of exasperation. "An A.T.S. They are cargo ships that move from one village to the next. They aren't for everyday Asperians though. At one point before the exile, only Praetorians and those of the High Court could use them."

Neeko kept pace behind them, a silent lookout for any danger they might walk into. The cat seemed complacent with her questions, making her want to push for more information. Despite the air of undisturbed surroundings, Camille kept her voice intentionally low, only loud enough for Theo to hear. "How many soldiers can they hold?"

"No idea, I've never seen his Royal Air Fleet, only a few passenger ships the high court sent out to collect goods or make a trade. These ships are built for war and complete destruction from what Vesyon told me—it'll be a feat if the compound survives long enough to allow us the honor of blowing it up. They may just get to it first."

Theo descended a narrow staircase straight down into a dark stone tunnel where they stood almost shoulder-to-shoulder in the pitch black. It was eerily quiet as they crept through the narrow passage, their feet a whisper of sound against the stone walkway. Camille gripped her dagger loosely in one hand, resting her other on the hilt of her sword. Theo seemed to be in the same frame of mind, as he was wielding a menacing curved dagger. They would smell Acher, possibly even hear him before they saw him, but they could never be too careful in the heavy press of darkness surrounding them.

Pushing their way through a sagging wooden door, they were entrenched in the past. "You think Acher's down here?" Camille asked incredulously, closing in behind Theo as they stood at the neck of a high-ceilinged hall.

"Not here, no. This back entrance to the vault moves through the old sanctuary quarters. I think Acher is in the greenhouse. He would've come through the front entrance."

Silent as a shadow, Theo grabbed an unlit wooden torch from the wall, his steps a visual path through the layers of dust and debris spread across the cobbled ground. Sparking his dagger against the flint stone in his hand, he caught flame to the torch end and moved into the looming darkness of the hall. "You coming?"

Her insides suddenly squirmed with discomfort as she became aware of a stark apprehension of the unknown extending down the long, open hallway. It was ludicrous, of course, to feel a lurking sense of fear in the narrow space, but, nonetheless, she felt it snake around the cavity of her organs and squeeze with unrelenting pressure.

"Um, I...I don't..." she mumbled unintelligibly uncertain of her reaction. Once again, her Praetorian response paralyzed her, evading her desperate plea for power as it had in the forest when the Equestrians attacked her.

Theo's lips turned downward in worry, his eyes squinting as though trying to read her thoughts. "You alright, Cam?"

Stark images flashed in front of Camille's eyes; she could see the ghost-like image of a man dressed in grey slacks and a billowing grey cloak. He seemed not just calm but eager as he stared down at her, his face alight with anticipation. The sharp kiss of cold steel against her shackled wrists and neck jolted her into a startling vision, while the voices ricocheted around her head in a wave of memories.

> *"She should be manageable now. The dosage coursing through her body is more than I've ever seen a Praetorian have," a familiar, oaky voice spoke out. The words drifted to Camille's ears slowly, jumbling and getting stuck in the hazy blur of her mind.*
>
> *"Why isn't it working then? What makes her different? You said this would be routine," another voice barked.*
>
> *"It should've been, but her biological structure is extremely different than any other I've come across."*
>
> *Camille felt a sharp pinch on the inside of her left wrist, followed by an intense warming sensation that traveled up her arm and into her chest. The voices continued to talk over her immobile body, but they faded into nothingness as the moderate heat turned into a roaring fire, one that consumed everything.*

"Camille?"

Camille jerked, her body convulsing once as it sprang back into the present. The bitter chill of the stone floor seeped into her clothing as she lay flat against the ground, her head pillowed in Theo's arms. "Cam, come back." His voice slipped through the haze of her memory as she struggled to regain composure.

She blinked rapidly, trudging her way out as though pulling her feet through knee deep mud. "What happened?" she murmured when she could talk again, her tongue feeling strangely heavy in her mouth. Lifting herself into a sitting position, she shook her head, the heaviness of her Praecollection making her vision swim.

"You stopped walking, then you collapsed." He paused, assessing her. "Praecollection?"

She nodded, rubbing at her face. It had been one with Metus, she was sure of it. "I'm fine. Let's keep moving."

Regaining her feet, she took several wobbly steps, though Theo didn't seem convinced of her strength. He kept time with her as she plowed down the hallway, the warming Praetorian response trickling back into place beneath her skin.

Neeko waited for them at a wide wooden door painted a deep blue, his yellowed stare assessing her as she approached.

"I'm fine," she whispered to the cat in a tone she wasn't certain sounded confident. Theo approached just behind her, the torchlight dancing across the weathered door, sprinkling the aged wood with bits of golden light. Dead center of the door was a brass knob larger than Camille's fist. Theo grasped the knob and turned, pressing the door open with a groan of age and neglect. A blast of fetid air assaulted Camille's nose, and she coughed in response.

"What's that smell?" She held a bent arm in front of her nose trying to block out the dank intensity. It reminded her of the heavy scent of mold and decomposition: sour yet extremely rich.

"Time," Theo replied, moving into the dark space and lighting several candle sconces along an arched wall as he walked. As he stepped further into the space, Camille saw high, arched beams expanding across the ceiling in a crisscross of support. Several stone benches in front of them created a sitting area facing a raised platform at the end of the room.

"Where are we?" Camille said in a hushed whisper as they moved through the narrow pathway of benches. She couldn't be sure why, but she felt surrounded by a sea of lingering souls. Her breath came out in short puffs of steam, the cold stone seeping the warmth straight from her core.

"The Worship sanctuary, but we don't often use this entry," Theo said as he moved toward the head of the room, apparently not feeling the same sense of thrumming power. "We came through a back entry of the vault. Vesyon requested we use a pathway Acher wouldn't. The worship sanctuary gives some people the creeps," Theo said with a grin, but she noticed the casual flick of wariness spark from the corner of his eye as he watched her.

"I can imagine why." Camille kept in line with Theo, not wanting to stray too far from the gentle warming glow of his torch. "I thought the compound was new, the underground an addition to the village up top."

"Oh no," Theo replied as he moved up the platform and past a flat stone table laden with dusty stone plates, cups, and several simplistic candle lamps. Ducking under a thick blanket of cobwebs surrounding the table, Theo led Camille toward the back of the room through a high arched doorway. "The compound has been here for quite some time. From what I know, Langhorn's great-grandfather helped build the original underground when he was a boy."

"Langhorn, the physician?"

"Yep, he grew up here in the reign of High King Lucas, High King LeMarc's father."

Glancing around the darkened hall, Camille shuddered with the creepy sense of unease as they exited the sanctuary room. They slipped into another vaulted ceiling room just off the main hall, with tiny alcoves lining either side of the room resembling small stone sleeping quarters. "So, Langhorn grew up in a dungeon?"

Theo chuckled lightly as they moved through another archway into a low ceiling space lined with wooden shelves. Neeko continued before them, his light-footed steps padding in silence across the stone floor.

"No, they didn't live in dungeons. Romeo Village was a place of worship for the Daeites. This was their temple for daily worship."

"Worship?" Camille asked, not understanding his meaning as she shuffled to keep up with his quick steps through the confined space. "Worship to what, the crown?"

"No!" Theo said sharply, stopping mid-step to glance back at Camille in shocked bewilderment. "You are so literal sometimes." The corner of his lips tilted downward with a glint of shock lurking in his deep-set sapphire gaze. She couldn't be sure if he was disappointed that she didn't remember basic history or that he was beginning to see the immense depth of her memory loss.

"Worship of the Mother Ma'Nada," Theo clarified. "The room we entered was a sacred Daeism burial ground."

"Oh," Camille replied as a shudder ran down her spine.

Theo turned away from her with a slight shake of his head before moving down a curved flight of stairs. Reaching a small square landing leading to another long extending hallway, Camille noticed a cobweb-covered statue nudged in the corner of the space. It was weathered with age yet so perfectly molded that its pristine artistry wasn't lost beneath the layers of dust. "Do you believe in the Mother?" Camille asked as she ran a single finger over the curved form of Ma'Nada's upturned cheek.

"Cam, we need to keep moving." Even as he pressed her to move, he stood next to her, his hand brushing gently against hers. She couldn't explain the reasoning behind it, but she felt a strong urge to link her fingers through his. Instead of giving in to the desire, she tucked her fingers against her body and crossed her arms over her chest.

"I don't believe a woman sprouted daughters from nowhere," he replied at last in the close press of dim light surrounding them, "but I do believe in the spiritual connection to the Mother. The stories are just stories, but their origin stems from something—a beginning."

Theo continued, "I don't know the first chapter, but I do know many tales at the center of the story to be true."

"Like what?" Camille asked, her voice soft yet insistent. Theo pulled her gently away from the ivory stone statue and led her down another dizzying number of hallways.

"The two cursed daughters Buvona stole for revenge against Fotrix," Theo spoke up after several minutes of silent walking. "They're real."

Neeko stood at the end of a hall, silently perched and waiting for them to catch up yet again.

"How do you know that?" Camille whispered.

"Because their remains lie in the sanctuary tomb we walked through when we entered the vault."

Camille's mouth gaped in shock, but before she could process Theo's revelation, a putrid stench hit her nose and Theo dropped into a crouch at the end of the hall. A slight scraping of metal on wood rang out from the depths of the empty corridor. He pulled her down beside him before tossing the torch back down the hall from the direction they had come, submerging their surroundings into pitch black.

"You think it's him?" Camille asked in a barely audible whisper, blindly grasping for Theo's hand in desperation to know that she wasn't alone.

"No idea. But if it is, Acher isn't alone. You smell that?"

She did: the putrid stench of Chimera wafted through the air with the promise of at least four beasts awaiting their arrival.

***

Vesyon shook his hands out as the wind pulled against the sleeves beneath his leather armor. His entire body felt tight with anticipation, making it hard to wiggle his fingers freely. Even the leather chest protector felt like too much. He hated being weighed down during a fight and usually found it unnecessary as a Praetorian, but the Chimera's presence required additional protection.

In their head-to-toe garb of green and white, iron and leather armor, the Romeo Village Rogues resembled little green bugs marching toward an inescapable slaughter. The massive black beast that was the High Court would flick them aside, killing each one of them upon impact. Vesyon knew by now that their plan was going to fail but was hesitant to show it for fear the soldiers scurrying around him would see. His confidence was flimsy at best, and he was struck with the desire to laugh sardonically as he watched three huge warships cut through the clouds in the distance. They needed more time, *months* of it, to prepare for what was already knocking at their door.

The entirety of their Rogue army crouched along the far south side of the compound, hunkering in the tall grass like lion cubs waiting to pounce. It was slightly laughable with their small numbers, but there was nothing else they could do. It was too late; the Chimera alone outnumbered Vesyon's troops, not to mention the hundreds of Equestrians bringing up the rear. The Rogues had a mere handful of men posted in the trees to gun down whomever they could. He hated to be the cynic, but this wasn't a promising outcome even with the plan to vacate the premises as soon as the alarm rang.

"Get that scowl off your face," Vesyon barked at Phillip as they passed through the town square. "You're scaring them."

"This was a bad idea," Phillip shot back in a hushed tone.

Together they moved toward the area where most of the troops were waiting. They'd left the gates to Romeo Village open, and the compound's entryway was impossible to miss. Now all they needed to do was wait for the invasion to begin.

"And it was mostly *your* idea," Phillip went on, eyes wide with worry. Neither Vesyon nor Phillip had seen Charlie in over an hour, and Vesyon hadn't missed the General's fingers drumming against his thigh as her absence stretched on.

Vesyon glared despite the justification of Phillip's fears. "The only option we have is to stand our ground. We know how much LeMarc is willing to sacrifice to get what he wants—but we still don't know *why*."

The pair of them moved through the waist high grass along the edges of the outer wall. Their boots crunched loudly in the frozen underbrush, the noise ricocheting through the silence.

"You think sacrificing our people—sending them to their *deaths*—will tell you why he wants this stupid plant so badly?"

Vesyon stopped suddenly and faced Phillip. "I'm sorry if you feel this is an unwarranted and unnecessary attack. I believe the opposite. This isn't only about his search for Ephidra Lily; it is to confirm that he's making a move. We've had eight years, Phillip. There was no other way to prepare for this."

Phillip glowered back at Vesyon, his head tilted downward. "You are sending my men to slaughter. They will die today, you know this."

"Then I will die as one of them!" Vesyon burst out.

"And Camille? You're willing to sacrifice her?" Phillip knew all too well that he'd hit a nerve, yet he continued. "She was never part of the plan, Captain. We shouldn't be standing to fight, we should be running from it. If you believe there's a purpose in this plan though, I *will* stand beside you and fight."

Vesyon nodded and extended his hand. "I believe this is the only way. The rebellion must breathe life again, and if this is the spark to set loose the flame, then we must make it."

Phillip took it without hesitation, grasping Vesyon's wrist in firm solidarity.

A thunderous boom rang out overhead as the mortar fire rained in from the proceeding ships. Cannon fire exploded into the main square of the village, pulverizing the weathered skeleton of the remaining structures.

"Charlie knows to fight only until the warning horn sounds for retreat, right?" Vesyon asked.

Theo was supposed to have been with him to keep a second set of Praetorian eyes on Charlie and Phillip, as he'd always been Vesyon's right hand in times of battle. He needed him, but Camille needed him more. There was no way he was going to allow Camille to stand on the front line, and Theo had been the only one he trusted to get her out of harm's way.

"Theo showed her several weeks ago where to retreat to; she knows to cut and run at the horn. She's very aware of how much time she has to get away from the village before the detonation of the underground. Once she's made it to safe ground, she will lead her troops to White Wall!" Phillip screamed as another cannonball hurtled over their heads into the crumbling foundation of Romeo Village.

A sharp, stabbing pain seared Vesyon's chest at the thought of Camille being forever trapped beneath the compound, a cavernous crypt without an exit. In his desperation to keep her alive and far removed from battle, he very well could have doomed her to death.

As the wind picked up speed and threw the western wind into their faces, Vesyon smelled the wretched stench of muddied fur, the heavy saltiness of filthy men, and something *floral?* "Do you smell that?"

"Amazingly, I do. The beast's foul stench is unlike anything. Dear Ma'Nada, it's horrible," Phillip said, covering his nostrils with a gloved hand.

"No, not the Chimera. I smell something else," Vesyon said, the first pricks of panic jabbing into his Praetorian awareness. "They aren't alone, Phillip. The Equestrians brought something else I've never confronted before."

Phillip didn't respond as they saw the horror unfurl before their eyes. The warships of LeMarc's Royal Air Fleet dotted the moonlit sky like hovering vultures: dark and formidable.

The main decks of each ship were topped with a towering mast, giving the general resemblance of a typical seaworthy vessel—but these flying battle weapons were anything but ordinary. From bow to keel, the seven ships were lined with shimmering copper and hardened iron plating. Five rows of gun port windows boasted a display of massive cannons, and on either side of the rudder and vertical stabilizers were twin turbine engines propelling the massive ships forward. They cut through the air like a knife; absolutely *nothing* would be able to stop their forward propulsion.

The previous rainfall and melting snow left the ground mushy and slick with squelching mud piles and icy slush. It wasn't ideal fighting ground, but it didn't bother Vesyon nearly as much as the fact that they had such small numbers up against LeMarc's army.

"I see intruders on foot to the west, men!" Phillip called out, pointing his sword and readying his battalion.

"Do you think Camille will make it out in time?" Phillip said to Vesyon before they began their stealthy march forward, hunkering in the weed thickets for cover.

"She will," Vesyon said, gritting his teeth together.

Phillip tossed him a stern expression. "She better."

The closest ship's gun deck opened for battle then, and any remaining conversation was gobbled up by devastating blasts of cannon fire.

***

Pressing her shoulder blades against the stone wall at her back, Camille felt the chill seep through to the core of her body. Theo pulled away from the corner of the wall as Neeko slipped into the shadows, scouting ahead before they pursued the distant sounds of intrusion. His fingers tentatively brushed against hers in the dark surrounding. She could smell the fresh, woodsy scent of him, and see a hint of panic sift through the carefully constructed veneer of his expression.

"I need you to promise you'll follow my every move, Cam. No matter what. Do you understand?"

She bobbed her chin, keeping her eyes locked with his. It was almost impossible to see the sharp outline of his features, but she saw the glimmer of silvery light in his eyes and clung to it.

"Listen to me. Vesyon is a smart man, and my every cell is loyal to him, but this wasn't part of the plan, having you be involved. If I tell you to run, you *run*." His thumb traced an invisible line up along her cheekbone, each stroke sending a rolling wave of desire throughout her entire body. "I've said it before, and I'll repeat it: I'm not losing you this time."

For the first time since Camille had met Theo, she felt the immense vulnerability he harbored, the open heart and fierce loyalty of a man willing to do whatever it took to protect those he cared for.

"What does Ad Astra per Aspera mean?" Camille blurted out, not quite understanding why the words popped into her head. Theo seemed slightly taken aback as well, but his smile grew wide as he looked at her, his teeth a mere slip of white in the shadows.

Glancing over his shoulder down the hall, he looked for the sleek shape of Neeko before he turned back to Camille. "It's quite fitting for the moment, actually. It means 'to the stars through difficulties.' It was our guiding force before the rebellion began and became something of a battle call for us Praetorians and Rogues. For us *heathens*," he said with a sly smile. "It was a way of saying that nothing could stop us; that we would push through to the very end no matter the consequences."

Her eyes glittered with unshed tears, and her voice stuck in her throat. They had been the last words Peter said to her before she left Sierra Village. The intention of his meaning to her became incredibly clear and an overwhelming desire to smile as much as cry crashed into her. He'd been giving her permission to go, to find her true purpose with the words of their cause as his final gift to her. She may not have had a choice in the matter, but she wouldn't have chosen a different route to where she stood.

Glancing up into the gentle depths of Theo's azure stare, she knew that despite the pain of not remembering everything about the man, she wanted to know who he'd become. A single tear slipped down her cheek in a quick hot trail, and she swiped it away with a flick of a finger. "You *won't* lose me," she said with marked surety.

His hand slid around the back of her neck, and he jerked her to his mouth, bruising her lips with a quick, passionate kiss. He pulled back, but only slightly, their breaths mingling together as he held her face close to his. "I won't let anything happen to you, okay? Do you trust me?"

"Yes."

Neeko mewed, a soft noise meant to gain their attention that snapped between them like a firecracker, effectively splitting them apart. Her heart thumped against the cavity of her chest, the tingling of Theo's kiss still warm on her skin.

Standing with him as he moved, they crept toward the greenhouse at the end of the hall. Without questioning her instinct,

Camille abruptly halted, her nose twitching with the incoming scent. "Theo," she said, her heart hammering in her chest. "Do you smell that?"

"I do," he whispered as they reached the cracked open door of the greenhouse. "Gunpowder."

Their time was running out; the Royal Air Fleet had arrived.

CHAPTER FIFTEEN
THE TRAITOR

Theo didn't *just* smell gunpowder; there was something else. It was sweet and difficult to identify, but as his mind focused on the varying notes his nose picked up, he couldn't seem to concentrate on anything past the horrid stench of the Chimera. Rotten and musky, like a dead fish after months of sunbathing: there was nothing else like it.

They moved as one unit down the empty hall, their steps silent across the stone.

As Theo opened his mouth to ask Camille if she smelled it also, a rush of warmth whooshed down the hall toward them, rumbling the ground with a jolting shake. The fleet had arrived, and, as Theo expected, Romeo wouldn't hold up for long beneath the pressure of constant cannon fire. They would need to find Acher and escape quickly before the crumbling weight of the compound crushed their only exit.

Neeko remained perched just outside the greenhouse waiting for Theo and Camille. His sleek form was a mere silhouette in the bright shaft of moonlight emitting from the cracked door. The greenhouse was a vast cave used initially for access to the underground river, but in the past eight years a man-made dam was built to enable a slower flow of water and promote the growth of crops. Several angled mirrors kept the room lit naturally, sending a tinge of brilliant light through the dappled layers of trees, vegetable crops, and wheat.

Acher was there, Theo could smell his presence through the open door, but he wasn't sure yet *where* he was. The greenhouse wasn't small by any means, and it left many locations to hide amongst the growing crops. Sounds of battle filtering through the open airways at the top of the cave were unmistakable: they were running out of time.

Theo readied himself and Camille before nudging the door open with the toe of his boot. The heavy metal door swung silently on its hinges, revealing a quaint picture of blue-tinted trees and silver strands of wheat swaying in the swirling breeze. A moonlit cobbled path led them from one garden block to the next, with wheat rows laid out in perfect lines to their right and vegetable patches to their left almost naked by comparison, the treasures having been picked during the harvest several weeks prior.

Heavy sounds of artillery and cannon fire boomed from above. In the secluded confinement of the greenhouse, Theo almost felt safe—or would have if not for the red glowing eyes of Chimera lurking near the river edge.

"I know you're down here, Acher! Come out and surrender and I won't be forced to harm you," Theo bellowed out, no longer caring about a surprise attack. They needed to grab Acher and head up top before the entire compound went up in flames. He didn't have time to be delicate or sly. Right now, he just wanted to be above ground, and he wasn't going to let Acher get in his way of escaping. It was tempting to forgo the plan entirely and just run for cover, but Theo wasn't one to back down or turn tail, even if the task at hand seemed utterly ludicrous. He would give the traitor one chance to surrender, and if he didn't come quietly, he'd move on to plan two: punch said traitor in the face and run like hell out of Romeo Village. The idea of hearing the pop and crunch of cartilage under his knuckles as he connected his fist to Acher's face made him smile, filling his entire body with a calm sense of determination.

The Lieutenant materialized from behind a tree, his jacket removed, and his sleeves yanked up haphazardly past his elbows. His hands were covered in dirt, his knees equally as dirty. To Theo's surprise, he appeared unperturbed and slightly drunk with self-imposed importance. His chin snapped upward, giving his head a slightly backward tilt, forcing him to glare down his nose at them as they moved toward him.

211

"Didn't realize that you were such an avid gardener," Theo said with an impish grin.

Acher snarled in response, his face slick with sweat. "*Where is it?* I know it's down here; tell me where it is!"

Theo sidestepped in front of Camille, his heart blasting out a rapid pace against the confines of his chest as four Chimera assembled behind Acher like trained dogs. It was something he'd never seen before; the beasts had always been wild and unteachable. It struck him not only as strange but intriguing—in a very worrisome way.

"I don't think I can tell you," Theo replied in a smooth, confident tone. He'd never liked Acher, but it was possible he could be wrong about the man. Despite Theo's ability to read people, he tried to not assume personality defects until he saw them in action. Acher was a seeker of power and glory; nothing more.

A fire raged above them, Theo could smell the sharpness of pine and singed wood wafting down the open airway with an alarming heat. The plan of securing Acher and getting out of the compound alive was becoming less of a viable outcome as the seconds ticked by.

"Figures Vesyon would tuck her away down here, with her watch dog no less," Acher said, taking another step toward them, his eyes darting back and forth around them as though the plant he was desperately seeking would appear suddenly. Neeko lurched out in front of Camille, hissing and spitting wildly as he clawed the open air. Acher glanced at him like a cute pet before ignoring him completely.

Theo snorted, backing up a step, his hand securely enveloping his dagger's hilt. "And I suppose you chose to miss all the action up top just to chat with us?"

Acher's face immediately contorted, his brow receding downward in a mass of furrowed wrinkles. "I will be rewarded for capturing you and finding the Ephidra Lily. Unlike *you*—both of you will be punished for your deceit and treason."

Theo let loose a mocking guffaw. "You're a moron."

Acher's eyes flashed as he whipped his arm downward, a long black cylinder sizzling with electricity in his hand. All four Chimera growled in response, seemingly controlled by Acher's weapon. "You need to watch your mouth, Praetorian. Always pranced through Romeo Village like you owned the place—*but you don't*. You're nothing but Praetorian scum, a broken and useless soldier. You both will get me what I want, and then—*then*—I'll let the beasts devour you for supper. Or you defy me, and I kill you now. Either way—you die."

He wasn't sure if it was Lieutenant's manic expression or the aggressive stare he was slinging in Camille's direction, but Theo decided then and there that he was going to murder Acher Greeves at the first opportunity and to hell with capturing him. The bastard could rot beneath the rubble of the compound for all he cared.

"Don't you *get* it, Acher?" Camille yelled at him. "There isn't any Ephidra Lily!"

The greenhouse was slowly filling with a toxic amount of smoke, and Theo would've taken off if he'd been confident Camille would follow and the beasts would leave them to their business. Looking over his shoulder at the open tunnel at the edge of the river bed, he was sure they could get to the opening in quick succession, but unlocking the gate halfway down the shaft would be a problem if they were being chased by four Chimera.

"What do you mean?" Acher barked, stepping out of the shadows of the tree line, his eyes blazing with panic.

"She means you're down here for no reason, idiot! There isn't any Ephidra Lily, and there never was!"

In a matter of seconds, Acher seemed to understand the ploy, and his expression morphed from irritation to full-blown rage.

With a sharp flick of his wrist, Acher jerked the black, cylindrical weapon so that it shot a spray of sparks upwards. The Chimera lurched into action, barreling past him toward Theo and Camille.

Neeko charged in front of them, his tiny cat paws digging into the ground as six-inch claws, sharp and menacing, emerged through his fur. His slim feline body exploded with cords of muscle, lengthening and growing before their eyes. Camille's jaw dropped in shock as the cat she'd known since arriving at Sierra Village transformed in seconds into a sleek, terrifying jaguar. The cat was well known for his quick change of form and knack for timing, and Theo guessed by the look on Camille's face that this was the first time she'd witnessed a Felius Metamorphi shift since her induced memory loss.

"Kill them," Acher said, his voice low and coolly detached.

The Chimera rocketed toward them, mouths opening with a roar.

In that frozen second before the imminent attack, Theo felt Camille's hand press into the small of his back, a gentle touch, a promise of trust and determination to stick by his side. He sighed in relief, an exhalation of pent up panic he hadn't realized he'd been holding. It was a small dose of *his* Camille reaching out to touch him, to make sure he knew she was beside him. Despite the loss of her memory, she was giving him crumbs of her former self—even if she didn't realize she was doing it.

Acher expected a blood bath, Theo was sure by the way the Lieutenant turned away from the fight to continue searching despite what they'd told him. It wouldn't go the way Acher expected. In seconds the Chimera beasts lay in a mass at their feet, the ground stained black with the remnants of their blood. It hadn't been brutal, but quick—several expertly sliced jugulars and it was done. Neeko growled at Acher, his shadowed form still and silent in the shade of the treetops.

"We don't have time, Acher! Enough of this. Admit defeat and come with us. Phillip will show you mercy if you come quietly," Theo barked over the growing chaos above their heads.

Acher ambled toward them, pulling out his gun as he moved. "I would never act against the High King. You can take your pardon, you piece of scum, and shove it up your—" Acher's bellow was cut off by a thunderous explosion overhead.

Rocks and metallic debris rained down on them, pummeling the cobbled stones and vegetable patches in a deadly spray.

"Let's go!" Theo said, snatching Camille's hand and pulling her away from the mass of falling rock.

"We can't leave him!" Camille gasped, watching as Acher dove back into the trees to duck away from a huge, tumbling rock. "I swore to Vesyon we would collect him."

"We aren't going to retrieve Acher; I don't care what Vesyon told you. My job was to ensure your safety by keeping you away from the battle, and if that meant killing Acher or detaining him, fine. But right now, I need to get you to safety, and there is no way I am risking that just to bring that bastard along. Now, *come on!*"

Theo yanked her down the cobblestone path littered with broken branches and twisted metal toward the river bank. Neeko dashed forward, his form small once again, hopping from one flattened, exposed rock in the river to the next before reaching the narrow tunnel space and disappearing down into the darkness of the water runoff.

Another explosion overhead boomed into the cavity of the greenhouse, the echo momentarily deafening Theo as he pulled Camille through the thigh-deep water toward the tunnel head. Camille's hand jerked out of his, and he looked back, not realizing that she was screaming at him until it was too late.

The fortified wall of the underwater river cracked into fissures, water dribbling out as a warning of release. There was no other way out; they wouldn't reach the main door to the greenhouse in time—nor could they escape the compound through the way they'd come before it crumbled beneath them. Grabbing her hand in a rush of hysteria, hoping that he could get them through the escape tunnel before the wall collapsed, Theo lunged forward as fast as possible through the water. Camille stumbled along behind him, screaming at him, but he heard nothing more than the loud blast of rock and metal raining down from above.

Just as his foot hit the metal grate of the tunnel and he lifted Camille out of the water, the wall behind them split open, and a flood of water jetted toward them. "Run!" Theo bellowed, but it didn't do them much use. The wall of water crashed into them, ripping their legs out from beneath them and hurtling them down the path without care of elbows, fingers, and face; ramming, colliding, and scraping against the edges of the tunnel.

Theo reached the locked gate first, his entire body slamming into the bars with a sickening thud. Camille crashed against him, the water pressing them with unrelenting force into the gated bars.

"What do we do now?" Camille yelled over the rush of water. It cascaded past them in a mad dash for release, the height of the water just above Theo's waist and nearly to Camille's chest. He needed to unlock the gate, but he wasn't confident he could open the bars against the restraining weight of water.

"I need to get the door unlocked."

"*It's locked?*" Camille shrieked, her eyes wide with panic.

The water began to rise, the pressure increasing on them as Theo made for the lock along the right side of the bars. Camille clung to the gate over his shoulder, trying to keep her head above the roaring rush when the water threatened to pull her under.

Locating the chain and lock wrapped around the bars, Theo

tried to pull the metal links apart but struggled to get enough leverage with the water pressing into his back.

"Help me with this!" Theo barked, jerking madly at the stubborn links.

"Move!" Camille said, her voice shaking with a tremor of chill. The water was icy cold and it billowed past them at a rapid speed, leaving their bodies to take the surge of ice against their backs with unrelenting force. Reaching out for the lock, Camille maneuvered herself between Theo and the gate, allowing her to move without having to hold onto the bars for support.

He watched her hand slip into her pack and deftly pull out a small pin, her fingers grasping it in a death grip. She took a deep breath and disappeared beneath the surface of the water as the level of rushing water rose to Theo's upper chest. With her back pressed against his abdomen, he felt her move, shoulders bunched and neck taut.

After what felt like five minutes, she jolted upward, her face breaking the surface with a gasp of air. "I got it. Help me with the chain," she panted as she bobbed up and down in the water, her feet no longer reaching the ground.

The chain came loose from the bars in a clang of metal, the links disappearing in the rush of water. Theo pushed against the bars to wrench open the passage, his arms straining with effort. It wouldn't budge. Camille braced her foot on the wall next to his, and together they shoved against the stubborn metal as the water rose even further. His head bumped along the roof of the tunnel, and he took a final gasp of air as the rushing water engulfed them and the bars twitched apart.

Without any remaining headspace, they heaved apart the bars, forcing the hinges to move. With a mere foot of space to squeeze between, Theo grasped Camille and wrapped her legs around his middle before they plunged through the opening, the surge of water shooting them down the tunnel into the depths of the passageway.

The water was cold—downright *frigid* if Theo allowed his brain to register the icy fingers encircling him. He could feel the bump and tremor of shivering shakes emulating from Camille's petite form, and he clutched onto her in reassurance. They catapulted in wild circles, his elbows, head, and back scraping against the lining of the tunnel with unforgiving force. Despite the blur of water surrounding them, he could see a brightness at the end of the passage, and his lungs burned with the need to breathe. When they reached the tunnel end, the current shot them through a narrowed archway and into the open stillness of a vast underground lake.

Their bodies flew several feet through the air before crashing into the surface of the lake, sending them through the inky water at a breakneck speed. Disentangling their bodies, Theo swam toward the surface, desperate for air. His face broke the surface, and he gasped with relief as air surged into his burning lungs. He gulped it greedily, for a moment dizzily unfocused and unable to think past breathing and keeping his head above water.

"Camille!" He bellowed on a gasp of oxygen, his mind and focus returning to him in a sudden pang of terror. Treading water in the expansive, inky lake, he desperately searched for her in every direction. Dread crept over his skin, and his mouth immediately went dry in panic. Bitter cold water surrounded his furiously churning limbs as he called for her again, "Camille! Where are you?"

"CAMILLE!" Theo screamed, his voice hoarse with dread.

A stitching pain stabbed into his abdomen as his panic shifted into high gear. What if she'd collided with the edges of the tunnel and hit her head? She could be beneath the water, struggling to breathe and yet unaware that she was about to drown.

"Here," she replied weakly, her head bobbing several feet behind him, just out from beneath the fall of water shooting from the tunnel. His heart hammering in the cavity of his chest, Theo heaved a sigh of relief.

He swam toward her, his arms and legs wind-milling easily through the water despite the heavy weight of terror still ricocheting through his body. Reaching her in a few seconds, he grasped her face and kissed her soundly, his legs kicking wildly beneath the surface to keep them afloat. "Dear Ma'Nada, I thought I'd lost you."

She smiled as their lips parted, the heat of her breathe fanning across his cheeks. "I thought I'd lost myself," she replied with a blue-lipped grin. His fingers entwined in the thick mat of her hair as he yanked her to him, their bodies sliding against each other beneath the surface of the water. He felt her chatter and twitch, but she clung to him as he did her for a few minutes of needed reassurance. They weren't lost; they had each other.

"I'm here," Theo found himself repeating, his cheek pressed firmly to hers as he held her. "I'm here."

She pulled back, lips quivering, and smiled at him. "Perhaps we should keep moving?"

He nodded, almost regretful to leave the fleeting moment, but they had little time left and needed to be moving if they were going to survive the night. They swam to the edge of the lake, the temperature of the air not much warmer than the water they moved through. Several torches lit the underground space, but it was sparse and dim, leaving their surroundings in shadow with nothing more than a sliver of orange to guide their way. Inky water sloshed against the ground as they emerged, the distant expanse of the lake disappearing into shadow behind them and jagged, angry stone teeth leering at them from overhead.

"Are we still in the compound?" Camille asked, shaking her limbs dry and ringing out her hair. Water pooled in black puddles on the stone around her feet as she shivered.

Appearing like a shadow on the ground at her feet, Neeko sidled up to her legs, entwining his body around her ankles as he cooed a sound of relief at the sight of her. Bending down, her face and hair dripping water all over his fur, Camille pressed her nose into the crook of the cat's neck and kissed him soundly several times before running her fingers over his ears again and again.

"I'm glad to see you can swim, too," Camille said with a brilliant smile, her straight white teeth a pearly glow in the dim torchlight. Despite Theo's slight pang of jealousy over the cat's immense fondness and reciprocated affection he had with Camille, he smiled at the intimacy. She may not outwardly show him love, but it was a relief to know that she could. Her memories of him might be few and far between, and she may never remember who he was or what they had been, but at least he knew her ability to show love had not been taken from her.

She was there—somewhere inside the broken membrane of her fractured self—and he would do whatever it took to find her again. Theo fought the urge to cradle her close and warm her up as he watched her fingers tremble while righting her weapons and hoisting her soggy pack onto her back. He knew the luxury of touching her wasn't something he could afford, despite how much he needed it.

Neeko shook out his coat, emitting a low purr as he headed

toward the cave opening.

"Still underground, and still in danger," Theo said, his voice clipped and as straight-forward as possible. She glanced at him, her mouth open in a pout-like bow, seemingly on the verge of saying something, but she remained silent. "Come on, we need to keep moving."

Camille nodded, ducking her head and eyes to the ground as she moved past him in pursuit of Neeko. Theo shook the droplets from his own hair and checked that he still had all his weapons, then took off at a jog up the steep slope of the cave after them. They had precious little time before the compound would collapse, and he didn't want to be underground when it did.

CHAPTER SIXTEEN
DEFIANCE

It wasn't a quick slaughter; it was a bloody, drawn-out battle. The first round of Chimera ripped past their hunkered positions, blasting through the tall grass like battle rams through thin sheets of paper into the main square of the village. After the Chimera came the Equestrians, and though Vesyon led his troops around behind them, their efforts were unnecessary—most of LeMarc's forces filed straight into the village like flies to a buzzing lamplight.

The truth remained, however, that there were just *too many* of them. The Equestrians scuttled across the damp ground, their boots marking out endless paths of forward motion like the ever-persistent march of ants. It seemed impossible to knock down their lines. Even if they decimated several hundred soldiers during the explosion, the Rogues would still be vastly outnumbered.

Two of the larger warships held back, firing with everything they had, killing Rogues and Equestrians alike. Bodies became the only barrier against the incoming swarm of beasts and cannon fire, a wall of matted, bloodied fur or tender flesh in uniforms painted the bright red of freshly drawn blood. There was no hope of winning; they just needed to push as many into the compound as possible before running like mad in the opposite direction and hoping to survive the night.

Vesyon pivoted toward an incoming Equestrian and flayed the man's chest wide open, spraying the ground with crimson. He watched as the soldier fell backward, mouth agape, his final gasping breath and familiar wide eyes of unbelieving shock locked on Vesyon's face. It made little sense to Vesyon—most of these men were young soldiers, barely old enough to have experienced war, let alone a battle of such proportions. The men dressed in black and red were little more than moving bodies at this point, flinging themselves at Vesyon's sword and him powerless to stop their trajectory toward death. He wondered if the men were genuinely loyal to the crown or if the High King, being a manipulative ruler, dangled the prize of their lives over their naïve heads. The outcome; one more body in a pack of pure innocence.

The pang of loss struck him across the chest as another soldier swung wildly at his head, missing by more than a foot. Vesyon scanned the mountain line where Camille and Theo were to exit for the millionth time, but they were nowhere to be seen. He knew that if she had appeared on the battlefield, she would have been noticed by now—a red beacon in the center of chaos.

A black stallion covered in blood charged toward him, his owner no longer seated across the top but draped to one side, his head gushing blood over its front flank. Sharp black eyes peered manically at Vesyon as the beast reared up, dislodging its owner to the ground in squelching *splat*.

"You!" Phillip bellowed to a soldier just right of Vesyon. "Take that stallion and ride to White Wall. Langhorn isn't prepared for this. Not if we are to follow. Send word to Sierra Village as soon as you get there. We're going to need back up."

"General, the frontline is broken," the soldier replied in a sharp bark. "I'm needed there to hold the line."

Phillip shook his head vehemently. "No soldier, I need you to warn White Wall. Langhorn needs to be prepared if the fight moves his direction and I have a feeling this won't be the end of it."

The young soldier gripped his sword with grim acceptance, grabbing the blood-slicked reigns from Phillip's hand before hoisting himself up into the saddle. Vesyon watched the soldier's back as he rode past the line of fire and straight out of the battle as though nothing could touch him. Perhaps one of them would live, Vesyon thought optimistically, but as the swarm of Chimera closed in on his location, his thoughts returned to Camille.

"Where *is* she?!" Vesyon asked himself as his blade cut a wide arc, severing multiple limbs from screaming Equestrians. His rising kill number was starting to weigh on his conscience much more than it usually did. It was one thing to decimate a herd of Chimera, but far different when they were weak, ill-experienced Asperians.

"Camille or Charlie? I haven't seen either of them," Phillip grunted, sinking his sword into an unusually large Equestrian's throat.

It was impossible to keep the mention of Camille from sending Vesyon's stomach into knots. There was no *not* thinking about her—she was everywhere. He should trust that Theo would keep her safe, but it felt like he'd released a child into a burning forest hoping they'd survive intact.

Vesyon turned as another Equestrian charged toward him. His fist connected with the soldier's nose, sending a shiver of impact through his arm as he smashed the bone up into the man's skull. The soldier went rigid and continued forward, falling straight onto his shattered face in the mud.

Beyond the trees just behind their battleground, Vesyon's gaze was pulled toward a glint of light. He saw Charlie charging toward a pack of Chimera, unconcerned about the sharpness of their fangs and claws as she raised her twin handguns high, firing with everything she had. "I see Charlie!" he shouted at Phillip, pointing with the tip of his sword. He was becoming increasingly worried about the sheer number of beasts surrounding them—never in all his years of fighting had he seen so many.

A thunderous explosion rent through the air just behind them as cannon fire struck one of the main buildings of the village. Red and orange flames billowed into the sky, a blast of heat and smoke so acrid it made Vesyon's eyes water. He felt the reverberation through the ground at his feet, a terrifying shake warning him of what was to come. Most of the buildings in the village square that weren't made of stone or brick had caught fire, sending billowing black smoke trails up to the thick grey clouds that hung low and bloated, belching a constant mist of frigid water on their heads.

"We can't wait for her any longer, Captain. We need to evacuate!"

As the moon shifted behind the layers of clouds, dipping below the horizon, the lights of Romeo Village flickered on full blast. The last beacon of hope surrounded by catastrophe.

Glancing around at the remaining troops on hand, he couldn't argue with Phillip's logic, despite the heavy weight of terror careening through his insides like a hungry eel. "The warning alarm hasn't gone off yet Phillip, we can't abandon our hold yet!" He knew Phillip understood his true meaning: he couldn't leave until he saw Camille. Having kept a close eye on the path down the mountainside, and in proximity to where Theo would lead her away from the line of fight, Vesyon was ready to go the second he saw her. His plan had worked as well as it was going to and Phillip was right, they needed to leave.

"We don't have a choice," Phillip replied, taking on two Equestrians that charged his direction. Vesyon grabbed one of the soldiers by the back of his head before plunging his sword straight through his back, low enough to plow past the ribs and straight up through the kidney. The Equestrian slumped in a heap at his feet, face slackened and dead on impact.

The lights of the village flickered again in a zip of color—orange, red, and yellow—before dying out completely. It was too late. Their count down and fuse would never go off without electricity to send the final message to detonate.

"We'll have to set it by hand," Vesyon barked loud enough for Phillip to hear.

The General's eyes flicked to the compound and back to Vesyon, his face a ragged mask of confidence. That facade shattered as his gaze flew to the ridge over Vesyon's shoulder. Vesyon turned in time to see Charlie's body fly several feet before crashing into the rocky hillside by a ravenous Chimera.

"*Go!*" Vesyon commanded Phillip, who had charged toward his daughter immediately.

"Get to the compound, Captain! Set the fuses! As soon as you're out, I'll call for the evacuation!" he called over his shoulder before disappearing amongst the mayhem.

Vesyon hesitated, glancing around at the mass destruction of the village and the many soldiers nearest him. He should stay and help the Rogues force more Equestrians into the area before they abandoned the grounds, but he had to ensure the explosion *would* happen—even if he were caught in the crossfire.

Vesyon raced toward the south side of the village, his boots slipping and sliding through the mud and snow-slicked ground. He felt unbalanced and uncoordinated, using his sword to steady himself as much as he could manage. He charged down a steep slope just east of his destination, hoping to loop around the back side and slip in without notice. He was relieved to find his path wasn't yet crawling with Chimera or Equestrians. Sliding through a narrow passageway along the outskirts of the square, he was in the compound within a few minutes.

Glowing orange lamps lit his way in the black corridor, his heavy boots skidding to a halt just outside the electrical room: a small closet filled to the brim with fuses connected to the entirety of Romeo Village. Each wire had a purpose and sent electricity to a specific location. He'd rigged the room several months ago with the fuses needed to set off the compound—each would fall in line after the countdown was complete. Without the countdown ticking away the seconds, however, Vesyon would have to set the delay switch off by hand. It would give him little time to escape the surrounding village—fifteen minutes if he calculated correctly.

Trying not to think of Camille stuck in the depths of the compound, Vesyon yanked the wires out, fumbling through the multi-colored metal pieces careful not to touch any of them with his bare hands. Locating the one he needed, with dagger poised to cut the wire, he stopped moving as he heard mumbled voices approached just outside the door.

"What do you mean you failed?!"

"I went to collect the Ephidra Lily, as the King Regent requested, but it wasn't down there. I sent the Chimera after them both, but they escaped," Acher said, his voice clearly distinguishable through the hollow door.

"It's a vault—how many exits can there possibly be?"

"Well," Acher squeaked, "there's more than one obviously."

A loud huff of frustration was followed by a harsh slap and a moan of pain. "Where?!"

Acher didn't respond at first, but another heavy blow got him talking. It sounded like knuckles crunching into delicate cartilage. No doubt Acher had a broken nose by this point.

"In the river tunnel," Acher mumbled through what sounded like a mouth full of blood.

"Soldier," the Equestrian barked at his comrades. "Take this pathetic traitor into the village square."

Hunched silently in the claustrophobic space, Vesyon had half a mind to duck out of the door and wring Acher's neck himself. The traitorous bastard deserved it no less, but as his fists bunched together, he thought better of it. Acher would be going to the village square—good riddance. It would go up in smoke and flame and crumble beneath his feet. Hopefully, it would be the last of him.

"To the King Regent sir?"

"No, the Night Raves will be there shortly and will know what to do with him."

Vesyon had no idea what a Night Rave was, but a nagging sense of dread burned like fire on his skin, sending a ripple of heat across his flesh. The horrid floral scent of an unknown origin screamed through his olfactory memory, and he froze in terror. He didn't want to believe it, didn't want to admit that he'd been wrong. Vesyon had created the lie of Ephidra Lily to entice LeMarc, to force him into the light again. Perhaps he'd been wrong to push so hard. If he was right about what a Night Rave *was*, they were in far deeper waters than he'd initially thought.

Vesyon waited a few beats for the men outside to walk farther away before digging the sharpened edge of his dagger into the wire he'd wiggled away from its confinement. He had little time to escape, but it was possible. His fastest time was three minutes and twenty-three seconds from the wire room to the door, and then he would have less than ten minutes to escape the village altogether. Taking one final, deep breath, Vesyon yanked the blade backward, effectively slicing the wire in two.

He crept out of the room with haste and turned toward the exit, immediately finding himself cornered by three Chimera.

"Shiat," he muttered. "Perfect timing, as always."

They growled in response, heavy spittle and drool slipping off their protruding jowls before splattering against the floor.

It's now or never, he thought as he dove forward, sliding between the legs of one Chimera to gain purchase on the opposite side.

Vesyon took off running, the three hungry Chimera on his tail. The hallways seemed longer and windier as he sprinted from narrow passage to narrow passage, zig-zagging his way through a maze of rock, stone, steel, and tile. Any second, the lights inside would blink off, and he'd be a goner, trapped inside the compound until it imploded on itself. His legs churned wildly at the idea, propelling him through the corridors at a rapid pace. Vesyon located the exit door at the end of the hallway. Blocking the door was another Chimera, swatting at the closed metal door as if trying to break through the four inches of steel. The Chimera whined pitifully, a sound Vesyon had never heard before.

"Hey!" Vesyon said as he ran closer, trying to get the Chimera's attention. "Come get me beast, I'm here for the taking!"

The Chimera snarled but didn't move.

For Vesyon to make it out alive, he needed to get through that door, and there was no way this Chimera was going to stop him. "*Move*, you big lump!"

That kicked the Chimera into gear. It reared up, lunging wildly at him as Vesyon launched himself around the beast's body. One solid front paw grasped hold of Vesyon midair, inadvertently flinging him toward the metal slab door. Vesyon braced for the impact of heavy steel against his Praetorian body, praying the collision wouldn't knock him off kilter so that he might not be able to escape.

***

Her clothing stuck to her body, and yet she wasn't cold in the least. She felt a thrumming warmth as they walked through the silent confines of the cave together, arms brushing against each other as they moved. There was no way to say what it was that she felt, but the minute her face had broken the surface of the lake below the compound, the first thought in her mind had been, *where is Theo?*

There was no sense lying to herself about the torrent of emotion boiling through her. Theo was not to be ignored, nor were the memories that flooded into her system. Glancing over at him as they walked, she explored the angles of his face, and the lines of worry etched into his brow. Her fingers itched to press down the creases of concern at the edges of his eyes, but she clenched her fists and kept them at her sides.

It wasn't the time to dive into their past, as much as she felt the sudden urge to do so, which also felt peculiar and strange. Theo's fingers brushed against the edge of her hand, and he took a step over a large rock, extending a hand to help her over the protruding barrier on their path. It wasn't needed, she could manage on her own, but she accepted the fingers stretched out before her and grasped hold. Their eyes connected and they paused for a mere moment, taking in each other's features and drinking in the single moment of silence together.

"I won't let anything happen to you, Camille. I'll always protect you."

"Always is a very long time, Theodore," Camille replied, softly jesting but also desperately needing a way to focus on him and not her sudden desire to break apart into tears of fear and worry.

He smiled at her use of his full name, pulled her close to his chest and kissed her temple gently. "There will never be enough time for me when it comes to being with you, my love."

She smiled then, words failing her as a blossoming warmth turned into a roaring fire within her chest.

"Let's go," he said with finality, obviously pained to have to pull away, but focused with clear intent on getting her to safety and as far away from the battle as possible.

Camille wasn't sure what to expect as Theo led her through the darkened cave entrance and out across the damp grassy plateau of the mountainside. The open fields below their perch were crawling with Chimera, Rogues, and Equestrians—hundreds dead but still hundreds more engaged in battle.

"That looks promising," Theo said, placing both hands on the weapons at his sides.

The sharp, chilly air bit into the lining of Camille's nose as she tried to take in what they were about to do next. The village was blazing with the hungry lick of fire, and as they watched the flames dance in eerie grace, the wailing cry of the warning alarm sounded. The fuses had been set, and they had fifteen minutes to escape the grounds. The Rogues would begin their mass exodus as well, and, hopefully, everyone would make it to safety before Romeo Village was no more.

"We need to get out of here," Theo said, shifting his weight and readying to go.

"Wait," Camille said, grasping his wrist, "look, over there!"

In the center of the village square where the fire remained, Metus was directing an Equestrian who led a line of shackled prisoners behind him. Even from a distance, she knew it was Metus with his perfectly groomed blonde hair and starkly clean uniform.

Theo shook his head ardently. "That's the *last* place we're going, Cam. We have fourteen minutes tops before the entire village goes up in flames. Absolutely not!"

"We can't just leave them to die! Those are Rogues, yes?"

Camille stood her ground, unwilling to accept the fact that any man would die because of her sudden appearance at Romeo. Her presence may not be the reason for the battle, but neither had it slowed down the quick precession of the High King's army.

Her words of compassion didn't seem to have any effect on Theo, who continued to edge in the opposite direction, away from the pandemonium of the battlefield.

"I can't let them die," Camille said with determination, breaking away from Theo and Neeko.

Theo pursued her, grasping her at the elbow with such harshness that she flinched. "What are you doing?" She barked out at him.

He flinched at her tone, but only slightly. "There's nothing you can do Cam. *Please*, stop!" The pleading panic swimming in his eyes did nothing to change her mind.

"They have no way to survive Theo, I have to help them."

"We're out of time, we have to leave. Now!"

"No," she said softly, her mind flashing with memories of those she'd killed in Charlie Town. Too many had died at the edge of her sword. She needed to know that she *could* save them, even if it meant dying alongside them if she to failed.

"I won't let them die. Not like this. And definitely not alone." She yanked her dagger free of its holster and carefully made her way down the rocky cliff side to the village square, not looking back to see if Theo followed.

CHAPTER SEVENTEEN
DESTRUCTION OF THE UNDERGROUND

"Success?"

Vesyon squinted through a single scrunched eye to see Phillip towering over him, covered in black Chimera blood. Sweat streamed down either side of Phillip's reddened, dirt-streaked face but it was the large puncture wound on his left upper arm that caught Vesyon's attention.

He lurched upwards in the muddied grass—he hadn't collided with the door, as Phillip had been opening it in that very same moment. Which meant—

"Close the door!" Vesyon yelled, gesturing at the Chimera barreling down the corridor about to descend.

Phillip slammed it shut just in time, sealing the beasts in as they yipped and growled on the other side.

"How the hell did you make it out?" Phillip gasped, seeming to struggle for each breath. Vesyon eyed the General warily, taking in every facet of Phillip's complexion and dilated pupils. Despite the darkened sky and dimly lit surroundings, Vesyon could see the penetrating symptoms of Chimera poisoning already taking hold within him.

"The fuses are set," Vesyon said quietly. "We have ten minutes to get out of here."

"Yes, we heard the alarm. We need to get the remaining men out; there's something else out there," Phillip said, swallowing loudly and beginning to wheeze.

Vesyon nodded; the floral scent he'd smelled before floated back through his senses. It was something he'd never encountered, not in battle. Every fiber in his Praetorian being screamed with worry as he pressed through the tree line, making his way beside Phillip back toward their men. With every footstep, every motion pushing him forward, Vesyon began to accept the inevitability of the evening. They were going to lose far more than what they'd bargained for. He wasn't sure now that it *had* been worth it.

His eyes shifted back toward the town square as the weight of reality began to set in. He had lost so much in his fight against the kingdom—family, friends, loved ones—but he kept pushing forward because he knew his goal would eat away at him until he reached it. More than anything in the world, he wanted to return to his home in White Wall, but he'd lose much more in the months to come for that to become a possibility. Vesyon glanced over at the puce tone of Phillip's skin and forced his emotions down. They both knew Phillip had only hours.

Cannon fire flew in every direction, reaching deafening heights as they pressed on through the snow-slicked grassy knolls. The wind whipped against their faces in a constant mist, sending the chill of their surroundings straight down to their bones. Phillip dodged and swayed, hammering at any Equestrian who stood in his way, but he was quickly losing the battle of remaining conscious.

"You need treatment!" Vesyon cried over the din.

"What for?" Phillip retorted, completely ignoring the suggestion. Turning his body away from an oncoming blast of shrapnel, Phillip groaned as he moved, every motion an obvious task to accomplish. "Most of the men Metus brought with him are standing guard at the perimeter. You can't go north or west as planned; you'll need to double back south and get to White Wall that way."

Vesyon blanched, noticing Phillip's use of *you* instead of *we*. "South? Are you sure that's a good idea?" He would have to ride through the open grasslands along the barrier wall of Dwaa without hope of cover before crossing over the Syene River. It wasn't an option Vesyon felt comfortable with, but he had little choice left.

"There's no other way," Phillip said. "Camille and Theo haven't been spotted yet, and you and my men can't wait any longer. You will have to regroup with them in White Wall."

"Can't we just—"

"Incoming!" Phillip screamed as the line broke and seven Chimera hurdled toward them.

The ground was almost impossible to traverse with muddied grass and puddles of gore. Vesyon slipped as a Chimera stormed close, snarling with deadly intention. Phillip jumped in front of Vesyon, and the beast's jaw snapped down with ferocity on his upper arm.

The General's scream sang through the air like an arrow loosed, and time seemed to stop as the Chimera's teeth dug hungrily into Phillip's flesh. Vesyon barely caught him as he slumped headfirst toward the ground but managed to crook his arm under his chest in time to keep Phillip on his feet.

Charlie charged forward out of nowhere, a battle cry escaping her blood-slicked lips. Her matted brown hair flew out behind her like an incoming flag of protection. With a swift yank of her sword, she sliced the Chimera's head clean off, spraying everyone with blood and bone.

With her face screwed up and mouth wide in a silent scream, she hacked away at the unmoving carcass. She didn't stop until the Chimera that had attacked her father was obliterated—a pile of fur and organs at her feet. Vesyon pushed up from the ground as he slid Phillip over to his side and Charlie rushed toward them.

"Is he ok?"

"He's breathing," Vesyon replied, their eyes meeting for a moment to convey the truth of what he meant. *He's breathing—for now.*

She blanched, set her jaw in understanding, and leaned over him, checking the heat of his skin and color of his eyes as though he wasn't as bad as he appeared to be. In watching her reaction, Vesyon was unable to miss several distant Chimera leaning over their fallen brethren—as Charlie was doing with Phillip.

"Are they mourning?" he asked aloud to himself, narrowing his eyes in bewildered shock. More than once during the battle, he'd seen the creatures express emotion in an unnerving way. The beasts hadn't just returned in full force from the original outbreak—they were evolving.

As Vesyon helped Phillip to his feet beside Charlie, he was immediately assaulted by a floral bouquet so intense he nearly gagged. He looked across the flat expanse of trampled grass and weeds to see a strikingly tall woman dressed from her neckline to the tops of her boots in thick red leather. Her raven hair was yanked back in a cluster of braids, and her smooth, olive skin seemed to glow against the bloated black clouds overhead. Her red leather chest protector was clamped securely in place and decorated with shiny gold buckles that winked like flickering fire as she moved. She wasn't scowling or nervous—no, her complexion was smooth, her lips relaxed, her seemingly crystalline blue eyes bright with the ease of a veteran warrior.

Vesyon surged forward, his sword raised high, angling toward her face. Instead of meeting his blade with one of her own, the woman pointed a short black cylinder at him, and a line of Chimera charged his direction, their fallen companions no longer their concern.

The woman reached down and lifted Charlie by the neck, bringing them face-to-face. Vesyon couldn't hear what the woman said to her as he fought off the group of Chimera, but after several seconds the woman in red tossed Charlie aside like a rag doll, no longer wanting to touch the girl or waste a second to rip the life out of her chest.

The woman's icy eyes scanned the battleground until they landed on Vesyon. She moved with steady purpose, the Chimera remaining stoic at her sides like harmless puppies. She stopped just out of reach of his sword, holding the black cylinder sparking with sinister intent.

"Where is she, Praetorian?"

Vesyon rose to his full height, only an inch over hers. "Who?" The single word expelled from his chest on a heavy exhalation of air. He wasn't exhausted, but he felt a weariness deep in his bones that made it difficult to breathe.

She snarled, her eyes flitting from icy blue to a deep vivid red. "Don't play with me, Vesyon. You know who we came here for."

He winced as his name flowed from her perfectly painted lips. Who was she—or more appropriately, *what* was she? The floral scent was overpowering with her closeness, mixed with something feral and purely animalistic. She wasn't an Asperian, though neither was she a Praetorian. He was staring into the eyes of LeMarc's future, and he shuddered at the realization.

"Where. Is. Camille?" she demanded, surging toward him with a hand to his neck. She slammed him into the muck. She wasn't just sturdy; she was a formidable force he had no chance of stopping.

232

She touched the black cylinder to his chest, and he was paralyzed as jolts of electricity raced through his entire body.

"Pathetic," the woman said venomously when she removed the cylinder and Vesyon collapsed into the squish of mud at his back. "It's no wonder the High King exiled you. He needs someone more substantial by his side, and you obviously aren't capable of fulfilling his needs like I am."

White spots rained before his eyes as he blinked through the dizziness. "Night Rave?" Vesyon whispered, his mind barely able to grasp what his Praetorian senses had already confirmed.

"Yes," she replied with a withering red glare before turning on her heel toward the village square, "but more importantly: *your replacement.*"

Vesyon scrambled unsteadily to his feet, but the woman was already gone. *He needed to find Camille before she did.*

Nearby Charlie was crawling through the mud to her father, mumbling empty words of blind hope as she fumbled through her pocket with manic persistence. Finding what she was searching for, she ripped off the protective seal and jammed the sharpened end of their antidote packs into Phillip's bared chest. It wouldn't stop the transformation, or remove the venom coursing through Phillip's body, but it would give them a few minutes of borrowed time to say their last words of goodbye.

"Let's get him out of here," Vesyon said thickly around the massive lump of fear lodged deep in his throat. Glancing toward the now-crumbling village square, he searched for the woman in red to be sure she was heading toward the center of destruction. They had precious minutes left until the compound would collapse upon itself; it wasn't a time to dally.

He found the Night Rave walking along the outer wall on the east side of the grounds, and managed a small smile knowing the comfort of what she was about to endure. His stomach then suddenly dropped like a lead ball, a fearful groan escaping his throat unlike anything he'd ever heard before.

He watched the spark of red hair duck in and out of the shadows, and then lean over a line of shackled Rogues. Even with her face hidden away from his line of sight, he knew it was her; could see it in the gentle slope of her shoulders and delicate long-fingered hands. *Camille had made it out of the compound,* he thought with a flood of relief, but this was quickly followed with the hollowed dread of *where* she was, and what was about to happen.

He raced toward her, boots trampling through the snow and mud without regard of himself or his surroundings. Chimera and Equestrians seemed to melt from his vision as he focused entirely on the spark and sizzle of her hair, the surrounding flames roaring with a warning. He had to get to her, had to pull her away from the structures he knew would crumble and melt like butter beneath her feet.

"Camille!" Vesyon yelled, but there was no way she could hear him—no way he could help her escape the fate that fast approached.

Don't lose her, my sweet girl, she is the only thing I have left in this world. He heard the soft, gentle voice of Jesabelle whisper in his ear as time around him slowed down. His legs felt like lead in his boots, but he kept moving, hoping, begging to any of the gods that would listen to him: *please don't let her die.* The clangor of swords and boom of cannon melted away, the shouts of battle became a droning hum in the background. His eyes remained glued on Camille's hunched form.

"I won't lose her, my love; I will protect her with every last fiber of my being," Vesyon said, repeating his final promise to Jesabelle like a prayer. He wouldn't let anything happen to Camille, not today. He was already losing Phillip and had lost the love of his life years ago; he wasn't going to let Camille slip out of his grasp—he couldn't.

"No!" he bellowed as the first rumbling explosion shook the ground beneath his feet. Tears unknowingly streamed down his cheeks, but it was far too late to stop the trajectory of his plan.

***

"Cam, we've gotta go!" Theo bellowed over the turmoil in the square. The fire was moving closer, the hungry mouth of flames like a groaning monster consuming everything in its path.

"Go then!" she shot back. "I won't let these soldiers die for no reason. I *will* save them, damn it!"

Camille gripped one of the soldier's wrists and inspected his shackles: just like the rest of them, they were rusted shut. As much as she tried, she couldn't rip them apart with her bare hands.

The men were urging her to leave them, too—all of them

Rogues, willing to die in exchange for her safety. It was heartbreaking to see the terror in their eyes as they urged her to run, begged her to leave them behind in their chains.

"It's okay, Camille—we know who you are, we've heard the stories," the young man before her said. "We're willing to die for what you started."

His wide blue eyes and scruffy blonde hair reminded her of Lunci, and she ached to brush it out of his face the way she'd done for Lunci so many times before. His gentle words stabbed at her heart, penetrating to the depths of her soul. *It was her fault.* These men fought for a cause she'd unknowingly started, a moment that she barely remembered. A day that would haunt her for days and years to come.

Camille grabbed the iron peg keeping the soldier attached to the wall and yanked on it with everything she had. Her fingers screamed for mercy, but she clung to the metal with fierce determination. With a final cry, Camille managed to wrench it from the stone with a satisfying *clunk*. She whipped around to face Theo, grinning victoriously. She could do this, she could rip them all free, and they could run as one unit. "I won't let you die, not like this. Do you hear me?"

"O-okay," said the Rogue, his expression transforming from the grim acceptance of death to one of renewed hope.

She began to tear at the pegs lining the stone wall, yanking on the chains with everything she had until they broke free. Theo started at the opposite end, while Neeko stood guard, his jaguar eyes on the watch for incoming attacks. Camille reached the final peg and pulled, her hands now bleeding from the effort, blackened smoke filling her lungs and threatening to suffocate her. The last one held fast, drilled so deep into the stone wall that she could barely keep her grip.

"It won't budge," she cried, tears flowing freely down her cheeks in sudden panic, "I can't, it's not moving!"

The man sitting on the ground nodded his head once, the stark pores of his face like polka dots in the smear of dirt across his cheeks. Reaching up with a shackled hand, he placed a calloused palm against her arm and smiled. "I've lived a full life dear child," the elderly man said, his voice a raspy, grating noise. Camille shook her head, but his hand remained firm. "You've done what you can, now get them out of here."

Theo pried the chain connecting the man to the others apart, and the shackled Rogues took off at a clipped run.

"I can save you," Camille begged. Tears flowed down her cheeks in a rush as she tugged against the shackle connecting the man to the wall. "I can keep trying." Smoke caught in her throat and made her choke, but she ignored the stinging pain and the flow of salty wetness streaming down her face.

"No; you must go," the elderly man said. His voice was a harsh whisper in the density of smoke, but she heard the tremor of panic beneath his determined layer of courage. "I'm not your responsibility, and this isn't your fault."

"I'm sorry," Camille said in despair, the blunt resignation of his life hollowing out all remaining words in her throat.

"We all have our time, my dear. And now isn't yours!"

Her eyes met his through a cloud of debris and sediment, the shaky cobblestone ground rumbling underfoot.

"Camille!" Theo bellowed from over her shoulder.

She felt a hand on her arm yanking her backward and onto her feet before another hand pressed her head to the warming heat of Theo's chest.

A loud, bursting wave exploded just behind them, sending flames and debris rocketing upwards. Camille was flung into the opposite building with a cloud of heat pressing into her exposed flesh. Her head slammed into the stone wall as she landed, sending a hot white light blasting through her vision before a thundering mass of crumbling stone, metal, and wood rained down from the skies.

CHAPTER EIGHTEEN
FAREWELL

"Captain! Did you hear me?" A soldier screamed at Vesyon over the blast of the explosion emitting from the compound. He stood like a glazed statue, his face growing hot from a cloud of fire and ash as he stared at the damage.

In Vesyon's haste to get to Camille, he hadn't heard Charlie scream at him to stop, hadn't felt her hands on his arm yanking him backward. He hadn't noticed when she jumped on his back and wrestled him to the ground. Vesyon was positive she'd acted on orders from Phillip—if not, she would have been more upset about the broken nose Vesyon had given her while trying to wrestle free of her grasp. The village grounds had catapulted into the air, the force of the explosion blasting his cheeks with bitter warmth as his face rose from the mud-slicked grass he'd landed in.

He had kicked Charlie unceremoniously off him, meaning to continue into the village, uncaring that the town square would be nothing but smoldering rock and crumbling buildings. There was no thought behind his actions; he just knew he needed to find Camille. Phillip's blood-soaked hand on his shoulder stopped him.

"She's gone Vesyon; we need to keep moving. Please," the General pleaded.

The cannon fire that had momentarily ceased picked up its cadence and Vesyon snapped back into his surroundings with a roar of frustration. His heart crumbled beneath his chest plate, a fierce stab of desolation crashing into him with a force he hadn't felt since losing Jesabelle.

Phillip placed a slick, blood-soaked hand on the back of Vesyon's neck and leaned into him, his legs barely able to hold him upright. "She's gone," Phillip repeated. "And I will be too, Captain. Please, I need you to stay with me here."

Vesyon nodded, uncertain of what else to do. He had to continue, he had to fight back—Vesyon would slowly and methodically kill LeMarc. The satisfaction of watching him perish would be the *only* salve to the heartache and anger surging through his body.

"Captain?" one of the Rogues screamed into his ear.

Vesyon looked at the brown-haired soldier, his chocolate eyes wide with sharp attention. The young man didn't seem afraid or worried, only determined to continue with the orders he'd been given.

"Yes?" Vesyon replied, his stare returning to the bursting explosions within the village.

"The General has given me orders to take the remaining men and head out. We are to relocate to White Wall, sir."

Vesyon nodded his entire body numb.

"Are you coming with us, Captain?" The Rogue screamed impatiently.

Vesyon turned to see Charlie administering another injection of antidote into Phillip's chest. Phillip had a single pack left, and once the venom finished its course through Phillip's veins there would be no stopping the outcome. Staying behind would do nothing to help the rebel cause; Romeo was gone and so was Camille.

"Head out with the remaining Rogues," Vesyon said to the young man eager to move, "I will catch up with you as soon as I can." The young man wavered for a mere moment, his eyes flitting to the General before nodding agreement to Vesyon's orders.

Vesyon should leave—he knew he should—but following through with the logical plan felt impossible. His boots remained glued to the spot, staring at the village square and begging to see her face just one last time.

***

She felt the soft tufts of Neeko's fur against her forearm, his body limp and unmoving. Theo had landed a few yards away, his hunched form groaning in pain. Another blast rang out on the opposite side of Romeo Village, causing her to duck her head, pressing her body over Neeko's. Constant, ringing deafness clouded her head like wads of cotton had been shoved into her ear cavity.

Fire and stone catapulted through the sky, raining debris and chunks of rock throughout the village square around them. She felt the blazing heat of fire close to her skin, almost as though her skin were melting like beeswax off her bones.

Hunching over the lifeless cat's body, Camille cradled his tiny head in her hands. "Neeko?" Camille asked, her voice a stuttering quiver. She felt the lax give of flesh beneath his blood-soaked fur, and her heart almost stopped. Her hand came away red and sticky; his head was bleeding profusely. "Neeko, *please stay with me. Please don't go!*"

Theo twitched upright, and Camille's head swam viciously as she turned to assess his wounds. He swore loudly, a grunting objection to the apparent pains in his head. Theo clutched the backside of his skull, wincing as he touched the swell of his hairline. He crawled on his hands and knees across the desecrated ground, his eyes never leaving hers. Shrapnel had split his cheek with a jagged line, and he had gashes along his neck and the back of his scalp, but he was breathing. He was alive.

"You all right?" he said brokenly, his voice box raspy and tight.

"Yeah," Camille replied, her words surprisingly strong despite the bitter smoke filling her lungs. "Neeko's not."

She bent to gather the small animal to her chest before Theo pulled himself up and leaned down to help her to her feet. With an arm around her waist, he led them through the rubble to the outskirts of the village.

"We need to move faster!" Theo said as they jogged, dodging smoking ruins and fallen Chimera. "This way!"

Another blast shot into the sky as they crossed into the dense grass surrounding the village. Camille glanced back to where the final soldier in chains had been, a man unwaveringly calm in the face of death. His body, still shackled to the wall, was now smoldering ash.

Anger flooded into her bloodstream, and her resulting cry was so savage it sounded more bestial than Asperian. She didn't care what it took to defeat the High King; she wouldn't let him do this again. Even if she died in the process, she was going to fight for Aspera—to fight for their freedom as much as her own.

Cannon fire zoomed loudly in the distance, but the clinking sounds of swords had died off almost entirely. The battle was over, yet neither side had won.

Glancing down at the tiny, fluffy ball in her arms, Camille began to understand why Vesyon had been so focused on keeping her away from the frontlines of battle. She loved Neeko; he'd been her only companion through many lonely days living in Sierra Village, and seeing him so lifeless in her arms made her insides squirm with molten frustration.

"Do you think they evacuated?" She asked as a cannonball zipped over their heads into the village grounds at their back.

"Yes, we need to get out of here."

Camille crunched through the tufts of dead grass, hand on her sword as she watched the shapes of Chimera move toward them in the distance. "We can't go that way!"

"No, we need to—" Theo stopped suddenly at the sound of Neeko mewling in her arms. His furry head swayed upward as though waking from a drug-induced sleep. Bright, yellowed eyes, glassy from the haze of confusion, blinked up at her face but didn't appear to see her at all.

"Hi little guy," she murmured in a rush of relief, looking down into his blood-slicked features. Neeko mewled again, louder this time as he shook his head as though to dislodge a bug, and his mouth stretched wide in a sleepy yawn. Camille set him in the grass, wary of the advancing Chimera.

Neeko took a few woozy steps, and, then, without warning, flexed and grew, his muscles bulging beneath the slick black fur still covered in a mess of blood and dirt. He coughed, grunted, and then growled before shaking his body in a flurry of flying blood and dirt.

"Not-So-Little-Guy," Camille said, smiling and hunching to embrace the jaguar. His body was warm, and covered in splotches of blood and thick globs of mud, but he was alive.

Neeko licked her face, nuzzling her cheek with affection before turning toward the north end of Romeo Village and loping away toward the surge of beasts.

"Follow him!" Theo bellowed, taking up his sword and dagger before lunging after Neeko.

She didn't advance more than a few sprinted steps before two Chimera dove at her, their fangs dripping with venom and paws churning the ground. She downed them in less than three minutes, but their brethren surged around the trio. One would go down, and two more would take its place.

"We need to move toward the east!" Theo hollered over the mass of growls and yips of pain. "Our horses are tethered along the eastern outskirts."

It was slow-going, but Camille held nothing back. She slashed throats and tore out chunks of hair as they charged in close. She kicked and stabbed everything in her proximity, knowing nothing but the never-ending slew of attack. Theo ducked and twisted behind her, narrowly avoiding the onslaught, throwing what weapons he could at the ravenous creatures.

There was a handful of Rogues in the distance faring no better. Camille watched as they too fought viciously, pushing toward the east side of the battlefield. Fending off the slash of teeth and swipe of a claw, she tripped and stepped over many bodies pock-marked in oozing puncture wounds. The ground glistened with the fresh fall of rain, but the liquid that shone was red. It covered the slick tendrils of grass poking through the piles of bodies like fragile flags in a sea of death.

Camille ducked in time to miss the lunge of an unusually large beast, catching the monster along the back of his hind legs with her sword. She whirled to face the Chimera rearing back toward her, but her eye caught sight of Vesyon charging toward her, Phillip and Charlie flanking him.

"Vesyon!" she screamed, though she wasn't sure if it was in welcoming relief or in a flood of panic at seeing the stampede of thundering Chimera behind him. Theo turned in time to see Vesyon and froze in bewildered shock—as did Camille. The Chimera had ceased their attacks on the others and raced toward Camille. Perhaps Vesyon had been wrong: maybe the High King *had* come for her, after all.

Power thrummed wildly through Camille's system, making her feel invincible as she realized she could lead the Chimera away, giving the remaining fighters a chance to escape.

Camille scanned the commotion, finding Neeko battling two Chimera nearby. "Neeko!" she yelled, and with a sharp swipe of his four-inch claws, both beasts were killed, and the jaguar was at her side. "Keep them safe," Camille said, pointing to Vesyon, Theo, Phillip, and Charlie.

His head turned sharply toward her, uncertainty flitting across his features.

"Thank you for protecting me, my friend," she said with a soft pat to the top of Neeko's head. He seemed wary of her words, but only for a moment as she ducked the attacks of Chimera, putting several feet of distance between them.

She turned without another word, not glancing back at Theo or Vesyon, unwilling to risk them stopping her or allowing her mind to keep her from doing what she knew she must.

Ducking under an advancing black beast, Camille ran up the hillside she and Theo had fled. The plateau just outside the cave opening would give her ample height advantage. If she could gain a foot or two over the Chimera, it'd be easier to knock off more at once. As she slapped back every advance of the beast, she began to notice their extreme hesitancy to go in for the kill. They attacked Theo with deadly intent, but with Camille, the Chimera held back. It was making it easier for her to kill them. Even if they'd been ordered not to kill her, she knew they'd pluck her up in an instant and take her straight to the High King if she faltered.

The ground gave way several times under her feet, but Camille dashed through the muddied plains as fast as her legs could carry her. She heard a strangled call from over her shoulder, but she wasn't positive if it was Theo or Vesyon. The air was biting and dense with the chilling mist seeping through the layers of her clothes. She bit down on her lower lip as she acknowledged that this was the end—she'd never see Theo, Vesyon, or Neeko again. She would fight and perhaps lose, but they would make it out alive—they would live. Gripping her sword with intense determination, she crawled up the last towering slope to the cave, and faced the droves of Chimera, screaming as loudly as possible, "*Come and get me!*"

Hundreds of heads twisted up to Camille's location. The beasts moved like a black wave of fur and fangs to pursue her and no one else.

She stared down at the pockmarked battlefield below, a cold trickle of terror snaking down her spine as the Chimera advanced. Reaching for her bow and holstering her sword, Camille took down several Chimera in succession with the snap of her bowline. She picked them off quickly, snagging two with a single shot, but she only had a small handful of arrows left.

"I'm coming, Camille!" someone cried from below, a man's voice, but one she couldn't place.

Another explosion vibrated through the ground, and Camille glanced over to see the high treetops near Romeo Village ablaze with fire. Two of the warships had begun their retreat, but one remained to lay waste to whatever structures were still standing. The entirety of Romeo's topside had crumbled into the depths of the compound, which belched heavy clouds of acrid smoke into the blackened sky.

"Camille!" the man called out again, much closer this time, and Camille spun to find Phillip fighting his way toward her.

He reached her in a matter of minutes, and she immediately saw that something wasn't right—his skin was pale and yellowed, and sweat poured down his face. His left arm and chest were a bloodied mess, and Camille immediately understood why he'd come to her rescue: Phillip had already been bitten.

"Take cover, Camille—get out of here!" Phillip coughed, slicing a Chimera straight up through the gut as it tried to attack Camille from behind.

"No!" Camille said, choking on the words fighting to escape. She'd unknowingly killed Phillip's wife in Charlie Town and now he was fighting for *her* life? "I never got to say how *sorry I am*. To make it up to you and Charlie!"

"You just did," Phillip said through labored breaths, slaying two more Chimera with a determined slice of his sword.

The Chimera numbers had dwindled, and the two of them were cornered against a ledge as the pile of dead bodies grew. She charged one advancing Chimera, her sword moving with such speed she was barely aware of her motions. The metal slashed through it's neck, spraying the ground in a waterfall of blood before the body slumped heavily at her feet.

Surrounded by a wall of bleeding and dead Chimera, silence enveloped them. Sweat dripped down Camille's face in rivers, but she paid it no mind. Her eyes flew to Phillip's, and she trembled with the emotion bubbling up to the surface.

"I remember her face," Camille said softly.

Phillip leaned heavily on his broad sword peering at her trembling expression, his face also dripping in sweat.

One final Chimera lunged over the tower of carcasses toward her, but she notched her final arrow and took aim. It rolled down the heaping pile of dead bodies to land at her feet, purging the last remnants of its life onto her boots.

"She was a beautiful woman. Charlie looks so much like her," Camille continued as Phillip slipped to his knees, unable to stand any longer.

Tears mixed with sweat on her face, dribbling down her cheeks in hot, wet rivers as she darted toward him to keep Phillip from pitching forward on his face. Her words were pointless; she knew it, but she still felt they had to be said. "I didn't know what I was doing. I never meant to hurt them."

"What happened to my wife, to my friends in Charlie Town—it wasn't your fault," Phillip said, hacking up thick chunks of blood and mucus. "I know that. Vesyon knows that. You need to accept it as well."

He lurched forward, scrambling for something in one of his many pockets. He unearthed a flattened, palm-sized bag tipped with a nasty, thorn-like cylinder. He jabbed it into his thigh and emitted a heavy sigh of relief.

Phillip peered up at Camille, his color almost returning to normal. His skin remained clammy, however, and turned red with fever. "It won't last long," he grunted. "I'd get that look of hope off your face, soldier. The antidote only works when you're able to remove the virus."

"Let's go, then! I can carry you," Camille said, reaching to help Phillip up.

He waved her off and shook his head as he swayed backward toward the ground. "He warned me about you," Phillip said, removing his chest protector with a grunt of satisfaction. "I promised myself I'd hate you after everything that's happened, but Vesyon told me I wouldn't be able to resist your charm. By Ma'Nada, he was right for once," he said dryly. "Even after all these years, I look at you and see *her* blazing through your eyes—the same genuine smile and spark of hope."

She stared at him, confused, but his lips twitched with a slight smile. "Your mother," he said, almost choking on the syllables. "You have the same determination to do right, to protect those around you even at the expense of yourself. Jesabelle would be proud of you, proud that you're still fighting."

244

He coughed loudly, spitting copious amounts of blood on the ground. The wound across his chest bloomed with color, and the poison spread like black ink through his veins. His once-bright eyes were now bloodshot, and his curling brown hair stuck to his sweat-slicked forehead. "Camille, please, you have to kill me. I will turn; I can feel it."

Camille shook her head violently. "No, I can't. What about Charlie?"

"She can take care of herself. Please—I don't want her to see me like this." His eyes started to fill with tears, and his skin flushed with the heat of fever.

"What about the antidote? Do you have more?"

Phillip shook his head. "That was my last one."

His eyes were almost entirely glossed over with red; he wouldn't be able to keep the venom at bay much longer. Soon his mind would recoil in agony, and he'd either die or transform into a monstrous beast.

Camille's eyes shot up toward the rim of dead Chimera as Vesyon, Theo, Neeko, and Charlie crested the pile.

"Do it. *Now*," Phillip commanded, placing his dagger in Camille's right hand.

"No!" Charlie screamed as she catapulted over the edge of the barrier wall, lumbering through the bleeding bodies toward Phillip. "Daddy, please! I can save you!"

Camille stared shakily down at Phillip, the dagger in her hand suddenly weighing a hundred pounds.

Phillip's eyes rolled back, and he slumped over, blotchy green face angled up to the misty night sky.

"Daddy, *no*!" Charlie hovered over her father's body, and then looked from Vesyon to Theo in desperation. "Help me, please, help us!"

Vesyon and Theo moved swiftly down the embankment, while Neeko remained above in jaguar form.

"Give me the blade, Camille. Theo, please hold Charlie back," Vesyon said. "The Chimera have moved down the mountain, seemingly having lost Camille's scent, but the Equestrians will be here any minute. We need to leave now while we have the chance to escape."

The venom started to rage through Phillip's veins, and he shook violently as though he was having a seizure. His body bucked and jerked beneath Camille's hand, red oozing from his mouth and nose as though his body was rejecting his own blood.

"No, please, no!" Charlie begged as Theo yanked her back. "You can't do this!"

Camille handed Vesyon the blade and stood, moving closer to the wall of putrid, stinking Chimera flesh to get away from what she was about to witness. Neeko growled from above, his warning loud and clear: The Equestrians were coming.

"I'll go!" Camille shouted. "Take Phillip with you and leave me. You could make it to White Wall—once the King Regent has me, this will all end."

"Yes," Charlie said in a manic rush of hope, her amber eyes sharp like a hawk searching for prey.

"No!" Theo and Vesyon said in unison.

"You will *not* hand yourself over to the King Regent! Not now. Not ever," Vesyon said sharply. "It wouldn't do anything to end this war, I promise you." He put his hand out to keep Camille back, his eyes forcing her feet to remain solidly where she stood.

Phillip lay before them in a pool of his own blood, drowning in a mountain of venom and about to die at Vesyon's hand. Camille watched as Vesyon grasped Phillip's hand tightly, their eyes connecting for a long moment.

"Forgive me, my friend," Vesyon murmured.

Phillip's voice was gone, but he blinked several times as if to say, *please end this torture.*

Vesyon lifted the knife up, angling it for the swiftest and least painful death. Camille couldn't avert her eyes and inhaled a shaky breath, filling her nose with the metallic tang of blood and slain beasts as Vesyon drove the dagger into Phillip's heart.

Without warning, a crushing weight slammed against Camille's back and she shot forward into the mud. She landed on her left side as sharp fangs clamped down on her right shoulder, arm, and abdomen. A violent scream burst from her lips as searing pain invaded her every cell, wrenching, tearing, and destroying until she saw only blackness.

CHAPTER NINETEEN
WHITE WALL

Vesyon was in motion the second the Chimera pounced on top of Camille, but he was too slow to save her from the beast's piercing bites. Her scream penetrated the silence as Theo rushed forward, slashing the Chimera's throat in one fluid motion.

"Cam! Oh, Ma'Nada!" Theo shoved manically at the gigantic animal as Vesyon managed to pull her free from underneath it.

The Chimera had bitten her, it's venom now coursing through her body. Together they assessed the damage and saw that it went clean to the bone, far worse than the wounds Phillip had endured.

"Camille, damn it! You don't get to die on me, you hear?!" Vesyon said in a rush. Each puncture was deathly black against her alabaster skin blood seeping from them staining her clothes.

Neeko growled loudly, racing back and forth from his lookout spot.

"We need to move!" Vesyon said, glancing over his shoulder to see Charlie still sprawled over her father's body. "Charlie, come on!"

Another explosion rang out as they quickly made their way over the pile of dead Chimera and down the hill. With the thankful protection of cloud and smoke cover, Vesyon's small group made their way east of the village grounds, and he silently thanked Phillip for allowing him to complete the plan they'd formulated. They'd held off the Chimera and Equestrians as long as they could, and it was far past the time to flee.

"They infiltrated the compound just like you predicted," Theo huffed beside Vesyon, dragging a sobbing Charlie along. "What now?"

"We'll make our way to White Wall," Vesyon said, readjusting Camille's limp and feverish body in his arms before bounding through the underbrush.

Neeko sprinted in front of Vesyon and bobbed his head around, pointing his snout in the direction of impending danger.

"Damn it!" Vesyon cursed, catching a whiff of that horrendous, floral scent at their backs. The Night Rave was coming, and judging by the multitude of footsteps, the woman in red had brought some friends.

Vesyon found the spot he'd prepared the previous evening, where several sturdy grey mares stood in waiting for them. "You *must* get her to the White Wall. No exceptions!" Vesyon said as Theo hopped onto the first horse and reached out for Camille.

"What's that strange smell?" Theo asked furtively, arranging a now somewhat conscious Camille behind him on the saddle. Vesyon moved to secure her while keeping an eye out over his shoulder for an incoming invasion.

"LeMarc's new regiment—Night Raves. I only saw the one but, there must be more. Theo, don't waste any time. Head west through the flatlands and keep a good distance from Dwaa. You must cross the Syene River and get Camille to Langhorn."

Vesyon mounted his own horse, adjusting his postion to face what sounded like a herd of Chimera charging through the forest toward himself, Charlie, and Neeko. Turning back to Theo, his face appeared like a ghost from the shadows. "You can lose them beyond the bridge past Syene. I'll join you when I can," Vesyon said, yanking Charlie up behind him on his horse.

Theo dug his heels in, and his mare shot forward, Camille's long copper tresses like a flag of fire in the wind.

There was little light so far from the fire of the compound. Darkness spread around them like a shroud, their last mode of protection giving them mere hours to the breaking of dawn.

Lifting his face to the swollen, rain-filled clouds hanging over his head like malevolent gods, he felt a tremor of hope. Camille would make it to White Wall, she would live, and the war for their freedom would continue.

***

Theo sped off through the trees on his mare, Jolie, while urging Camille to hold on tight. The massive snow-laden pines gave way to open, crisp meadows and rolling hills, providing his enemies with a more unobstructed view. The clouds had dwindled, but he still could only make out a sliver of moonlight behind the low hanging clouds.

Theo glanced over his shoulder and saw them: five Night Raves closing in, each riding a pure black stallion.

They were clothed in deep red leather, some with more skin showing than covered. There were three women and two men, all sporting a tight gold and silver choker around their necks. They were packed down with swords, axes, bows, and rifles.

"Give her to us," a Night Rave called out, her voice a menacing hiss.

Jolie pressed forward as fast as her muscular body could manage, her hooves thundering through the meadow hills and kicking up dirt and grass in her wake.

"Are they close enough to shoot down?" he yelled back to Camille, who was fumbling with his bow.

"Almost," she replied, twisting to get a better look. Theo heard the creaking pull of an arrow against his bowstring, and then the reverberating shock as one of his arrows took flight. There was no chance of him looking back, but the sharp exhalation of breath from Camille let him know she'd missed.

Theo pulled Jolie's reins to the right, toward the Syene River. If he got to it in time, he could cut the tethers of the bridge once they'd crossed and the Night Raves would be forced to find another way.

Another snap and a stumbling crash from behind—Camille had downed a Night Rave. He knew she was struggling; he could feel the blaze of her body against him like a blanket of coals pressed to his back, yet she continued to fire.

"I only have three arrows left," she screamed into Theo's ear, her legs losing grip when Jolie leaped over a mound of sharp boulders.

"Stay with me, Cam!" Theo said, reaching back to steady her.

They catapulted through a sea of thick bushes and over a tumbled tree, barely able to make out their surroundings in the dark night.

One Night Rave pulled in close, his arm outstretched. Without a word, Camille snatched a dagger from Theo's belt loop and chucked it at the Night Rave, sending him tumbling off his horse into a thicket of weeds.

Camille leaned against Theo, keeping her hands linked in front of his abdomen. "Theo," she murmured, barely loud enough for him to hear, "thank you for everything."

"Don't you do that! You hold on, damn it!" He felt her nod against his back, but she was fading fast. A racking shiver tumbled through her system as the fever set into her bones: the final calling card of the Chimera virus before it took over completely. Praetorian or not, she would eventually succumb.

Jolie bolted up the final yards of the hillside, immediately sliding to a stop at the edge of a cliff. Several hundred feet below them was the rushing Syene River, cascading with vicious force through the jagged valley walls. The treacherous crossing was as Theo feared—an old wooden bridge that looked ready to crumble at the slightest weight.

"Really?!" Theo barked out, urging the mare forward.

Jolie balked at the rotted wood but acquiesced as the remaining three Night Raves gained on them.

"Halt, Praetorian! Don't move another step!" one of the Night Raves bellowed as they vaulted closer.

Camille notched another arrow and let it fly, with a resulting crash telling Theo she'd hit her mark.

"You've been warned!" another Night Rave seethed, notching her own wooden bow with a steel-plated arrow and following them across the bridge on foot.

"Go, go!" Theo said, kicking Jolie in the sides and praying the planks beneath them held. The grey mare cleared the bridge and Theo leaped off the horse tugging Camille down with him. Yanking two daggers from his saddle, he tossed one at Camille and charged toward the bridge. "We need to cut the ropes!"

"No!" screeched the Night Rave who was already on the bridge charging toward them, but it was too late—with a few more zealous cuts, the rope handles were severed, and the rickety bridge gave way.

Theo watched as the Night Rave tumbled into the rapids below and dodged an arrow that zoomed past his cheek from the remaining Night Rave still crouched on the opposite side.

"Camille, come on," Theo said, grabbing her hand and half dragging her into the woods behind Jolie.

"I can't go any further," she said once they were hidden by the underbrush. Her legs gave out, and she tumbled to the ground in a mess of blood and sweat.

"Cam! Wait—*please*! *Hold on*!" Theo cried, crouching to gather her into his arms. "We're almost there, we're almost to the doctor—" His eyes searched her face, but she didn't move or speak. With shaking hands, he caressed the soft sides of her cheeks, feeling the burning fire raging beneath the surface. Tears welled up in his eyes, but he brushed them away in fierce, sharp swipes.

"I love you, Cam. Dear Ma'Nada, I love you," he sobbed, pulling her limp form against his chest. "I won't let you die, not now! You don't get to leave me this time—do you hear me!"

He gripped her face and kissed her burning lips before a firm determination flooded his system. After lifting her onto Jolie, he climbed up behind her and nudged the mare toward White Wall. "Fly my sweet girl," he cooed in Jolie's ear. "Take us home!"

***

An amber sun rose majestically over the horizon, its gentle glow highlighting the sheen of sweat on Camille's chalk-white face.

Amazingly, the fever seemed to be breaking, but Camille's breathing remained shallow and intermittent. Usually, an Asperian would be howling bloody murder as their body underwent the steps to become a Chimera, but Camille hadn't made a sound.

Just as the sun began its climb across the sky, Theo and Camille crested over the hills of White Wall territory. The vaulted walls of the city cast dark and looming shadows over the ground, the main village zigzagging up the mountainside.

The climb toward the outer wall seemed endless, and Theo felt as though Camille was slipping out of his grasp with every pound of Jolie's hoof against the muddied path. "Hold tight, my love. Almost there."

Despite the darkness of the looming village, White Wall was a place of rebuilding and recovery for anyone suffering from the virus. No one questioned the methods of the old man at the top of the keep; it was with unshakable faith that anyone who was sick or in need of a remedy sought out Langhorn. He was the most knowledgeable doctor in Aspera, and one of the few citizens who remained free of the High King's far-reaching control.

Camille would be in good hands with Langhorn, although Theo was still worried about how long she'd been under. He could tell her body was fiercely fighting the venom, but only Langhorn's assurances would make him feel better.

Jolie's hooves clopped loudly on the white cobblestones of the village square as they entered. Maneuvering Jolie along the twisting streets, he urged her faster with increasing determination. Once they'd reached the tallest tower, Theo slipped from the horse's back and threw the doors open, leading Jolie and Camille straight into the main hall. A group of Rogues were gathered around a table at the far end of the room, equally as blood-soaked and spent as he was..

"Theo, is that you?" a Rogue said, rushing forward with a look of extreme concern as he took in Camille's condition. "Send word for Langhorn—we need to get this girl to the infirmary."

"She's been bitten," Theo said. "We must hurry—"

"I'm here," said an elderly man, approaching from a side entrance. "Where is she?"

Theo cradled her close as he walked over to Langhorn. The old man's piercing stare was bright with intelligence, his eyes a soft, mossy green. Relief flooded Theo's body at the mere sight of the legendary doctor.

The old man didn't ask for an explanation as he traced the edges of Camille's face, his eyes widening and narrowing as he assessed the damage. He took in the greyish pigment of her clammy skin and the garish holes along her arm, chest, and abdomen before motioning for Theo to follow. The old man moved with haste, his long grey and white robe—tied with a silver sash—billowing out behind him like a sail when he walked.

Langhorn moved with purpose, striding swiftly down the maze of hallways and stairs as though he were a leaf floating down a brisk stream. Never second guessing, never careening off the road map stamped in his head. Langhorn knew the caverns, hallways, corners, and crevices of his home like nobody else.

They burrowed deep into the belly of the mountainside, finally arriving at a seemingly old wooden door, reinforced by a thick slab of iron on the other side.

Langhorn went inside and beckoned for Theo to follow. "Put her there, on the examining table."

Theo listened and watched as Langhorn bustled around Camille, scribbling things on a tiny slip of paper as he stripped the blood-soaked clothes from her wounds. He carefully doused the puncture holes with various ointments, before wrapping the open wounds in a thick cushion of bandages.

Camille didn't move an inch during the entire process. Her skin had returned to a nearly-normal, pinkish hue during the cleansing, but she was still extremely dirty and bruised all over.

"She's going to be okay, right?" Theo asked, aching to touch her, to feel the warmth of her skin beneath his fingertips, but he refrained. Not that he cared if Langhorn saw. Theo was worried his ability to maintain control would falter. The wall keeping back his emotions was perilously close to crumbling, and he feared a single touch of her skin would send him down a darkened path of aching guilt and regret.

"Of course; Camille's a strong little bird. It would take more than a few Chimera bites to do her in," Langhorn said brightly, continuing to clean the dozen or so other small cuts she'd sustained on her face and limbs.

The door suddenly burst open behind them, nearly flying off the hinges as Vesyon and Neeko bounded into the room. Langhorn didn't even pause in his cleaning and wrapping, working methodically to address every wound with precision.

"How is she?" Vesyon asked as he moved swiftly to her side.

"Fine, she's just fine," Langhorn said calmly.

Theo watched as Vesyon pulled one of Camille's hands into his grasp, and a small pit of jealousy formed in his belly. He'd seen them touch, hug, and hold each other many times before in moments of extreme emotion and in the comfort of friendship. They were close, he knew that, but still, it irked him. Something about the blazing heat of panic swimming openly across Vesyon's face rang an alarm in Theo's pricked awareness.

"Theo," Langhorn said, startling him out of his envious reverie. "You and Vesyon should go up to the kitchens and find something to eat."

Langhorn's words sounded foreign to Theo's tender ears, and it took him much longer than usual to register their meaning. "Yeah—okay."

"I'll summon several of my healers this morning, and by tomorrow she'll be good as new!" Langhorn said as he turned to wash his hands in the porcelain basin along the opposite wall.

The promise of sustenance was enticing, and Theo knew his presence would only be a nuisance to the flutter of healers and caretakers. He waited for Vesyon to join him, observing with a sharp eye the way his friend was doting on Camille in a tender way he'd never seen before. He'd always suspected Vesyon loved her, but, standing there in that small medical room, with Camille's life hanging in the balance, had proven *just how much*. And it made Theo sick.

CHAPTER TWENTY
BROKEN BOND

Langhorn waited for Theo to turn away before shooting Vesyon a look of concern. He knew Camille would be all right, but he wasn't sure what effect the Chimera venom would have on her system. He needed to run blood tests and thoroughly assess her vitals because something about her now-pinkish complexion had him confused.

"See you in the kitchens?" Vesyon said, his brow furrowed and eyes flooded with the shadows of concern.

"Be there in a hop, skip, and a jump. Just need to finish a couple things here," Langhorn responded in a sing-song, cheerful voice, not wanting to raise the alarm if Theo were still close enough to hear.

Vesyon took the cue and let himself out after Theo, a frown darkening his handsome features.

In the wake of their absence, a humming silence fell over the room, and Langhorn stared down at the motionless girl before him. A soft sigh escaped his mouth, his hand trembling for a mere moment as he brought the tips of his fingers to his lips. "I've missed you, child," Langhorn whispered, feeling the sharp, tingling prick of wetness burn at the edges of his eyes. He brushed it away in one quick swipe. It'd been a very long time since he'd last seen his granddaughter, and even though she wasn't awake now, it felt wonderful to have her home again.

With her complexion shining bright like the fresh pink of a newborn, he went about the process of collecting data. He slipped

255

a thin, hollowed out steel needle into her arm and drew out several ounces of blood. He took each wound in turn: cleaning, suturing—if needed—covering in ointment or compress, and bandaging. He knew Maggie, would be in soon to do a thorough clean and dress of Camille, but Langhorn preferred to do a detailed first assessment of his patients. Most wouldn't receive such focused treatment even though, within the perimeters of White Wall, every patient was considered essential to Langhorn.

Camille, of course, was an exceptionally rare occurrence, and an intriguing puzzle—even for Langhorn. Despite his intense desire to stay until she woke, he knew discussing his suspicions of her recovery with Vesyon was the main priority.

"It's good to see you, dear child," he said as he brushed a hand over her rosy cheek. Something glinted in his eye line as he stepped closer: the silver chain of her medallion. Langhorn grasped it, examining the amulet with curiosity as a rivulet of chills snaked down his spine. It was as clean and shiny as the day she'd first received it, but it felt icy to the touch. He frowned, placing the necklace back against the pale, smooth skin along her collar bone.

Knowing there was a mountain of information from the past few weeks waiting for him upstairs with Vesyon, Langhorn made his way up through the maze of hallways toward the kitchen, shaking his head in pure astonishment.

***

Vesyon watched as Theo downed two bowls of honey-soaked oatmeal, two slices of buttered bread, and half an apple before saying a word. After years of eating the same meal every day at Romeo Village, he was certain Theo wouldn't be the only Rogue taking advantage of the open and fully stocked kitchens at White Wall.

Vesyon shook his head at the way Theo's foot tapped out an impatient beat on the floor; he was evidently anxious to return to Camille.

Langhorn emerged at the top of the stairs, his hair wild and flying about his face, a slight smile perking up the corner of his lips. He turned toward them without seeing, as though he knew where to find Vesyon without looking. His slippered feet floated silently across the expansive kitchen hall. He took a seat next to Theo and across from Vesyon, placing his hand on Theo's shoulder to lower himself gently to the bench. They exchanged quiet pleasantries as the cook served Langhorn his usual breakfast, but Vesyon could tell Theo didn't want to be sitting with them any longer as the small talk ended. The cobalt stare twitching from right to left, up and down, and all around the room gave him the look of a caged animal. He needed to see her, to feel at ease, an emotion Vesyon understood all too well.

"You look tired beyond belief, Theo. Go rest. I'll come to find you when she wakes," Vesyon said, knowing full well he'd find Theo right by her side. Theo nodded once, then quietly excused himself before trudging up the stairwell without another word.

After the stern look Langhorn had given Vesyon in the lab, he knew there were some difficult topics to discuss that Theo need not be present for.

Steam coiled up from Langhorn's green ceramic mug, filling the air with the earthy scent of his morning herbs and lifelong necessity. Sitting across from Vesyon, Langhorn took his time dipping the wide-mouthed spoon into his honeyed oatmeal, allowing the milk to swallow the metal disk into its belly before pulling a steaming spoonful up to his puckered lips. Vesyon understood Langhorn's love for his slow morning ritual and gave him time to settle into his breakfast before pouncing on the status of Camille.

"I promise you, she's fine—or will be once the virus is fully expelled from her body." Langhorn waved his hands over his head as though swatting at an annoying bug, but the motion only managed to fan his wild, grey hair around. "In a few days she will, most likely, be back to a semblance of her normal self, but it will take weeks for her to fully recover."

Something in his eyes made Vesyon uneasy. Despite Langhorn's sincerity, the elderly doctor was holding something back. "'Most likely?'" Vesyon repeated, not being one to dance around a topic.

"Well, to be honest, her status is quite odd. The medallion..." Langhorn began, his unruly eyebrows reaching toward one another as he frowned.

"What about it?" Vesyon snapped out, unable to control the pitch of panic in his voice.

Langhorn took another small bite of his oatmeal, his calm expression unreadable to Vesyon's sharp inquisition. "Your medallion sends off a sort of pulse, a *vibration*. You probably can't sense it—in the same way I no longer smell the herbal scent clinging to my skin—but it's there. I, however, can *feel* the live quality of the Ephidra Lily pulsing through the metal when I handle it. It's the Praetorian virus battling against its bonds of restriction. Most Praetorians don't know this, but that Blood Bond you carry around your neck wasn't intended to be a promise of protection to the High King; it's actually your only wall of safety."

"Safety from the virus, yes I know."

Langhorn shook his head, his mossy eyes narrowed with intent. "No—safety from yourself. Without it, the Praetorian Virus would overwhelm you with its intoxicating power. You'd become an unchained Praetorian, losing complete control of your humanity."

Vesyon nodded, already understanding this clearly and yet struggling to wrap his head around why Langhorn was telling him. "I know this already. What's so bizarre about her medallion?"

"Her medallion has no pulse, no vibration at all—just like when you rescued her from LeMarc eight years ago. I had thought that instance was a fluke, perhaps because she'd been so weak. But it appears I was wrong. The medallion is doing absolutely nothing for her, and I'm almost certain the virus within her bloodstream hasn't had many restrictions for quite a long time."

Vesyon's eyes widened. "Are you saying she's no longer a Praetorian?"

"I can't honestly say what I think," Langhorn said, sipping his tea. "I need to do more research to be certain. Most unchained Praetorians are unable to control their emotional functions. One specific emotion would take over, leaving the Praetorian to be a shell of the person they once were. This is different though, something I've never seen. I don't believe she was ever *just* a Praetorian, to begin with."

"What do you mean? How's that possible?"

Langhorn opened his mouth as though to respond, but instead snapped his lips closed again on a lengthy pause, gathering his cloak more firmly around his thin shoulders. Despite the plethora of lines scrolled across his features, he carried himself with a young air as though a twenty-year-old man lived within a ninety-year-old body. There was age and wisdom in his almond-shaped eyes but also an abundance of vitality. "Did you happen to see them?"

"Them?" Vesyon asked, his stomach dropping like a lead ball in his gut. He watched as Langhorn's expression glittered with wild excitement in the way they always did when explaining a new theory. It was remarkable to watch his massive enthusiasm, sometimes even awe-inspiring. In some instances, it was terrifying. In moments of discovery and quick judgment, especially when concerning an Asperian life, Langhorn could make some of the most impossible decisions. It was the requirement of being a successful physician: cold-hearted ruthlessness in dire situations.

"LeMarc's new army. They're called Night Raves—unyielding from what I have heard."

"How did you know about them?" Vesyon asked, bewildered so far beyond surprise he wasn't yet able to be angry Langhorn hadn't sent word of what he'd known.

"Well, I haven't known for long," Langhorn said matter-of-factly, obviously recognizing a possible flicker of heat in Vesyon's words that could flare into full-blown fury. "I found out recently *what* they are. I had no idea if they would be at Romeo Village or not. But from the look on your face, they were absolutely there."

Not able to process the information fast enough to respond, Vesyon merely nodded. "Why is this relevant?" Vesyon asked, trying to keep his voice under control, but it was useless. He saw the gleam of exuberance flutter through Langhorn's expression and felt the burning heat filtering through his own system at a rapid pace. "No," he said, desperate to halt the information he was undoubtedly about to hear. "It's not possible; it can't be possible."

The puzzle pieces unwillingly slipped together in his head, and he knew without Langhorn uttering a single word what he was about to say.

"It's just a theory, a possibility. I can't be certain, not until I do more tests," Langhorn replied, appearing uncertain for the first time. The old man's lips twitched in apparent acknowledgment of what he was about to say to Vesyon, but he bravely continued, knowing that it wasn't going to end well.

"Remember how I discovered the Praetorian virus?" Langhorn began lightly, as though they were talking about the weather. "And when I told you about the Dai'Cia Kingdom and my dalliance with Queen Isis before I met my wife?" He said it with a straight face, but Vesyon knew it was difficult for Langhorn to talk about his past so openly.

"They're incredible beings, the Dai'Cian—bred as soldiers from birth," he continued, taking a small sip inbetween sentences to give Vesyon ample time to take in the information. "They are strong and powerful, with an immune system unlike anything I've ever encountered. I was curious to see what made them so incredibly different than Asperians. Geographically speaking, they aren't so far north of us to be considered out of reach. I wanted to know what made them...*them*. My small curiosity turned into a much larger experiment, which led me to create the Praetorian virus in the first place. It was something I never should've explored," he said, sighing into his mug. "I had no intention of allowing my discovery about the effects of Dai'Cia blood to fall into the wrong hands, but it did. Anyways, my point is that Night Raves aren't created, Vesyon—they're born. A Dai'Cia native and an Asperian mating is the only way to birth a true Night Rave."

Vesyon's head spun. "But I *know* Camille; I watched her grow up. There were no signs of her being anything but a normal, Asperian child."

Langhorn's frank stare leveled on Vesyon as he set his teacup back on the smooth wooden table. "I know this is hard to hear, but think about it: we don't know who Camille's birth father is. Jesabelle came back to us after seven years serving with the High King as an Equestrian, and she was already six months pregnant. It very likely could've been on her travels, or it could have happened—"

"No," Vesyon said, shaking his head violently, not allowing Langhorn to finish his thought. "I refuse to believe—"

"That Camille's father was a Dai'Cian native? That LeMarc has something to do with it? It's not hard to believe; the facts are all there. It's just hard to hear."

"Camille *isn't* like them!" Vesyon practically roared. "Jesabelle would've told us if that were the case!"

Langhorn glanced away in somber silence, pinching his lower lip between his thumb and pointer finger before allowing his fingers to slip down the expanse of his short, grey beard. "I don't know that she would have."

Vesyon inhaled through his nose, tamping his anger down. "If Camille *is* indeed a Night Rave, then why is she so different from the ones I saw last night?"

"I have a theory," Langhorn started, green eyes bright with intensity.

Vesyon rubbed at his jawline. "Another theory!?"

"All theories exist on the road to truth. Come on, my boy—did I teach you nothing in your younger years?" Langhorn scolded. "Praetorians are created, yes? The strength you've acquired is incredibly powerful and requires control from an outside source. Dai'Cian natives are powerful from *birth*; they grow up learning about their power and how to control it. Now, think of any muscle in your body, and how it grows stronger if you use it every day. Imagine that the muscle continues to get stronger, but you suddenly have a cap on how much strength you're allowed to use. If that cap ever gets removed, you'll have a surge of power you're no longer used to handling.

"I believe that Camille was unknowingly forced to cap her power the day she became a Praetorian. The Ephidra Lily in her body maintained a steady level of power, strength, and ability—"

"But Charlie Town—"

"Was the result of removing that cap of power, yes," Langhorn finished.

Vesyon's head began to swim with the information. "But her medallion," he said, clinging to his last crumb of hope. "You said you can't remove the power of a Blood Bond without obliterating the bond. The bond is still around her neck; it hasn't been removed."

"I don't think it ever was removed Vesyon, I think it was *destroyed*. And I believe the Chimera virus has something to do with it."

"No, that can't be possible," Vesyon said, shaking his head back and forth. "The bonds are unbreakable."

Langhorn took a moment to sip his tea, allowing the steam to drift about his head as he breathed in the earthy tang of it. "Charlie Town wasn't a coincidence; it was a purposeful attack by LeMarc. He knows what she is, and he found a way to push her past the restraint of the bond. It goes without question that he's been trying to create an army of Night Raves like her to follow his command. And the bond is not unbreakable, Vesyon; you know very well that it can, indeed, be broken."

Vesyon ignored the last comment and focused instead on information he was willing to listen to. "Then why the Ephidra Lily? Why wait until this moment to search for it?"

"Your Blood Bond is infused with Ephidra Lily. It's your wall of protection against yourself, yes, but can also be used as a weapon against you. A collar, so to speak, created to force submission if the owner is so inclined to do so. If done correctly your strength wouldn't be hindered, but your ability to move without his command would be."

"I see where you're going with this," Vesyon said, remembering in retrospect the thin metal collars secured tightly around the Night Raves' necks.

"When you have an army of powerful and well-trained soldiers, you need a way to control them, to bend them to your will without stripping away their power. Ephidra Lily, when handled properly, isn't just a bonding agent; it's a carrier of information. If I tell it to carry a virus to specific areas within the body, it will. If I tell the Ephidra Lily to attack the body, it will. He must've discovered a way to use this against his army to maintain control over them."

Vesyon eyed the remnants of food in front of him, and his stomach roiled. He pulled out his old worn pipe and the small leather bag of tobacco, craving the familiar, calming ritual and the fragrant taste of the leaves on his lips. "You're absolutely sure about this?"

"I am more than I'm not. Camille wasn't created to be a soldier—she was born," Langhorn said with exuberance. "She was already healing from the Chimera bites by the time I saw her. Such a heavy dose of their venom would kill off any normal Praetorian. All clues point to it, and there's no denying the truth when faced with the fact."

Vesyon's head fell forward so that his long black hair covered his eyes. She was still Camille, still a woman he loved and cared deeply for—but if he were honest with himself, he was also a bit afraid of her now. With such incredible power at her beck and call, there was no telling what she was capable of. He'd been a fool to believe she'd reigned in her emotions when at any moment she could flip a switch and be consumed by her own strength and power. His reasoning for keeping her in the dark about her past would no longer be temporary. There was no telling what she'd do once she learned the full truth of what happened in Charlie Town or why he'd waited seven years to rescue her from the LeMarc's dungeon.

"What can we do to prevent another Charlie Town incident from happening? If she has no sense of control, how can we be sure she's safe?"

Langhorn shrugged. "You know very well we can't. To protect each other against her is to remove her ability to live a free life. The Dai'Cian live free and without any restraints on their power. We have to trust that she'll learn control and take precautions against the possibility of it happening again."

"I've observed her the past few days, and she *has* been in control." Vesyon's tone was forceful, as though it were a struggle for him to accept this new information.

Langhorn lifted his eyes to Vesyon's. "It doesn't mean she'll remain that way. We both know blood rage isn't a Praetorian ability. Not a single Praetorian has been able to achieve the level of power and strength Camille did that night," Langhorn said with exasperation. "LeMarc used Camille's power for his convenience, and he'll do so again. Ephidra Lily is something he needs, Camille is the other, and he won't stop until he has both within his grasp. She isn't like the rest of you, and to be honest, I can already see she's unlike the Dai'Cia as well. There's something incredible about her, and LeMarc knows that. He never really wanted Praetorians; he desired a powerful soldier to do his bidding without question, someone lacking in compassion, brimming with ruthlessness. Night Raves are the perfect soldiers in LeMarc's eyes, and Camille was going to be his golden jewel."

"LeMarc will *never* have her again," Vesyon said with finality. "Not after what he did to Jesabelle." Vesyon's voice croaked as a Praecollection washed over him in a swirl of memories he'd never been able to sufficiently suppress—of Jesabelle's smile, her emerald eyes, and her sweet, soft-spoken demeanor.

He once thought love would bring Jesabelle back, but the hold of LeMarc's tightly wrapped bonds kept her soul out of sight.

"Do you think Camille knows what she is?" Vesyon asked, trying to pull his mind away from the surge of protectiveness building inside him. He blew out a puff of bluish smoke, allowing it to waft in lazy curls up toward the roof.

"I don't think she has a clue, but I *do* believe her mind will soon awaken to all we forced her to forget," Langhorn murmured. "She'll find out what we did. You understand that, right?"

Vesyon balled his hands into fists. "That's what I'm afraid of."

"I will need to run more tests. It's been too long since I've seen Camille; there is so much I don't know. Only her blood can reveal the truth. Until then, I won't know for certain what will happen. I honestly don't know if this is a natural effect or a side effect from our meddling."

Vesyon nodded in response, but his glare remained fixed forward as though he were no longer seeing the deep grooves of the table from years of use but the memories of long ago playing painfully through his mind.

"She wouldn't have recovered if we hadn't taken her memories Vesyon, you must know that."

Their eyes connected for a mere moment, but Vesyon knew Langhorn's words were a hollow comfort. There'd be no way to see if they'd helped her or harmed her after rescuing her from the clutches of LeMarc. Only time would tell, and so far, the truth was becoming a more substantial burden to bear by the day.

"What about Phillip?" Langhorn questioned softly. To change the subject away from a festering open wound, Langhorn guided Vesyon into a different one.

His grey eyes shot upward to Langhorn's face, a flicker of pain dappled in his features. "Phillip's gone. Charlie decided to stay behind."

Langhorn stared at him for several long seconds, neither betraying emotion nor offering comfort. The mossy glare remained stoic and unchanging. "I'm sorry to hear that. I know how close you were to the General."

Vesyon felt the heat of tears slide down his cheeks, and he couldn't muster the strength to wipe them away. His reasons to fight for his freedom were slipping away, buried beneath the pain of those friends and loved ones he'd lost along the way.

"The village, is it gone?" Langhorn asked, his tone low in cadence and purposefully under his breath.

Vesyon rubbed a hand down his face, ridding himself of the sharp prickling desire to let loose on his emotions and give in to the anguish building within his chest. He nodded, rubbing his thumbs deep into the groove just beneath his eyebrows. "It's rubble. There's no reason for LeMarc to go back in search of Ephidra Lily. I'm not positive if Acher made it out alive—" Vesyon said, stopping suddenly at Langhorn's sudden intake of air.

"Acher?" Langhorn asked, his tone uncharacteristically sharp.

Vesyon nodded, feeling the weariness of the last few weeks press into his flesh, the heavy weight so evenly distributed across his mind and body that he felt a massive sense of relief just sitting down and closing his eyes for the barest moment. "Yes, Acher was the leak to the crown. I'm surprised your inside man didn't fill us in on that detail."

His tone was clipped and short, with a hefty dose of acidity to it. Of all the reasons to have someone on the inside of the High Court, the greatest was to extract pertinent information. Langhorn had his secrets, mountains of them, and Vesyon would never dream of trying to crack the vault to his chunk of history. It was the current issues that bothered him to no end, the blatant disregard for people around them because Langhorn felt the knowledge was on a need to know basis—he being the only one that really needed to know.

"Well," Langhorn said, his eyes drifting toward the edge of his teacup in obvious misdirection. "It wasn't that important of a detail." He waved in an off-hand gesture as though they were talking about a small disagreement like their favorite color.

"Langhorn," Vesyon warned. He felt his cheeks flame with heat as the black most assuredly slipped from his eyes and down the angular planes of his face. "That small detail might have caused us far more deaths than we had to afford. It would have been helpful to know," he said with a growl, feeling the energetic zip of Praetorian anger surge through his system.

Langhorn didn't seem to mind or notice his change of tone. Instead, the doctor sipped his tea, smiling blandly and without humor in his general direction but remained quiet.

"You aren't going to tell me his name, are you?" Vesyon asked. He drummed his fingers in quick succession on the panel of wood, thumping out a steady purr of sound, but it didn't appear to affect Langhorn in the least.

"My source tells me what I need to know, and nothing more. He told me to be ready to destroy the village when LeMarc started his search for Ephidra Lily. *That* is the information I needed and what we prepared for. I can't ask him for more than that."

Vesyon snorted in response, lifting a mug of lukewarm tea to his lips. "I don't see how you can expect me to blindly trust someone I don't even know." The tea leaves were bitter and sharp on his tongue, leaving an unwelcome aftertaste coating his mouth. He craved more of the smooth, earthy tang of his pipe leaves but refrained.

The elderly man glared at Vesyon, green eyes sharply piercing. "I haven't once asked you to trust someone you don't know. I have asked you to trust me."

"It's not the same thing Langhorn, you know that."

One green eye peered at Vesyon from beneath the thick tuft of his shaggy grey brows, but Langhorn didn't respond. He nodded and sipped his tea, knowing that to argue with Vesyon on this account would get him nowhere.

"You need to rest, my boy," he finally said, pushing away the empty mug and shifting his weight to stand.

"I don't even know if it's possible to find sleep tonight."

There would be little rest for all of those within the gates of White Wall. It would be impossible to pretend ignorance of a rebellion now well underfoot. The slow game of waiting was now in the past; the fight for freedom had well and truly sparked flame again.

Langhorn tucked his hands into the wide-billowed ends of his sleeves and bowed slightly to Vesyon in a bid of farewell. "Be at ease Vesyon, for the moment at least. You are here, Camille is here, you're all safe." The old man's lips quirked upward in a smile before his slippered feet shuffled him silently out of the dining hall.

"Safe," Vesyon repeated, his voice sounding hollowed and foreign in his own ears. "For the moment."

CHAPTER TWENTY - ONE
DEMONS WITHIN

She was breathing so incredibly slow that it hurt Theo to watch. Her chest rose and fell with slight, almost imperceptible motions. His eyes were beginning to ache as he strained to ensure she was indeed breathing. Langhorn had told him she would be alright. "You better not be incorrect, doc," Theo said, gripping the side of the bed, his fingers white from the pressure.

Despite his terror of her never waking, she appeared in decently good health. Her soft porcelain skin practically glowed in the room's lamplight, a sheen of pink across the plains of her cheeks and nose, with a spray of freckles where the sun had touched her most. Every surface of her skin that had been marred during the battle at Romeo had healed, which was beyond incredible—even for a Praetorian.

Lifting the tattered sleeve of his grubby tunic, Theo spotted several scabbed wounds, and a couple of deeper cuts still oozing beneath the layers of bandages. Camille didn't have a single mark on her anywhere. It seemed unnatural even to him, but then again Camille had always been faster at everything.

Growing up together she'd been the faster runner, the stronger contender in hand-to-hand combat, and by far the best hunter. She'd been trapping rabbits and shooting down dinner from the sky at the age of six, and it seemed natural to everyone around her because it's Camille. It wasn't until they pledged their loyalty to the crown by taking the bond that he finally felt he was equal to her.

The difference had been night and day; one day he could barely keep up and the next he was pushing past her.

Despite his sudden ability to maintain speed with her, there were still so many things in which he fell markedly behind in. Theo healed rather quickly, but he rarely walked away without any scars. His skin was a field of history; any wound deep enough to gush in blood left a mark of his adventures. The worst was the jagged line from his temple down the side of his cheek, a calling card from an angry Asperian unwilling to die because the High King demanded it.

It had been the first time Theo had questioned his actions so thoroughly that he almost hadn't followed through. Vesyon had saved him from making the final decision, and Jesabelle had carried his bleeding body to the closest village to manage the deep gash as best she could. He'd been more than lucky; if the blade had sliced down his face a hairs width closer to his eye, he would have lost it.

The scar remained and never healed completely, although it lessened its ostentatious display over the years. It reminded Theo to take every order he was given with serious intent. If he half-assed his responsibilities, he'd find a blade or a bullet hitting a more permanent mark. He no longer was one to believe in the fight for LeMarc's kingdom though; his honor and sense of duty lay with Vesyon and Langhorn in the rebuilding of the rebellion. He had his doubts, still. Looking down at Camille's body, barely breathing, he felt that perhaps fighting hand to hand combat for freedom against such a powerful king wasn't the smartest option.

"Dear Ma'Nada, let her wake up. Let her be alright, please dear Mother," Theo prayed. He scooted as close to her bedside as he could, gripping her hand like a lifeline of support. There was no way he'd be able to survive without her; he'd never be able to forgive himself for failing to protect her.

His heart paused in his chest as he watched her breathing stop. "Cam?" He tentatively shook her shoulder. Nothing happened. He stood quickly, kicking his chair out as he leaned over her. Placing one finger beneath her nostrils, he waited for the heat of her exhalation but felt nothing whatsoever. "Camille, damn it, don't you dare die on me!"

Tears fell freely down his cheeks unchecked and without notice. Words tumbled thickly from his mouth as he leaned over her, begging the Mother for help. Her skin felt cold to the touch, as did her medallion. It was wrong but he wasn't willing to accept it; she wasn't going to die, she couldn't.

Thick auburn hair glistened around her head like a wreath of fire about her face, alive and fiercely demanding of attention. He couldn't stop himself from touching it as he spoke utter nonsense to her, running his fingers through the silky strands to feel close to her, to absorb her within him just one last time.

"Cam, please, I can't do this without you," he begged, leaning his forehead upon hers gently, willing her to take another breath. "Please darling, come back." There was nothing, just pure and empty silence.

He heard her then, a soft sigh of breath through her lips, and then, without warning, she was violently awake. "Theo!" She croaked, her voice ragged with weariness and hours of misuse. She jolted upright in bed, almost slamming her skull against his. Her hair flew wildly around her shoulders, creating a lion's mane of vibrant auburn, cinnamon, strawberry, and ruby to curl about her pallid face. Her eyes blazed with sudden heat, a sharp inky black sliding over the glossy surface before settling into a brilliant emerald with flecks of gold and a ring of forest green encircling the iris.

"Holy Ma'Nada, you're alive," Theo said on a whisper, tears streaming down his cheeks in relief. She appeared not to notice his emotional response as she stared at him, her own expression a mask of shock mixed with a tinge of horror. "What is it?" Theo asked, beginning to take note of a tremor rippling through her body.

"I saw her," Camille said, her voice raspy but firm. "Theo, I saw my mother in Charlie Town."

He shook his head in bewilderment, unable to comprehend what he'd just heard. "You what?"

"I saw my mother!" She repeated vehemently. "She's alive. I saw her face—she wasn't quite..." she said in a rambling mess, her words running into nothing as her eyes glossed over in deep thought. Her lips scrunched into a bow, and he saw her descend into the depths of her mind.

"She wasn't what?" Theo pressed.

Her green eyes turned toward him with such unbridled fear that he suddenly felt desperate to crush her to his chest and rock her into safety. Instead, he took her hands in his and sat as close as he could to her on the bed, slowly coaxing the words lodged in her throat.

"She wasn't herself Theo, but then again, neither was I," she finished lamely as her right hand pressed two fingers to the side of her temple. "How long have I been asleep?"

"A little over a day."

Camille's face lit up with unbridled excitement. "Then she is still there, in Charlie Town!" She burst out loudly without restraint. "We must go; we must find her!"

Theo's eyes squinted at her, trying to assess what it was that she was remembering and why it was suddenly so urgent to her. "Cam," he started gently. "It's not possible for Jesabelle to be in Charlie Town right now."

"She is, I swear! I saw her there Theo, I found her!"

"Cam," Theo started again, coming to a clear understanding of what was happening. "The last time you were in Charlie Town was over eight years ago."

She blinked at him, her head tilting questioningly to one side. "No." She stated it firmly as though it were the most obvious thing in the world that Theo was wrong. "I...I was just with..." she said as a cloud of confusion washed over her features. "I was just— Lunci," she said slowly, as though trying the name out on her tongue. "I was just with Lunci."

Her eyebrows drew together, the long elegant slants scrunching close in seeming desperation to join.

"Anything else that you remember?" Theo pressed, trying not to sound as desperate as he felt. "What happened after being with Lunci?"

"After?" Camille said in a hushed whisper. He watched a storm of panic shift through her features. The sides of her lips twitched downward, twisting her features from hope and surprised shock into doubt and fearful worry. "I was...I saw her. My mother was at Charlie Town."

She said it with such conviction that Theo had no doubt she meant it. "What else?"

"They attacked her Theo." Without warning, her eyes flashed deadly with a surge of black spilling past the fleshy lining of her eyes and into the once bright pink flush of her cheeks.

"Hey sweetheart, it's ok. There's no need to get angry. You're in White Wall. You're safe." His hand extended toward her but stopped mid-air when a snarling growl rumble from the back of her throat.

"Did you know?" Her black eyes locked on him with deadly intent. He felt the hair on the back of his neck rise as he subtly leaned away from her, his Praetorian response slipping down his spine in preparation.

"Did I know what?" he asked warily.

Her voice rippled with accusation and fury, her body tensing, but fluid in motion, like a predator ready to pounce. "What they did to her? They attacked her. She was their Praetorian! They dragged her out into the street by her hair, stripped her of her clothes, and beat her. They put their disgusting, filthy hands on her." Camille began to shake, the muscles beneath the skin twitching and shaking uncontrollably as she spoke. "She begged for them to stop, not wanting to hurt them, but they wouldn't listen. They called her a monster, Theo. They whipped her, beat her, sliced into her flesh. They murdered her," she said on a gulp of air, and a slight, croaked hesitation as though she were confused again.

"Cam, I don't know what you are..." Theo started to say, but she turned on him in an instant, jumping out from beneath the sheets of her bed. She stood before him in a blaze of fury, her breaths exploding out of her airways like a charging steed.

"I know what it is they did!"

The infirmary floors were shiny white and brilliantly clean beneath the blooming pink outlines of her toes. She was naked except for a pair of thin cotton shorts and a slim white cotton tank top. The black shock of her Praetorian response spilled like a tidal wave into the fiery red roots of her hairline and down her neck as she stood before him, the rage of her past thrumming through her like an unstoppable fire burning everything in its wake.

Short quick breaths puffed out from between her lips as she glared at him through black, emotionless eyes. The depth of her silence dared him to speak, but he was unable to formulate a single word. He couldn't breathe. A choked cry clawed its way up his throat, but nothing escaped his lips when he opened his mouth wide to scream.

It was then that she smiled—a smooth and unemotional action without an ounce of humanity displayed. It was the most terrifying expression Theo had ever seen painted across Camille's features. "I killed them," she purred, taking slow, menacing steps toward him.

"I killed every single one of those treacherous Asperians. The men. The women. The children. They all deserved to die."

Theo shook his head slowly, uncertain of what to do. It'd been a very long time since he'd feared for his life, but as he watched Camille slink toward him, her eyes pure black and swimming in hatred, he felt a familiar panic surge like bile in the back of his throat. She was lost to him, crushed beneath the tangled lies of her past and completely unreachable as the fury swallowed her whole.

***

Vesyon stood on the balcony just off the main living quarters of his old room. It had felt beyond good to walk into the familiar space, run his fingers over the old worn books and disarray of papers, grasp the simple items he had once held so dear. With the wondrous delight of coming home, he was struck silent with the sudden sharp taste of loneliness. Standing alone in the home he'd grown up in with Jesabelle—it was welcoming and horribly bittersweet.

He walked straight out to the balcony, needing to get some fresh air, and lost track of time as he pulled out his worn wooden pipe and packed his favorite tobacco down the chamber in rhythmic repetition. Smoke billowed from between his lips, bringing a slow and needed peace to his mind.

"May I join you?" Langhorn asked from the edge of the balcony behind him. Vesyon hadn't heard him enter. The old man had moved silently like a cloud on a persistent breeze. It didn't matter, he was finally home, and for once Vesyon felt safe in the comfort of his surroundings. He nodded at the old man and Langhorn floated toward him, his feet moving beneath the billowing material of his cloak.

Reaching into one sleeve, Langhorn pulled out a narrow, ivory pipe the length of Vesyon's forearm, carved with the most delicate details around the base of the pipe end. Langhorn rarely smoked with Vesyon, but when he did, he staunchly smoked his private reserve of cannabis. Vesyon had smoked the old man's leaf once or twice in his life, but it made his mind fuzzy in a way that made him not understand the appeal. *It eases the ache in my bones,* Langhorn would say, but Vesyon believed it was more about the gentle ease of his mind that made Langhorn delight in the delicate leaf from time to time.

"There's one more thing," Langhorn said, reaching into his other sleeve and pulling out a thin parchment envelope. The broken red seal across the front the mark of the High Court.

"What's this?" Vesyon asked with an edge to his voice. He eyed the envelope and array of parchment with a strong sense of foreboding.

"Open it," Langhorn replied dryly before he inhaled heavily on his pipe, allowing the smoke to sit comfortably in his chest before blowing out gentle blueish rings.

Vesyon reached inside the envelope and pulled out a piece of parchment folded into thirds. Two tiny slips of paper fluttered into his hand as he unfolded the letter, and his eyes flicked up to Langhorn's in trepidation. He quickly read through the perfectly looped words across the top and felt the blood drain from his face. "How?" Vesyon asked, his tongue suddenly heavy in his mouth as the sweet taste of tobacco turned to ash on his taste buds.

"He's made his next move."

Vesyon reread the words delicately written in beautiful green ink, but the heading was the only content he seemed able to process. His heart slammed against his chest as a rolling wave of Praecollection poured into him. He didn't want to remember, didn't want to see what his mind was forcing him to endure, but the memories were unstoppable. His vision blurred from the intense pain drumming behind his eyes, and he tossed the letter onto the balcony railing, wishing a gust of wind would whip it away from him. "This can't be possible. He exiled Praetorians, all of us!"

Langhorn nodded, staring out at the swirling loops of smoke drifting lazily through the early evening air, purposely giving Vesyon time to collect himself. "*You* may not believe what's written on that page, but the rest of Aspera will. And when they receive *their* letters, there will be nothing to stop him from yanking every Asperian he wants into Alpha Quarter."

"He needs Ephidra Lily to continue what he's started—you said that yourself. He didn't find any."

"I told you the war would begin when he began to search for *more*, he's run through the supply he stole from me. We're too late, Vesyon. The war for Aspera has truly begun, and there's nothing we can do to stop its forward trajectory."

Vesyon glanced at the heading again, wishing more than

anything that he imagined the words as he read them:

> *The High Court cordially demands you attend the Thirteenth Aspera Munera Praetorian Trials.*

"No," Vesyon said, resolutely slamming a palm on the marble banister. "I won't let him do this. If he's going to pull more innocent Asperians into the fight, then I'll go to the trials to challenge it."

"By yourself, hmm?" Langhorn said in a mocking jest.

"Don't be ridiculous, you know I can't take down the crown by myself," Vesyon shot back.

"Not all the men in Romeo Village are enough, Vesyon. We need to extend our reach into other territories outside our borders."

Vesyon grunted in response, slamming his pipe against the flattened expanse of his palm. "There's no one else besides Phillip's men that I am certain I can count on. Those beyond the border would kill us just as quickly as they'd kill LeMarc. We have no allies."

"Oh posh," Langhorn snorted in response. "I know the old treaties would hold tight for those outside Aspera. Many remain loyal to the true heir, the rightful High King of the Five Shores!"

"Oh, dear Ma'Nada," Vesyon said on a sigh of exasperation. He'd heard the story so many times in his life that it'd become a joke how seriously some Asperians took it, including Langhorn. "Now is not the time for imaginary stories or make-believe. Don't you think 'the chosen one' story-line fated to lead the people to salvation is a bit old?" Taking in a deep breath of the crisp night air, Vesyon could taste the slight chill of blossoming winter. He felt the icy tendrils grip at his vocal chords, and it chilled him down to the bone.

Langhorn shook his head, his brows drawn together. "For a man so determined to live a life of freedom and happiness, you're sure going about it strangely. The prophecy lays out the truth my boy; the true born Lowenhaar will take the throne."

"Screw the prophecy, you old man. For all Aspera knows, LeMarc *is* a true born. He states that fact himself."

"Just because the High King says something is true, are you going to believe him?"

Vesyon stared daggers at Langhorn before relighting his pipe and taking an extra-long drag on the smoldering leaves. "It doesn't matter what I believe. The last thing Aspera needs is another heavy-handed ruler forcing his or her thoughts over this land. The people need freedom, Langhorn, and they want to have a voice. The prophecy you cling to is an old myth. Just a story to tell children at night to ensure hope exists. LeMarc is the High King. The only savior Aspera will have are those willing to fight against the crown, not some prophesied child born some sixty years ago. Aspera doesn't need to bow to yet another monarchy focused on its own agenda and not the true needs of the people."

"That crown is the only thing holding Aspera together," Langhorn said in a clipped tone as Vesyon snorted, sufficiently cutting him off.

"That's total hogwash. The people hold this land together."

"You forget that I was there. I saw when High King Lucas's brother Logan sent his wife Vivienne away from Alpha Quarter. I was the physician meant to help her through the birthing, but she abandoned her station before the child was due," Langhorn snapped back in a harsh whisper.

Vesyon shook his head in a wearisome way. "Yes, but you didn't. Vivienne disappeared, and she died along with her unborn child. There's no proof the heir is alive. There's no savior or chosen one. There will be an army of men and women, Praetorians and Rogues, that will fight to the death for the land and the life they deserve. We don't need a High King or Queen to lead us."

"And if you take LeMarc down, remove the monster from the throne, what then? Who will rule Aspera if not the heir to the crown?"

He didn't have an answer for that and hadn't allowed himself to think of what life would be once LeMarc was gone entirely. There was so little he did want, and in the smallest form, he was desperate for the pure simplicity of solitude. A moment's peace living out his long days in White Wall in his old living quarters. It was an impossible dream, he knew that, but it was far more realistic to him than searching for the promised heir to take a crown they had no clue what to do with.

"I have no time to concern myself with what will come next. First, we must defeat a High King. When we win, the land and its people will decide on the structure of rule. I have nothing to do with what is decided. I'm promised to Camille and her safety, and I will live to serve her."

"Horse shiat!"

Vesyon's eyes blazed with anger as he whirled on the man. "You're out of line, old man!"

"No, you are! Do you have any idea what you're saying! Aspera needs a leader, a voice to lead them to victory. If not the heir to the throne, then an honorable Asperian to show them how to achieve what they are fighting for. You can't honestly think that existing fulfill a single promise you made many years ago is a life worth living. You are meant to lead."

"I don't want to be their leader," Vesyon replied curtly.

"Vesyon," Langhorn said, his tone soft and pleading. "You have to come to terms that Jesabelle is gone; she will never be with us again. I understand you made her a promise to protect Camille, but you can do more than that. You can protect Camille's future as well as her present. Both of you could live in peace. Is that not what you want for her?"

Vesyon ignored his words and hunched his shoulders in annoyance. "Aspera will find a way."

Langhorn snorted. "Say what you want, child, but once you remove one snake another will slithered into his place. Unless someone is willing to step forward and enforce a new way of life, you can't stop it. The absence of a ruler will cause a vacuum of power if no structure is enforced. If not the rightful heir to the throne, then what? If freedom is what you see for this land, a country ruled by the people, then *you* need to be the front runner of that."

"You're telling me to raise an army against LeMarc and head into Alpha Quarter, stating my right to destroy the crown? What would that achieve? That sounds like suicide even for a Praetorian."

"Sounds like the beginning of a plan to me," Langhorn replied, his lips quirking with a sly smile.

"Be careful old man. You don't know what LeMarc is capable of," Vesyon said, the darkness of his past floating like ghosts in the deep well of his eyes.

"I know more than you can imagine," Langhorn stated firmly, though without sharpness. Vesyon eyed the man out of the corner of his peripheral vision, but let the comment lay. There was much about Langhorn that Vesyon would never know, and it sparked renewed interest in the man he'd always thought of as his mentor and substitute father.

"I don't care about growing our troops beyond what we have now, we have *her*, and no one knows what she's capable of. You should have seen her, Langhorn," Vesyon said, his eyes alight with wistful excitement looking out over the dark expanse of the Aspera lands before him. If he hadn't been so terrified when he'd first seen Camille after the explosion of Romeo Village, Vesyon would have smiled in sweet relief and swelling pride watching her battle more Chimera than he'd ever seen anyone battle at one time. Her strength and ferocity had blazed like wildfire across the battlefield, pulling the horde of beasts toward her like a homing beacon. There'd been no stopping her.

Langhorn pursed his thin lips in silent response as Vesyon's eyes zeroed in on the fluttering parchment before him on the banister.

"I know that look," Langhorn said grimly. "And you need to think about what he's already taken from you before you blaze ahead without a plan. What *else* are you willing to lose in your quest to defeat him? This isn't the time to rush into battle alone. We need to build our strength before we continue this path. Romeo Village isn't enough. There needs to be strong support of Aspera's loyalists on our side. Whiskey Wharf, Echo Colony, Sierra Village, Delta Square—they will all stand strong behind the true High King of Aspera."

Vesyon stared straight at Langhorn, his expression one of sharp determination. Without hesitation, he replied with complete and untainted honesty, "Langhorn—I'm willing to lose everything I have if it means that man falls from the throne."

Nodding in grim understanding, Langhorn took one final pull on his long-necked pipe and blew the fragrant smoke out in a soft, billowing cloud. "We will need to go to the trials, but we must not do this openly. We need to see how far along he has come in building his army of Night Raves. There must be preparation and discovery before we make our move. We will build our army one village at a time."

Vesyon nodded his head slowly, knowing without a doubt that Langhorn spoke the truth. "Yes, we must prepare for Alpha Quarter."

"Will you bring her with you?" Langhorn asked, his eyes searching, though without assumption.

"I don't believe I can afford to leave her behind," Vesyon replied carefully. Langhorn wasn't an idiot. Just like Phillip, he knew the truth behind Vesyon's words.

"Then Theo must join."

"Yes, of course," Vesyon replied instinctively.

"As will I," Langhorn stated firmly.

Vesyon chuckled softly, the blazing heat of his anger simmering to a manageable level. "Yes, I don't believe I could keep you away from such an event, could I?"

Footsteps raced across the interior of his room and Vesyon's head turned just in time to see one of Langhorn's assistants skid into view, her charcoal eyes bright with unrestrained excitement. "What is it?" Langhorn asked, taking a few steps toward the young woman in obvious worry. "Has something happened?"

"Yes," she said, her voice brimming with fascination but also a note of apprehension. "The girl is awake, Doctor, and she's asking for Vesyon."

"That's wonderful news, Maggie," Langhorn exclaimed, glancing from the young girl of seventeen to Vesyon and then back again.

"There's more, Doctor," Maggie's short black hair swung forward over her features as she ducked her head in silent request to continue.

"Please my dear, continue."

"Um, well..." she started, nervously hopping from foot to foot. "She isn't really in a great state of mind. She is quite furious and um, Theo is struggling to keep her restrained. I tried to dose her with valerian serum to induce sleep as you suggested, but I wasn't successful. I am hoping Theo was," she said meekly, as though chastising herself for her inability to combat a mighty Praetorian.

"Oh dear," Langhorn said with a soft sigh. "Looks like we might have a long night ahead of us."

Vesyon nodded slowly, uncertain of what they'd find after walking into the surgery ward. A tremor of fear, long ago buried, resurfaced as they rushed down the silent hallways of White Wall. It'd been eight years since the destruction of Charlie Town, and yet the familiar taste of terror exploded throughout Vesyon's system as he struggled to reign in his internal dread. Would there be any essence of his Camille left or had the demons finally consumed her whole?

EPILOGUE
SILVER PRISON

Green ink dripped from the metal-tipped pen staining the parchment beneath Emma's fingertips. Her mouth felt as dry as if she'd swallowed an entire gallon of salted biscuits, and her bright blue eyes blinked rapidly as she stared at the name written neatly across the page. She pushed her mousy brown hair away from her face, ensuring she'd read the words correctly.

There'd been a moment of excitement and glee when an Equestrian had come to her parent's home that afternoon, requesting Miss Emma Donner's appearance at the High Court. She was only sixteen, barely legal under Asperian Law—yet she went up to the High Court with an eager grin on her face, hoping the High King's request would be followed with an easy task and some sort of payment. The fall season had been dreary and fruitless, a grim warning of the winter to come, and her family needed money.

The High King had been a sight to behold, and it was a bit shocking to see him at first. He was beyond tall, with a charismatic smile bolstered by the deepest dimples she'd ever seen on a man. Thick black hair tousled perfectly over his dark olive skin, the messy array of curls the only mark of wildness. There was no crown atop his head, but it didn't diminish the air of power he managed to exude in his posture and undeniable confidence.

He wore a fitted black doublet, gold threading, and fixtures sewn into the fabric blinking brilliantly across his chest and shoulders as he moved toward her. Black breeches clung to his legs and thighs, his sturdy leather boots shined to perfection, but obviously worn, the scuffed edges a mere hint of their constant use. A thick gold necklace sat over his chest, spanning the length of his shoulders, the obsidian and sapphire stones flickering with movement. It was hard not to stare, though Emma kept her eyes cast downward as best she could. Despite the ebony depths of his eyes, his attractive features brought her attention up to his face again and again. He was an impossible man not to stare at, and despite her fear of punishment, she felt herself smiling back at him as he offered her a hand in welcome.

Bowing as gracefully as possible, Emma leaned toward his proffered hand and kissed the hefty ruby ring sitting on his left pinky. She'd always wondered about the rumors that he was in hiding, but he graciously greeted her at the front door of his throne room, leading her himself to the sitting room she was now occupying. His conversational tone had been pleasant, his questions simple, his smile divine. The High King offered her a cup of rose tea, which she'd gracefully accepted while trying to keep her giddiness to a minimum. As she sipped the delicious concoction and listened to his lilting voice, she didn't think there was anything wrong with what he was asking her to do, especially as he was offering to pay her for her services.

"Take this list, my dear, and in your perfect calligraphy I want you to write each name on its own slip of paper and put them into their respective envelopes."

An Equestrian stood just outside the small room, but the High King had closed the doors, giving Emma an excellent opportunity to take in her stunning surroundings without being watched. There was an open bay window overlooking Black Bottom Lake, and Emma peeked up from her desk to admire the way the structures of Alpha Quarter glittered in the late morning sun. It was beautiful, and, as a native of Delta Village, Emma had never thought her stars would lead her to such a breathtaking moment. She shifted in the soft, red leather chair and pulled her utensils closer, narrowing her eyes in a moment of intense concentration.

The High King had requested her presence because of her beautiful penmanship and was offering her family a year's amount of Moon Tax prepaid. Her entire family would be able to eat everything they gathered and grew for a whole year. It seemed too good to be true. She had been chosen by the High King.

With a smile on her rose painted lips, she dipped her metal-tipped pen into the vial of deep emerald ink and got to work with enthusiasm.

It wasn't until her eyes had skimmed the twelfth name on the list that her pen stilled and her mouth seized up. Her eyes flipped from the record before her to others pushed to the side to make sure she was reading it right. One paper had two-hundred names listed and was called *Families to Attend*. A second list was labeled *Audience Attendees and Possible Volunteers,* which had over one-thousand names listed. On the last record, there were only twenty names written down in scrawled black lettering. The stark label read: *Aspera Munera - Praetorian Trials*.

Twelve lines down from the top she read the name *Luke Donner*—her twin brother. It couldn't be true; it wasn't possible. Emma wasn't an idiot; she knew full well that being inside the walls of the High Court was an honor as much as it was a danger. She needed to get the job done and vacate the premises with her note of reward snug in hand, but to do that, she had to write down every name listed on a slip of paper and drop it into its coordinating envelope.

Her pen remained frozen until the entirety of green ink held in the feed had dripped all over the tabletop. A flash of flame from the shifting wood pieces in the crackling hearth nearby sparked an idea in her head, and before she knew what she was doing, she'd taken the envelope with her brother's name on it and thrown it into the fire. She grabbed a blank envelope from the stack and carefully began to write a different name on the back, but before she could finish, the heavy wooden door behind her opened.

Fear stilted her movements, though she tried to appear natural as she politely turned to greet them.

"Hello," Emma squeaked, swallowing down the lump in her throat as she saw who'd entered.

"Why would you do that, my dear?" the High King said, his tone clear and controlled. "Each and every name chosen for the Praetorian Trials is done so carefully, specifically, and with clear intent. To toss aside a single name is to disrespect the kingdom. Are you trying to disrespect me?"

"No, Your Majesty," Emma said, trembling from head to toe.

"I don't think you *do* respect me, or the kingdom. If you did, you'd know that I chose you specifically for this job, just as I chose your brother. To go against my wishes is to go against Aspera, and I don't tolerate traitors of any kind."

"I'm sorry, Your Majesty. I didn't mean any disrespect."

The High King reached across the table and lifted the last envelope Emma had been working on. "You should've completed the job I asked of you, dear. I have a feeling you might not like the direction you're about to head in."

Emma wasn't even able to register his statement before a chilly metal collar was clipped tightly around her neck and a sharp, stabbing pain seared through her chest. Her body convulsed, and she flew back onto the floor, but the pain didn't cease. Her eyes went wide as she watched a gloved hand shove a thin metal tool straight into her ribcage, the pain so acute she knew she was close to passing out.

"Please, please, make it stop! Don't kill me, I don't want to die!"

"Oh, my sweet girl," the High King said as he leaned over her hunched body, grasping the pen still clenched in her hand. "You aren't going to die—far from it. I'm giving you a gift, a token of forgiveness. You see, I didn't ask you here for your penmanship. The letters have already gone out."

Emma's mouth fell open as her vision went blurry.

"Your family will be so happy once they receive *your* letter."

"My letter?"

"Yes. The letter you wrote to your family telling them about your devotion to your High King. You've decided to remain in my service, to serve your king as a dutiful subject should. But don't worry; your family will never come looking for you. They will be very well taken care of, never having to pay the Moon Tax again. Your brother, I can only assume, has already received his letter. He will take part in the Praetorian Aspera Munera. And *you*—you will help me populate my new army."

High King LeMarc's words ran together in Emma's brain as her blood pumped frantically through her veins. Every bone felt like it was on fire, like it was being ground to fine dust under the crushing pressure of a thousand stones. Moving wasn't an option, so instead, Emma remained slumped on the wooden floor, staring at the beautiful reds and oranges of a brilliant sunrise through the bay window.

"The Ephidra Lily serum has fully spread through her system by now. You may take her down to the dungeon holding." The High King said to his guard. "I would like to watch her punishment myself before she's shipped out with the others."

As the High King rattled off his demands to the guard, Emma watched brilliant rays of sun spread its orange fingers across the glory of Alpha Quarter. Her pain was beginning to recede, and she allowed herself a moment of relief until she realized the soldier regarding her *wasn't* an Equestrian.

"I'll be certain to make sure she's well taken care of," the man said, his red leather attire loud and squeaky as he approached Emma and told her to stand.

She attempted to move, but her legs still felt like wobbly jam.

"Move, you Asperian lump!" the guard barked, pulling the short metal rod from his hip and touching it to the choker around her neck. Electric shocks raced through her extremities, sending wave after wave of anguish through her body. She wanted to scream, to beg, but all words failed her as the guard kept the metallic rod held against her neck restraint.

"Now," the guard said, "on your feet. I can do this all day, little girl, but your punishment will be more enjoyable for me to partake in if you're awake. I like to hear my conquests scream."

As soon as he removed the rod from her collar, the pain evaporated, and she scrambled to her feet, staring at her reflection in the window. Tears slipped down her cheeks as her new reality settled in—this was no nightmare, at least not one she'd be waking up from. She was no longer just a subject of the High King's court. She was his captive—without hope of rescue.

ABOUT THE AUTHOR

Jessie McSpadden grew up in San Diego and went to school to work in film. After moving to Los Angeles, she found herself without a job and an abundance of time. She turned her mind toward writing. Praetorian Rising was born of her love of music, life experience, obsession with food, and a little bit of fantasy dreaming. Jessie now lives in Los Angeles with her family and pug. She works in the film industry by day and a writes every possible minute in-between.

Made in the USA
Columbia, SC
28 September 2019